Benjamin One Feather saw it all . . . the great fire sweeping the plains, driving all living creatures before it . . . the limping wolf that survived and the black toad leaping from the wolf's forehead into the flames . . . the great medicine wheel spinning out of control, being torn apart.

But no one could tell him its meaning—not his father, who knew both the ways of the whites and Indians . . . not the beautiful White Crane, who gave herself in passion and in love . . . not the bluecoats who were enemies and those who were his friends . . . not his tribe, the Crow, or his mother's, the Nez Percé, or the Blackfoot, or Sioux, or Cheyenne. . . .

None could go where that vision led except him alone . . .

THE VISION OF BENJAMIN ONE FEATHER

THE VISION OF BENJAMIN ONE FEATHER

Paul A. Hawkins

SIGNET
Published by the Penguin Group
Penguin Books USA Inc., 375 Hudson Street,
New York, New York 10014, U.S.A.
Penguin Books Ltd, 27 Wrights Lane, London W8 5TZ, England
Penguin Books Australia Ltd, Ringwood, Victoria, Australia
Penguin Books Canada Ltd, 10 Alcorn Avenue,
Toronto, Ontario, Canada M4V 3B2
Penguin Books (N.Z.) Ltd, 182-190 Wairau Road,
Auckland 10, New Zealand

Penguin Books Ltd, Registered Offices:
Harmondsworth, Middlesex, England

First published by Signet, an imprint of Dutton Signet, a division
of Penguin Books USA Inc.

First Printing, October, 1993
10 9 8 7 6 5 4 3 2 1

Cover art by John Leone.

REGISTERED TRADEMARK—MARCA REGISTRADA

Printed in the United States of America

To my three children, Paul, Janet,
and Christopher

AUTHOR'S NOTE

Although this novel is fiction, many of the incidents in it are historical events that happened in the Idaho and Montana territories during the period from 1870–1877. The depiction of some men and women has been fictionalized to enhance the plot lines of the story, but is not intended to impugn their character in any way.

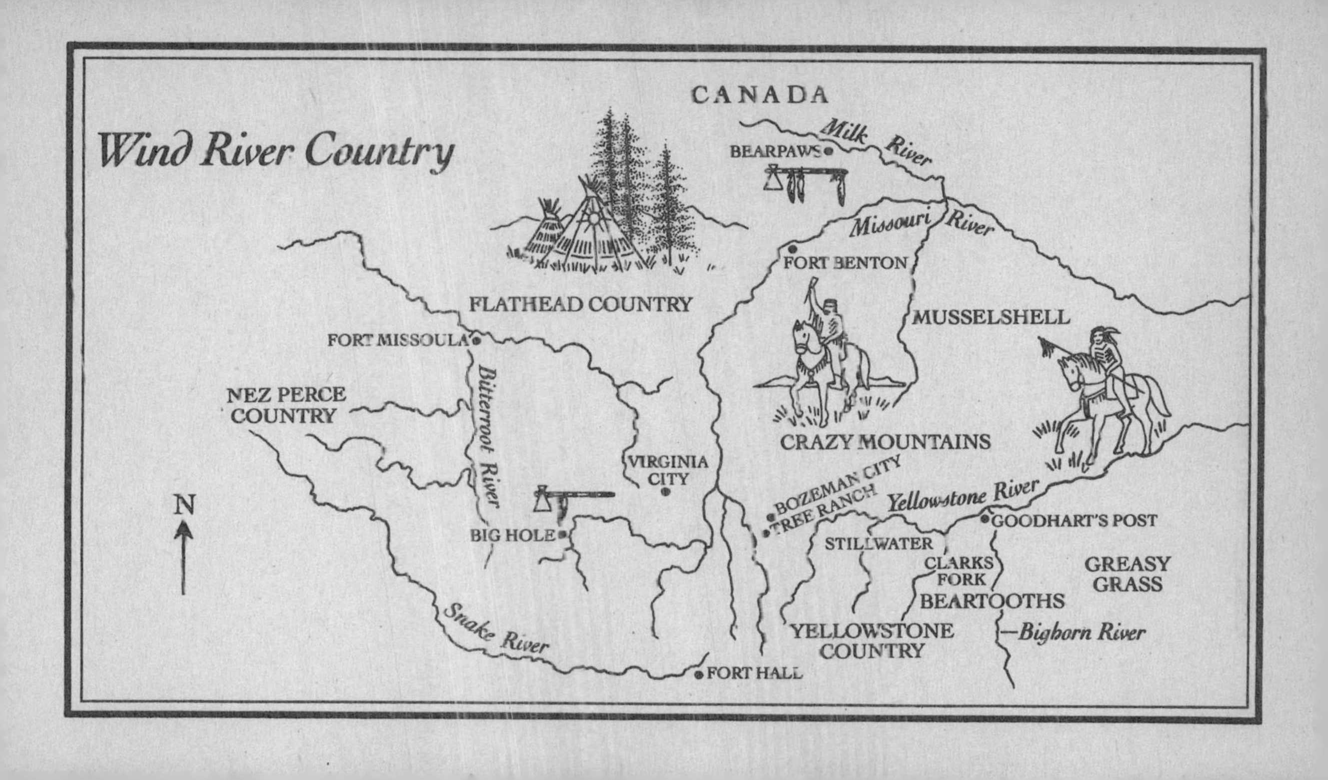
Wind River Country
CANADA
Milk River
BEARPAWS
Missouri River
FORT BENTON
FLATHEAD COUNTRY
MUSSELSHELL
FORT MISSOULA
NEZ PERCE
COUNTRY
Bitterroot River
CRAZY MOUNTAINS
VIRGINIA
CITY
BOZEMAN CITY
TREE RANCH
Yellowstone River
GOODHART'S POST
N
BIG HOLE
STILLWATER
CLARKS
FORK
GREASY
GRASS
BEARTOOTHS
Bighorn River
YELLOWSTONE
COUNTRY
Snake River
FORT HALL

I love a people who are honest without laws, who have no jails and no poorhouses.

I love a people who keep the commandments without ever having read them or heard them preached from the pulpit.

—George Catlin, painter

PROLOGUE

The old holy man, Ten Sleeps, sat in the shadow of his lodge quietly contemplating Chief Man Called Tree. Finally: "I have known you many winters, too many to remember. I have watched over you as if you were my son, watched you gain honors, raise a family, and become a chief among the Absaroke. You cast a long shadow, Man Called Tree. Now, as you once did, your eldest son has counted coup on the Pekony."

"Ei, he has become a brave."

Ten Sleeps paused. His eyelids fluttered once and he nodded. "A brave, yes, and do you know he has been touched by the spirits of the Great Medicine Wheel?"

"Touched? No." It was Ben Tree's turn to pause. Ten Sleep's face, a mass of wrinkles, was expressionless. Man Called Tree finally said, "He made mention of visiting the old sacred place, nothing more."

"Benjamin One Feather will soon become a vision-seeker."

"You have foreseen this?" asked Man Called Tree.

"No. I have made no medicine for him. It is what I believe. Long ago, this happened to another young man. Ei, I have seen this happen only once before."

"And to whom did this happen? Is this man within our tribe?"

A faint smile parted the thin lips of Ten Sleeps and he answered, "You are listening to him now. I am that man."

Man Called Tree replied, "I learned long ago never to doubt your words, brother."

"I am too old to watch the boy. Not many winters left. You must give Benjamin One Feather guidance."

"I have always tried to give guidance and learning to my three children," said Man Called Tree.

"Without a vision, you have done well."

"I never sought a vision. By the blessing of the Great One Above, and by my own wits, I survived."

Ten Sleeps nodded and then said, "Benjamin One Feather has never sought a vision either, but a powerful one will come to him before the snow covers his moccasins. You must see that he does not stray from within the confines of The Great Circle and what he seeks."

"Ei, and what might that be, my brother?" asked Man Called Tree.

Ten Sleeps smiled faintly. "What most seek but never attain. The wisdom and understanding contained in each of The Four Great Directions."

"Making the circle?"

"Ei."

"By the powers!" exclaimed Man Called Tree. "Does the young man know of this . . . this challenge?"

"The seed is within him now, as it was with me," answered Ten Sleeps. "I believe the seed will blossom before the end of the Hungry Moons. How powerful his medicine will be, and how wisely he uses it, only the Great Spirit knows."

ONE

Montana Territory, September 1869

By the time Benjamin One Feather was thirteen years old and preparing for his first journey into the white man's land, he had heard many of the legends about his adopted father, who was known to the Absaroke and other Indian tribes as Man Called Tree. Man Called Tree had big medicine. There were over fifty tipis in his village. At thirty-five he was a powerful young chief among the Crow, or Bird People, who lived and hunted along the beautiful valleys and mountains of the Echeta Casha, the great Yellowstone River basin. But these stories that Benjamin One Feather proudly listened to with great fascination, and with his own fertile imagination coursing the high canyons of the Beartooth, were never told to him by his great stepfather or even his mother, Rainbow, a Nez Percé *palojami*, a beautiful one, from the Land of the Winding Waters. These stories always came from other Crow children who had overheard the legends around the night fires, tales that were constantly repeated by their fathers and brothers.

So it was told that Benjamin One Feather's father had been a relentless and much-feared warrior among the hairy-faced people who lived far over the mountains to the south and west, that he had counted coup on them many times, long before becoming a human being and a great Crow chief and spokesman for the Bird People. So it was told that even the Pekonies, the Piegan-Blackfeet across the Yellowstone to the north, knew of Man Called Tree, a man who was half-white and half-Osage. For many moons these fearless and cunning Blackfeet people, as well as a few foolish white men, had tried to count coup on him. All of these efforts had been fruitless because, according to the Crow, Man Called Tree's medicine was too powerful: the tree, the coyote, and the sun, very strong medicine, indeed. For the tree was most formidable, firmly rooted, thick in the trunk, its branches unbending; the coyote was the most cunning animal of all; and Masaka, the sun, ruled the Great Hanging Road between Mother Earth and the Kingdom of the Great Spirit. Benjamin One Feather and his younger breed brother, White Moon, the blood son of Man Called Tree, had asked about some of these mysterious legends, but their father and mother always told them the same thing: it was bad medicine to recall the past and disturb the spirits of the dead.

Only when Benjamin One Feather became older did he finally realize that both his mother and father's ancient days were too sorrowfully disheartening to recall, that they both had buried the past in scattered graves across the frontier wilderness. Some of this past was about Benjamin One Feather himself, for his blood father, Henri Bilodeau, had died when Benjamin was only one year old. After that, Rainbow, his Nez Percé mother, had taken Man Called Tree for her husband. Before this marriage a white man had murdered Tree's first woman, Little Hoop, a Crow maiden only seventeen years old, and this was another one of the legends: that Man Called Tree had crucified and scalped the killer of his wife. Benjamin One Feather knew that his younger sister, Little Blue Hoop, had been named after this first woman, Little Hoop, but he had been told nothing about the Crow maiden's death; he knew only what he had heard. This, too was part of his father's buried, legendary past.

Since Benjamin was the eldest son, it was he who had the privilege of accompanying Man Called Tree into the white man's world on this long trip down to Fort Hall in the Idaho territory, and for the first time he would actually see some of these many strange things that he had only heard about in the legends. So, during the Moon of the Drying Grass, with eight braves from the village riding along with them, Benjamin One Feather and Man Called Tree headed up the Yellowstone river for Bozeman City, arriving at the pass overlooking the Gallatin Valley six sleeps later. Man Called Tree told the Crow men that he and Benjamin would return by the passing of one moon, that he would look for them at the mountain gorge at that time; additionally, he would return with gifts for everyone.

That the young chief would honor his Indian brothers this way was nothing unusual, for he was a wealthy man among the whites as well as his adopted Absaroke people. This wealth was the very reason he was returning to one of his old homes, Fort Hall in the Idaho territory, where for many years he had been a silent partner with Englishman James Digby, the trading post owner and operator of freight lines to Fort Boise and Virginia City. Only two days past, Man Called Tree had received a distressing message by trail runners that Digby had died, that white men wanted Tree to come out of the mountains once again, this time to settle the estate, all of which had been left solely to him. Only a few people knew that Ben Tree (the name by which he was known in the white man's land) had shared business ventures with James Digby for fifteen years, ever since Ben's father and brother were murdered by roadsters. After that episode in his life, Ben Tree had liquidated the family freight business at Independence and Fort Laramie. When he returned to a permanent life with the Crow, he put the proceeds into Digby's capable hands to initiate new stage and freight lines both east and north from Fort Hall.

Ben had not visited the ancient outpost for six years, receiving only periodic reports in the Yellowstone when Digby delivered an occasional message or an accounting. There were several reasons for Ben Tree's infrequent visits to Fort Hall, first and foremost being that he despised the white man's so-called civilization and the continuing depredations that it brought to the land of his Indian brothers. Second, frontier memories were as long as the evening shadows. Even after six years, any number of disreputables waited along the trail, eager to enhance their own reputation by killing the notorious gunman Ben Tree, the man considered most responsible for the demise of Henry Plummer and his gang of roadsters only a few years back in the territory of the gold fields. Here, again, more legend.

Benjamin One Feather knew very little about these controversial events: how his father, in his own personal quest for a killer, had uncovered damaging evidence against Plummer and his cohorts that eventually led to the formation of the vigilantes. What Benjamin did know was that his father was a famous man to many people. What he didn't know was that to many, his father was also an infamous, unforgiving renegade.

Even so, in the clutter and turmoil of booming Bozeman City, no one recognized Ben Tree. Here was a man and his son in customary frontier dress of fringed and beaded buckskins, who obviously had come down from the high country somewhere, a distant fort, or an Indian village, wherever, and they were outfitting themselves with clothing, pants, coats, hats, and boots. When they left the stores wearing their purchases, they appeared no different in the bustling boardwalk crowd than anyone else. Benjamin One Feather knew the difference. This was the first time that he was wearing leather boots, and they were clumsily awkward on small feet that had never known anything but the well-molded feel of skin moccasins. And his woolen pants were ridiculously baggy and uncomfortable, flapping uselessly around his thin legs like the wings of a molting goose. The broad-brimmed gray hat pleased him, though, for he had seen white men on the Yellowstone wearing these, sometimes decorated with bright beaded bands. He thought these hats were rather fetching. He told his father that once back in the village he would adapt his more to his own taste, with appropriate decorations of skins, feathers, and beads. He would be envied by his brothers.

By nightfall, Benjamin had seen many strange customs of the hairy-faced people, and experienced some of these himself. These *shoyapee*, as his mother called them in her native Nez Percé tongue, wore hats of different kinds, some like his own, others with floppy sides, and the most unusual of all, the black ones with tiny useless brims and tops rounded off like riverside hummocks. Other observations too: Instead of sitting down and smoking pipe in the circle, these men carried their pipes about in their mouths at all times, often making conversation without even removing them. This custom, Benjamin thought, must require much practice. Other *shoyapee* chewed the tobacco instead of smoking it, and spat brown streams of juice into the dusty street. They seemed to make themselves purposefully ugly with brown stains about their mouths and whiskers, but as Man Called Tree told him, this was a custom among the hairy-faced people. They were "civilized."

As was the room where they sat down to eat that night, taking their food from big white plates, using knives and small spears to fetch up the portions, and then watching some of these same men wipe their mouths and noses with pieces of white cloth that they sometimes hid in their pockets. Some even picked at their teeth with small splinters of wood. Oddly, they later left the eating place chewing on these tiny slivers as though they were tasty morsels, when in fact, as Benjamin discovered, these tiny sticks had no flavor at all. While many of the *shoyapee* differed in their dress, they all had one thing in common: They carried holstered pistols of various kinds around their waists. Benjamin One Feather saw no one, however, who wore a pistol as low on his hip as did his father, and Man Called Tree's holster was neatly strapped to his thigh by a thong of leather.

Before they left on the stage for Virginia City, Ben Tree made several stops, one at the bank, one at the livery stable where they had left the two horses, then at the smithy's where he inquired about some land owned by Bill Coonrad on Six Mile Creek, a man that Woman Called Bird, or Bird Rutledge, had told Ben about. This Cree woman, Bird, had been a friend of his father. The smithy, Donald Blodgett, said that Coonrad was probably down at his diggings in Alder Gulch but that he still owned the land, a homestead of one-hundred-sixty acres, and he certainly did remember the breed, Bird Rutledge, who had used the property one summer ago for her horse-trading business. That she had shot and killed a man and been forced to flee was a terrible tragedy, Blodgett told Tree, because the enterprising young woman had been so successful in the short time that she was in the Gallatin. Furthermore, Bird Rutledge was well liked by everyone. No one could understand what had happened that night at Coonrad's place.

Blodgett gave his fire at the forge a boost and turned back to Ben Tree. "She must have had a damned good reason to do something like that," he said. "Nobody 'round here ever figured it out, not to my knowledge. Never did catch up with her, either." He had a curious look on his hardy face. "Did you know the Rutledge woman?"

"Ei, I knew her, an old acquaintance," he replied. Of course, Ben Tree also knew the reason for the killing. The man she had shot was a disreputable trader by the name of Jubal McComber, who had tried to blackmail Woman Called Bird for a crime that she hadn't committed. Ben Tree had met the young Rutledge woman and her Cree mother at Manuel's post on the Yellowstone during the Moon of the Drying Grass in 1867, shortly after they escaped from the Sioux who had captured them during Red Cloud's war. "Take it from me," Ben told Blodgett, "she shot that fellow in self-defense, and that comes from the horse's mouth."

"Is that so?" returned the smithy, scratching his beard. "Well then, don't make much sense does it, the way she upped and ran away? Seems to me—"

"That she should have waited around and explained it?" Ben Tree asked. "That she could have gotten a fair hearing from the fort people?"

"Something like that, I suppose," Blodgett said. "That McComber, from what I hear, was a no-account, anyways."

"A white no-account," Ben said wryly, "and our friend Bird Rutledge was a breed. I reckon that might have had something to do with her hitting the trail, ei? I understand that there were hard feelings running around here at the time, hangings and such."

"Hard feelings?" Pausing for a moment, recollecting, Blodgett finally said, "Oh, you must mean the vigilantes down Virginia City way. Hell, that ruckus is over and done. The law's down there now, and we even have a constable's office here in Bozeman. No, I knew that woman pretty well. She just wasn't the running kind, not that one, no siree. She had something stuck in her craw, that's the way I figure. Anyways, I lost some good business on that one. She was in here every week with horses to be shod. Woman knew what she was about, she did." He paused and stared inquisitively at Ben Tree again. "You interested in Coonrad's place, too, horses and such? Is that it?"

"I know the place, but I have a little more than just horses in mind," Ben Tree said. "Does he still plan on leaving?"

"Talks about it all the time when he's here," Donald Blodgett answered. "Figures this may be his last season at the mine. Reckon by now he has enough stashed in the bank to make a break of it. He's done well, I reckon, better than most of 'em down there. He saves it. No drinker, no gambler, if you know what I mean."

"Then, maybe I'll have a parley with him on my way back," Ben said. "Or look him up down at the Gulch if I have time. But if perchance I miss him, you tell him I was in looking to make a deal on that property. I'm going to file on that land next to his, and I'd like to have the whole creek bottom, plus some grazing rights on the bench."

"Well, I sure will tell him if he drops in," Blodgett said. "But that acreage of his is next to nowhere, you know, butts right up against the mountains. If lonely is what you want, that's it. Reckon the bench grass above is heady, if that's what you have in mind, running a few cattle, breeding horses. It's open range, you know. Who shall I tell him was inquiring . . . your name?"

"Ben Tree," replied Ben, smiling and offering his hand.

Donald Blodgett readily shook hands, but his eyes suddenly widened in surprise. Yes, this was the man, all right: That faint scar blazed across his cheek. A gun duel somewhere down in the Hell Gate country, he remembered, a dead man left behind. "Ben Tree? *The* Ben Tree?" he cautiously inquired. "Are you coming in here to settle?"

Ben, sensing Blodgett's slight apprehension, merely laughed. More often than not, the mention of his name drew a curious response. "No, not at all," he replied. "No, I have no wish to be a part of this. Let's just say

I'm looking down the trail a ways, an investment, that's all. If you can't beat 'em, join 'em.'' With a deep, disapproving frown, he motioned to the bustling town around them. ''Mr. Blodgett, I was riding this land when the sound of an ax scared the hell out of me . . . could hear it ten miles away . . . no trail, only what you made yourself through the bluestem and grama. Beautiful, lonely country. I used to take all of this personal-like, being young and a bit hotheaded, you might say, downright selfish for a fact. Didn't like to see it marked and divided, and by jingo, now I'm a part of it myself.''

''Yes, I suppose I understand how you feel,'' Donald Blodgett said. ''Heard you were up around here from time to time . . . heard a few stories about you. I pay them no mind, understand. Knew your family's brand, I did, the Tree mules, when I was back in Missouri, just a kid.''

''Time comes when a man has to start thinking about family,'' Ben went on, ''and time is running a short wick for my kind of people. No, that Six Mile country's not for me, Mr. Blodgett, it's for my boys, this one here and the one back down the Yellowstone.''

Donald Blodgett quickly sized up Benjamin One Feather, a young boy with dark, shining eyes, his long hair neatly swept back and tied under his hat with a thin piece of rawhide. A breed? Except for a slight coloration, more olive than copper, and those penetrating, dark, inquisitive eyes, who could possibly guess? Oh, black hair, yes, but there were many handsome frontier lads about with black hair and not a lick of Indian blood in them. Ah, but the boy's stature, straight as a hickory staff, and his demeanor, attentive to everything around him. Blodgett said, ''But he's only a boy, this one. Does he speak English?''

Grinning at Benjamin, Ben Tree plunked the boy's hat with a finger. ''Ei, a boy today, but a man before we know it. What do you say, Benjamin? This man is Mr. Blodgett. What will you tell him?''

Benjamin One Feather promptly held out his hand. ''I am pleased to meet you, Mr. Blodgett. My name is Benjamin. My brothers call me Benjamin One Feather, and I don't think these ponies like what you do to their hooves. If ponies were meant to wear iron shoes, the Great Spirit would have made it so in the beginning."

Both Blodgett and Ben Tree were amused, and Blodgett quickly returned, "But, Benjamin, I see *you're* shod in new boots. So tell me, what's the difference?"

"The difference, sir, is that I only wear these boots because it is the custom among your people. It is not by necessity."

"Smart boy," commented Blodgett, winking at him. "You don't look much Injun, son, and you sure don't talk like one, either."

Ben Tree said with a touch of pride, "He can tell you the same thing in two other languages, Absaroke and Nez Percé. Ei, he has learned well, writes and reads better than his father. He knows the difference between riding point and riding drag, and when his day comes, he'll not be fooled by any man."

The Oliver stage layover in Virginia City was overnight, and once again young Benjamin had opportunity to witness some of the madness of the white people, the crazies, as some of his older Crow brothers called them. As in Bozeman City, there were many different types of *shoyapee* here on the one long street, some of them lounging in the cool evening air, talking in groups in front of the stores and saloons, and in other places leaning across long tables, drinking, and smoking their pipes. Others were playing games with colored cards. In one of these big rooms there were large bowls for those men who chewed tobacco to spit into, and Benjamin observed that they did so readily but frequently missed their mark, leaving dirty stains on the floor. This, he thought, was not a good custom, for in his village such a vile habit inside a lodge would never be permitted. This custom of standing and drinking at the long table was also foreign to Benjamin. If their feet were tired from work, why did they do this when there were so many fine places to sit and take rest?

And their thirst seemed unending, as though they had been on a hot, dusty trail from dawn to dusk without water. Fresh water, one good drink, filled the belly, slaked the thirst, and made one ready to ride again, refreshed and of sound mind. But this water, what his father called "Taos lightning," didn't seem to refresh the men. Instead, it did strange things to them. Some of these crazy *shoyapee* laughed loudly and even danced; others cried; others wanted to fight with their friends; and some went outside and vomited everything they had just drunk. This, Benjamin remembered, only happened to his people when they ate too much fresh liver. It was not a good sight to see, or a feeling to experience, either.

They didn't tarry in any of these places, since his father had no desire to participate in what he so despised. Man Called Tree was only searching for another man by the name of Arthur Clawson, and by the time they were ready to eat supper, he had found him. Mr. Clawson, an attorney, joined them in the big room with tables and white plates at the Goodrich Hotel where they were staying the night. Man Called Tree said this man was an associate of another attorney, Wilbur Fisk Sanders, whose uncle, Sidney Edgerton, had been governor of the Montana territory. Clawson was very important because his speciality was property deeds and land sales. He was a young man with a small beard and he wore spectacles, strange eyepieces with thin wires that went behind his ears and hid in his long hair.

Arthur Clawson amused Benjamin. He laughed and smiled a lot, and Benjamin thought this was a good sign, for this man, unlike some of the others he had watched, seemed untroubled by the furor of the street and the staggering walks of the crazies. He carried a gun, too, but it was a small one, barely protruding from his vest pocket. This was undoubtedly the smallest weapon Benjamin had ever seen, and when he finally asked about it, Mr. Clawson carefully shucked the two fat bullets and showed it to him. It was called a "derringer." No more than a toy, it was nonetheless deadly at close range. It had two silver barrels and a shiny black handle, and when Man Called Tree took it, it completely disappeared in his big hand. This was a useless weapon for animals, his father said, for its accuracy was limited to only ten or twelve paces. Its only purpose was to kill men, something that Benjamin was told frequently happened in the white man's civilization. This was the way *they* counted coup.

After their supper they went to Clawson's office, where they studied and marked maps and signed long documents which Man Called Tree read carefully. These were the papers and plats of the land Arthur Clawson would file for the homestead in the Gallatin at Six Mile Creek, including rights to all the water and eight thousand acres of grazing land adjacent, with the option to purchase at one dollar per acre when the land office approved the sale. This, explained Clawson, would take money, political pressure, and time, perhaps six months' worth, but with these papers signed and filed it was as good as done. Ben Tree had first priority on the range land. In due time all of these legal matters would be sent to the bank in Bozeman City, where Ben was planning to have his funds from Fort Hall transferred. When this latter transaction was completed, Arthur Clawson jokingly said that Ben Tree probably would have enough money on deposit even to control the bank. This made Benjamin One Feather proud. His father did have big medicine, even in the white man's civilization.

Later that night, when they were ready for their high beds and fat pillows, Man Called Tree spoke serious words to Benjamin, ones that he didn't fully understand. Benjamin knew they were true, though, for his father never spoke with two tongues; the Yellowstone Crow who followed him knew this to be true. His vision was as long as his medicine was strong. He said that the days of the early people, the ancient ones, were sadly numbered, and that while he had fought against this for many years, the face of the land was changing. There was nothing anyone could do about this now. Even this town, he said, would one day be gone, because Mother Earth's bounty of gold was not endless. So change for all people was inevitable, red and white alike.

The changes that he had already witnessed were devastating to his way of life, but he warned that people must adapt or wither on the vine like wild grapes in the winter. This was one of the reasons that he spent many long nights by the fire teaching his three children how to read and write, why he always brought new books to the lodge. Since the white man had come to mark and divide the land, only those who fully understood the written word would profit. This is also why he was talking to the lawyer of deeds and titles and the bankers; for the time will soon come, he said, when the land purveyors will discover who the real master of their game is in the Gallatin Valley—Ben Tree.

"Someday you may choose to leave the village," Man Called Tree said. "Our Yellowstone land is being marked, too, into what these government people call 'a reservation.' There will be more concessions, but by my life, the treaty writers will not cheat us as they have others. Such a limited life may not suit you. What I've done this day is given you and your brother most of the property rights to this land along Six Mile Creek across the gateway into the Gallatin canyon . . . water, the fields, and the mountains. You'll have a lot of land for ranching. I was here a few times, long ago. I know this country, Benjamin. In time, you can beat these people at their own game. They'll not make beggars of you as they have others. You'll own the land and your voices will be powerful and strong, for by law it will be signed, sealed, and delivered. When the dark cloud comes, this may be your future, the only good one you may have. If this is my last quarrel with the white man, I want to be able to say that I've won it. Do you understand?"

Benjamin One Feather nodded. He understood most of what his father was trying to tell him, but much like him, he was happy in the Yellowstone and wanted nothing more. But his father had wisdom. His sight was far beyond the palms of his hands. Who knew how long the trail was, anymore? "What shall we do with all of this land?" he finally asked.

"When the iron road comes here," Man Called Tree said, "you'll know what to do. Before I came here, a man named Jim Bridger told me about this country. It's always good medicine to listen to a man who has been over the mountain."

"Yes, I know this man," Benjamin said.

"You've heard legends about him many times, how he made long tracks up here many years ago and covered them when he left. It was his words that I always remembered: 'This is a land of grass and water, pure as mountain honey.' Ei, that's what he told me. What did you see on that one range I showed you when we came down here today? Buffalo?"

"No, some of the white man's cows and horses."

"Ei, the buffalo are almost gone from these hills, now.

When the buffalo is finished, so is the Indian. He must adjust or die. Do you remember what the man who puts iron on the ponies' hooves asked me about the land above Six Mile Creek, what I might do with it?"

"That was Mr. Blodgett," Benjamin said. "Yes, he said you could run a few cattle at that place."

"Ei, you are right again, son," Man Called Tree replied with a proud smile. "But what I had in mind was thousands, not just a few. And somewhere down the trail, what will the fire wagons on the iron road do?"

Benjamin One Feather grinned and said confidently, "Carry the cows away to hungry people."

Man Called Tree slapped his son on the shoulder. "That is the future, Benjamin. Now you understand, and it will be yours if you want it."

The stage ride to Fort Hall was monotonously long and tortuous, through sagebrush flats, along winding creek and river bottoms flanked by yellowing alders and aspen, and down into the wide valleys where eagles were soaring southward toward the great rift of the Snake River basin. Man Called Tree, pointing to a distant, bluish range of westward mountains, told Benjamin that over there was the Land of the Winding Waters, home of the Nez Percé where Benjamin was born; the land of many brothers, Gray Hawk, Young Joseph, Ollocut, White Bird, and Looking Glass; the land where he had once taken Benjamin for long rides down along the Tahmonmah or Salmon River. It was a land of peaceful Nez Percé who long ago had saved the Lewis and Clark expedition from starvation, who had given them fresh stock and pointed the way to the Columbia, and who had supplied them with boats to make the voyage to the west coast, and regrettably, whose lands and culture were now being picked apart, piece by piece, by the very people they had once befriended. Man Called Tree said Benjamin's mother, Rainbow, knew these legends better than he did, but it pained her *simikia,* her inner self, too much to tell them anymore.

At other places, where there were stage stations for food and lodging and changing of horses, Man Called Tree pointed out mountains and rivers that he knew long ago from journeys he had made with his father and brother, another time with Jim Bridger, and the strangest trip of all, one with a young Jesuit blackrobe taking medicines to the Flathead Indians over the Bitterroot mountains. Still another time he had ridden with Henri Bilodeau, Benjamin's blood father. Benjamin was both delighted and impressed with these stories, was proud to have such a great father who had been an important part of what would never be again. By the time they reached Fort Hall he had envisioned himself a part of this beautiful wild country, and in his imagination he thought that he, too, could take a good pony and a pack and perhaps find a mysterious place where no man had been before him.

But once off the stage his visions fled, for here at Fort Hall was another place of "civilization," crude, rough, and bustling with whiskered men again, doing many of the same things that he had seen in the Montana territory; a few women, too, in long dresses and shawls, children in tow, and wagons and freighters by the dozens, most of them drawn by mules. For the first time on his trip he saw in the distance a few tipis—large white lodges of Shoshoni and Bannock Indians who came here to trade in the late summer. Man Called Tree said that in another moon only a few hundred people would be in this place, only the hardiest. The wagon trains only stopped to rest here before moving on along the Oregon Trail, and the Indians always moved away to their winter villages. This was a crossroad on the frontier, a place of permanence only for a few merchants and others who had been buried in the nearby hills, including his father Thaddeus and his twin, Will. Many years ago they had been killed by white outlaws near here, but Man Called Tree, with clouded eyes, said no more about this, and Benjamin knew that it was another one of the ancient, bad-medicine legends his father wanted to forget.

Father and adopted son spent one night at the old post, sharing the big bed in James Digby's quarters. The next morning Benjamin One Feather was introduced to yet another of the white man's innovations, a breakfast of bacon, eggs, and hot biscuits, all prepared by his father, who laughed heartily when his boy commented how good Ben was at cooking their food. This was truly a woman's work and not meant for a warrior. Benjamin had never tasted these eggs from the fat birds called chickens, and these chickens when cooked were as delicious as sage grouse, or so his father said, and of course Benjamin knew this must be true.

Shortly afterward another man, this one called Jediah Howe, arrived, and he and Man Called Tree sat down in the big office of James Digby, where they carefully inspected several ledgers and signed more papers. By the time they were through, Man Called Tree, Digby's silent partner, was even more wealthy than before. Jediah Howe was commissioned to dispose of the freight and stage business and the big four-room house; funds from the safe and the bank were to be transferred to Bozeman City, and this alone was over a hundred and fifty thousand dollars—to Benjamin's notion, a fortune. But if this pleased Man Called Tree, he failed to show it. Throughout the whole transaction he was quite somber, absolutely emotionless as if in the trance of a holy man, and Benjamin wondered why he saw no trace of happiness on his father's face. Later, Man Called Tree explained his curious behavior to his son. There were several reasons for it.

First, James Digby's death was sad enough, but his passing also marked the end of an era, for he had been at the trading post since its conception in 1834. When the lucrative fur trading days came to an end, Digby bought his property from the Hudson Bay Company, doggedly held on during the lean years, mostly trading with Indians and the few remaining trappers, until the riches of the great migration west finally began pouring in.

Second, even though Man Called Tree had contributed all of his own inherited money, and had established the stage and freight line, he felt some remorse, for his personal participation had been negligible. He had fled from his responsibilities, taking refuge in the mountains where he found sanctuary among the Bird People. He didn't explain further to Benjamin that this had been dictated partly by circumstance, that in those days there were dozens of white men prepared to shoot him on sight, that only his elusiveness, his cunning, and skill had prevented this from ever happening. But Benjamin One Feather sensed what had happened to his father, and those many fireside legends seemed to substantiate it. Only along the Yellowstone was his father truly a happy man, with his family and his beloved Crow friends. To Benjamin this was not legend, it was fact.

Before they left on the stage that morning, Man Called Tree and Benjamin took a walk to a nearby hillside. The last of the summer's flowers were there, mostly late-blooming gentian, beautiful blue petals curling up from the dryness of Mother Earth. Ben told his son to pick a large bouquet, as many flowers as he could hold in his small hands, and without questioning, Benjamin One Feather did as he was told. Then he dutifully followed his father to another hill, where they soon came down into a small meadow. A fence surrounded this place and there were many markers, both wood and stone, inside it. It was a white man's burial ground. Here were the people who had been left behind, the newborn, the young, the old, all interred in the shadows of the distant Tetons.

Man Called Tree knew this cemetery, and directly he stopped and placed his hand on his son's shoulder. Pointing, he said, "This is one of the reasons I brought you along on this trip. Here lies your real father, a good man, one that you should be proud to claim." The wooden cross was simply marked: HENRI BILODEAU. Next to it was a tiny grave with a like marker: INFANT BILODEAU. "This was your Nez Percé brother you never knew," Man Called Tree said. "He was born before his time, and I helped bury him. It rained that day, son, and no one could see our tears. You came a year later to take his place."

Removing his white man's hat, Benjamin One Feather bent low and distributed the gentians evenly over the graves. Speaking in Nez Percé, he said, "*Niez kunu,* are you there, my family? Hear me then, for I honor you, my father and brother, as I honor my father who brought me to see your resting place. *Taz alago,* good-bye, and sleep well. May the Great Spirit be with you always."

A week later, Ben Tree and his son were back in Virginia City, en route home to the Echeta Casha, once again stopping overnight and meeting with the lawyer, Arthur Clawson. Clawson, as empowered, had ridden down to

Alder Gulch and met with Bill Coonrad regarding the homestead cabin and corrals on Six Mile Creek in the Gallatin, and Clawson was happy to report the sale of the property to Ben for the sum of fifteen hundred dollars. Coonrad had agreed to winter in the cabin and pick up his money from the bank in the spring, when he planned on returning to Kentucky. What surprised Clawson was that his influential senior partner, Wilbur Sanders, knew all about their client Ben Tree, and had prepared a special memorandum for the land office to expedite the acquisition of the new homestead and rights to the adjacent eight thousand acres.

Clawson, a puzzled look on his face, said to Ben Tree, "He offered no explanation, but he seemed to think this was a matter of great urgency after I mentioned the documents we had prepared. In fact, he was somewhat disappointed I hadn't informed him earlier of your visit. I take it he wanted to see you, something of a personal nature. I told him that you were coming back in several weeks, but he's down in Bannack now. Do you know Mr. Sanders?"

"Only by reputation," said Ben reflectively. "I recall he was a pretty good lawyer five or six years back, all that vigilante business, probably before your time here."

"That's true, yes, before I practiced with Mr. Sanders," replied Clawson. "And he has so many political matters on his mind these days, a man of great influence. . . . Well, it surprised me when he was so keen about this kind of business." Clawson, still puzzled, shook his head. "Well, you must have made an impression on him at some time, because the last thing he told me was to take good care of you . . . something about owing you a debt of gratitude."

"Just a small matter a long time ago," Ben said, a fleeting vision of five outlaws marching up a frozen street to the gallows racing through his mind. And one of them had been the killer of his father and brother. He had almost forgotten that cold December day of death and retribution. The grisly image faded away like a misty cloud and he heard himself saying, "Some things are best forgotten, Mr. Clawson. Just draw the shade and blow out the lantern, ei?"

Benjamin One Feather wondered about this evasive

conversation on the part of his father, but he suspected it was more of the bad-medicine past. He recalled that there was a mysterious legend once told by the shaman, Ten Sleeps, in which Man Called Tree goes into the white man's gold country to fulfill a prophecy. Ten Sleeps was old now, so old that his skin cracked when he walked about in the tipi, but he remembered this legend. He said that Man Called Tree once had lost his *iraaxe,* his soul, because of these white men and what they had done to his family. Man Called Tree was very troubled and not at peace with himself. Ten Sleeps made medicine and told Man Called Tree about a dream he had had, a vision of many riders, their faces painted black with death, their hands painted red with blood. This was in the Moon of Ice on the River. He said that in this dream Man Called Tree rode into a terrible storm, with many dark clouds around him, to meet these strange riders. But Man Called Tree had made his moccasins ready and had big medicine. His face was painted half-black and half-red. When he came riding out of the big storm, there were many horses running away but they had no riders. These men had become lost somewhere on the Great Hanging Road, in that great void between Mother Earth and the Milky Way.

This was the end of Ten Sleeps' story, but those who listened knew that this was a true legend, for Man Called Tree had indeed gone away during the Moon of Ice on the River, and when he returned to the village he was at peace with himself. He had reclaimed his *iraaxe.*

Benjamin One Feather knew Virginia City wasn't a place of good memories for Man Called Tree, and he was happy to be back on the stage early the next morning. Their village on the Clarks Fork of the Yellowstone was getting closer. Back in Bozeman City, they made only a short stop in town. No more noisy hotels, his father said, so after a brief chat with Donald Blodgett at the smithy shed they picked up their horses and packs at the livery and bought a few food supplies for a one-night stay at the Coonrad homestead, quarters less hectic and more palatable to their frontier taste. Ben Tree found the key to the cabin right where Arthur Clawson had told him it would be, over a rafter in the horse shed, and within a short time father and son had settled in, had a fire going in the iron stove and their bedrolls spread across the two wooden bunks.

Before dark set in, Ben inspected the corrals near the creek, found the lodgepoles surrounding the bottom in good condition and in no need of immediate work. He decided, however, that in due time he would fence both homesteads and erect a large gate where the ruts of the trail entered, facing the property frontage. He would erect his mark here, the sign of the tree. Benjamin One Feather could see that what Jim Bridger had said was true, for this land was rich and fertile, the meadow grass almost knee-high. His father allowed that with irrigation meadows within the homestead would produce three hundred acres of good hay, and he told Benjamin that by the following summer he would initiate the first phase of the new Tree ranch, purchasing a few head of seed stock, fencing the bottom, and marking boundaries on the spacious upper lands.

This, he said, was only the beginning. The future would be up to the sons of Tree and what they would make of it, either accepting a monthly handout of chuckaway on the great reservation or raising and selling their own cattle in the Gallatin. Chuckaway—a ration of flour, bacon, and beans supplied by the government—had an ominous, distasteful sound. Benjamin One Feather did not like this, and so, as his great father had done, he decided to live within his Indian heritage for as many moons as the Great Spirit would allow, while also vowing never to accept chuckaway from the white man at the Crow agency.

It was now the Moon of the Changing Seasons, the time when Man Called Tree promised that he and Benjamin would meet the Crow braves back near the east pass of the Gallatin. They were saddling their ponies, preparing to leave on this brisk October morning, when a lone rider appeared down the trail, heading up toward the cabin. Shortly, the man hailed them with a wave of his hand. Then, dismounting some distance away, he gave his horse a pat on the rump and it went over to the creek to drink. When the stranger finally came near, Benjamin could see that he was young and long in the limbs, his moustache thin and stringy, and he wore a floppy hat. A bandanna was curled loosely around his neck and hung down over the front part of his canvas duster.

"Hello," he said, walking up, swinging his long arms. "Are you Mr. Ben Tree?"

"I'm known as Ben Tree," Ben answered. "And who might you be, son?"

"Name is Claybourn Moore, sir, but my friends call me just plain old Clay." Removing his gloves, he went on. "Fellow down at the blacksmith barn said I might catch up with you out here." He shook hands with Ben Tree, and Ben then introduced him to young Benjamin. Clay Moore grinned and said, "Looks like I caught you two just in time. That Blodgett said you moved in a hurry."

"Ei," Ben Tree nodded. "A man has to strike while the iron's hot to catch up with me in this country. And what brings you way out here?"

"Well, matter of fact, a couple of things," answered Moore. "Blodgett says you're fixing to do a little work up here, and I was wondering if you might need an extra hand. I'm sorta good with critters and such, worked down at Barney O'Keefe's spread for a while, and I'm over at Stuart's ranch at the present, back over toward the Three Forks a piece. I can do about anything you'd be wanting done, if you're hiring and so obliged."

Ben nodded and said, "Ei, we'll be doing some work here come next spring, but Bill Coonrad's coming back for the winter, so there'll be nothing until after that, I reckon about April next or so." Ben Tree threw his canvas bedroll on his horse and began to secure it. "What are you doing for this Mr. Stuart?"

"Droving, mostly up in the hills, moving stock back and forth, looking for the best grass," Moore replied.

"You don't like it over there?"

"Don't mind the work, no, not at all," said Moore with a smile. "It's the bunkhouse that I don't much cater to, rowdies and such. Liquor don't set with me much. More of a loner, I reckon. Something like this would suit me just fine. That's about it, Mr. Tree."

Ben paused and closely studied the young man for a moment. What he saw was an image somewhat like his own of about fifteen years past: a raw-boned, eager youngster seeking opportunity and challenge, a loose, limber rider with keen blue eyes that never strayed when he talked. "You know how to make fence? Handle those timbers, make jacks and string poles?"

"Hell, yes!" responded Clay Moore, his blue eyes lighting up as he laughed. "I've sure done that more'n once, I have. I'd say a jack fence is one of my specialties."

"What's Stuart paying these days?"

"Dollar a day and vittles, two dollars haying."

"Well, I *will* need a hand, but like I told you, come next spring," Ben said. "If you can hold on through the winter at Stuart's spread, I'll be back for a day or two in April, no more, only to get things under way, so you check in regular with Mr. Blodgett about that time. You'll get your chance to see what you can do. You'll have to take care of your own larder, but I'll pay you two dollars a day straight and make a bonus if the job around here is done right and proper. How does that sound?"

"Mighty fine to me, Mr. Tree," Moore said, his grin broadening. "And I'll sure keep in touch with the blacksmith."

"Good enough," Ben Tree said. "We'll mark out this bottom next spring, see how you do. Now, you said you had a couple of things on your mind, ei? So what's the other?"

Hesitating, Clay Moore sighed, then said haltingly, "Well . . . I reckon this'll sound . . . crazy as a bedbug to you, but I just wanted to . . . meet you right personal. You see, I had an ornery older brother, a downright no-account for a fact, no respect for our ma—she's a washerwoman down at Virginia City, and he whomped me more'n once, too. Maybe you remember him. His name was Gad Moore. You shot and killed him over at Cottonwood a few years back."

Ben Tree suddenly sagged, devastated inside by this abrupt and startling revelation, this dark shadow from his past. "Yes, a young man no older than yourself," he finally said with a sigh. "Yes, I remember him, and I'm damned sorry about it, but by jingo, the boy didn't give me much choice. I tried to talk him down, get out of there. Yes, I remember, and I'm sorry it had to happen that way."

Moore brushed away the apology. "Oh, everybody

heard the story, and how you went and paid twenty dollars to have him put under right proper. He deserved what he got, all right. That's the true story. Those no-accounts he was running with pitched in five hundred dollars for him to kill you. Didn't know that, did you? I found it out later, when the dam broke loose down there and they strung up Plummer's gang. No, ain't no use feeling sorry about Gad, Mr. Tree, 'cause he wasn't worth a whit, anyways. You're damned lucky he didn't bushwhack you with a shotgun. He had a mean streak in him a mile wide."

What a strange twist of fate, Ben thought, staring sorrowfully above his horse at Claybourn Moore. Here was a young drover seeking employment from the very man who had killed his brother. And Ben obviously felt more remorse about the ancient disaster than Clay Moore did. Ben Tree looked down at Benjamin's serious face, reaching out for some solace and understanding from his son. "What do you say, Benjamin? You've heard this man's story, and now he wants to work for us."

Benjamin One Feather was silent for a moment, making judgment. Finally: "You did him no wrong. His brother dishonored him and his mother. I think he should work. He's honest, and he has more sense than his brother did. *Sepekuse,*" he finished in Nez Percé. So let it be done.

"*Tasnig,*" replied Ben with a sad smile. It is decided.

The three of them rode back to Bozeman City together, where Clay Moore headed west toward the Three Forks country and Man Called Tree and his son trailed to the east, back to the Yellowstone Valley.

Benjamin One Feather's childhood was speeding quickly, and as he grew tall and straight like his adopted father, his face began to reflect the beauty of his Nez Percé mother, Rainbow, the *palojami* from the Land of the Shell People. He was a handsome, fearless young man, straight of nose and with wide-set dark eyes; he had inherited the firm chin and light skin of the Frenchman, Henri Bilodeau. He had been blessed by Akabatatdia, the Maker of Everything, with ability, appearance, and intelligence, but unlike his parents he had seen little strife or tragedy in his sheltered life among the Crow.

Much of this was because Man Called Tree had made it so. Man Called Tree and the chiefs who followed him lived by preference in the isolated valleys of the Yellowstone, along the lower Big Horn, Clarks Fork and Stillwater rivers, only occasionally traveling as far south as the Wind, where they sometimes intermingled with the friendly Shoshoni. They seldom met other Crow brothers who wandered across the Echeta Casha in the plains below the Bull mountains or even those who roamed the lower Rosebud and Big Horn reservation land. They were content to live in their traditional lands.

By purposely shunning the white man's civilization, Man Called Tree's followers had little contact or confrontation with either the bluecoats or immigrants. Even though Man Called Tree's village was friendly, Benjamin One Feather knew that some of these occasional white passersby went out of their way to please his father. And others went out of their way to avoid him. He made no quarrels with the bluecoats, nor did they bother him, even on the unceded land along the upper Yellowstone. For these reasons, there were no contentious forts in the Crow country, nor any blackrobe missions, for long ago Man Called Tree had spoken to these cross-bearers, telling them that there was nothing spiritual they could give the Absaroke that the Absaroke didn't already have. Nor was there any gold, as Man Called Tree told those foolish hairy-faced ones who dared to come into the land seeking it. They always left, and usually in a hurry. And so Benjamin One Feather's legacy was a childhood of peace and happiness.

Throughout the growing years, he had excelled in the games of the youngsters: shooting buffalo chips with the bow, the kickball, riding contests, and wrestling. He was among the first to ride backward like a contrary, which brought great amusement to his father. Often Benjamin One Feather had been the leader in the village raids on the meat-makers, when the boys, their faces blackened in disguise, their bodies naked and greased so they couldn't be held, raced in on the squaws unexpectedly, snatching choice portions of buffalo from the racks. Later, in the forest, they built their fires and roasted the stolen bounty, all the while bragging of their prowess in thievery. They were like little old men talking in the council. "Who got this meat?" "Benjamin One Feather." "He is the best meat-getter of us all." "Give him the best piece." "Yes, he shall have the best." "I will steal a better piece next time, no matter how many lumps I get." And when finished with their feast, the little men would sit silently, waiting for the first one to rise to drink water or relieve himself of it, and whoever that one was, they would pounce upon him and wipe their greasy hands on his body. After cleansing themselves in the river and returning victoriously to the village, Benjamin One Feather was always the most successful in dodging the stones and buffalo-tail whisks of the irate old women. Among the young he was the pipe-carrier, the leader, and the admiring girls said Benjamin had been touched by the Trickster, Esaccawata, Old Man Coyote himself. They vied for his attention and affection.

As he passed into young manhood, Benjamin One Feather participated fully in all phases of village life. He was now a member of the Iaxuxke, the Fox society, one of the military-social clubs for young men seeking honor and prestige. So was his young brother, White Moon. This, in the eyes of their pretty fifteen year-old sister, Little Blue Hoop, gave them great esteem, even though Man Called Tree had been a Big Dog member when he was a young brave. Other societies were the Muddy Hands and the Lumpwoods. Little Blue Hoop, slender and willowy, and with the attractive Nez Percé features of her mother, detested the Lumpwoods. This on account of Bear Gets Up, a young brave who continually flirted with her despite her pointed aloofness and disdain of him.

She told Benjamin One Feather that she was not being haughty just because her father was such a great chief, or that Bear Gets Up was beneath her station in life. Simply, she had no desire for a husband such as Bear Gets Up, or any of the other Lumpwoods who chided her because she ignored the advances of their fellow member. She just considered him *irise,* dumb, and extremely crude, to the point of being outright lewd. Once, he had made gestures to his crotch. Bear Gets Up ate fish, she told her brother, and this was one of the worst of insults. And she sang a little song, "IAXUXKE ITUM BAKIWAKE," in a quavering tremolo to keep the chagrined Lumpwoods at their distance. 'The Foxes are good-looking. I'll make *them* my sweethearts.' This made Benjamin One Feather chuckle, and he promised that he and his fellow Foxes would look out for her, that no Lumpwood would dare try to kidnap her during the time of the Taking of Women, the annual event of wife-snatching. This promise was made with some levity on the part of Benjamin, for he realized that because of Chief Man Called Tree's prominence, Little Blue Hoop would be spared such embarrassment. Any brave who wanted her for a wife would have to secure the chief's permission, as well as an assortment of rich gifts. Bear Gets Up was a courageous young man, strong in deeds, but he was a brave of little means.

By the time he was eighteen Benjamin One Feather had shot buffalo, stolen ponies from the Cheyenne, and eluded a band of Sioux in the upper Big Horn country, but he had never personally counted coup on an enemy. This finally came about in a strange and unexpected way during the Moon of the Red Blooming Lilies, July, when he and a group of the Foxes rode along with some food-gatherers down into the Yellowstone bottom to search for tubers and berries. Chokecherry and serviceberry were just beginning to ripen, and in the green meadows above the river the squaws always found a bountiful supply of elk thistle, yampa onion, and red turnip to fetch out with their dibbles. Even though this was labor for badly needed food it most often was an enjoyable, festive occasion. While the sixteen women went about their work in small, gossiping groups, joking and laughing, the young Fox men served as lookouts, usually banding together on the perimeters or ranging their ponies far in advance of the women who were busy filling their parfleches. Later they always came together to share the food they had brought, and if the day happened to be warm and sunny everyone bathed in the river before returning to the village. These were happy, carefree forays, sometimes even the beginnings of a village romance or a clandestine affair in the bushes, but rarely an occasion fraught with the threat of violence.

In late afternoon, when a few of the women had put their parfleches and digging sticks to the side and were bathing, Old Dog Jumps came riding into the cottonwood trees where Benjamin One Feather and his brothers were seated in a circle, talking. Reining his pony around, Old Dog Jumps pointed downriver. Eight riders were coming, he reported excitedly, following the tracks of the women's ponies along the bottom land. He said these riders were wandering Piegan, probably scouts coming from the Buffalo country somewhere below, because he saw no packs with them. They were armed with rifles.

Sitting Elk, the Fox leader, immediately stood. He possessed the symbolic forked stick of authority, a small shaft decorated with beaded strips of rawhide and fox fur, and instantly he was making decisions. He spoke clearly, without a trace of alarm in his voice. "We will not run and hide from these Pekonies. They are on our side of the river, far from their land. Now they plan mischief with our women. They follow their tracks. They want their ponies, and are not afraid to steal a woman or two to make it a good bargain." He looked around at the other Foxes. "There are six of us and eight of them. Ei, and we have rifles, too, so if they are looking for some mischief, we will give it to them." Holding his leader's staff aloft, he said with authority, "*Ictua wapaxaxiky*!" I poke it in their eyes! Motioning to Benjamin One Feather and Old Dog Jumps, he told them to ride quietly around in back of the Blackfeet, to surprise them from the rear. Sitting Elk then quickly dispatched Benjamin's brother, White Moon, to alert the women, to tell them to find hiding places in the trees and leave their ponies in the clearing to serve as decoys, for he was allowing that the Piegan would come charging in, trying to drive the horses out across the bottom upriver. "*Ikye*!" he called. "Attention, make your moccasins ready!" Checking his rifle, he ran off in a crouch toward the head of the clearing, the remaining two brother Foxes close behind.

The Piegan appeared about five minutes later, but not as Sitting Elk had anticipated. These Pekonies were extremely cautious, sitting on their ponies in the shadows of the cottonwoods, silently contemplating the sixteen Crow ponies grazing in the meadow. Spread out through the brush and trees, the Piegan apparently were in no great haste to make a dash across the open clearing. Something was amiss. Obviously their suspicion had been aroused by the missing women, the absence of the magpie chatter always so common among maidens. Instead, the woods were strangely silent. Only the sounds of a few birds, and the nearby rippling of the river, could be heard. Near the front, one of the men made sign, and another slid off his pony and trotted toward the river. Directly he returned, shaking his head. Suddenly, from behind them, Benjamin's shrill war cry shattered the stillness, sending the Piegan bolting directly toward the pastured Crow ponies. Then two shots echoed through the bottom, and one of the advancing Pekonies toppled from his horse.

To avoid the ambush, four of the enemy broke off toward the river, driving horses ahead of them while the remaining three Piegan unexpectedly dashed straight ahead into the hidden Absaroke. The women hiding in the brush by the river couldn't believe their eyes when they saw their own ponies approaching. Leaping out, they frantically waved their arms, successfully turning the spooked animals back toward the dense woods. Unfortunately one of the maidens, young White Crane, daughter of Shoots Far Arrow, was struck a blow in the back of her head by one of the charging Piegan. As she reeled away, a brave seized her by her long hair and dragged her into the water. From the trees there was more gunfire, and another riderless Piegan pony trotted across the clearing.

Meanwhile, Benjamin One Feather, riding hard behind the Pekonies closest to the river, managed to catch the brave who was attempting to hike White Crane onto his horse. Half-dazed, she was hanging partway over the front of the saddle when Benjamin came in, slashing out with his rifle barrel. He smashed the Pekony across the side of the head, sending both him and White Crane splashing into the water.

When the man came up thrashing wildly, trying to grasp his pony's foreleg, Benjamin One Feather had already wheeled about and was on top of him again. With another crushing blow, he tumbled the brave backward into the river right on top of White Crane. Blood swirled around in the eddy, and the Blackfeet came up floating on his back. One eyeball, resting on his broken cheekbone, was staring eerily up at the late-afternoon sun. Then White Crane popped up like a cork, her dress floating up over her hips, exposing her long brown legs. Her beads had curled halfway around her face, but the sudden dip had revived her, and in between gasps and spitting water she managed to say, "*Aho,*" thanks. Benjamin leaped down, plucked her from the water, and hoisted her into the saddle of the stricken man's pony. "*Hiya!*" he cried, and giving it a slap on the rump, he sent it running down the bank toward safety.

By the time he returned to the clearing, the furor was over. His younger brother, White Moon, had ridden off through the trees to round up the women's horses. Sitting

Elk, bleeding from a blow to his cheek, and Old Dog Jumps were near the edge of the clearing, squatting over a dead Pekony, removing his hair. At the far end of the meadow, the other two Foxes and some of the girls were scalping and stripping the body of the Piegan brave shot at the very beginning of the short battle. From what Benjamin One Feather could determine, Sitting Elk was the only casualty among the Crow, and his wound, luckily, was superficial. White Crane bore no mark where she'd been struck. While the women had lost four of their mounts, the net loss was only one, for the three dead Piegans' horses were left behind.

Later, when White Crane rode back in, Benjamin discovered that his riverside victim's horse was a fine gray mare with a good saddle, plus a new Winchester rifle secured in a beaded elkskin scabbard. This not only made Benjamin One Feather a coup counter, but a gun-snatcher as well. Other kudos were to come his way, too. He had rescued one of his sisters, thus becoming an *akbapicere*, one who saves someone. Probably less meaningful to him, as a coup-counter he could now take a bride.

So what had begun as merely a routine food-gathering venture had suddenly turned into a war party *aratsiwe*, a homecoming. Sitting Elk dispatched White Moon to alert the village crier and Fox Society, for these other members at home would mount up and join them in the triumphant processional into camp, to the beating of the drums, the tremolo of the women, and howling of the dogs.

After the preparations were made, an eagle bone whistle pierced the air. Their faces blackened and scalp sticks held high, the braves came riding in, dust swirling from the rush of their ponies' hooves. Swaying lines of dancing and chanting women began to form, and in his exuberance Benjamin One Feather could not resist one final ride-around. He charged away, crossing over the back of his pony four times to each side and raising the tremolos to a shrieking crescendo. The lines of the stomping women swelled to over a hundred; more drums were beating; eagle-bone whistles sounded again; and rattles and bells joined the rhythm. Soon the Fox braves came dancing in a file, their faces black, vermilion streaks on their bare chests and backs, their feathers, beads, and strips of fur dangling, their dew-claw rattles and scalp-sticks shaking, and all this sent the squaws and maidens into a squealing frenzy. Benjamin One Feather had never felt such exhilaration in his life. To be honored in such a way was beyond his imagination.

That night, long after the *aratsiwe,* Man Called Tree presented his son with an eagle feather and spoke wise words to him. "You have honored our people and they have responded, ei? I'm proud of you, but in this joy remember that you've also dishonored those across the Echeta Casha. From this moon on you'll have to have the eye of an eagle, the cunning of a coyote, and the heart of a wolf. I know this from experience. They'll be after your hair, and don't you ever forget it."

Benjamin One Feather took these new honors of a brave warrior in stride, but with some kind admonishment from his family. Each morning the crier would call out, '*Bire daxua hia, bire daxua kok,*' take to the water, get up and bathe, and Man Called Tree would remind Benjamin to be sure to look in the water to see if his head was bigger than his body. This was not the only reminder. Little Blue Hoop told him not to hold his head too high, lest the rain fall into his nose and choke him. But she was protective, too, warning Benjamin about the maidens who were forever flirting with him: the virtuous ones, and others less virtuous who had already taken lovers in the bushes; those who did fine bead and quill work and others who were slovenly and poor tipi managers. He laughingly dismissed some of this sisterly advice and imparted some of his own. "I watch you, too, my little sister," he told her, speaking in English. "Don't be so careless that you fall into the same trap that Old Man Coyote has so cunningly set for others. He always gets the unsuspecting. You're not above this, either."

"I'm no longer a child," she returned flippantly. "I know my way."

"Ei, I'm aware of this," he said with a smile. There was a teasing gleam in his dark eyes. "And so are my brothers. The roundness of your bottom hasn't gone unnoticed."

"*Aho*!" she exclaimed, smiling. "Thanks. I will take this as a compliment, my brother, for what you say is true, and I'm proud of it. I have the body of a woman, but only the right man may claim it. It would be well to remind you that the trap works both ways. Ei, and you are no more safe than I. My eyes don't deceive me, either. If you go strutting around like a prairie chicken in the spring, I will disown you, cast you aside like a fish."

They enjoyed this gentle chiding, the bantering back and forth in both Absaroke and English, but in reality each one was only seeking the best of life for the other, and Benjamin's love for his Nez Percé sister was so deep he gladly would have died for her. Man Called Tree's family was bonded by love and honor, and this was good.

Among the young women who watched Benjamin, White Crane, daughter of Shoots Far Arrow, was the most ubiquitous and one of the most attractive. Rather tall for her sixteen years, she had a boyish beauty about her, finely chiseled features, a sharp and well-defined face, a little fatness in the cheeks, a straight nose with barely a flare at the nostrils, and a clear complexion. Since he had plucked her from the grasp of the Blackfeet that July day, she seemed to buzz about him like a honey bee, seeking sustenance, a nectar that he wasn't yet fully prepared to give. On occasion she spoke a few pleasant words, nothing the least suggestive, and for a time Benjamin passed this off as gratitude, her own peculiar way of thanking him for saving her life or honor, maybe both.

Benjamin One Feather's response to her attentions was polite. He wasn't snobbish or conceited, never purposely avoided her, even though she seemed to pop up at the most unexpected times. It was as though she had the all-seeing eyes of Owl Maker, the witch above whose magic could penetrate the very depths of the blackest forest, or see through the hides of the finest tipi. Often, when he was in front of the Fox lodge talking with his brothers, White Crane would pass by, accompanied by other maidens, and she would smile at him. Another time at the pony herd, he was singling out horses for his father, and when he turned, White Crane was there, too, fetching ponies for her brother, Little Bull Runs. Yet another time he was washing his face in the creek, and when he rose up, water dripping down, there she was again, sitting cross-legged across the stream, smiling at him as usual. *"Kahe,"* she simply said. Hello. Welcome. After this last encounter, Benjamin One Feather took extra precaution when he went to the woods to relieve himself, lest he look up in the process of urinating and discover White Crane standing there with another "*Kahe.*"

One afternoon, Benjamin finally took White Crane's brother aside and explained his predicament. This woman was everywhere, drawn to him like a moth to the flame. Little Bull Runs listened attentively for a while and then broke out laughing, as if this were one of the best stories he had heard in years. Little Bull Runs was a member of the Lumpwoods, and while he was a friend and Crow brother of Benjamin One Feather, he really had no sympathy for him. Understanding, yes, since he well knew the aims of his younger sister, White Crane. These maidens were all alike, and after their first menses had only one thing on their minds. White Crane had set her sights on taking a man for a husband or lover, and she wanted one that suited her discriminating taste.

Grinning like a fat frog, Little Bull Runs said to Benjamin One Feather, "I think you are the man my sister wants. I would tell her no; that is, if this man didn't meet my expectations. But even if you are a Fox, I see no dishonor in you. In fact, I like you. Already you have big medicine, so if you choose to mount my sister, do so. You and your father have plenty of ponies, and I know your gifts to me and my father will be good ones. My mother will gladly accept food and meat from your tipis. Would you have me discourage my sister for all of this? Am I a fool? *Eyah*, this would be like pulling the teeth of Old Man Coyote."

Mouth agape, Benjamin One Feather was dumbfounded. It angered him that his plea for help and understanding had met such a callous, materialistic rebuff, that Little Bull Runs ignored the fact that Benjamin was not ready for such a relationship, that he had too many other tribal matters and ambitions on his mind. Turning on his heel, he said in Nez Percé the only retort that came to his mind, "*Enimkinikai neksep!*" Go to Hell, foreigner! Of course, Benjamin knew that the Lumpwood didn't understand this insult, any more than he understood Ben's predicament.

But Benjamin gained a temporary reprieve from his romantic dilemma during the Moon of the Black Berries, when he and his brother accompanied Man Called Tree on the yearly visitation to the ranch in the Gallatin Valley. It was a short trip, only long enough to meet Clay Moore's new wife, arrange for the construction of a bunkhouse, and take care of business at the bank. Benjamin was proud to say that he had been right about Claybourn Moore during that long-ago first meeting. This young man was industrious, possessed common sense, and was thoroughly honest, and with these attributes had slowly but surely brought the ranch into financial stability. Another full-time drover had been hired, a new mower and hay-stacker acquired, the seed stock had multiplied from forty head to almost six hundred in five years, and Moore's horse sales also had proliferated. Profit, less all expenses, was near seven thousand dollars. For the young drover's efforts, Man Called Tree gave him a five-hundred-dollar bonus, and wedding gifts of one hundred dollars each for him and his bride, Ruth.

If Benjamin One Feather believed that his two-week absence would cool White Crane's ardor, he was sadly mistaken, for one of the first faces that he saw when he rode back into the village was that of the comely maiden. There she was, standing with others of her kind, staring directly at him, her dark eyes dancing with pleasure. Her hand came up in greeting, and while this was at some considerable distance, he clearly saw her mouth the word *kahe*. What else could he do but graciously acknowledge this? Lest there be any misconception of conceit or pomposity on his part, he finally managed a weak smile and casually returned her welcome with a passing wave of his hand. This was only the proper response to a young woman so smitten with romantic notions. Now Benjamin realized that he was in a real quandary, and to deny that White Crane had worked his mind into a state of befuddled confusion would have been an outright lie. She was spreading her blanket for him, and the equilibrium of his well-organized life was beginning to lose some of its balance. What could he possibly do to dissuade her that would not offend her or belittle her own worth? The maiden was faultless. She was pretty, immaculately clean, her hair beautifully kept, and her grace was mature and womanly. By jingo, he had taken note of all of this, too!

While Benjamin One Feather knew the intentions of

this calculating woman, regrettably he couldn't comprehend his own muddled intentions. Why the timidity, the reluctance on his part to accept White Crane's generosity, her surreptitious invitation to romance? This was disconcerting, an embarrassment. And that her brother found such humor in the situation was absolutely outrageous. If Little Bull Runs let the rest of the Lumpwoods in on this little game everyone might be laughing and passing snide remarks his way, if not about his manhood then some other ridiculous accusation—maybe that he was a berdache, no less, a woman-man. Benjamin One Feather shrank at the thought of such humiliation.

When, in desperation, and seeking some parental advice, Benjamin finally approached Man Called Tree about White Crane, all he received was a fatherly pat on the back, a Nez Percé *taz, taz,*—take it easy, these things happen to all young people, and in time they disperse like seeds in the wind. What seems a mountain one day, may be a small hill the next. Man Called Tree neglected to tell his son that he had encountered a similar situation when he had first lived with the Crow, that when he was bedridden with a Pekony arrow wound in his hip, a conniving brother had moved his pretty sister into Man Called Tree's lodge to help nurse him back to health. That he had tried to avoid her loving attention only to end up taking her for his wife. Man Called Tree, trying to take the matter more seriously, asked, "What do you know about this girl? What have you talked about?"

Benjamin One Feather heaved a breath of exasperation. "That's just it, we've talked about nothing. I barely know her, but I can't escape seeing her. She's here, she's there, flitting about like a butterfly. She's beginning to follow me around like a camp puppy. She knows nothing about talk. An occasional hello, and that's it. To ignore her would be impolite."

"No more than infatuation, perhaps," suggested Man Called Tree. "Idolatry, maybe, what with you saving her from the Blackfeet. I can understand that, a thankful young lady."

Benjamin shook his head doubtfully. "I don't read 'thanks' in those eyes; no, that's not what I read at all. It's more like a *hungry* look, sometimes with a spark of fire. Would you call that infatuation? No, the woman embarrasses me, father. My Fox brothers see this too.''

Suppressing a smile, Man Called Tree reflected momentarily on long-ago days when Little Hoop, his first woman, had given him the same sensation, that rush of color she used to bring to his face with just one, small suggestive gesture. Love had not come easily for him either, but it did come, and it flowered beautifully. ''Well, my son,'' he concluded, ''I'll tell you this. You'll never know anything about this girl unless you communicate something more than *kahe*. Ei, some conversation would help matters, maybe clear up this little problem. Then you can each go your own way, if that's what you decide.''

''She seems so darned young,'' commented Benjamin. ''What can she know about conversation?''

His father's brow arched in surprise. ''Young? You're thinking like a white man, again, Benjamin. Indian women are wise beyond their years . . . already up and grown by thirteen or fourteen, sometimes not in body, but in mind. They're born to the land, and they get a good taste of it a damned sight quicker than a white girl. Look at your own sister, fifteen, a young woman, and smart as a whip.'' He finally chuckled and gave his son a bolstering pat of confidence. ''You're so outspoken about everything else under the sun, I didn't realize you were so shy about women.''

Benjamin One Feather blushed. ''I'm not shy. I just don't know whether I'm prepared for this sort of thing. Inexperience, as it must be.''

''Well, this subject of women is one thing that I can't prepare you for,'' Man Called Tree said. ''You see, I learned long ago that only a woman can teach you about a woman. This much, I do know: They're a highly unpredictable and loving lot, most often always a step ahead of you, mind-readers, all of them. And don't go telling your mother I said this, either, but once you let a woman in your life, once your heart gets in the way of your mind, you're a goner, and that's a fact.''

Benjamin One Feather grinned at his father. ''I think that mother would enjoy hearing something like this. It sounds like a profession of love.''

Pressing his fingers to his lips, Man Called Tree whispered back, "Maybe so, maybe not. Like I said, they're a highly unpredictable lot. They can turn words inside out and make them come out like a love song. Ei, that's a woman for you, Benjamin. Show me a man who understands one, and I'll show you a braggart or a liar, maybe both."

Later, when Benjamin left, he considered some of what his father had told him. Perhaps he would indeed have to initiate some communication, verbal, precise, and intimidating, in retaliation to the only type of communication that White Crane seemed to know, a body language solely devoted to the covetous shift of her dark eyes, the twist of a hip, the glide of long legs, and the *kahe* of her pursed lips. Somehow he must conclude this flirtation without embarrassment or shame to White Crane or himself, and this called for strategy and cunning.

White Crane, however, was not without her own strategy. So far she had only employed what *Bakukure,* the One Above, had given her: a lithe, slender figure, a beguiling smile, and the doe-eyed innocence of a fawn. What she knew of these young men in the village came from keen observation and from gossip, and of course the advice she continually received from her sister companions, many of whom were experienced in such matters. Around the circle of bead and quill work, the making of robes, food-gathering, or evening strolling, the talk, accompanied by much giggling, usually centered on the opposite sex. If one maiden innocently inquired, there was always another, sometimes several, who had a ready answer and explanation. "But how do you know this?" someone would ask. "An old woman told me," would be a likely reply, and everyone would break out in giggles. It seemed to White Crane that none of her sisters ever admitted to first-hand knowledge, but this was the custom, to say that "someone else told me"; my *iraxaxe,* or shadow; or my *akse,* parents; and most ridiculous of all, Old Man Coyote, the devious Trickster, the master of logic who always knew how to turn wrong into right.

White Crane quietly absorbed these many different ploys and suggestions of her sisters, some of which were no more than common sense, others quite funny, and some quite crude. Do not gabble incessantly like a goose, for no man likes this; only speak when you have carefully chosen your words; observe your intended man, learn his likes and dislikes, uncover his weaknesses, and play on all of these accordingly; pretend innocence; talk of his interests, not your own; try to be with him when he is alone. And there were others: Compliment him on his accomplishments, ignore his shortcomings; comb your hair morning and night; scent yourself and be ready at all times with a clean body. (Giggling, here.) Wash your feet, too. (More giggling.) Hide his moccasins and loincloth under your bed robes. (Much laughter.) Never have the breath of a buffalo. (Repugnant sighs.) If you feel his hardness against you, do not be surprised, think nothing of it. (Peals of laughter.)

Otter Woman, a vivacious and mischievous one, cautioned all in this talking group not to be misled by the latter suggestion, for all wasn't as it seemed. She said that once she had heard of a maiden loving a brave under a big pine tree, holding him close, making powerful kisses. This woman (not Otter Woman, of course) became highly embarrassed when she discovered this hardness was not what she had thought—it was his *maxaxore*, his dew-claw club rattle pressing against her middle. (More hilarity.) And on and on.

By the time of the Moon of the Drying Grass, White Crane's want had become an obsession, but some good fortune finally came her way. She noticed, with some amusement, that the dogs had found a new marking post near the perimeter of the village to piss on. Big Cloud That Rides Over the Mountain had placed a buffalo skull on a stump. The white skull, facing inward, meant that meat was needed, and Big Cloud, whose special medicine was in the Buffalo hunt, was alerting the villagers to make their preparations. Four scouts from the Muddy Hands were already searching for likely curly cow herds in the eastern valleys, where the surround would be conducted. The people who would participate, the hunters, the butchers, and the fleshers, had already been chosen, and Shoots Far Arrow's family was among them. This was to be the last hunt before Cold Maker settled his icy hands over the vast land of the Absaroke, and much smoked meat and pemmican were always needed during the time of the Hungry Moons. When winter came, other selected hunters would take to the mountains for fresh meat from the elk and deer, the blackhorns being forgotten until late spring when the great hunt for bulls began.

White Crane was happy because this marked the first time she was accompanying her family on the buffalo trail. The hunt itself didn't interest her that much; it was only a means to an end. Benjamin One Feather was going, too, and this meant only one thing: another good opportunity to press her suit, the chance to fetch him to her bosom. From what she had heard, everyone came together like a family on the trail, and during the time of the hunting camp there was no protocol because of all the frenzied activity. A good time to escape watchful eyes, a good time to find romance in some secluded place. Her hopes were running as high as the late summer clouds.

The sighting of buffalo in meadows not too far from the lower Big Horn River pleased others besides White Crane; particularly, Man Called Tree. This place was close to Manuel's fort, the old trading outpost now occupied by John Goodhart, his half-Crow wife Molly, and their son James. These people were close friends of Man Called Tree and his family, had been for many moons. They exchanged visits several times each year, and the Absaroke often traded with Goodhart and sold him ponies. This ancient post, now a small ranch, was also where the breed woman, Bird Rutledge, and her mother had found refuge after they had escaped from the Sioux during Red Cloud's victorious war with the bluecoats over the Bozeman trail. It was a pleasant place to visit, because the Goodharts politely made their land available for a stopover feast and celebration with the Bird People. When Man Called Tree learned of the proximity of the blackhorns to Manuel's post, he allowed that Rainbow and Little Blue Hoop would enjoy the cozy comfort of the warm companionship of Molly Goodhart rather than live at the buffalo camp. Rainbow and Little Blue Hoop were delighted by the suggestion.

So, with preparations for the trail already completed, the hunting party left the next morning for the Big Horn River. Led by the buffalo hunter/shaman Big Cloud, there were almost fifty people in the group, twenty-five hunters and scouts, the rest, women and older children. Over a hundred ponies were in the procession, carrying riders and packs, and some pulling travois loaded with lodge-poles and tipi coverings. Near the front, not too far out of sight of Benjamin One Feather, rode the pretty maiden, White Crane.

Near sundown of the second day, the Absaroke arrived at the Goodharts, tired and weary from a warm and very long day on the trail. Man Called Tree had pushed them hard. But he had wanted it this way, to camp safely for the night in familiar surroundings, old friends around, good water for baths and corrals for the ponies. For those people who had not been here before, he knew that the comfort and hospitality provided by the Goodharts would more than compensate for the day's exhausting trail ride. And John Goodhart, a jovial, congenial host, was prepared for the hunters. Since the buffalo scouts had alerted him several days before, he and his son James already had carved out a large fire pit for the night fire. The ground around it, where the Crow women would erect their tipis, had been strewn with fresh straw.

Activity soon abounded. Within a short time the lodges were up, Crows bathed in the nearby river, and a fire was blazing in the pit. Sometime later Goodhart, James, Benjamin, and Man Called Tree brought from the shed a side of beef, the white man's buffalo that Goodhart had butchered two days before. This was good, and when the Absaroke women, all refreshed and dressed for the night's celebration, saw them coming to the fire with the meat, they set up their usual tremolo, a sound of joy before any feast. Molly Goodhart was probably the happiest of all, for these were her people. Even though she was a breed Crow, she knew their customs, their language, their songs, and as she busied herself she talked and laughed with each person she met. Finally the great slabs of beef were placed on a giant grid over the hot coals, and a huge cauldron of Molly's bean-and-bacon soup stewed beside the roasting meat. When the women saw this they happily rushed back to their packs, where they dug out cups and bowls. This was an unexpected treat, a gracious gesture on the part of their hosts, and a great gift to be shared by all.

James Goodhart, who had just seen his twenty-first birthday, understood the Absaroke language almost as well as his visiting brothers, but found little need of the tongue when he was with Man Called Tree's family. With the exception of Rainbow they all spoke English fluently, but only among themselves. Joining Benjamin and White Moon, James sat with them some distance back from the fire where they were eating and joking. Since boyhood these three had shared many meals together, had ridden on hunts into the piney hills, and had spread their blankets under the stars. All three were handsome young men, now, with only James's long brown hair, which he knotted at the back with leather, setting him apart from his two Nez Percé brothers.

Soon afterward, Little Blue Hoop brought her friend to see this breed Crow, James, a man she had known since she was a child. But now she was no longer a child, and secretly, for a year, she had fancied James. Little Blue Hoop confessed this to Walking Woman, telling her this was the reason she ignored the young braves in her village. Her heart was set on this man. Walking Woman was impressed, too, and unaware that James spoke Absaroke, knowing only that he was more white than Indian, she said at length to Little Hoop, "Yes, he is a handsome one. Your eyes tell the truth. This man is a good one." Everyone abruptly turned and stared at her, surprised by this inadvertent declaration. When James politely said, "*Aho,*" thanks in Absaroke, both Little Blue Hoop and Walking Woman, giggling, covered their faces in shame. Finally White Moon emitted a small snicker, and then everyone started to laugh.

Benjamin One Feather, amused by the disclosure, said aside to James, "I didn't know this, my friend, but it seems my little sister admires you. I think you must be the first one she's paid any attention to. Let me know if this nonsense becomes embarrassing. I'll speak with her."

James Goodhart only laughed. No, he was not embarrassed. Like Benjamin he was amused, but also flattered. And for the first time he noticed that Little Blue Hoop was not the same child whom he once had carried around on his shoulders. Almost overnight, it seemed, she had become a young woman, and a very pretty one at that. Reaching back, he tousled her hair and said, "*Aho, bi itsi,*" thanks, good woman. This brought a broad smile of relief to Little Blue Hoop's pretty face; Walking Woman covered her mouth and giggled again.

After the feast, several of the Absaroke men appeared with their skin-covered drums, and one of the women, Red Bead, motioned people back to make a clearing for dancing. There were enthusiastic shouts and a few yip-yips from the men as she called out *popute disua,* the owl dance. Benjamin One Feather, White Moon, and James, sat to the side of the circle with Man Called Tree and his woman, Rainbow. When the drums began to beat, Red Bead, seizing a stick, went dancing around the great circle making small, rhythmic steps to the side. She was a large woman in her rear and it jiggled like jelly, bringing gleeful shrieks of encouragement from the crowd. When she heard this stimulating outcry, she shook her bottom even more furiously. Soon, she came to the beautiful Rainbow, Man Called Tree's Nez Percé wife, and repeatedly struck her with the stick until Rainbow, laughing, leaped out and began the identical step. Everyone clapped and howled when Red Bead suddenly whipped her stick on Man Called Tree, their great leader. He too hastily jumped out, placing his arm around his woman, and they sidestepped around the circle clockwise, keeping time with the quickening beat of the drums.

Directly, Red Bead started to thrash all of the seated women, and they also went into the circle, linking arms and joining with Man Called Tree and Rainbow. White Crane was among them, nimbly swaying, her flashing dark eyes on Benjamin One Feather, and it took only a moment for James Goodhart to notice this romantically enticing display. Nudging his longtime friend, he asked in English, "Who is that one, the tall, pretty one who keeps looking at you? I sure don't remember seeing her before."

Benjamin, feigning innocence, said, "I think her name is White Crane. First time she's been so far out of the village. Just a girl, James, it amounts to nothing."

"Is that so?" his friend replied curiously. "Well, she sure has her eyes on you. No little girl to my notion, either. By damned, look at that smile!"

"It's really nothing," Benjamin repeated weakly, following the dance closely and anticipating what was about to happen in the circle. And directly, it did happen. The fat little woman, Red Bead, called out again, and all the dancing women suddenly were reaching out, grabbing men for their partners. Benjamin One Feather found his arm around White Crane, and her arm in turn was firmly around his waist, her fingers digging into his ribs. When he came full-circle, he stared helplessly over his shoulder at a grinning James Goodhart, who shouted out over the din of drums and rustling feet, "Ei, so it's nothing, Benjamin, nothing at all!"

White Moon, seated next to James, explained, "She has been waiting for this for one full moon. If Benjamin doesn't dodge her arrow, I'll soon have a sister-in-law. This woman is out to get him, make no mistake about it. Ei, a sister-in-law! I can't believe it."

James, laughing, finding great humor in this, had no opportunity to answer. Another circle was forming, moving counterclockwise, and he was quickly pulled into it by a smiling, exuberant Little Blue Hoop.

White Moon sadly shook his head as he watched them hop away. "*Eyah*, and maybe a brother-in-law, too," he muttered to himself.

For a time this dance went on, and then another followed with only women performing. When everyone was tired, they took water and listened to Big Cloud talk about his vision of the buffalo hunt; what the land would look like; how many buffalo cows were to be taken; and in great detail, every move contemplated by him and his hunters. Someone then told a humorous story; another man related the legend of how Old Man Coyote and two red-eyed ducks had created the world, making Mother Earth from small bits of mud. All this while White Crane, smiling contentedly, sat by Benjamin One Feather, as snugly as decorum would permit. Since Little Blue Hoop likewise had found a place near James, Benjamin pretended it was nothing.

Ultimately the leader of the Fox society, Sitting Elk, stood up and pointed to Benjamin One Feather, saying, "My brother tells the best story of all, the one about the prairie chicken and the bear. Some of you have heard this legend. It is very old, but no one but Benjamin One Feather tells it so well. I've heard this story in our lodge. Hear him speak the words and do his great dance."

Recoiling in embarrassment, Benjamin fell back,

shaking his head and protesting the suggestion. He had told the story in the Fox lodge only to make his brothers laugh, and they did, but the thought of playing the clown in front of all these people, including his parents and White Crane, no less, left him utterly speechless. But the people around the circle were clapping and calling out his name with great enthusiasm, giving him encouragement. So he finally stood by himself in the clearing next to the two drummers. Amidst some sighs and teasing taunts from the women, he removed his beaded, buckskin shirt, baring himself to the waist. Red Bead leaped up, shaking her bottom, and shouted gleefully, "Everything!" and all of the squaws and maidens squealed in delight. Benjamin One Feather grinned crookedly and tossed her his strings of beads. More laughter. Then, catching his breath, he began.

"In the beginning, at the time of creation, it was thus, after Old Man Coyote had brought many animals into being. A few of them were sitting together, a bull buffalo, a wolf, and a bear, all made by Old Man Coyote. But the bear wasn't happy with his appearance. He thought himself ugly and ungainly, ei, his front legs were shorter than his back legs, and he told Old Man Coyote that he was offended. Old Man Coyote said, 'But why? *I* am satisfied, for I am the one who made you.' 'No,' protested the bear, 'I by myself have grown, but maybe you can improve me. If you made me, show me your power, make something so that I may see for myself that you have made me, too.'

"So Old Man Coyote said, 'All right, I will make a bird for you,' and he did. From the bear, he took a claw to make feet. He took from the wolf another claw and made a beak; from the buffalo, he took muscle for body; hair from a wooly worm for webs in the feet, and he plucked leaves from the box elder for a fancy tail, and lo, this was the prairie chicken. But Old Man Coyote wasn't satisfied with this bird. It was too plain, and it had nothing to do. It just sat there clucking. So he said, 'Come here, bird, I will make you better.' He took white and gray dust, a touch of red, and painted the chicken. He made the chicken's tail to rattle, and when this was done he told the bird what his purpose in life should be. 'When the Blackfeet come roaming around to steal ponies, you shall crouch down thusly, rattle your wings and frighten them away.' " Benjamin squatted, stretched out his hands behind his butt, and began to flutter menacingly around the circle, as the men with the drums pounded on them resoundingly.

Leaping up, Benjamin said, "But the chicken said, 'Is this all I have to do, frighten the Pekony?' Old Man Coyote told him, 'No, it would be better if you puffed out your feathers and your face, then did the dance. Do it for fun, in the morning and at sunset, do it for your own pleasure, do it so everyone admires you, too. You may save the bad dance for the Pekony.' " Everyone laughed at this, and Benjamin crouched again, puffed out his cheeks, and hopped, strutted, and clapped his hands together behind his bottom. Once again the drummers picked up his steps and accompanied him. As Benjamin held up his hands for quiet, the drums softened, and he went on with the story.

"This pleased the prairie chicken greatly. He was satisfied, but the bear was still ill-tempered. He asked Old Man Coyote, 'If you made me, why did you not make me a dancer, too? You have treated me unfairly. Come, give me some of that power, or I will take back that claw of mine from the chicken.' Old Man Coyote said to the bear, 'Why, you said that you grew yourself, so if this is so, choose your own mode of dance. Look not to me to do it.' This bear envied the chicken his mode of dance, and he told Old Man Coyote that it would give him great pleasure to be able to dance like that pretty bird. Old Man Coyote finally said, 'All right, you shall dance, you have that power. I give it to you now.' And the bear went to a tree, where he found a grouse hiding. This grouse had the power of a drum, and the bear said, 'I will have music when I dance, and this will make me a better dancer than the chicken bird.' This little grouse made sounds, beating his wings like a drum, and the bear danced forward, one foot, the other foot."

Hopping clumsily about, the drums beating with him, Benjamin danced about like a drunken man, staggering into the women, snarling and clawing at them, and they fell back, shrieking, throwing straw at him. Once again he positioned himself in the clearing and held up his hands. "The chicken laughed loudly at this foolish bear.'' Benjamin yowled into the warm night air. ''The chicken said, 'This was a very poor dance.' And indeed it was, and even Old Man Coyote pulled back his whiskers and grinned.'' And, mimicking Old Man Coyote, Benjamin, grinning evilly, went around the circle again, trying to entice the cowering women into his grasp.

''This didn't please the bear, being laughed at so much, so he thought he would eat this chicken and be rid of him once and for all. But Old Man Coyote was there and he admonished the bear. He said, 'Bear, you are too mean and ill of temper. You act like a Pekony. You even smell like a Pekony. You should not live among these other animals, so I will send you to the forest to live. The bear protested, saying, 'But what shall I find to eat in the forest? I will starve to death.' 'No,' Old Man Coyote said, 'I will make you to eat the roots and berries found there.' The bear growled and said, 'What about meat? I love meat. You mean I can have none?' Old Man Coyote said to him, 'You will eat the meat you find on the ground, the remains of ones who have left this earth for another place. Yes, to the forest you must go.' This news pleased the prairie chicken, to be rid of such a beast, and he began dancing wildly.'' Benjamin leaped about madly, flapping his arms, fanning his tail, and putting his chin low to the ground like a prairie chicken.

''But to be sent away, this displeased the bear. He had no other choice, so he went dancing off into the woods to hide in shame. And my brothers and sisters, this is where we find the bear to this very day, like the Pekony, in the forest afraid to show his face.'' Grunting and staggering away, Benjamin One Feather disappeared into the darkness beyond the tipis.

Though Benjamin thought he had played the part of the clown by such a foolishly animated display of storytelling, it proved otherwise. This serious young brave, a coup-counter and gun-snatcher, also was a man who had the knack of bringing amusement to his brothers, and when he returned from the darkness the people accorded him applause and tremolos. Red Bead came shaking and dancing around him and replaced his beads around his neck. He bowed graciously and said aloud, ''This is a true story I've told you—an old Pekony man said this was so.''

And everyone laughed again, for any humorous or demeaning reference to the enemy Blackfeet was a matter of great levity to the Crow. And later, when Benjamin had found his place in the circle, White Crane, who cleverly had found her place beside him, leaned close and said to him. "You were the most handsome and the best of all the storytellers."

Benjamin felt good about this compliment, but he was still embarrassed about his antics in the clearing. He said to her, "*Aho,* but my Fox brother, Sitting Elk, gave me no choice. One day I'll get even with him. I felt foolish playing the clown. *Eyah,* this isn't my way."

White Crane, carefully choosing words of praise, gently protested, saying, "No, no, you showed great spirit, one not too proud to make others laugh. You bring fresh happiness, like the morning sun. I think that your nose is on your face, not in the sky. This is good, what I've always seen in you with my own eyes. Benjamin One Feather, hear me, people love a person for what he is, not what he pretends to be. This is good that you can show many faces, a man for all people. I was happy to see this. Someday, you will be a chief."

Benjamin One Feather gave her an incredulous stare. This young maiden who seldom spoke anything but *kahe,* who said more with her body than her lips, was now professing herself like some sage from the smoky shadows of a medicine lodge. "You surprise me," he finally said with a grin. "I have seen you, too, but I didn't know you possessed such words . . . such thoughts."

White Crane smiled at him, her hand tracing across his knee. "There is an old saying, is there not? 'Still waters run deep.' " And with a small, mischievous gleam in her eyes, the same one that Benjamin had faltered under before, she whispered, "*Kahe,*" welcome.

THREE

Four Absaroke scouts rode out ahead before dawn. They were gone three suns and two sleeps, and when they came back they reported sighting only one village of meat-makers, a small encampment of thirty enemy Sioux lodges on the other side of the Rosebud Mountains. This was a two-day ride from where Big Cloud's herd of buffalo had been sighted earlier, and it was agreed by the buffalo chief and Man Called Tree that these Tetons, probably an Oglala band from far upriver, presented no immediate threat to the Absaroke. Besides, many of the Sioux were too busy harassing the bluecoat soldiers over along the Powder River to concern themselves with counting coup on a few hunter Crows. Man Called Tree allowed that these Sioux, by necessity, were now more interested in making meat than making war, only taking a brief respite from the trouble in the Black Hills farther east where one of the Indian's bitterest enemies, Lt. Col. George Custer, the one they called Yellow Hair or Long Hair, recently had led gold-seekers into the land in violation of the latest Fort Laramie treaty.

This distressing news had come to Man Called Tree from John Goodhart several nights before at Manuel's post. The Sioux were now calling the sacred Paha Sapa trail the Thieves' Road, and Goodhart prophecied that within another year the entire reservation country to the east would be aflame with renewed hostilities. Battles would be won and lost by the Absaroke's bitter enemies, the Sioux and Cheyenne, but Man Called Tree knew the inevitable outcome—the bluecoat's government would eventually prevail, another nail would be driven into the coffin of the Indian nation, and yet another in a series of meaningless treaties would be signed.

Man Called Tree allowed that his bitter skepticism was warranted, for he had been a part of the dying frontier too long. Broken treaties were a part of his life and the lives of his brothers. As a young man he had warned the Nez Percé against the paper of Gov. Isaac Stevens in the Washington territory, and ultimately three-fourths of their land was needlessly signed away. And one by one, he had watched other tribes inextricably drawn into bloody death struggles from which there was no escape but humiliating surrender and the ignoble lassitude of reservation life. All of this in the name of progress, the juggernaut which no man, red or white, could stop. He advised Benjamin to avoid bluecoats, treaty-makers, and agents, for they all were harbingers of the plague.

The Crow hunter camp was made at the Place Where the Cranes Rest, a wide bend of the Big Horn flanked by green meadows and towering cottonwoods, an area of the river where migrating waterfowl congregated during the Geese Going Moon. This was traditional Absaroke land. There were several nearby knolls where the Wolf lookouts would always be stationed, and the village site itself was only three miles from the blackhorn grounds. With fresh water at hand, a supply of firewood in the bottom, and lush pasture for the ponies, this was a good camp for the four or five days of the hunt. The twenty-two lodges were erected in a semicircle. At the south end of the new village, close to the river, some of the women immediately went to work making green willow racks for curing those portions of the meat to be dried and smoked. If the first frosts came and the weather cooled, some of the meat would be carefully packed and taken back fresh to the main village. But in the Moon of the Changing Seasons no one could predict the weather; one day was hot, one day cold, and this is the way it had always been in the Land of the Big Sky. Whatever, no meat was to be wasted by spoiling. Among the Absaroke, who also knew the bad smell of hunger, wasted meat was a sin.

On the first afternoon Big Cloud, carrying his feathered staff and sacred buffalo pipe, went out with several scouts, including Benjamin One Feather, to locate the curly cows and plan strategy for the following morning. And, as it had been foretold in his story during the night's stay at the Goodharts', the buffalo were feeding in a flat bottom of grama grass near some small, rolling hills, at the base of one of which was a huge, tepid wallow. But Big Cloud's amazing vision was not vision alone. Some of it was experience, for at sixty years of age he had been here many times, and he knew the blackhorn country as well as he did the familiar wrinkles on his aged face. This had been his position of wisdom with the Bird People for twenty-five years. He was making medicine for the hunts long before Man Called Tree came to live with the Crow.

The night before the first hunt is never a good night for restful sleep. The hunter is gripped by anxiety, his robes filled with itchy anticipation. It was this way for Benjamin One Feather, who had been selected to be among the hunters on the first surround prepared by Big Cloud. Tossing and turning all night under his bedding, he was finally up at dawn, stirring the embers of the tipi night fire, and making himself ready by checking his rifle and ammunition and testing the sharpness of his knife. There were other chores, too. Since his mother and sister had been left behind at the Goodharts', there were no women to manage Man Called Tree's lodge, and Benjamin did what had to be done, heating water for coffee, scrounging for food to cook, searching the packs for utensils. After waking his father and brother, he then rushed away to the river to wash and fetch more water.

The sun was barely touching the eastern hills toward the distant Rosebud Mountains, the air cool and misty along the cold Big Horn River. Even though he hadn't tarried at the stream, by the time he returned to the tipi he heard the shrill laughter of women inside. Directly his father came bounding out, laughing too, leaping about on one foot as he tried to slip on a moccasin. His great wash towel was draped around his neck, and he bounced away toward the river jovially shouting out the crier's morning call, *"bire daxua hia, bire daxua kok!"* Get up and bathe, get water on your body! Benjamin stood by in quiet amazement as White Moon next came tumbling out, jerking at his leggings, and more shrieks of laughter followed from inside the lodge. When he warily poked his head inside, he saw White Crane and Walking Woman busy over the fire, giggling and shifting pots back and forth, preparing to cook breakfast.

Before Benjamin could even utter a word, White Crane leaped up, smiling broadly, and greeted him just as he had fully expected. *"Kahe!"* she murmured. But then unexpectedly, and to his disbelief, she kissed him on the lips, to another accompanying joyous howl from Walking Woman. Grasping Benjamin firmly, White Crane led him to the side and seated him on the robes. He was speechless, but she was not. "Sit here and prepare to eat," White Crane commanded. "Your mother and sister are gone from this place. You have no woman to do these things. From this day until the hunt is ended, I will be your woman. Walking Woman will help me take care of Chief Man Called Tree and his son, White Moon. She will watch to see that you don't pinch me when I work." Shrieking hilariously again, Walking Woman beat madly on a pan with a wooden spoon.

"But," Benjamin protested, trying to find his tongue, "I wouldn't do such a thing . . . it wouldn't enter my mind."

"This, I think, is your problem, Benjamin One Feather," White Crane said, turning back to the fire. "Sometimes you think too much, and are afraid to do what you're really thinking. You waste time thinking so much."

Benjamin, thoroughly befuddled, scratched his head, crossed his legs, and said nothing. In such a short time, how could this woman have come to read his mind so readily? Where did her quick words come from? Ei, it was just as his father had spoke: These women were all mind-readers, the whole lot of them, always a step ahead, and he suddenly felt, as Man Called Tree had warned, that he was fast becoming one of those "goners." He stared glumly at the fire, completely squelched.

But breakfast was a happy occasion. The two women were free-spirited, chatting excitedly between themselves as they worked over the fire, for this was an honor, and one that their parents willingly approved of, to be of help in the chief's lodge. Later, when the men were prepared to leave, Man Called Tree, delighted with the women's assistance, said, "It pleases me to have good cooks around in the morning, ones of good cheer. It makes for a better day, the belly full and the heart light. I will send a gift to your lodges, and I pledge the first two buffalo in your names."

This was good, and the young women smiled and nodded their heads in approval. White Crane finally said, politely, "We are pleased to hear you say this. It is an honor for us to be here. We honor you, Man Called Tree, and wish you good hunting."

He laughed heartily and said, "*Aho,* but aren't you the one they call White Crane? I think I've heard about you, the daughter of Shoots Far Arrow, yes, the one who sat by my eldest son at the dance. Did you come to honor only me this morning, or have my eyes deceived me? I see you looking another way, more often than not, ei?"

Walking Woman emitted a small giggle, but White Crane only smiled back at Man Called Tree. Undaunted, she did not falter or blush, but spoke clearly in return. "Your eyes, my chief, are better than those of your son. I walk in his shadow. He doesn't see me."

"Ho, I like your spirit!" Man Called Tree replied. "You're not the silent one I was led to believe." He looked over at Benjamin, who was shouldering his rifle at the tipi entrance, eager to be gone and to be free of this needless complimentary breakfast banter. "Ei, Benjamin, this is a little more than a *kahe.* What is this talk? What will you say to this, that my eyes are truly better?"

Seized by the challenge of the moment, Benjamin One Feather reacted with impulsive assertiveness. In one swift move, his rifle swept from his hand, hurtling toward his father. Man Called Tree snatched it in midair. Striding over to the smiling White Crane, Benjamin pressed a firm, lasting kiss on her lips, and for a second she hung limply in his arms. He finally pushed her back, saying, "One only deserves another, but better, ei?" And facing back to his astonished father and awestruck brother, he said, "Come, we shall see who had the best eyes this day, not in the tipi, but on the range."

* * *

They were buffalo hunters, good ones, among the best on the northern plains, and Big Cloud's strategy was perfectly sound this early morning, albeit under conditions not necessarily to his choosing. The herd of several hundred was badly scattered throughout the grassy flat, a few head even grazing on the small hills above the giant wallow. He was not interested in making a chase of it, dispersing the blackhorns, running them until their meat toughened. He wanted a selective few cut out, the surround effectively mounted to take only the choice specimens.

For the moment the buffalo chief sat silently on his pony holding his staff, contemplating the situation in the long, peaceful valley below. For this hunt, he finally decided, it would be best to split some of the blackhorns and leave the greater number of animals at the lower end unmolested, to be contested another day. This was going to take delicate timing, he said, because the splitting riders would have to quietly file their ponies through the selected area, flattened as close to their saddles as possible to keep from alarming the herd. Other hunters would be stationed on either flank, and at a given signal from Big Cloud the converging of the surround would begin.

Be selective. Take only the young bulls, yearlings, and dry cows without calves. This was Big Cloud's order. From his medicine bundle he took out powder and threw it to the Four Winds, then presented his medicine pipe to the heavens and motioned his twelve hunters to their positions.

Among those threading their way through the stragglers was Benjamin One Feather. All the while he hung as low as he could over his saddle, his eyes warily on the heavy beasts milling and snorting to either side. A few were beginning to trot away, their tails lifted in alarm. This was not necessarily a new experience for him, hunting buffalo, but it marked the first time that he found himself so precariously close to the quarry and unable to shoot. When badly frightened, these animals were as contrary as a mule. They ran in sheer panic, sometimes rushing headlong into the best buffalo pony, toppling both horse and rider. Benjamin had seen this happen several times, the hunters luckily coming away with only minor bruises, but with great embarrassment. Lest this happen to him, Benjamin always implicitly adhered to his father's instructions: Never run a pony ahead of the quarry on a close-quarter kill; stay well behind the front shoulder; preferably, shoot from the right side, and always veer the pony left after firing. Another admonishment: Waste no meat; when possible, place the shot directly behind the ear.

Finally, at the signal of Big Cloud's waving robe, the men in the midst of the lower group of animals reined to the right, cutting out at least forty head. When they came up high in their saddles, waving rifles and yelling, buffalo began to bolt in all directions. Coming down on their flanks were the riders who had sat patiently on the far-off fringe, only awaiting Big Cloud's signal. They came in firing. In the confusion, Benjamin guardedly pulled up, expecting some of the blackhorns to come pounding back toward him, but they already had taken their lead from a few matron cows and gone charging swiftly up the small valley toward Big Cloud and his men, who were stationed at the end of the surround.

Immediately Benjamin took off, trying to catch up, his eyes out for eligible targets. He passed up two cows with trailing calves, but by the end of the ragged chase, when the buffalo finally had broken the trap and were fleeing into the coulees, Benjamin One Feather had killed three young bulls. Several of the Crow went riding away, trying to pick off the loners. Now a heavy cloud of dust hovered over the area. Benjamin heard a few excited shouts, some victorious yelping, and he sensed that this first foray had been successful enough. Down below, the main herd was thundering toward the open valley, mere black specks on the dusty plain. In another place, he saw a great flight of frightened prairie chickens sailing away over the Greasy Grass.

Soon Big Cloud came riding by. He was smiling. There would be no hungry people in the village this winter. By his count twenty-nine buffalo had been slain, and no hunter injured. Better yet, no one had killed a herd bull, and there were no abandoned calves running about. This was a good beginning, he said, but tomorrow the ride would be longer, the hunt more difficult, and fewer animals taken. However, now was a time for labor. He dispatched a rider to return to camp for pack ponies and women to help with the dressing of the kill. White Moon soon appeared and spoke to his older brother. He had shot two dry cows, and Man Called Three had killed a bull and a yearling. Benjamin said this was good, and he slid off his horse, unsheathed his knife, and went to work, smiling, allowing that his father's eyes were no better than his own. This was something White Crane could ponder.

Later that day, when Benjamin One Feather came riding into the village, he was greeted by none other than White Crane, who was already helping to flesh hides. After she had given him his customary *kahe*, he proudly pointed to his eyes and held up three fingers to make the sign of the curly cow with forked thumbs from his forehead. He also made the sign of his father, the forked stick, spiraling into outthrust branches, but he only held up two fingers. She knew what he meant, and she smiled. Then, as he rode by to turn his pony loose in the remuda, he made more sign, pointing to his eyes again, and in turn to her. When he touched the back of his saddle she yelled gleefully, threw aside her fleshing knife, and eagerly leaped up behind him, for this was the customary ride for sweethearts. He had met her challenge.

And that night, during all the happy confusion of the celebration, while everyone was feasting on ribs and hump basted with chokecherry and plum Benjamin One Feather and White Crane slipped away and walked together under the heavy canopy of the trees along the river. Benjamin, his emotions still slightly askew, knew from the moment he had touched his saddle, inviting her to join him, that he had succumbed to her charms. Now the last vestiges of resistance had been shredded. But he had decided this was good; it was his choice, made freely and willingly; he would never admit to coercion. There was a manly feeling surging inside him now, and after all, "a man without a woman is like a man without a pony,"—this, another of his father's sage observations.

And here he was, walking hand in hand with his sweetheart, not saying much of anything consequential, wondering if the small, nagging ache in the pit of his stomach had anything to do with love, or need of it, or if it was only a simple case of gorging himself on too many ribs.

What did he know about love, anyway? Admittedly, nothing. Was it merely a state of the mind? Or the heart? Or secrets between the thighs? No matter; thinking too much again, as White Crane had told him. And in his troubled mind he found himself mimicking her sweet singsong voice: *This is your problem, Benjamin One Feather, you think too much, and are afraid to do what you're really thinking.* Yah, yah, yah, these mind-reading women! But how she had stunned him, he the reluctant lover, this *bi itsi,* good woman, more woman than he had once thought.

Loving him, White Crane saw the smile on his face and said, "You are happy? I see something in your face that tells me this. Is it not so?"

"Ei," he agreed, "I'm happy enough. Your conversation pleases me. Your words aren't without meaning. This is good. First I saw you, but how could I escape this? You were like a butterfly, everywhere. Did you think I was some one-eyed hibernating gopher who had not seen the sun in six months? And then I heard you speak intelligent words after believing you had no tongue. Ei, a quick tongue, too, one as sharp as my knife." He laughed, nervously kicking at pebbles along the moonlit trail. "You please my father, too. He says you are a good woman to have around in the tipi. He finds great humor in some of what you say."

"That I please only you is best," White Crane said. Then, with some innocence, "Was I so obvious? Like a butterfly? Hmmm, did you not like what you saw? Did you not know that my eyes were for no other man but you? This must please you, ei?"

"This is true," he admitted. "Yes, you do please me. It is also true that you were obvious. My skin was hot. I was embarrassed. I think you take great joy in this."

"For this I'm sorry, but you must know that it takes honey to catch a fly. You didn't come after me with your medicine flute, so I made you aware of me. You are no longer embarrassed? You now admit you like to look at me, as I believed?"

Laughing at her devious probe, he replied, "Ei, you are pretty enough. Everyone knows this. Others feast their eyes on you, too. I see this. Perhaps I'm the lucky fly, but you didn't fool me. I came by my own accord.

And you know that I would not tootle on a flute. It would look foolish, and that's not my way. It would only serve to call more attention to you, ei."

"Our men say it's bad medicine to be jealous," White Crane said. "Do you believe this?"

"If a woman is true, there is no reason for a man to be jealous," Benjamin One Feather answered quickly, with the sound of authority. But in truth he knew nothing of jealousy or love, because he had experienced neither. He laughed and said, "Sometimes, jealousy is more bad luck than bad medicine. I will tell you a story about this Pekony who had such a beautiful woman that he would not pitch his tipi near the village. . . ."

"Will you dance for me, too?" she asked jokingly.

"*Ikye!*" he whispered harshly. "Attention, listen, this isn't a story where I dance. This man wouldn't pitch his tipi around the others because his woman was so beautiful. Yes, he feared that some other Pekony was going to steal her, ei. Or as you say, pinch her. One night some smart Absaroke braves who were out to steal ponies saw this. This man had no protection from the village, so these Absaroke sneaked up in the night and stole the ponies picketed in the back of the jealous man's tipi, No one was around to sound the alarm, ei. And all the other Pekony men laughed when they found out his ponies were stolen, for any man too jealous of his wife to be sociable with them around the fire deserved to have his ponies stolen."

"*Eyah,*" she laughed. "And I suppose an old Pekony man told you this story?"

"This is true," Benjamin said with a grin. She was so close, her cheek almost touching his, that he could smell the fresh mint on her slender neck. "Yes, this is the story as I heard it."

White Crane then said slyly, "But I wonder if this woman possessed something better for her man than just talk around the fire with other men? What do you think of such a notion?"

"The old Pekony said nothing about such matters."

"I shall tell you the reason, the true story," White Crane said, tossing her head saucily. "This woman was wise. So it was told, she knew how to please her man to keep him beside her. Each night she hid his moccasins and breechclout under her robes. It was better for him to be bare under these robes with her than bare outside with his friends, who surely would have laughed even louder than when a few of his old ponies were stolen."

Benjamin One Feather stopped dead in his tracks and stared down at her. In surprised amusement he asked, "Now, woman called White Crane, whoever told you such a crazy thing like that? It's a ridiculous story."

"I shall say the same as you," replied White Crane, her eyes sparking mischievously. "An old Pekony woman told me this. And this is a true story. I will only deny it when the evergreens turn yellow."

"Ei," he laughed. "And may they never turn yellow for one who shoots such a quick arrow as you. Each moment you bring a new surprise."

White Crane stopped abruptly, tilted her head upward and kissed him, her minty aroma flooding his senses. "I only try to please you. Tell me, when did you first see me with loving eyes? Was I so hard to catch, to ride the pony with you? Because I didn't speak, did you think that I was shy? Or are you the shy one? No, I cannot believe one so brave as you could be shy. Cautious? Yes, this is better. A cautious warrior."

"Sometimes the rocks in the creek are slippery," Benjamin said. "Ei, I'm no Crazy Dog. One must always be careful about making the wrong step. And if I told you about the first time I saw you, I'm afraid you would find it hard to believe. That I would have had such a thought about you under such circumstances is too hard to believe, like another Old Man Coyote story."

"Then, tell me," she said. "If I am to be your woman, I demand to know."

"No, no," Benjamin teasingly replied, rubbing noses with her. But he acquiesced, as she knew he would. "Well," he sighed, "if you must know, it was the day I saved you from the Pekony at the river, or maybe before, I can't recall."

"This is not so!" she exclaimed with surprise. "I never saw you looking at me, not once, not on that horrible day or before."

"Ei, but I *had* seen you," Benjamin admitted. "I just couldn't bring myself to believe it, not until you fell in the water, and ho, what I then saw I truly believed, although it didn't strike me until later. In the middle of battle, I had no time to dwell on it.'' His grin broadened.

Pinching him, she asked curiously, ''You have dwelled on this for three moons? A secret kept only to yourself and not revealed to me? What did you see this day to make it so?''

''A woman in fright who was pretty,'' Benjamin honestly replied. ''A woman whose unseen beauty was a sight to behold. Had it not been for the moment I would have shielded my eyes, for only Akbatatdia could have made such long and beautiful legs.''

''Ei, you are a coyote disguised as a prairie chicken,'' she said, smiling. ''You can hide no longer, for I know what you are, a clever one. My heart is only for you, clever coyote,''

''An honest coyote to confess that I had such thoughts,'' said Benjamin. ''I say it again, you are beautiful.''

White Crane suddenly stepped back from him and held her arms wide. ''Then what you secretly admire, you shall finally see,'' she said. ''Do you know what I wear under this dress tonight? Nothing!'' And with that, she pulled the elkskin dress away from her shoulders and let it drop to the ground. What she said was true. Now only the long strands of red and white beads hung down between her firm breasts. Turning slowly in the moonlight, White Crane displayed all the fullness of her beautiful young body to him. Indeed, the Maker of Everything had blessed this woman in every respect, in every minute detail. With a thousand crickets making music in the shadowy thickets, Benjamin One Feather stood there speechless, unable to find one single note of joyous accompaniment. He had heard many Praise Songs in his life, but there was not one he could think of befitting this lovely occasion. Standing in front of him was the goddess of the forest, and he was transfixed.

''My heart is like a breath feather,'' White Crane said softly. ''Before you I am unashamed, yes, to be your woman so long as you shall have me, be it tonight or forever. Come and cover me, or leave me as I am. Do as you wish, for from this moon on, it will be for you to decide.'' She waited. Then, her generous smile slowly began to widen, and a small laugh finally escaped her. "*Ikye*, Benjamin One Feather!" she harshly whispered. "By the goodness of the Great Spirit, don't think on this *too* long or I will catch a chill!"

He dismissed all further thoughts or consequences.

Shortly after dawn, Benjamin One Feather, back in his robes, heard the sound of voices outside the lodge. His first sleepy thought was that White Crane and her friend, Walking Woman, were coming once again to prepare breakfast, to send Man Called Tree's men away on the day's hunt. But hunting was of no concern to a weary Benjamin. Fortunately, this was not his day to seek out and kill buffalo. He and several of the other braves had been selected to attend the camp, to police the perimeter of the village, and relieve some of the Wolf lookouts at their posts. By sharing these duties, they would enable everyone to participate in the hunt.

This was good, particularly for Benjamin, because for reasons known only to him he believed that today something much less strenuous than the hunt was more to his liking. During the night, most of his strength had been left in the Big Horn River bottom, wrested from his sinewy body by a lovely doe-eyed creature, turned vixen, who had wasted him away like a spent bee. To his astonishment, and pleasure, he discovered that White Crane was a desirous woman, not one to be denied. The beautiful long legs that had captivated him so had become her weapon of the night, vise-like smooth saplings, a trap sprung around his middle, unrelenting in its grip, and she had turned his spine to jelly in a night of blanket love never to be forgotten.

Outside the voices grew louder, more excited, and Benjamin looked over toward his father, who now was crawling from under his robe, rubbing the night's sleep from his eyes. They dressed hastily and left the tipi, only to encounter a group of men gesturing and arguing among themselves. Jumps High, one of the Wolves, was pointing upriver. White Moon, Benjamin's brother, who had been one of the night guards, was shrugging helplessly. When Man Called Tree finally silenced the men, Sitting Elk spoke up and explained. Someone, probably Sioux, had stolen fourteen ponies from the remuda—ponies badly needed to pack meat back to the main village. They had to be recovered.

Jumps High said the tracks went up the Big Horn River trail and appeared to be only four or five hours old. No one had seen or heard the thieves, not even White Moon, who vehemently denied that he had fallen asleep on the job. Fix the blame on no one, Man Called Tree told the group, but give credit to the thieves for being so clever and so cunningly bold. Now it was up to the Absaroke to prove themselves more clever. He quickly appointed four men not assigned to Big Cloud's hunting party for the day and ordered them to take up the chase. They were to take their strongest ponies and enough food to last three sleeps.

The chief said only four men could be spared without disrupting the camp. These ponies were important and vital, but Man Called Tree wanted no interruption in the hunt, since the well-being of the entire main village depended upon an adequate supply of meat for the winter. The four chasers named were two Lumpwoods, Little Bull Runs and Bear Gets Up, and two Fox brothers, Sitting Elk and Benjamin One Feather. Who was to carry the pipe? White Crane's brother, Little Bull Runs, nominated Benjamin.

The others quickly agreed that Benjamin could lead them, and within fifteen minutes they were off and riding up the Big Horn River trail, following the tracks of the stolen ponies. In the excitement of the moment Benjamin One Feather found renewed vitality, but the few small beads of perspiration White Crane had left in him were already popping out on his forehead. He would take much water this day.

After several hours of riding, some of it spent backtracking to pick up the thieves' well-covered trail, Benjamin One Feather determined that it was unlikely these men were from the Sioux hunting village over beyond the Rosebud Mountains to the east. Their direction was almost due south, sometimes along the river bottom, at other times up along the foothills, where the pony tracks mingled and became confused with the heavy buffalo sign. And ultimately, when Benjamin came to the fork of the Little Big Horn, he became convinced their quarry was from another village, perhaps a large, permanent hostile encampment on unceded land, but just how far he did not know. What he did know, however, was that prior to making their own hunting camp, the Crow scouts had thoroughly covered this area and found no enemies within a three-day ride.

Toward midday, when the four braves huddled to eat and drink water, Benjamin told them it was good the thieves' village was so far away, because these men they were following would certainly have to stop and rest for the night, maybe even a second night. Pushing the stolen ponies too hard was foolish because, as clever as the enemy appeared to be, there never was any profit in coming home with a herd of broken-down or sore-footed horses. For the present, he said, he thought it wise to follow slowly and cautiously, in case a few of the men came back to set up an ambuscade, a favorite ploy of the Sioux.

In fact, Benjamin became so cautious that he spread out his braves in a single file fifty yards apart, and since part of his medicine in his neck pouch was the tiny skull of a sparrow hawk, a bird with unerring sight, he elected to take the point, the forward place and the most dangerous. He took this position not because he was fearless, but because he believed that there was no man with better eyes than his, with one possible exception: Man Called Tree.

But the keen eyes of Benjamin did not ultimately alert him to the nearness of the thieves. It was his ears. Near dark, just when he was about to halt the pursuit and take rest for the night, he heard the faint whinny of a pony, and he knew that he had overtaken the enemy. Reining about, he slowly walked his horse back to meet his brothers coming up from behind. When they were all together in the fading light, they agreed that their own ponies needed some rest, and that any ride back down the trail at night was ill-advised. So they planned to make a wide circuit around the camp, find a resting place of their own, and somehow try to determine how many braves they faced. Benjamin One Feather finally motioned them toward the valley, and they rode quietly to the east, ultimately returning to the river almost two miles above where he had heard the pony.

After the four Absaroke found a secluded place in the

dark timber, they munched on dried berries and strips of buffalo, only recently smoked on the racks at their hunting camp. Sitting Elk and Bear Gets Up were appointed to investigate the whereabouts of the enemy, to ascertain the odds in case of an outright fight, something that Benjamin badly wanted to avoid. He was more interested in stealing back the horses than in taking scalps, but Bear Gets Up said that he had an uncle who had been killed by the Sioux near the Little Big Horn River, that his uncle's spirit was still in the valley calling for revenge, and that if he had a chance to count coup, he would. Benjamin quietly reminded him that he was the pipe-carrier, and it was against his medicine to count coup if it in any way jeopardized the safety of the others. This was immediately agreed upon, as Bear Gets Up and Sitting Elk went sneaking away into the darkness to the wooded area below.

Resting back against a big cottonwood trunk, Benjamin curled his blanket around him and prepared to wait. Nothing more could be done until his two brothers returned. He checked his rifle once, a sixteen-shot Henry repeater, then rested it across his lap. To the side of him Little Bull Runs, also shrouded in a blanket, finally asked, "Is it safe to sleep?"

"Ei," said Benjamin, "we are well above them. They won't move until they're rested. We are the shadows of their souls now, and this is good. Sleep, if you must. When our brothers come back, we'll make our plans."

"And you? What will you do?" Little Bull Runs asked.

"I'm too nervous to sleep," Benjamin truthfully admitted. "I'll only rest after our brothers return with news of who these braves are, and how many. Maybe then I can spread my blanket for a short while."

Little Bull Runs, smothering a laugh in his blanket, said, "After last night I should think you *would* be tired, too. As for myself, I did little but eat and smoke the pipe last night. I thought I might talk with you, share a pipe, but I saw you not." He paused and sighed. "Nor did I see my sister, White Crane."

Benjamin One Feather gritted his teeth. Little Bull Runs was playing foxy, tossing him a morsel, trying to draw him out, but he refused to take the bait. The Indian's methodically circuitous way of arriving at a point, the pyramid of insinuation, had always irked him. Benjamin bluntly answered, "We were walking around the village, talking, as now we must."

"Oh, I saw her," his companion said. "She disturbed my rest coming in as late as she did. I don't like the sound of her humming little Fox songs in the night. Your sister does this, too, sometimes, to put me in my place, I think."

"I shall caution these women," Benjamin said with a smile. "No more songs."

"My sister was drying her hair by the tipi fire."

Benjamin only grunted in response. That both he and White Crane had bathed together in the backwaters of the Big Horn wasn't a matter he wished to divulge.

"I thought it strange that she went swimming in the middle of the night. I asked nothing. I went back to sleep. What do you say to this?"

Benjamin One Feather smiled again, suddenly beginning to pleasure in the little game they were playing. "That she went swimming, or that you went back to sleep?"

Little Bull Runs chuckled and pulled his blanket close. "You're beginning to sound like Old Man Coyote, talking with two tongues."

"And you Cirape, his inquiring coyote brother, ei?"

"A fair exchange," returned Little Bull Runs. Curling up on his side, he added, "When she decides to share a tipi with you, Benjamin One Feather, I want that Winchester rifle you took from the Blackfeet that day. After the marriage celebration, of course."

"You shall have it," was the reply.

The woodland bottom fell quiet, and despite Benjamin's anxiety he found himself nodding off, his eyelids heavy from the long day's ride and the short sleep of the night before. Almost two hours passed before he heard a rustling nearby. Sitting Elk and Bear Gets Up were returning, the soft pads of their moccasins scuffing the fallen leaves and twigs cluttering the ancient river trail. Their breath was short, and they rested before telling what they had seen.

The news was mixed—both good and bad. The stolen ponies, Sitting Elk said, were being carefully guarded by three braves in a small meadow near the banks of the

Little Big Horn, while in an adjacent grove of trees three more men were asleep. These braves were not Sioux as everyone had thought—they were Cheyenne warriors prepared for battle (their ponies being painted on the legs and rumps), and they were probably destined to join others of their kind farther up the trail, or they could be heading for Morning Star's village.

Sitting Elk said that this great Cheyenne leader often camped late in the summer along the upper Rosebud and Tongue river country. This was true, Benjamin agreed, for once, when he was scouting, he had seen a huge village of Northern Cheyenne at this place. He was later told that the village belonged to Dull Knife, the name given to Morning Star by the Sioux, whom he often joined with to battle the invading bluecoats. Everyone knew that Dull Knife had a deep hatred for the soldiers because they had destroyed the village of Black Kettle, the Southern Cheyenne chief, down on the Washita, killing many women and children while they slept in their tipis. Morning Star repeatedly had vowed vengeance upon the leader of these particular bluecoats, Long Hair Custer. But everyone detested the bluecoats, for wherever they went big trouble came with them, and more trouble followed because the hairy-faced ones always came in their shadows.

But this was not Benjamin One Feather's fight. Although he also hated soldiers who used such despicable tactics, the Cheyenne and Sioux never had been friends of the Crow, either. These tribes, along with the Arapaho, Blackfeet, and Gros Ventre, had warred for too many moons against the outnumbered Bird People, and had punished them at every opportunity. No, Benjamin One Feather wasn't about to give any quarter to the clever Cheyenne camped below. Where they had come from he had no idea, but he vowed to his brothers that these unfriendlies with battle feathers would not reach their destination with stolen Crow ponies. However, the matter at hand was how to outwit them.

After listening to Sitting Elk, Benjamin nodded thoughtfully and finally held up his hand. "I have considered what our brother says. For a time I thought it best to wait for Masaka to show his face, hide ourselves along the trail in ambush. But these Cheyenne are too contrary, and the land here is too wide for an ambush. We must claim our ponies while it's dark, make a surprise for these men. This is better. There are four of us, six of them. Ei, but in the darkness, they don't know where we are, so the odds become more even. And these braves won't wait for daylight. When the bellies of our stolen ponies are full, the Cheyenne will be ready to travel again, for they always have to be alert for someone following. They will be moving soon, so we must waste no more time here."

Bear Gets Up asked, "Who among us has the medicine of the owl? Who can be guided so well in the darkness to help us?"

Sitting Elk quickly answered, "I possess the claw of an owl in my pouch. Also the hair of an otter and the foot of a frog. My vision was one of water and darkness. By the medicine of the otter I came from a place of great darkness, riding a white pony with marks of lightning on its four legs. An owl with horns came and led me into the safety of the mountains. This was one of my signs. I have such medicine."

"Ei, this will surely help us," Benjamin One Feather said. "With the blessing of the moon, we shall take some of this medicine and use it on the butts of these pony thieves. We shall come at them from the least likely way—by water and darkness." The three brother Absaroke stared curiously at Benjamin One Feather for a moment, but he quickly enlightened them. "Sitting Elk and Bear Gets Up will find themselves each a piece of driftwood, sturdy and long, ei, big enough to rest their rifles upon. Leave their ponies upstream a short way." Simultaneously everyone said, "Ahhh!" Benjamin smiled at them, for they now knew his mind. "Yes, to float silently down to where the men are resting near the bank," he said. "Little Bull Runs and I will come into the warriors where the ponies are. And there will be one call, the hoot of the long-eared owl." Benjamin leaned close and hooted low, "Who-who, whooo, whooo, whooo. Ei?"

"That is a very good call, brother," Bear Gets Up said with a chuckle. And cupping his hands, he answered and flapped his blanket like the soft wing-beat of an owl. "What do you say to this?"

"Yes, that's it," Benjamin replied. "We'll wait for

your call. At that moment, we'll know that you and Sitting Elk are ready. Wait three counts. Each man must pick a close target and make his shot true. If this is so, we'll have only two Cheyenne left to worry about."

"You carry the pipe well," Sitting Elk said with a smile. "All this day I have felt in need of a bath, and now I shall have it."

Little Bull Runs could not resist shooting one more arrow into the proud hide of Benjamin One Feather. Grinning, he said to the others, "I should think that the one who carries the pipe is more suited for a bath in the night. In this, our leader has some experience."

These words were meaningless to Sitting Elk and Bear Gets Up, and Benjamin, who found little humor in his present situation, made no reply. His final words were, "Make your moccasins ready."

They made themselves ready and soon departed, trailing their ponies behind. At a point some distance above the Cheyenne, Sitting Elk and Bear Gets Up waved and turned toward the river. It was now only a matter of time, and fate. Benjamin came within sight of the stolen ponies much sooner than he had expected, and he softly backtracked into the shadows of the cottonwoods. From this position he could barely see the grazing horses, and he saw nothing of the three guards. Making sign, he told Little Bull Runs to climb the nearest tree, to see if he could look down on the remuda and position himself well enough to shoot. This Little Bull Runs did, and finally motioned down to Benjamin that, indeed, there were still three men, one to the right and two to the left, but it was too difficult to make a clean shot from the tree.

Wasting no more time, Benjamin waved Little Bull Runs down, telling him to crawl around the guard on the right side, and that he himself would watch the others. Little Bull Runs silently began to snake his way through the tall bunch grass, and in moments he was out of sight. Likewise Benjamin One Feather hunkered down. Using the cover of some rose bushes, he soon came within sight of his quarry; not only could he see the two men huddled in their blankets, he could also see the river to his left, the moon playing its light across the silent eddies. This, he allowed, was a stroke of good fortune, for now he was able to watch for his companions, and certainly would spot them when they floated by through the bright shaft of moonlight.

Shortly thereafter, Benjamin was alarmed when one of the Cheyenne suddenly stood and took several steps directly toward him, and this was only twenty paces away! But just as suddenly this man stopped, threw aside his blanket, and began to urinate in the grass. Directly the brave turned, called out a few words, and someone answered from the other side, presumably the guard that Little Bull Runs was watching. Then, except for the calls of crickets and the croak of a frog, everything was silent again. When Benjamin glanced back at the river, he saw two dark forms float by, and it was only a few minutes later when he finally heard the hoot of a great-horned owl.

Taking careful aim on the nearest form, right between the shoulders, Benjamin counted to three and pulled the trigger of his Henry. Shots came from the river and across the remuda, and horses began to bolt in all directions, kicking and snorting, breaking brush, but most of them running downriver. A second figure loomed up in front of him, and he fired another round. This man flew over backward as though struck by lightning. Jacking in another shell, Benjamin leaped through the darkness toward the river, only to be met head-on by a mounted Cheyenne, who almost toppled him with his pony. By the time Benjamin had recovered he could only manage a quick shot through the black cottonwood grove, and he missed. He heard several shouts at the river's edge, ran that way first to discover Sitting Elk and Bear Gets Up both astride two dead Cheyenne. His brothers were already carving scalps. Bear Gets Up had avenged the death of his uncle.

A few confused ponies were still milling about in the meadow, and Benjamin deftly dodged through them, leaping over the body of the second brave he had slain. He saw no sight of Little Bull Runs, and with good reason. Suddenly, by the light of the moon, he came upon another stricken Cheyenne, badly wounded, gasping, weakly waving a revolver in an outstretched hand. Benjamin kicked the gun away. Nearby was Benjamin's Absaroke brother, Little Bull Runs, lying on his side, curled up like a woolly worm, bleeding from his chest and breathing his last. Benjamin One Feather, tears flooding his eyes, bent down and took him up into his arms.

Little Bull Runs smiled faintly. He knew someone had come to help him on his new journey. This was good. "Pistol . . . had a pistol," he mumbled, and those were his last words. Little Bull Runs, who had seen only twenty winters, was going home on another trail. Lowering him back to Mother Earth, Benjamin One Feather returned to the dying Cheyenne. He sucked deeply for wind, slipped his knife from its sheath, and violently plunged it into his enemy's chest. He threw back his head, and the wailing cry of anguish for his dead Crow brother echoed through the dark bottoms of the Little Big Horn.

The sun was crimson, dying against the buff-colored foothills of the river, when Benjamin One Feather and his two companions approached the hunting village. There would be no *aratsiwe* this day, no drums to beat, no chants, no parade of the scalp sticks. But at first, when the people down below saw all of the Crow ponies running to rejoin the herd, there were joyous shouts. They also saw the painted enemy ponies, five of them, decorated with bright colors, horses of war, a sight which brought more happy outcries. But then the gathering Absaroke grew hushed, for at the back of the horses, seated silently on their unmoving mounts, were only three of their brothers, and behind them was a lone pony carrying a blanket-draped body. This procession came no farther. Even though these Crow braves had their faces painted black because they had victoriously counted coup, they could not ride into the village to make the women dance and sing Praise Songs. Suffering a grievous loss, they were remaining on the hillside to fast and mourn a lost brother. People were shifting about uneasily, straining their eyes, looking for loved ones, but the blackened faces of the returning men were masked, not only in victory, but in death. The villagers knew that someone had lost his medicine, that someone had ascended the Great Hanging Road.

Finally the pipe-carrier, Benjamin One Feather, the one responsible to come forward with the news, slowly approached, his pony in a brisk, side-stepping gait, feathers and two fresh scalps dangling from its bridle. It was his father, Man Called Tree, who met him at the perimeter of the village. They talked quietly, and when Benjamin had related the story, he reined about, ready to return to his two friends on the small hill. A young woman came running to his side, momentarily looked up into his eyes. It was White Crane, but her mounted man was somber and unsmiling, and he only sadly shook his head, offered no words. There was no *kahe* forthcoming from White Crane, for she knew in an instant that her brother, Little Bull Runs, was the blanket-covered brave on the pony that stood alone. She read her man's eyes well. Wailing and tearing at her long black hair, she fled back to her father's tipi, and Benjamin One Feather groaned miserably, his heart heavy, his soul empty.

On a nearby knoll, Benjamin sat disconsolately with Sitting Elk and Bear Gets Up. Since there was no crier in the camp, Man Called Tree, who had received the news, was obligated to tell it to the awaiting Absaroke. His voice carried loud and clear, and Benjamin listened as the chief began to relate the story in sequence. Only at the end would the despairing outcries of the women reach the heavens.

"Hear this news, my people. This is a time to mourn and rejoice, a time to share sadness and happiness, and we will bear them together at the will of Akbatatdia. Our four young men traveled one sun and one moon with his blessing. On the Little Big Horn River they caught up with the men who stole our ponies. This was a party of six Cheyenne warriors, who were going someplace to make war. Over there, you see their ponies. When these warriors rested at night, our braves made medicine to steal our ponies back. They did so, but could find no way to do this without fighting. Our men fought with great cunning. Each counted coup, killing five of the enemy. They took five scalps, five rifles, one pistol, and captured those five ponies of the Cheyenne. In this battle our brother, Little Bull Runs, the son of Shoots Far Arrow, shot one enemy and mortally wounded him. While he was upon him, the enemy shot back. Little Bull Runs died honorably. He spoke his last words in battle. What Akbatatdia gives, he also takes. Speak well of Little Bull Runs while you mourn, and take heart that our other brothers avenged him and returned safely. This is now finished."

Crying women rushed away toward the tipi of Shoots Far Arrow and his woman, Covers Her Face, to grieve in front of the lodge. Some were shrieking at the sky, others were on their knees, striking the ground. Shoots Far Arrow, his chin outthrust, moved slowly through them and walked toward the hill to take his son from the pony. Several other men followed. Benjamin One Feather approached Shoots Far Arrow, carrying a folded red Cheyenne blanket. After a customary greeting, Benjamin carefully placed the blanket at the feet of Shoots Far Arrow. Kneeling and unfolding it, he displayed a rifle, a pistol, and a scalp, the latter either to be mounted on the symbolic stick or burned in ceremony. Benjamin said only one sentence to Shoots Far Arrow. "I laid my heart on the ground beside your son."

During the Moon of the Falling Leaves, Benjamin One Feather and six other braves left for Manuel's old trading post to pick up a load of staples that John and James Goodhart had freighted up the Yellowstone. These were supplies of dried beans, flour, coffee, cornmeal, and salt, ordered earlier by Man Called Tree, to be distributed to the people of his village before Cold Maker bared his white teeth. Along with the abundant supply of buffalo meat, dried fruits, and pemmican, this would help fill the bellies of the Absaroke through the winter months. And winter was not that far off. The first frosts already had touched the Echeta Casha bottoms, and Wind Maker harshly followed, his strong breath leaving the stricken trees waving with barren arms.

The round trip to Manuel's post always took four suns, and on this occasion it was a journey readily welcomed by Benjamin One Feather, for his recent days in the village had been sorely troubled by the continued mourning of Shoots Far Arrow and his family. This had tested his soul. He needed to get away from the torment of sorrow. While White Crane's beautiful long locks, shorn at the buffalo camp, were beginning to show signs of healing, there was still a great emptiness in her heart, and her eyes were dark pools of sadness. Benjamin, pained by this, made brief, consoling conversation with her, but to little avail. They both knew that it would be the Moon of Ice on the River before he could properly present marriage gifts at the tipi of Shoots Far Arrow. Still mounted outside Shoots Far Arrow's lodge on a feathered shaft was a weathered Cheyenne scalp, flicking back and forth in the autumn breeze like a frazzled pony tail. A few of the village dogs came daily to piss on the pole. No one objected, and the lament for Little Bull Runs continued.

For the first night's stop on the trail, Benjamin One Feather told his Crow brothers about a place that his father had once shown him, the Rocks where the Swallows Live, and here they camped, building a great fire out of driftwood, spreading their robes under the protection of the cliff outcropping. The fifteen pack ponies were tethered to a long rope in between two cottonwood trees, well within sight of the camp. Before dark set in the young braves paired off, dutifully sharing the guard. Though this was always routine it was now more accentuated, for there were those along on this trip who had been at the buffalo camp during the Moon of the Drying Grass, and they had not forgotten the Cheyenne pony raid and its tragic consequence. No particular thought was given to the possibility of the Cheyenne being this far north during the Hungry Moons, but there were other coup-counters about.

Benjamin One Feather knew the habits of hostiles like the Pekonies and Big Bellies, who occasionally ventured down from the Musselshell and Missouri rivers to make mischief. And they had been making a good game of it lately, sneaking regularly around the bluecoat patrols from Fort Maginnis to steal stock from neighboring Indian villages. Additionally, there were new targets for theft—the few isolated cattle spreads in the Judith Basin, where several harried ranchers were not only contending with Indian raids, but also discovering that the vastness and the inclement weather of the wilderness range presented other problems. Cattle, unlike the furry-coated blackhorns, were not indigenous to the land, and when Cold Maker came down from the Queen Mother's Land he often put ice in their veins. Sometimes they died. Other times they strayed across the broad land and simply got lost. This made the wolves happy, filled their bellies.

The first riverside campout by the Rocks of the Swallows passed without incident, and with an early departure Benjamin One Feather and his brothers allowed that they would reach the Goodharts' post by late afternoon. Two riders, Stone Calf and Running Red Horse, were sent ahead to scout downriver. Toward midday they came galloping back with unusual news: Fourteen troopers with packhorses were coming up the Bozeman Trail, only two bends away, while on the other side of the river, riding the same direction, was a larger column of soldiers. This surprised everyone, to encounter bluecoats so far from their forts this late in the year, particularly since the Sioux, Cheyenne, and Arapaho were far to the south, already in their winter villages.

After a brief discussion, Sitting Elk, who was carrying the pipe, suggested they meet with the longknives and find out their business. He moved on ahead, taking Benjamin One Feather with him. His Fox brother knew the white man's language, although frequently, in such encounters, Benjamin feigned ignorance, a good trick taught to him by Man Called Tree. It was told that most often the white man was loose with his tongue; he talked too much, and one could learn more by listening and making sign than in engaging in outright conversation. Many of these bluecoats had noses as long as their sabres. They were always seeking information but seldom offered any.

Shortly afterward, the two groups met near a stand of aspen. There was no officer with this small contingent of bluecoats. Their platoon leader was a tall man with red whiskers, and he wore three stripes on his heavy coat. Another man alongside the sergeant, dressed in a similar army coat but wearing buckskin leggings over his woolen pants, was a breed Piegan interpreter. He came forward, said "*Hau,*" and passed sign, identifying himself as Flat Nose. Far across the river with the other troopers was the leader of the soldiers, a lieutenant. Flat Nose said that they were all returning to Fort Maginnis after an unsuccessful search for thirty mules and nine horses stolen on the trail between Fort Maginnis and Fort Ellis. The Indians had been clever, Flat Nose said, splitting the herd when they came down the Musselshell river country. They covered their tracks well and finally eluded the troopers in the Bull Mountains. The soldier-leader across the river thought the horse thieves were Crow.

The red-whiskered sergeant finally spoke up, addressing Flat Nose. "These boys are Crows, aren't they?" he said. "Well, ask them if they've seen any sign of shod stock up the trail . . . how far they've come. These devils always know what's going on, maybe even had a hand in it."

Flat Nose made sign again to Sitting Elk, relating most of what the sergeant had said. Benjamin One Feather, sitting his pony to the side, muttered a few words in Absaroke, informing his brother of the soldier Three Stripe's insinuation. Nodding, Sitting Elk, then replied, "We saw no tracks. We have come one sleep from our village up the river. We passed no one, going or coming."

After the Piegan breed had translated this into broken English, Three Stripes pointed to the string of ponies trailing behind the Crow. He said, "Ask them where they're going with all those horses with empty packs. And what the hell are they doing here, anyways?"

Once again sign passed between Flat Nose and Sitting Elk, but Benjamin One Feather, although annoyed by the unpleasant beginning of this conversation, said nothing. He disliked the attitude of Three Stripes, wanted to speak out and tell him that it was none of his damned business what the Crow were doing on free land. True, this was part of the Bozeman Trail and a route of free passage, but it was still the ancestral land of the Absaroke. Additionally, Benjamin resented these particular bluecoats from Fort Maginnis. In the severe cold of winter, soldiers from this fort had killed almost one hundred and seventy-three women, children, and old men in Chief Heavy Runner's friendly Piegan village several years back. More deplorable, many of those Pekony were sick abed in their tipis with small pox. Even though the Pekonies were ancient enemies of the Absaroke, this atrocity had angered all of the neighboring tribes, friends and foes alike, and no one respected the Fort Maginnis bluecoats.

Flat Nose, glancing across at Three Stripes, said finally, "I think Crows no help. Plenty no talk, see no mules. Village up there, one-day ride. You want look?"

The sergeant nodded approvingly and replied, "It's on the way back. I reckon it might be a good idea. I'll check with the lieutenant, see what he figures is best. Ain't much profit wasting more time here with these poor dog-eaters. If some of their Crow kin got our stock, they wouldn't be telling us anyways, would they? Hell, no, they're all thicker than fleas on a dog's back."

The Piegan grinned, saying, "Maybe they go steal mules back from brothers. Next time come, you see ponies, plenty army mules."

Three Stripes laughed heartily. "You're probably right. You dirty little buggers are all alike, aren't you, stealing from one another? Come on, let's move out of here."

Benjamin One Feather, no longer able to contain himself, moved his mount directly in the path of the sergeant. Angered by the soldier's arrogance and his demeaning references, Benjamin was not about to let this pass uncontested. He said evenly, in English, "You'll be wasting more time if you go to my village. I don't advise it. We don't have any use for mules. Use your eyes, sergeant. Do you see any mules for packing here? Ei, and we speak the truth. We don't eat dogs, and we aren't dirty. We don't trust soldiers who shoot sleeping people in their tipis, either, so I advise you to stay on the trail. You'll not be welcome in our village. Our people are hungry. They may decide to eat your liver."

The sergeant's face exploded in brilliant color, matching the hue of his red whiskers. Taken aback by Benjamin's stern and unexpected redress, he was momentarily speechless. Then, gathering himself, he said sarcastically, "Well, by gawd, it looks like I've done been talking to the wrong buck, now haven't I? Look it here, Flat Nose, we got ourselves a smart-talking Injun, and an ornery one, at that." Staring stonily at Benjamin, he added, "Now, why didn't you speak up, boy? Where in the hell did you get your learning? Save us all a lot of time, passing these hands back and forth, if you'd talked up in the first place."

"Why should I speak with someone who has so little respect for my people?" Benjamin One Feather asked. "You understand nothing."

"And you're a sassy one to boot, ain't you?" said Three Stripes, nudging his horse forward. "Sassy and right crazy. Seems to me *you're* the one not understanding much. Your people are friendlies, ain't they? Horse thieves, maybe, but friendlies, no less. Now tell me, boy, when did we ever go bothering you, eh?''

Benjamin replied hotly, ''You bother anyone when it suits your purpose. Everyone in our great land knows this.''

Staring darkly at Benjamin One Feather, the sergeant said, ''Boy, what you need is a little dressing down, someone to put you in your proper place. I reckon you'll be getting it one of these days, too, carrying on this way. This ain't *your* great land anymore, either.'' He abruptly reined about and motioned his small troop forward. Calling out to Benjamin, he said, ''What's your name? I want to remember you, so I can call you out next time, see if there's more to you than mouth.''

''Benjamin One Feather, son of Man Called Tree,'' Benjamin answered without hesitation. ''I'll be ready any time you so choose.''

''Oh, ho!'' shouted Three Stripes. ''A chip off the old block, eh? Might a known it. Your old man has grit, for sure, no doubt about that. Well, my name is Sergeant Bevis Ketchum, and don't be forgetting it, you hear? Next time we meet, I might take a notion to take you down a notch or two, knock you off that saddle and get some respect.''

''You'll get no respect from me,'' Benjamin called back. ''It will be your pony that goes home with an empty saddle, not mine.'' He defiantly lifted a clinched fist as Bevis Ketchum rode by, grinning and tipping a salute with his faded blue cavalry hat.

When the rest of the troopers had trotted away, Benjamin One Feather's brothers gathered around him, eagerly awaiting his words. It was obvious that this brief conversation with the bluecoat had been laced with misunderstanding and animosity. What had their brother said to the red-whiskered one that had colored him like a paint brush? Benjamin One Feather first related the derogatory remarks of Three Stripes. This brought angry grunts of disapproval from the Crow. They did not eat dogs, nor were they devils! But when Benjamin told them that he had vowed the Absaroke would eat Three Stripes' liver if he ever came to their village, they howled in delight, gleefully slapping their hands against their thighs. The very thought of eating a white man's liver was hilarious.

While this brought a smile to Benjamin One Feather's grim face, he had a strong suspicion that this was not the last he would see of Bevis Ketchum. Somewhere down the trail another confrontation with this Indian-hater was highly likely. And the next time it might be more than words that they would exchange. Whatever, Benjamin One Feather believed strongly in himself; he was prepared, for as his father had predicted he now possessed the eye of an eagle, the cunning of a coyote, and the heart of a wolf. If need be, he would stomp Three Stripes Ketchum into the ground like a piss ant.

After the troopers had disappeared around the bend, the seven young braves moved on and, as they had anticipated, arrived at Manuel's old trading post late that same day. John Goodhart, James, and Molly gave them their usual hearty welcome, and after exchanging news they shared a pot-luck supper in the big cabin. Goodhart reported that traffic along the trail had come to a standstill, only two pack outfits and one small wagon train having passed the stockade in the month since Man Called Tree's people had last visited. For the most part the Lakota and Cheyenne were peacefully quiet on their wintering grounds, but he predicted that this would change by the Moon of the Greening Grass, when the gold-seekers intensified their migration into the Powder River and Black Hills country. The wagon train that had only recently gone by was headed for Sioux country, eight miners with it. Their luck had panned out in Last Chance Gulch, and reports of the new diggings in the Dakota territory had sent them packing, treaty violations notwithstanding. Others would follow, eventually precipitating another bloody clash between the white men and the Indians; this a certainty, opined Goodhart.

So another night passed, and shortly after dawn, preparations to leave were under way. The morning was sunny but brisk, the meadow grass around the post heavily bent under a fresh coat of hoar frost. The Crow ponies, anxious to be on the trail again, trotted nervously around the big corral, blowing steam and snorting. A few of the men walked in amongst them, singling out the packers. Young James Goodhart had brought his own horse and a pack mule down to the big cabin, and was busy securing camping equipment and his canvas bedroll. He had decided to make the trip back with his friends to visit for a week with Man Called Tree's family. Although this was always a standing invitation, James's decision to make use of it so late in the year came as no great surprise to Benjamin One Feather. Love was calling, a plaintive note on a cold November day.

Benjamin knew that, just like him, James had been snared in the web of romance. This was glaringly obvious after the Crow returned from the buffalo hunt in September. Little Blue Hoop, in her week-long stay at the Goodharts, had made her beautiful presence readily known, and when Benjamin came riding in from the hunt there she was, hanging on James's arm like a gate post, her smile unabashed, broad, and revealing. James didn't seem to mind, either. In fact he was grinning like a happy coyote.

Benjamin understood. His half-breed friend had let his heart displace his mind, and he too had become a "goner." While Benjamin found some humor in this, he did not chide James about it at the time, only expressed some concern about the consequences, wondered how his sister would adjust to life outside her own village. This had not been discussed, said James. But when Benjamin had mentioned this to Little Blue Hoop, she'd happily pointed to Molly Goodhart. Had not *her* life been a good one? Look at all the years she had been with John Goodhart. This silenced Benjamin. How could he possibly respond to that? As his father had said, these women were always a step ahead, and he decided to say nothing more about the matter.

Because of the supplies they were now packing, Sitting Elk elected to avoid the main trail. Instead he would travel the benchland, eventually cutting across the foothills down to Rock Creek at its confluence with the Clarks Fork, the location of the Crow village. While this was a more cumbersome route, it was easily scouted and less dangerous than the timbered bottom of the valley. The staples so generously provided by Man Called Tree were much too valuable to risk losing in a trailside ambush, a chance taken by anyone, summer or winter. This country above the river was broad and wide, interspersed with small grassy coulees where juniper, sage, and ponderosa clustered. Below some of the protected bluffs and sheltered draws a few stands of aspen were still flashing the last of their golden leaves, their trunks glistening white in the morning sun.

Toward midday, White Moon and Old Dog Jumps came riding back from the point to tell Sitting Elk that a band of fifty antelope were scattered across the near horizon. Why not make some meat on the way home? It would be easy to sneak behind the pronghorns and flag a few toward the pack train. Since fresh meat for the evening meal was a good thought, and the antelope were directly in their line of travel, Sitting Elk sent Stone Calf back with White Moon and Old Dog Jumps to spook them out. James Goodhart, armed with a Spencer repeater, and Benjamin One Feather, shouldering his Henry, slipped off their ponies and walked a half-mile ahead, where they parted and found cover in clumps of sage.

Meantime, Sitting Elk, Red Running Horse, and Bear Gets Up took the pack train aside into a meadow of bunch grass and waited. Not long afterward a series of shots erupted across the flat, and the waiting men jumped up in time to see a few white-and-tan streaks flashing through the high sage. Moments later, when it was quiet, they filed the ponies back in the direction of Benjamin One Feather and James Goodhart. Directly, Sitting Elk saw them approaching. They had smiles on their faces, and were conversing with great animation. Benjamin One Feather held up four fingers, more than enough meat for their meal, some left to take home, plus four good hides to tan.

That night, camped in an aspen hollow, the men huddled in their red and blue blankets around a big fire and told stories humorous, tragic, and smutty. They enjoyed a grand feast prepared by their breed brother, James, who produced good medicine from his pack: two loaves of the white man's bread that his mother had baked, a jar of chokecherry jam, and a large skillet in which he fried antelope steaks and liver. They had never eaten such tasty meat, thickly covered with cornmeal and cooked in bacon grease. This was even better grease than elk marrow. The meat was so delicious that they left little to store in their pouches for the next day. The greatest belch of the night was made by White Moon, and for this honorable feat Sitting Elk exempted him from guard duty.

When they finally took rest under their robes, their bellies full and their minds uncluttered, they were contented young men, thankful that Bakukure, the One Above, had blessed them another day. Benjamin One Feather promised himself that he would offer up a more proper thanks for this caring brotherhood at the next sweat in the Lodge of the Hot Rocks. He would make steam rise from the rocks, offer it up to Masaka, the Sun, and pray that he and his brothers might live such a good life until the next winter. That night he heard the wolves talking in the distant hills, but he slept well.

The next morning it was cold again, Masaka's orange face too weak to penetrate the chilly air, and the men wasted little time packing the ponies and moving out across the frosty foothills to the west. Traveling at a trot, they were only a few miles from where they had spread their blankets when Old Dog Jumps came back from his forward position to report a strange sight. He had found a dead eagle and coyote lying not too far apart in his path, and they were unmarked, mysteriously stricken by some unknown power. He was mystified. But when Benjamin One Feather came upon the bizarre scene and carefully inspected the coyote, it took him only a moment to explain the mystery. His friend, Stone Calf, also knew what had happened. Cursing lowly, Stone Calf leaped back onto his pony and began to make a wide circuit around the area.

These animals, Benjamin told his other brothers, had been poisoned, and that meant only one thing: Somewhere close by on their land, a wolfer had spread his blanket, and this was bad medicine. Shortly, Stone Calf called out, and Benjamin and James rode over to see what he had found. It was as suspected: Part of the carcass of an antelope was lying in a clump of juniper, this the wolfer's poisoned bait. The area around it had been carefully brush-swept, and no tracks other than coyote's were near the bait. But some distance away, Benjamin discovered the imprints of boots. There was no doubt, now, that a wolfer had come into the Absaroke country with his poison and his heavy, steel-jawed traps.

That Stone Calf was incensed by this was understandable, because his father, Red Plume, had lost two of his dogs to a wolfer's poison only a year past on Big Porcupine Creek, across the Yellowstone. Worse yet, Raven Wing, only a small boy, had stepped into a hidden trap, mangling his foot, and he still walked with a slight limp. All of this was deplorable to Benjamin One Feather. These wolfers, who came during the Time of the Hungry Moons when pelts were prime, were a recent phenomenon on the land. In only a short time they had stirred the wrath of every tribe in the territory. A few of these intrepid hide hunters, ones whom the Indians were able to catch, had been shot and scalped. In retaliation, the wolfers had taken to shooting Indians on sight.

Sitting Elk, also cursing the wolfer, recovered the poisoned eagle. This majestic bird, the source of great medicine, wasn't destined to die such an ignoble death. This powerful creature would not be wasted, he declared, and he told White Moon to pluck its valuable tail feathers for later ceremonial use in the medicine lodge. He also decided it was best to report the presence of the trapper to the council when his men arrived back at the village. With the packs to worry about, his braves had no time to make a search themselves this day. In due time a war party would be dispatched to seek out and destroy the interloper and his traps. But before they moved ahead, White Moon and Stone Calf returned to the poisoned antelope carcass and covered it with rocks and brush. No more prairie victims this day, they vowed.

While this was good, it gave little satisfaction to Stone Calf. His mind was filled with dark shadows. He had stood helplessly by on Big Porcupine that day as one of his father's dogs died in violent spasms. He vividly remembered this. With vengeance in his voice, he told White Moon that he wanted to be on the war party; he wanted to see this dog-killer be made to eat his own poison and die with his belly on fire.

However proper and wise Sitting Elk's plan was, that of letting the council determine the wolfer's fate, it didn't come to pass. Toward midday, when the Crow packers were less than twenty miles from their village, they saw a trace of ominous smoke drifting down from a small canyon to the southwest. Benjamin One Feather knew this place. So did Sitting Elk. Benjamin said it was called Spirit Creek Valley, because near the entrance was a giant medicine wheel used by the ancient people, and beyond this spread of holy rocks was their burial ground. Benjamin even knew of one great man placed on a scaffold there, Buffalo Horn, a powerful maker of medicine who had long ago saved Man Called Tree from blood poisoning when he had been shot by the Pekonies. No one came to this valley to spread a blanket, no one would dare. This was sacred ground. Who would be so ignorant to do such a thing, to displease the spirits of the dead? And who would be so foolish to make camp so close to the village of Man Called Tree?

Of course, everyone listening to Benjamin One Feather knew the answer. Spirit Creek Valley had no meaning to a wolfer, for how would he know of such Absaroke customs? Neither plums, chokecherries, nor buffalo berries were picked along the bottom of this holy place. Nor had any tree felt the bite of an ax. Quiet, secluded, far from the trail, what better place for a wolfer to camp, where he could go about his business unmolested? But not this day. Sitting Elk, thoroughly angered by the trapper's transgression and now aware of his location, immediately changed his plan, ordering Benjamin One Feather, Stone Calf, and Old Dog Jumps to flush the wolfer out and then either frighten him away or kill him. He also cautioned them to tread lightly, to be prepared for the unexpected. By reputation a wolfer was as dangerous as his prey, and merciless to Indians.

Once near the small valley, Benjamin One Feather and Old Dog Jumps rode a wide circle around the area of smoke. Stone Calf, who left his pony tied near the rocks of the medicine wheel, crept stealthily up the creek bottom, staying in the cover of the trees. The three men were preparing to converge on the camp from two sides. But when Benjamin and Old Dog Jumps ultimately rode into the edge of the small clearing, they encountered not one wolfer but two, and the men were so busy stacking freshly cut aspen logs, fashioning a crude lean-to shelter, that they failed to notice the two Indians. A large tent was pitched to the side. In front of it near the fire, stirring a ladle in a blackened pot, was a blanket-draped Indian woman. She looked up and saw the two Crow sitting on their ponies in the shadows of the aspen grove. Her face was expressionless. She made no motion, shouted no alarm, only returned the silent stares of Benjamin One Feather and Old Dog Jumps.

Laboring with the logs, the two bearded, buckskinned wolfers were totally unaware they were being observed by the young Absaroke braves. Benjamin One Feather, his rifle resting handily across the pommel of his saddle, had been shifting his keen eyes curiously back and forth between the two men and the woman. What he found so startling was that the woman was Nez Percé. Her unparted hair with a small forelock was swept back and tied behind her neck, and she wore shell earrings, identical to those worn by Benjamin's mother, Rainbow. When Benjamin One Feather spoke out, saying *"Kaiziyeuycu,"* "greetings" in Nez Percé, her dark eyes immediately widened. Simultaneously, the two wolfers leaped aside and scrambled for their nearby rifles.

"Ikye!" warned Benjamin, flying out of his saddle. Old Dog Jumps, snatching his rifle, did the same, and scrambled in behind a tree. One of the wolfers bolted to the side and took cover behind the logs. The other man, clutching his weapon, hurdled the fire, bowling over the Nez Percé woman and thwarting Benjamin's aim at his back. The man flung himself into the brush and then, from the trees, Benjamin heard him yell, "Amos! Amos, you hear me?"

And a surly growl came from behind the logs. "Aye, I hear ye."

"You hang low there, hear? I'll take the Injun on the right. You get the other one, eh? Ain't no way they can get out of those trees. Just keep your eyes peeled, and if that rascal moves, bust down on him."

Benjamin One Feather, listening closely, apprised Old Dog Jumps of the white man's words, and they both flattened themselves in the damp grass behind the aspens. Meantime, the frightened squaw had crawled out of the line of fire and disappeared inside the tent. Benjamin whispered over to Old Dog Jumps. "Don't move and make yourself a target. They're the ones who are trapped, not us. Wait for Stone Calf to come in behind them."

"What about the woman?" Old Dog Jumps asked.

"Don't worry about her," Benjamin replied. "She

isn't here by choice, not at all, so she won't help them. This one is a Nez Percé woman."

"Ahh!" murmured Old Dog Jumps. "You could not shoot because of her. Now I understand."

Directly, a shot came from the edge of the clearing, and a bullet splintered the base of the tree that Benjamin was hiding behind. The man yelled, "Git outta there, you damned heathens, and make a run for it. Go on, git!" A second bullet whined by, creasing the thin aspen bark and ricocheting harmlessly through the brush. But Benjamin One Feather and Old Dog Jumps refused to move. Moments later, moments that seemed like an eternity, Benjamin finally heard the bark of a pine squirrel, knew immediately that this was Stone Calf positioning himself along the creek bottom. Shortly another round exploded farther back in the trees, followed by a screaming war cry. Benjamin called over to Old Dog Jumps, "*Ikye*! Watch the logs!"

Cracking brush, the first wolfer came staggering out, grasping at his side, but before he could reach the clearing, Stone Calf, brandishing his knife, leaped on his back. Falling together, they thrashed about, rolling into the open opposite the fire. As Stone Calf raised his knife to make a fatal plunge, the wolfer behind the logs finally jumped up and leveled his rifle on Stone Calf. This was precisely what Benjamin and Old Dog Jumps had been expecting, and they both fired simultaneously. Stumbling away, the white man called Amos fell to his knees, but he did manage to turn and pull the trigger for one shot. Old Dog Jumps, closing in on the stricken man, took a bullet in the thigh, the impact tumbling him over near the logs. When Stone Calf and Benjamin saw their brother go down, they immediately rushed to his side, fearing the worst. Old Dog Jumps, however, came up crawling and dragged himself over to the dead wolfer to spit in his face. Only then did he sit back and grab at his bleeding leg.

Benjamin One Feather quickly stripped away Old Dog Jumps' buckskin, exposing the wound to discover that the ball had penetrated the edge of the thigh, exiting just below the buttock. A clean hole without bone splinters, but bleeding badly. But before he could do anything, a hand clutched his shoulder, pulling him away. It was the

Nez Percé woman. "*Koiimzi,*" she said, nodding toward the tent. "Take him, hurry, over there. The *shoyapee* have medicine in their bundle. I will make a compress, stop the bleeding. I know about these things."

"*Sepekuse,*" replied Benjamin One Feather. So be it. Supporting Old Dog Jumps on their shoulders, Benjamin and Stone Calf carried their comrade to the tent, where he sprawled out on the robes. Old Dog Jumps cursed once. "It burns," he moaned, but then he was silent and complained no more.

Stone Calf, surprised at the woman's presence, asked excitedly, "Who is this woman? How did she come here? What's she saying?"

"Nez Percé," answered Benjamin One Feather. "The people of my mother from far away over the mountains, the Land of the Winding Waters. Don't be alarmed." Then he shrugged. "Who knows how she came here? Not by her own accord, I think, but in time we'll find out."

Stone Calf, staring down apprehensively at the woman, who by now was busy tearing strips of cloth, asked Benjamin, "But how can she do this? Can she cure his wound?" Stone Calf thought she was too young and pretty to be a medicine woman, for only the ancient ones knew about such matters.

"Perhaps better than we," said Benjamin. "I think she is now carrying the pipe."

The Nez Percé woman looked up at Benjamin One Feather and said, "They call me Two Shell Woman. Bring me hot water from the fire. Do this now, and hurry!"

"*Tasnig,*" replied Benjamin, "It is done," and he hurried away to the fire to fetch the water. As she had said, it was there, steaming in a pail beside the stew she had been cooking when Benjamin and Old Dog Jumps first came upon the camp. When he returned, Two Shell Woman was disinfecting the oozing wound with alcohol from a small bottle. Benjamin spoke up with a small worry. "I have herbs and chokecherry powder in my pouch to staunch the flow; yarrow leaves, too, a good balm."

Two Shell Woman, shaking her head, answered, "No, I don't need them. It is not the best, anymore. Ei, what I shall do here is better." She motioned Benjamin down beside her. "Here, hold his leg back. We must bind both sides, put on these compresses. Be quick, and do as I say."

Old Dog Jumps, feeling the cool air at his exposed crotch, nervously tried to cover his breechclout, but Two Shell Woman quickly swept his hand away. "*Nyah!*" she exclaimed. "At a time like this, you think of modesty! What do you have to hide? Keep away, we must put balm on each side."

Between clinched teeth, Old Dog Jumps said, "What does she say? All the time she talks and I understand nothing."

The seriousness of the moment notwithstanding, Benjamin One Feather could not contain himself. He chuckled and said, "She says, 'Keep your hands away from your crotch. You have nothing so great to hide.' She says this is not the time to be feeling there."

Mortified, Old Dog Jumps turned his head away and cursed again. Holding the swatches firmly, Benjamin watched closely as Two Shell Woman deftly pressed patches on the two holes, then wrapped cloth tightly around Old Dog Jumps' leg. After this was done, she took two buckskin strips and fashioned tourniquets both above and below the bandage. She explained to Benjamin One Feather that these should be released every half-hour to prevent Old Dog Jumps' circulation from being cut off.

When this was finished she disappeared outside the tent, directly returned with a bowl of her stew and a large wooden spoon. In sign, she demanded that Old Dog Jumps sit up and eat. This, she said, was good venison stew that she had made, and it would be good for his strength. Old Dog Jumps wasn't that hungry, but nevertheless he dutifully began eating as he had been told. She left a second time, and when Benjamin and Stone Calf later followed, they found her angrily poking the faces of the two dead wolfers with a firebrand. Their eyes had been burned out, and all that remained were empty sockets and seared flesh. And both of the trappers had been scalped. Looking up at a startled Benjamin One Feather, her black eyes narrowed and she said bitterly that these men were *cultis shoyapee,* no-goods, and that it would be wise to leave this place soon. There was another one of their kind somewhere in the hills, setting a trap line.

This surprising disclosure set Benjamin and Stone Calf hurriedly to work. They helped Old Dog Jumps out of the tent and rounded up their ponies. Two Shell Woman sternly refused to let Old Dog Jumps get on his horse, making sign that this would be bad for his wound. Instead, she came forward with her own pony trailing a travois. Benjamin One Feather and Stone Calf began to strap Old Dog Jumps into the big hide cradle, and the Nez Percé woman came to supervise. Looking down at Old Dog Jumps, she managed only the barest thread of a smile. *''Tekash,''* she said, then hurried away to other tasks. Benjamin One Feather shook his head and laughed.

''Now what does she say?'' Old Dog Jumps asked.

''Cradle-board baby,'' Benjamin One Feather answered, grinning. ''She says that you are her cradle-board baby.''

Old Dog Jumps, embarrassed and disgruntled, started to protest, but his brothers had turned away to secure their rifles in the scabbards on the ponies, leaving him alone to stare up into an empty sky. Two Shell Woman, not satisfied to leave the camp as it was, scooped up hot coals in the pail and threw several buckets into the tent, along with all the scrap wood she could find. Gathering up the wolfers' rifles and knifes, she placed them in the travois under the blanket of Old Dog Jumps. The extra ponies—four of them—she claimed as her sole property, and with her bundle of personal goods she finally mounted, advising the two Crow brothers that it was now time to leave. She was ready. Since Two Shell Woman apparently had assumed control of the pipe, they both did as she ordered; they moved ahead toward the awaiting pack train back in the foothills, stopping only at the medicine wheel, where Two Shell Woman left the wolfers' scalps on the cold, sun-bleached rocks.

The wind was blowing here, and the locks of newly scalped hair fluttered in it. Two Shell Woman, facing into the stiff breeze, told Benjamin One Feather this was Hattia Tinukin, the Death Wind, showing his appreciation for her offering. She said this was a place of bad medicine for white men. Benjamin One Feather, staring at the bloody scalps, allowed that this was most certainly true.

By the time Sitting Elk and his Crow packers were riding down to Rock Creek, Benjamin had heard most of Two Shell Woman's story. Slender, and possessing the comely features of most Nez Percé women, she was twenty-two years old. Earlier in the year her husband, Spotted Pony, had been killed in an ambush by the Salish-Flathead. She was taken captive and lived for a time in the valley land above the place called Hell Gate. The wolfer named Samuel, the one killed by Stone Calf, had bought her from the Flatheads for five pieces of gold and two ponies during the Moon of the Drying Grass. Two times she had tried to escape, only to be caught and beaten. She displayed to Benjamin a livid scar just below her hairline, where the wolfer had struck her with a trap chain. Now my *simikia* is lost, wandering outside my body, Two Shell Woman lamented. These men had made her unclean, and she feared that if she ever saw her people again they would shun her, put her out on the prairie, make her an outcast. Not only had she lost her soul, but her people as well.

However, she was both surprised and happy when Benjamin One Feather told her that his mother was Nez Percé, and that she would be welcome in Man Called Tree's village. The mention of Man Called Tree surprised her even more, for she had heard legends of this renowned chief, the man whom the Nez Percé called Pootoosway, the great Medicine Tree. Benjamin One Feather said that his father had many friends among the Nez Percé, that if she pleaded her case to him he would intervene on her behalf. When her people came again to hunt buffalo, Benjamin promised that he would return her to their good graces, by the will of his father and the Great Spirit. This was good, and for the first time in many moons Two Shell Woman smiled broadly.

Many people soon came running and moaning when they saw the strange Nez Percé woman trailing her travois, with Old Dog Jumps lying in it. But their alarm quickly changed to happy relief when they gathered close to the young Fox brave. He was resting back, hands clasped behind his head, smiling and enjoying all the attention, refusing to give any indication of the throbbing pain in his thigh. Sitting Elk told the crier what had happened in the nearby hills, and the news was quickly related to the gathering crowd. By sundown everyone knew the story of the packers and wolfers, and how the new woman had come to their village.

Man Called Tree's wife, Rainbow, took Two Shell Woman to the second tipi, to stay with Little Blue Hoop and the old widow, Looks Far Away. They made Two Shell Woman welcome, as Benjamin One Feather knew they would, but she wasn't content until she had gone back to Old Dog Jumps' family lodge to attend the young brave's leg. Man Called Tree and Rainbow went with her, taking disinfectants and astringents. Examining the wound they found heartening signs: the bleeding almost halted, and only minor swelling around the punctures. As Rainbow and Two Shell Woman bathed Old Dog Jumps and reapplied the bandages and new medicinals, he elected to say nothing this time, nor did he move his hand protectively to his crotch, nor did he understand anything being said by his friends. Here he was in his own Crow village with a painful wound, and everyone around him was speaking Nez Percé, even his great chief, Man Called Tree. Old Dog Jumps thought perhaps that it was just as well to remain silent and ask no questions. Yes, better to be quiet around this attractive, forceful young woman, and do her bidding.

Meantime, all of the supplies brought back from downriver were finally unloaded at the Lumpwoods' lodge, from whence they were to be distributed the next day to the people of the village. It was here, while Benjamin One Feather and his brothers were unpacking the ponies, that White Crane and Little Blue Hoop came seeking their sweethearts to bid them welcome. James Goodheart, noticing Little Blue Hoop near the ponies, modestly smiled and called a greeting to her, then discreetly stepped away to make quiet conversation with her next to the big tipi. She suspected the reason why he had come, but he told her anyway: to talk to her father; to tell him that after the Season of the Hungry Moons he wanted to make her his wife. Smiling happily, Little Blue Hoop gave him a hug, and then they strolled away arm-in-arm, toward the edge of the village.

White Crane's greeting to Benjamin One Feather was much less inhibited. Dispensing with her usual *kahe*, she boldly walked through the workers and, to everyone's surprise, eagerly flung her arms around Benjamin, planting a powerful kiss upon his lips. His brothers stopped unloading and momentarily stared at the two bold lovers. Then they began to yip like crazy coyotes and Stone Calf, still elated at the demise of the hated wolfers, stomped wildly around the couple, crouching low and strutting like a prairie chicken, mimicking Benjamin's great bird dance. White Crane quickly pulled her young lover away, kicking a long leg out at Stone Calf, who finished off his prancing improvisation by lewdly palming his stomach.

Amid the good-natured laughter White Crane cried out, "Eat fish!", and she finally managed to catch Stone Calf in the rear with her moccasin. Taking Benjamin to the side, she smiled broadly and pointed toward the tipi of her father, Shoots Far Arrow. By the last lowering rays of Masaka, Benjamin One Feather saw what she meant, now understood the meaning of her renewed spirit and exuberance. For there, in the long shadows, he saw that the feathered scalp pole in front of the lodge was gone. The time of mourning was over.

FIVE

It was midmorning, the skies leaden, heavy clouds drifting down the distant Yellowstone river bottom. The three young braves had stopped at the Medicine Wheel. "The scalps are gone," Benjamin One Feather observed. "They were placed here at the north end of the rocks."

His two Fox brothers, Red Running Horse and Hides Alone, were silent on their ponies, staring at the giant wheel. Its lichen-covered boulders lay deeply embedded in the coldness of Mother Earth, its great rock spokes fanning out in the Four Great Directions. The young warriors were more interested in this mysterious place, its history, its symbolism, than they were in the missing scalps. After accompanying James Goodhart halfway back to Manuel's post, Benjamin One Feather had detoured to the site on the return trip to their village to show his curious brothers the Sacred Wheel.

"Maybe Wind Maker blew the scalps away," Red Running Horse suggested halfheartedly. He was awed by the size of the great circle. Contemplating the symbolic rocks, he sought guidance and understanding. "I have listened to stories about these great wheels, old stories, nothing more. What does it say?"

Benjamin One Feather ultimately spoke, explaining what he knew, what little he had heard, fragmentary legends told to him by others. At one time many of the old tribes had used these wheels in ceremony, and this one was the symbol of the Universe. The ancient ones had made big medicine here, so he was told. Pointing to the four stations, Benjamin said that within the Universe there was the Way of the Four Great Directions. He knew nothing of the ceremonies, but his father's revelations had come down from Buffalo Horn, a holy chief whose spirit dwelled in the valley above.

"Everyone knows the four directions," said Hides Alone, "but I don't understand the meaning of all of this. What can I learn from these old stones? They do not sing songs anymore. They are old and silent as the mountains themselves."

"Ei, they sing songs," Benjamin One Feather replied, "but only those with wisdom can understand them, the old ones who have participated." He thought for a moment, trying to recall some of what his father had said. He had taught him lore and traditions, but it seemed so long ago now. Finally: "Some things, I remember. Each direction has its own special meaning, my brothers, a sign, a virtue, for north, south, east, and west. It is said this wheel teaches us to understand ourselves. Any man who perceives only one of these directions is only a partial man, ei? To be a total person, one must understand them all, travel around the complete circle. This is representative of the Great Hoop, the Circle of Life to bind a tribe together, so some say."

Staring at the stone circle, Red Running Horse adjusted his otter skin hat and, pulling it close to his ears, said apprehensively, "Then I will be only part of a man the rest of my life. I know nothing, and I tell you, this is not a place for us to tarry. Ghosts are about. Only spirits come to a place like this. I feel cold just sitting here. My butt is cold in my saddle. Both the spirits of the dead and the weather are after me. It's time we leave this holy place, my brothers. There's a feel of snow in the air, and we are not wanted here. Our medicine is not worthy."

Hides Alone questioned Benjamin One Feather. "Who is so great that he understands this great circle? Tell me that. Only the ancient ones have such big medicine, and they have been dying like flies in the frost. Ei, I must make a prayer in the Lodge of the Willows that I shall live this long to attain wisdom, to be able to make the journey around the Great Hoop."

Benjamin One Feather smiled at him. "This is the medicine of the hoop. So it's told, we must grow by seeking and observing the virtues in each of the directions, not one or two, but all of them."

"Come, come," Red Running Horse interjected, "this is too mysterious, and we know so little. And we didn't come here to understand ourselves. We came to see this sacred place, and now we find that the wolfers' scalps are gone. This is not good. The spirits may not like this any more than us questioning the medicine in these old rocks. I think we should leave before bad luck befalls us."

"But who took these scalps from the spirits?" asked Hides Alone with a defensive air. "Certainly, not we. We can't gain the ill will of the spirits for this deed. The Nez Percé woman, Two Shell Woman, will be plenty angry when she hears of this. I shall blame it on varmints."

"Varmints!" scoffed Benjamin One Feather. "No, I think not, my brother. They are all in their winter dens, sleeping, hiding from Cold Maker. Ravens, perhaps. They make meals of flesh and hide."

Red Running Horse said, "Or a varmint with two legs, perhaps—the other man our brothers on the war party failed to catch. Maybe he came back and did this, you know. They dig up everything valuable, and what is of no use, they bury. This is what I say."

If not varmints or the great ravens, Benjamin One Feather allowed that Red Running Horse's assumption might be correct. Undoubtedly the missing wolfer, before fleeing, could have removed the two scalps just as he had buried the bodies of his partners under a rock pile in the creek bottom. There was nothing left at the campsite, only a few scattered ashes where the tent had once stood, and these would soon disappear when Wind Maker came. Fearful that any presence of the two trappers in the sacred burial ground would upset the spirits, the war party had uncovered the grave site and carefully replaced all the rocks along the creek. They thoroughly cleaned the camp, removed the few aspen logs, and made it holy again, then took the stiffened bodies of the white men out of the valley and back to the high plains, where they left them for the wolves and coyotes.

"Ei," Benjamin One Feather finally said, "Red Running Horse is right. It's best we ride on and not displease the ancient ones' rest. The other wolfer was no fool. He had no food or shelter left, so he moved out of this place soon after we left, probably rode across the Yellowstone. If he got past the Pekonies, by now he's back to the place called Rocky Point. This Rocky Point is where all of these men live, up near the Mother River at Fort Benton where the fire boats come. They make wood for the fire boats when the weather is warm. Ei, and when the weather is cold and the boats no longer run, they come and make trouble for us." Reining about, he motioned the other two braves ahead, and they left in a brisk trot for the distant mountain pass leading down into the Clarks Fork valley.

Under threatening skies and Wind Maker's cold breath, they threaded their horses and two pack ponies through the broken stands of ponderosa and fir, coming out on a long, high ridge where traces of early-winter snow still remained. They headed for a small cleft to the right that would eventually lead them down a long draw to the valley floor. After following the ridge a short time, Red Running Horse, in the lead, stopped near the mouth of the cleft and pointed to the ground. Coming up behind him, Benjamin One Feather quickly slid from his saddle and bent low, inspecting the impressions in the snow.

There were two sets of sign, side by side, meandering off to the right—fresh elk tracks, and by their great size these were two bulls, now off by themselves after the end of the rutting season. This was good: two elk at hand, and only fifteen miles from the village.

Rifles ready, all three of the men walked along trailing their ponies, following the tracks along the ridge until they disappeared into a small pocket below. It was a dense thicket of buckbrush, fir, and aspen, well protected from Wind Maker, and fortunately for the three Crow braves, upwind. These elk, Benjamin One Feather told his companions, were bedded down for the afternoon not too far below, probably in the aspen. There was no indication that the two bulls had passed through to the bench on the other side. After a short discussion, Benjamin volunteered to play dog and penetrate the broad thicket of buckbrush from the lower end, while Red Running Horse and Hides Alone posted themselves near the upper end where they could get clean shots if the animals bolted up-country. Tethering their ponies and two packers in the pine, they silently departed, Benjamin carefully picking his way through the trees to the left, his two companions staying to the right, below the brow of the ridge and out of sight.

Benjamin One Feather had barely entered the pocket when he caught a faint odor of elk, a pungent, gassy aroma, but his view was almost totally obscured by the trees and downfall. He could see absolutely nothing. Moving quietly ahead, he finally came upon a windblown, dead fir, its splintered trunk arched up toward the sky. Carefully finding a footing, he crept a few yards up the fallen tree until he could look through the tangle of pine and aspen.

Almost dead ahead, not more than thirty paces, was a six-point bull, its head thrown high, its glistening black nose pointing directly at him. Precariously high on the log, Benjamin had no chance of bringing his rifle to his shoulder without losing his balance. And even at that, it would have made little difference, because in an instant the huge bull was in motion, making several gigantic leaps and showing only his yellowish-white rump to Benjamin One Feather. The sound of brush cracking to his left indicated the presence of the other elk, but Benjamin saw little more than a flash of golden brown fleeing through the grove. Leaping down, his blood pumping wildly, Benjamin started to run, hurdling logs, his quick eyes searching for any opening ahead for a possible shot in the offing.

A short time later, rifle fire came from the timbered hillside, then a series of wheezing grunts from a stricken animal, the breaking of limbs and dry brush. Suddenly, it was quiet. Benjamin heard only the throb of his heart, like pounding hooves within his body. Finally, there was a victorious outcry up above from Hides Alone. Benjamin One Feather took a deep breath and trotted away in that direction.

When Benjamin came upon Hides Alone, his brother was bent low over a fallen elk, his sharp knife busy, the great stomach paunch already tumbled out into the thin skiff of snow. But this was not the bull Benjamin had first seen. This was a smaller animal, a four-point, fat and sleek, a bull that obviously had been without a harem of cows during the recent rut. "You have done well, brother," he said to Hides Alone. "He'll be tender. The old women will be happy for this one, ei?" Looking around for Red Running Horse, Benjamin asked, "What happened to the other one, the herd bull?"

Resting back on his haunches, Hides Alone replied, "Wounded. How badly, I don't know. Red Running Horse is that way, taking a look. Some blood up there, but not much. Maybe he bleeds from the inside and will lie down soon."

The wind had died, and thin, powdery flakes of snow were beginning to fall in the high country. Benjamin One Feather left to retrieve the ponies. By the time he had returned, Red Running Horse was back and helping Hides Alone to dress out the young bull. Benjamin asked him, "You had no luck with the big one?"

Shaking his head, Red Running Horse said wearily, "He was running up the ridge through the big trees, far ahead of me. By nightfall, he may be in the land of the Shoshoni. I don't know. He has the heart of a wolf."

Without hesitation, Benjamin One Feather said, "I'll mount up and follow him. Once in good cover, he may lie down and stiffen."

Red Running Horse pointed to the heavens. "The snow, brother. I think we should pack these ponies and go down to the village."

"Ei, you are right," Benjamin answered. "But it's not good to waste such a fine animal as this one, to leave him for the wolves to tear apart. I saw him clearly through the trees. He's too great a specimen for a fate like that. I tell you, only Akbatatdia could have given him horns so large."

Hides Alone, pointing his knife at Benjamin, laughed. "You can't eat those horns, my friend, and his meat may be as tough as your moccasins. I think you should come back with us. The day is too short. If you find him, what then? He's a big one. We will have to pack him on our own ponies, and I don't like the thought of walking down the valley in the snow."

But Benjamin One Feather was already astraddle his horse. He told his Fox brothers, "If I don't catch up with this bull, I'll be back in the village by dark. If not, come back early tomorrow and look for my smoke in the basin. I shall sleep the night with his spirit, for I vow he'll not become a meal for any pack of wolves." Reining about, he passed the sign of peace to his brothers and rode up the ridge.

As he ambled along watching the tracks ahead of him, Benjamin began to have doubts. Perhaps his brothers were right—he should be returning to the warmth of a tipi instead of trekking across the mountains in search of a wounded bull elk. But oddly, he sensed that this was something more than just the wasting of an animal, a needless death, a death without purpose. For most certainly this elk was going to die, and die slowly, that in itself a tragedy. Drawn forward by a compelling force, one that he could not fully comprehend, Benjamin One Feather pushed on, occasionally stopping to examine the tracks, the gait of the animal, to see whether it had come to a staggered step, how much blood had been spilled, and where the bull was headed.

Now the snow had turned into a curtain of white fluff, great flakes shrouding the tree limbs, and fearful of losing the track, Benjamin kicked his pony into a trot. This elk had already confused him. Badly wounded, it was traveling uphill, this a strange happenstance, for these animals when hurt invariably headed down, usually toward water when they could find it. And now the snow was becoming the great creature's ally, threatening to obliterate the very trail Benjamin One Feather was following.

Nearly an hour later, Benjamin was approaching a large stand of ponderosa near the utmost crest of the ridge, and inside this grove stood the largest tree of them all. Towering skyward, its heavy boughs formed a huge canopy, under which the thick grass was untouched by snow. Here, in the deepening shadows, rested the bull elk, lying down, its massive head propped low against its chest. Pulling his rifle from the scabbard, Benjamin slowly dismounted and walked close to the dying animal. It weakly raised its head once, then helplessly nodded back. A small trickle of blood was coming from one nostril.

Benjamin One Feather crouched a short distance away and stared at the great stricken beast. Even near death it was majestically beautiful. Compassion and grief suddenly swept over Benjamin and he said brokenly, "So, this is the great place you have come to die, ei? You knew where you were going all this time, and you've waited for me to join you. Ei, it was in your mind that you would not die alone, and it pleases you that I've finally come. I know this. Your spirit holds hands with mine. Your soul has come to my soul, never to turn away. Your thoughts have become mine. All the way up here I've pondered on this. Ei, now I know what brought me this far, and why.

"It wasn't for your meat alone, ei? You wanted me to share in your death and rebirth. This is your mind, I know. You are too great to die all alone on a winter mountaintop. If you could speak, this is what you would tell me. Yes, and you would forgive those who have taken you from Mother Earth to another place. Listen, brother, I understand. Yes, and I have a tear for you. Hear me speak, great one, for from this day on you will be my medicine. You have purposely called me here, and by my hand no harm will ever come to any of your brothers, this I pledge in the name of Bakukure, the One Above."

With tears streaming, Benjamin One Feather took hold of the big rack and pulled the elk over on its side. He crouched sadly beside it, and moments later heard its last breath. Only after he had gathered a huge bundle of wood and struck a fire could he once again approach the dead bull. The terrible sadness gripping him was incomprehensible. What was happening to him? Only once in his young life had he experienced such inner turmoil—at the death of his Lumpwood friend, Little Bull Runs—but that was a human death. He could only imagine that in some mysterious way a spell had been cast upon him, his *iraaxe* seared by the hand of Akbatatdia, the Maker of Everything. If there was meaning in this disheartening experience, Benjamin was at a loss to explain it.

With a cry of despair, he finally slid his skinning knife into the thick underside of the elk, carved upward to the brisket, and emptied the ponderous mass of innards onto the ground. Later, when he found sleep beneath the big ponderosa, his mind was troubled and he was not at peace with himself.

When Benjamin, half-frozen, stirred in the middle of the night to replenish the fire, a white elk with antlers black as ebony and tines of glowing ice was standing across from him in the shadows of the giant tree. Feeling both fright and wonderment, Benjamin One Feather began to nervously edge back against the gnarled trunk, reaching for his rifle. How had this majestic creature come to the fire so silently? And what was its purpose in the glade? Its great body was like a transparent glaze of ice against the backdrop of falling snow and mountain darkness. And then to Benjamin's amazement, the beast smiled and spoke to him. "Be not afraid, Benjamin One Feather, I am as you see me, Shining Elk. I carry the medicine of death and rebirth. I am what has been, what you have taken for sustenance, and what is, and I come from the rising sun."

Heart pounding, Benjamin asked haltingly, "Why are you here? What is your purpose? You've scared the wits out of me! Had you been my enemy, I would be dead."

"Fright is not my purpose," Shining Elk said, raising a glistening black hoof in front of Benjamin. "I have come to guide you on your journey across the Sacred Mountain, across the Sacred River which is the Spirit of Life and is in the Great Direction of the East."

Benjamin One Feather stared curiously at the white elk. "Of what journey do you speak? I have planned no journey, only one back to my village in the morning when my brothers return. I only stayed up here on this mountain to keep the wolves from stealing your brother over there." Benjamin nodded toward the dead elk at the edge of the clearing. "Are you his spirit?"

The Spirit Elk spoke again. "I am the spirit of all animals living and dead, for as I have told you, I possess the medicine of both death and rebirth. I come not to haunt but to guide and enlighten you." Standing tall, his great tines radiating like silver spires, he called Benjamin One Feather from his robe, told him to mount up and prepare to ride.

"But what is this journey? Where are you taking me?" As Benjamin One Feather leaped onto Spirit Elk's back he was apprehensive, for the great backward sweep of the elk's antlers came perilously close to his head. "I have never ridden this way . . . nothing to grasp." Tightening his legs around the rib cage of the elk, he suddenly felt the wind and snow at his face, yet he was not cold, and when he stared down from space he was not frightened. He saw his small fire fading from view in the glade of ponderosa pine.

After a race through the gray heavens, they came into light, Masaka shining like a huge ball of fire in the east. They rode in that direction, to finally come down in a rush of wind and settle to rest on a cliff of the Sacred Mountains. Sitting nearby on the limb of a dead pine was Brown Hawk. Suddenly, the hawk flew from the limb and soared high, making three half-circles in the sky before coming back to roost. Nearby, a red fox barked three times. When Spirit Elk lowered his antlers, a scorching shaft of white light shot out, and the fox mysteriously disappeared in a plume of smoke.

Then, for the first time, Benjamin One Feather noticed two small men huddled at the base of the dead tree. Little people of the trees, they were dressed in white buckskin, their faces painted green. They called to Benjamin One Feather to dismount and join them, and he did. One of the little men was holding a medicine pipe, the other mixing sweet grass and kinnikinnick, and when this was done the pipe was lit from an ember of their small fire.

"This is Mother Earth," one of the tiny men said, offering the pipe to Benjamin. "Take it and become part of her."

Benjamin One Feather said, "*Aho,*" and after puffing the pipe three times, returned it. Pointing to the east, one of the men asked Benjamin One Feather what he saw beyond the Sacred River on the distant plain. Benjamin stared eastward, shielding his eyes against the glowing red of Masaka. Masaka was now fire, prairie fire, waves of flame licking across the benevolent apron of Mother Earth. Animals were fleeing in panic before the billowing smoke and flames: buffalo, antelope, deer, coyote, rabbit, badger, prairie dog, and mice, all being chased by mounted dark shadows in the fire.

Out of these shadows, Benjamin saw materialize a limping wolf, hobbling on three legs. It took sanctuary behind a large white boulder. The fire swept over the great rock, leaving the wolf unharmed, but a small black toad leaped from the head of the wolf and was burned to a cinder. Benjamin shrank back, horrified.

"We must do something to help these animals!" he shouted in alarm to the men. He felt his own soul burning. When he turned, the little people of the trees were gone and only two mice now sat beside him, their whiskers twitching.

The Spirit Elk spoke from the side, saying, "You now have the medicine to help all creatures, both the four-legged and the two-legged in the East and in the West. The medicine pipe has given you this power. Go now, spread your wings and use it." But Benjamin One Feather hesitated, thinking about what he must do to stop the conflagration from consuming all of what was before him, the land, the trees, and the creatures. He was searching for wisdom, the great Medicine Wheel spinning in his mind's eye, violently out of control, the hoop being torn apart, the heat of prairie fire in his face, and he courageously hurled himself from the cliff, resolutely flapping his arms, seeking balance.

Suddenly awake, gasping, jerking upright, Benjamin One Feather stared into the night fire in front of him. It crackled and spit. A large limb, oozing with pitch, had burst into flame, its heat searing the side of his face. Wiping the small pebbles of sweat from his forehead, he moved to the side and heaved a great sigh. A brief wave of loneliness swept through him, the one great feeling common to all creatures, but he was at peace inside. He had never before had such a powerful dream.

Benjamin looked all around him, searching the shadows for reality. He was alone in a great sacred circle untouched by the snow, the broad canopy over him forming the lodge of all his feelings, thoughts, fantasies, and dreams. Alone but not alone. To his side he saw a mouse on its haunches, preening its whiskers. When he instinctively reached out to touch his brother, it darted into a small hole at the base of one of the ponderosa's roots. Only then did he realize that he had experienced a powerful vision.

The next morning, his brother White Moon and his two Fox friends, Sitting Elk and Red Running Horse, rode with him down from the mountains. A few of the villagers came running when they saw the pack ponies carrying the quarters of the bull elk. On the last horse was its magnificent head, its tremendous antlers fanning out over the pony's flanks. There were many exclamations. Old Dog Jumps came wobbling out, supporting his healing thigh with a cane, and he shouted words of praise to Benjamin. This was a great prize that would have made any hunter proud and happy, but Benjamin's face showed only a look of quiet containment.

He barely smiled, and the small conversation he made was spoken calmly and without a shred of emotion. Gracious and giving, he told his Fox brothers to distribute the meat to those in the village who needed it. He told White Moon to take the liver and great hide to the tipi of Shoots Far Arrow. The hide, when tanned, would make a beautiful dress for White Crane. Benjamin One Feather said that only the horns were of value to him, that he would keep them for sentimental reasons. No one seemed to understand this, for these antlers could be put to great practical use for many things: tools, ornaments, handles for knives and weapons. But his brothers asked no questions, and Benjamin One Feather offered no explanation.

White Crane eagerly awaited his arrival, her fearful anxiety over his night alone in the cold mountains now turned to joy. Half-hidden in her winter robe, she gave him her usual *kahe* and nuzzled her nose against his cold cheek. Happiness radiated in her eyes as she whispered into his ear, "The Great One answered my prayer. Since you were alone, I thought it best to say something for you. You were in my mind like a picture in a mirror."

Benjamin smiled and squeezed her arm. "You have no mirror, but someday I shall buy you one. Ei, so you can see your own pretty face."

"I don't need it," she said softly. "It is told that in every man there is a mirror of a woman. So you see, I don't need this mirror so long as I am that woman within you."

Benjamin One Feather, no longer surprised by her quick tongue, simply shook his head. "This is told, you say. And who tells it?" And he immediately knew that he should not have asked such a foolish question, and he repeated in unison with her, "An old Pekony woman told me this."

She laughed, saying, "So, if you knew, why did you ask?"

"Only to see your smile, one that brings great warmth on such a cold day." Benjamin dumped his saddle, and two small boys dressed in furs, looking like little elves from an enchanted forest, took his pony away to the herd. Hoisting his tack and bedding over his shoulder, he walked slowly toward the lodges of Man Called Tree, White Crane by his side carrying his rifle and scabbard. Benjamin said to White Crane, "So, what did you ask the One Above that he so answered your prayer?"

"To protect you, of course. Yes, to keep you from the wolf and the silvertip bear, the big-humped one."

Benjamin One Feather smiled down at her. "I saw neither. But the mountains were good to me. I did see the great Spirit Elk. Ei, and in a deep dream, he spoke to me. Shining Elk came in the night."

"The Spirit Elk!" she exclaimed. "But he's only of legends, a mystery. Your dream must have been very powerful, my lover. Shining Elk is beyond the sky."

"A dream so powerful it left me shaking. Many signs came to me up there, so many I cannot explain them all, some good, some bad. But this I know, I now possess the medicine of the Spirit Elk. What more, I don't know." A strange light was swimming in his eyes, a glow of reverence. "I shall prepare myself in the sweat lodge, then speak of these things to Ten Sleeps. He knows of such matters, and I know nothing."

"Ten Sleeps! The old holy one?" She sighed in quiet amazement. "Then a vision came to you, more than a dream. . . ."

"Ei, this must be so," said Benjamin One Feather. "I'll be guided by what he tells me when he explains the meaning of all of this."

"But tell me!" White Crane pleaded, jumping in front of him. "You understood nothing? Tell me some of it, the best parts!"

Benjamin shrugged helplessly. He could offer no explanation, not even to the woman he loved, but he tried, relating from the beginning the magnetic pull that had led him to the great ponderosa, and then all of the extraordinary events that followed. She sighed, and Benjamin, tossing his saddle and bedroll beside the third tipi, turned and kissed her lightly on the forehead. He said, "I have thought about nothing else since all of this happened, and I have no answers, not yet. The elk took me up that mountain as though it were meant to be. His spirit came back with me, this I do believe."

At that moment, Two Shell Woman came out of the second tipi and greeted Benjamin and White Crane. "Here," she said, speaking in Nez Percé, "I will take your things and put them away. Talk with your sweetheart. She has missed you and feared for your safety. I saw it in her eyes. Men go away too much. For any reason they go, always an excuse. They don't understand the needs of women." She stopped at the flap and looked back over her shoulder. "Hides Alone tells me you went back to those old rocks. My scalps were gone. He says the evil *shoyapee* came back in the night and stole them. The *shoyapee* will be cursed now until he dies. His life is wasted forever."

"What did she say?" White Crane asked.

"She says I go away too much, and I don't understand you."

"She is wise," said White Crane with a smile.

"She's also angry about the wolfers' scalps. Hides Alone told her they were missing at the big hoop."

"You went back to the Medicine Wheel?" White Crane stared incredulously at Benjamin. "You went back to that sacred place? But why?"

"Ei, on the way home the other day," Benjamin admitted. "My brothers had only heard of it. They wanted to see it. We only ventured there, not to the burial grounds."

"Well then, listen to me, Benjamin One Feather," she said, grasping him by the arm. "You must tell this to Ten Sleeps. This is important. My father says that the old man was there once at ceremonies with the ancient ones. He knows the medicine there. Yes, and I think somewhere within that hoop lies the answer to your vision. You may have been touched by that place . . . for the best, I pray."

Near the end of the Geese Going Moon, a group of Lumpwoods came back from a woodcutting expedition in the nearby mountains. They were also trailing freshly cut lodgepoles, which they placed in the bushes out of sight behind Shoots Far Arrow's tipi. White Crane had asked these young men to help with her new lodge in the name of Little Bull Runs, and they were pleased to do this in honor of their late brother.

Despite the recent mourning period for Little Bull Runs, the matter of preparing a handsome lodge for Benjamin One Feather had never been out of White Crane's mind. So, during the time when she knew it was improper to be romantically involved with him, she and other members of her clan had spent some of their spare time working on the great hides that would be pulled taut over the fourteen slender poles brought in by the Lumpwoods. Some of her women companions gently chided her. Was this not presumptuous, the making of a tipi before any exchange of marriage gifts? This could be bad medicine. What if there was some unforeseen happenstance, and the marriage fell apart? And what made her so certain that she had actually captivated Benjamin One Feather, that he was really committed to this union? Was he as serious as she? If something went awry, her shame would be the gossip of the village.

Undaunted by these suppositions, White Crane pressed on with her preparations, admonishing her sisters to work more and talk less. Her love for Benjamin One Feather was too powerful to be denied, and she predicted that she would live with him before the Moon of Ice on the River.

White Crane wanted to surprise Benjamin One Feather, to show him that she was more wife than he expected. Not only could she revere her man, honor him and love him passionately, she could also be a fine manager of the new lodge, assume her duties willingly and eagerly. Already she had stored bundles of meadow hay and fronds of pine and cedar for the base of her bed, and she possessed three fine blankets and a newly tanned buffalo robe for coverings. She brought up rocks from The Rapids to make the fire pit. These she stored behind her father's lodge with the long poles.

Two Shell Woman, who knew something of these plans from the Nez Percé words of Little Blue Hoop and Rainbow, came one evening and presented a great gift to White Crane, a cast-iron pot with a lid that she had taken from the wolfer camp. This big kettle could be buried in hot coals and used for baking bannack, a bread of flour, baking soda, and water. When laced with dried berries or plums this made a delicious pastry that would impress any young man, particularly Benjamin One Feather, whose mother often used this recipe. All of this was good. White Crane was leaving nothing to chance. She had even kept track of her menses cycle so that when she took her man into his new lodge she would be clean and he could not be left wanting. Nor she.

So it came to pass, three days after Benjamin One Feather's night on the mountain, that he arrived at Chief Shoots Far Arrow's tipi to claim his woman. The family and Bear clan were expecting him, the chief's lodge had been readied. White Crane and her mother, Covers Her Face, were seated at the back with a few clan relatives, mostly women and girls. White Crane was smiling. Her father, at the entrance, nodded and said *kahe,* then gestured graciously to Benjamin and his brother, White Moon, when he saw the five ponies and the gifts piled high on several of them. The presents were quickly unloaded and brought inside, arranged neatly to the side of the fire, and then everyone assumed their places, Shoots Far Arrow and Benjamin sitting to the front facing each other. The chief took the ceremonial pipe from one of the clan and politely passed it to Benjamin, who after taking several puffs, returned it to Shoots Far Arrow.

With a friendly smile, Shoots Far Arrow finally said, "Your presence here is no surprise. My daughter has talked of nothing else since the Moon of the Red Cherries." There were a few giggles from the women in the back. He went on, saying, "I am honored to have you in my tipi. You are welcome here. I have smoked with your father many times and he speaks well of you. Your deeds speak even better, my son, and this is good. You have strong medicine." Shoots Far Arrow turned and looked back at his daughter. "Is this the man you wish to have for a husband?"

White Crane nodded. "Yes, my father, this is Benjamin One Feather. With your permission, he has come to claim me as his wife."

"Ei," Shoots Far Arrow said, smiling, "I think his purpose here is clear enough." Everyone laughed, including Benjamin One Feather. Shoots Far Arrow continued. "White Crane is an intelligent daughter, a good one. Sometimes, too intelligent. She has learned to speak as well as listen. She tells me you have had a vision of the Spirit Elk, and soon you will go into the medicine lodge and talk with Ten Sleeps about the Sacred Wheel.

This pleases me. As our people pass up the Long Road, so do many of our traditions. It is good to honor the traditions, my son.

"Spirit Elk is a symbol of understanding and enlightenment. This is a good sign for this marriage. When you fully understand your vision, you must come and smoke with me again, tell me of it, the true meaning. Ei, and it is good you kept the horns from the elk on the mountain, did not misuse them. This shows understanding. The horns symbolize lightning. Torn apart, they are meaningless. But scrapings from these horns would be good medicine for your bundle when it is fully prepared."

Benjamin nodded and looked beyond Shoots Far Arrow to the back of the tipi where White Crane was sitting, still smiling. She winked. Benjamin One Feather, not surprised by her usual audacity, replied to Shoots Far Arrow, "I will heed your wise words. It pleases me to be in your lodge, to ask for your daughter to be my wife. I also have thought about this many moons. I come to seek your blessing." He gestured to the side. "I bring these gifts, and the ponies outside, to honor your lodge on this occasion, but there is one among them I wish to present to you personally." White Moon, standing to the side, came forward with a Winchester rifle and placed it near the lap of Shoots Far Arrow. The chief appraised it, then turned back to Benjamin One Feather with a questioning look. Benjamin explained. "This is a fine repeater, couped from the Pekony who tried to take your daughter at the Big River. It shoots the new shells. I once promised this to your son, Little Bull Runs. My heart is both heavy and light. In his name, I now offer it to you. He was my friend, my brother Absaroke. May it be a lasting bond between us in his memory."

Several of the people in the clan sighed and others murmured expressions of approval. This was indeed a generous gift, and one of great sentimental value. Shoots Far Arrow's firm jaw flexed several times. He was touched by the significance of Benjamin's offering, and by his kind words. Clearing his throat, he said, "I accept it proudly. By the sign of Spirit Elk who gives rebirth, I have lost one son and gained a new one. Ei, this pleases me greatly, Benjamin One Feather."

Benjamin, smiling broadly at the happiness in the chief's

face, said, "Ei, and I have gained another father." The two men reached over and clasped hands, as everyone around the circle laughed and clapped enthusiastically. Several of the older women wiped tears from their eyes, but they were smiling, too. Benjamin and Shoots Far Arrow talked quietly for several minutes. Then they finally stood, and Benjamin One Feather addressed the small gathering. "Then, my friends, if these gifts are accepted, the family of Man Called Tree will be honored to have your clan at our celebration feast tonight."

"So it is agreed," said Shoots Far Arrow, with a pass of his hand.

"Will you accept White Crane in exchange?" someone jokingly shouted. More hilarity, and everyone gathered around, offering congratulations to Benjamin One Feather, Shoots Far Arrow, and White Crane. The men smoked and the women drank hot herbal tea. But some women did not. Instead they hurried out of the tipi to a selected spot on the village perimeter, and began to erect White Crane's lodge.

Ten Sleeps, an ancient man heavy with wrinkles and slow of walk, had listened carefully to Benjamin's dream story in the dimness of his lodge, and after a second hearing sent the young brave away, telling him to return when the moon had passed over the tipi two times. Ten Sleeps told Benjamin One Feather that this was a powerful vision, one that required meditation and more preparation on the holy man's part to explain.

After this time had passed Benjamin returned, bringing with him, as ordered, the scrapings of elk horns, a hawk feather, and a buffalo tooth, items needed for the making of his new medicine pouch. He also brought a bowl of antelope stew and several pieces of bannack prepared by his beautiful woman, White Crane, to present as a gift to Ten Sleeps. This was good, for many of the holy man's teeth were missing, and chewing food had become a problem. Through a snaggled smile, he gratefully nodded; he was indeed pleased at Benjamin One Feather's gesture. Setting the food to the side, the medicine man said this gift showed that Benjamin possessed great kindness in his heart. After several more gracious nods and an *aho,* he went to the tipi flap and carefully whisked the entrance with his buffalo tail to keep away evil spirits.

After this had been attended to, Ten Sleeps took dried sweet grass and sage from his sacred bundle and cupped it in his hands. Moaning a low chant, he sprinkled it into his fire, filling the air with a delicate aroma. This, Benjamin One Feather knew, was to please the spirits of the dead, to honor the bereaved, all beings whether animal or human. Then the old man settled himself on his robes and closed his heavy lids. Benjamin One Feather thought it was a long meditation, long enough to feather a prairie chicken, before the holy man finally spoke.

"*Barak-batse*, my son," he began in a low whisper. "It is true what you believe. By this vision you have had, your medicine is indeed of the Spirit Elk. I believe that this is because you shared your soul with one of his kind and now the elk spirit dwells within your body. Now, when you pray to Bakukure in the Lodge of the Steaming Rocks you must also ask Spirit Elk for guidance. He is part of you. One cup of water on the rocks will always be for him. Ei, one for Masaka, one for Bakukure, and one for the Great Elk, the one who came to you at a sacred pine tree on the mountain. Hear my words. You should return to this holy place in the Moon of the Red Cherries and make a sacrifice, a giveaway. Look for another sign. If you see it, then you will know you have been truly blessed. For this the dust of the elk horns—is your strongest medicine."

Ten Sleeps passed his hands over the elk scrapings in the small pouch in front of him. After throwing dried holy grass into the fire, he closed his eyes again, shook his head, and said prophetically, "I also see some evil in this dream, *burak-batse*. This is what the Hawk warns us . . . the three marks in the sky, the red fox, and the limping wolf. Evil may come out of the fire to try and do you harm. I see this. The medicine of Spirit Elk destroys the Fox. But the wolf . . . now this is the sign of battle, power, and cunning, and the fire is the sign of the living spirit of the people. Beware of this wolf. What happens here is not clear, is yet to come. A conflict of many people.

"The little toad you saw leaping away, burning into nothing? This, I believe, is a lost shadow, but not from your body. A soul is lost. When it is your time to go to the Great Lodge of Bakukure, the sign will be lightning. Your medicine is that powerful. Since evil may come from the shadows, we ask for the power of Hawk to guard you and to be part of the hawk medicine you already possess." He then passed his bony hands over the hawk feather.

To Benjamin One Feather these were confusing words, and signs he didn't fully understand. He asked Ten Sleeps, "But how do I know of such evils in my life? Are these people? Where does this evil come from?"

"What this evil is, only you will know when the time comes, but your medicine is strong. The fire was from the East. In your dreams you were already turning on the Sacred Hoop, seeking help from the Four Great Ways. This is because you have already joined the gift of the mind with the gift of your heart through the help of Spirit Elk. So says the dream. You have become a seeker. This is good. Since you seek more wisdom, here is the tooth of the Great Buffalo that has tasted the holiness of Mother Earth." Once again, he made a motion over the tooth resting beside the small pouch.

"Ei, I understand this medicine, but not the vision," Benjamin replied.

"Did you not see what was on the plain coming from the flames? Did you not see the dark shadows?"

"I saw horrible things," recalled Benjamin One Feather. "A bad dream, that part of it. As you say, evil signs. My heart was heavy."

"Then understand this," Ten Sleeps said. "In all men there is both good and evil. But out of balance, one may destroy the other. I believe that the power of the Great Hoop brought you this vision. Twice you stood before it and contemplated. You were touched by a spirit. The Great Circle teaches us to seek out understanding in all directions, to find the balance between good and evil and become a whole person. When you have reached full understanding of the medicine of men and the Great Directions, you will never be threatened by the actions or decisions of other people. By your dream, the Spirit Elk gave you the most powerful medicine . . . to help others and destroy dark shadows. Now, you must go out and seek what has been so spoken and foretold. Be guided by the faith in the great medicine you now possess. This is rare for one so young, my brother. Many go through the Sun Dance Lodge seeking such visions and signs, the rituals of earth and spiritual renewal.''

Still somewhat perplexed, Benjamin One Feather thanked Ten Sleeps and returned to his tipi to ponder this new anxiety in his young life, his destiny and the relevance of his vision to it. For the present, his medicine was good but his vision was too short, clouded by vagueness and incomprehension on his part, not that of the holy man. This had become a riddle. How could anyone foresee the future? His future. And if the fire was coming from the east, when? Nothing seemed that predictable. And when he vainly tried to explain all of what had transpired in the lodge of Ten Sleeps to White Crane, she said exactly what he was thinking: What does it all mean? She sat before him on the robes in their splendid new tipi. The fire was leaping and crackling. Crossing her long legs, she said, ''Tell me.''

''He said I would know when the time comes,'' Benjamin replied with a deep sigh of frustration. ''I possess powerful medicine, enough to carry me through trouble, even the fire of battle. He says that within the hoop there is learning. I must go out and seek it.''

''Who can see beyond the horizon?'' she asked skeptically. ''This old man speaks words of wisdom, but they are too mysterious, my husband, too foreboding. This is what I perceive. I have no medicine, but I shall watch you like a hawk to keep you from doing something foolish, from becoming a crazy dog, one who would throw his life away for any cause or prophecy. I don't want my man in trouble. Do you hear me, Benjamin One Feather?''

''Yes, my ears are better than my vision,'' he said with a wry smile. Oh, how he admired and loved this woman! ''Yes, you I fully understand. Your bark is well heard, and I know your bite.''

White Crane returned smartly, ''This is good, Benjamin One Feather. You see, within *my* circle you are already learning. Listen to what I say, for I may teach you more than you have ever dreamed.'' She joyously leaped upon him and he fell back on the pile of robes, laughing as he happily took her into his arms.

SIX

''Pony soldiers coming,'' Red Running Horse motioned, reining up his horse. ''Down the river trail.''

The young men and women who were in the bottom making winter wood stood aside as he threaded through the logs searching out Benjamin One Feather. And Benjamin soon came, carrying a crosscut saw over his shoulder, another innovation Man Called Tree had introduced to his people. With these new saws and axes, making wood was no longer solely the task of the women. Now everyone joined in, cutting the poles, bundling and dragging them back up the trail to the village—fat chunks of dried cottonwood and pine to be stacked neatly alongside the tipis. Benjamin One Feather looked up at Red Running Horse inquisitively. He asked, ''How many of these riders?''

''Two abreast, maybe twelve or more,'' was the answer. ''Beyond the far bend of the river.''

Why longknives would be about after the Moon of Falling Leaves was a curious happenstance, since there had been very little activity along the cold banks of the Yellowstone in early winter. But then again, Benjamin was not too surprised. Once accustomed to the contrary frontier weather, these soldiers had quickly adapted. Garbed in buffalo coats and heavy woolens, they were now apt to show up most anywhere within a two- or three-day ride from their forts, wherever business or circumstance took them. Calling to his Fox brothers, Benjamin One Feather ordered them to disperse in the timber, to take positions on either side of the trail. A few of the young women hid, others gathered at the nearby fire and pulled their blankets about them and waited. Then Sitting Elk came and joined Benjamin and Red Running Horse near the trailside.

"Maybe a scouting patrol," suggested Sitting Elk, a doubtful tone to his voice.

"Who knows what these bluecoats are up to," put in Red Running Horse. And with a laugh he added, "Perhaps the Pekony stole some of their mules again, and have blamed the Crow. Ei, maybe these pony soldiers are going down the river to Plenty Coups' people."

Sitting Elk smiled and said, "Ei! Stolen ponies, indeed!"

"When my father first came to live in the Echeta Casha he saw no bluecoats for many winters at a time," Benjamin One Feather said reflectively. "Now they come with regularity, like grasshoppers, and even after the grasshoppers are long dead in the frost."

"A plague," said Sitting Elk.

"Ei, this is what my father says," Benjamin One Feather agreed. "Avoid them like a plague. He says one will find more peace by avoiding bluecoats, agents, and the treaties they bring. Time and events, my brothers, have proved the wisdom of Man Called Tree's words."

Sitting Elk nodded but said apprehensively, "Our chief has great vision, but I fear time and events are not on our side anymore. I often listened with envy to the legends of the old people. Ei, now many are dead. They walk the sacred path with firm steps. In our time the steps are faltering. This I see."

"I concede nothing to these foreigners," Benjamin One Feather said boldly. "Never!"

"Nor do I," returned Sitting Elk, affectionately patting Benjamin on the shoulder. And directly he pointed up the trail. "Ah, here come our soldiers now. So, we shall soon see what they are about this winter's morning."

"Ei, they come, and I see two of our old friends with

them,'' Benjamin said. ''There is the Piegan, Flat Nose, and the sergeant, Three Stripes. See his red beard flying like feathers on his chin. I think Wind Maker has blown us a bad omen, but one that I'll enjoy contending with. This is the one who is called Ketchum, eh?''

''The very one, brother, the one who vows to remove you from your saddle,'' replied Sitting Elk. He laughed derisively and spat to the side.

The troopers drew close and their leader, a young lieutenant, held up his hand as he pulled up in front of the three young Crow braves. Directly behind him, smiling, was Bevis Ketchum, a muffler under his cavalry hat pulled down over his ears. Another man, obviously a civilian from his attire of buckskin pants and heavy jacket, sat on a shaggy mount next to the Piegan interpreter, Flat Nose. It was the lieutenant who spoke first, pointing to the nearby fire and then to his eyes. ''Saw your smoke back there,'' he said. Then turning to Flat Nose, he said, ''Ask them how far to their village.''

Flat Nose raised a mitten to Benjamin One Feather and said, ''Hau,'' and was acknowledged. He then said brokenly to the young officer, ''You talk him. He know how. Talk you plenty good.''

''The young buck,'' interjected Sgt. Bevis Ketchum, ''is the son of their chief. He speaks English, sir, but he likes to play dumb.''

After a quick glance at Ketchum, the lieutenant looked down at Benjamin One Feather. ''So, you speak English. That's good. And what do they call you?''

''Benjamin One Feather,'' was the quick reply. ''What name do you go by?''

''Lieutenant Zachary Hockett, Company H, Fort Maginnis,''

''Are you interested in making wood this morning, Mr. Hockett?'' Benjamin asked lightly. ''Or do you wish to warm yourselves by our fire?'' He made a sweeping gesture toward the fire, where some of the women stood silently watching.

''Neither,'' Hockett replied, smiling. ''You speak well, Mr. Benjamin One Feather, and quite readily.''

Sergeant Ketchum grinned and said, ''He's a regular caution, sir. Riles real easy, too.''

The officer held up his hand. ''Well, sir, I'm looking

for your village. Have reason to believe a young woman is there, a Nez Percé woman. I want to talk to your chief about her, a serious matter.''

''What could be so serious to bring you all the way down here?'' Benjamin asked, quickly translating to his friends. But he now knew, as did they, the purpose of the visit, and Sitting Elk grunted disapprovingly, casting a sidelong glance over at the women.

''I thought I would discuss the matter with your father, Man Called Tree,'' answered Hockett. ''That would be the proper procedure. Where is your village? How far?''

''I speak for my father,'' Benjamin One Feather said. ''Soldiers from your fort are not welcome in our village, any village in this land. Our people, our brothers, have not forgotten the massacre of sick Pekony women and children in Chief Heavy Runner's village four years ago. Your Major Baker and his men slaughtered one hundred-seventy innocent people.'' He paused and pointed at Sergeant Ketchum. ''Your man there, the red-bearded one, once told me that he would teach me some respect. Ei, we all know the kind of respect he and his kind teach. This is not our way. No, I won't take you to our village.''

Obviously stunned, the lieutenant protested weakly, ''But that Baker affair was before my time.'' Searching for words, startled at such a damning accusal, especially from a young Crow brave whose mortal enemies were the Piegan Blackfeet, Hockett finally managed, ''And Major Baker is no longer at our fort. It was all a horrible mistake, the whole affair. . . .''

''Whatever, but not forgotten or forgiven,'' said Benjamin.

Sergeant Ketchum interjected loudly, ''See, sir, what did I tell you! He's a damned caution. Move him aside, and we'll find the village on our own. Hell, we can follow those drag trails right up to their tipis.''

At that moment, the civilian sitting to the side of Flat Nose suddenly came up in his saddle and shouted, ''By gawd, there she is! Right over there! That's her, all right, the little wench! She's the one! I'd know that one in the dark of night!'' And he pointed toward the fire where Two Shell Woman was standing among the other young women.

"Are you sure?" Hockett said, turning back. "Are you sure this is the woman?"

"Certain as the day is long, Mr. Hockett," he declared. "Hell's fire, you think I'd forgit a woman like this 'un? Damned lucky she didn't git my gizzard, too!"

Benjamin One Feather addressed Hockett as he dismounted. "Who is this man? What is he accusing her of?"

"His name is Ulis Birdwell, a trapper," Hockett replied. "Which squaw is he pointing at, anyhow? Good Lord, they all look and dress alike. He claims she killed his brother Amos and another trapper by the name of Sam Hanks. Made off with their horses and all their gears, trapping paraphernalia and such. Yes, up one of these river canyons ten days ago. That's what he charges. Now, which one is she? Point her out. There'll have to be a court of inquiry. This is the law, and we're obliged to follow it."

"A trapper!" exclaimed Benjamin One Feather. "What kind of a trapper? There are no furs left in our land. Anyone knows that. That man is no trapper, Lieutenant. He's a damned wolfer, and I'll take exception to his story." He turned angrily and stared at Ulis Birdwell. "You're a lying wolfer, a man who spreads poison, aren't you? What is your word worth against this woman? How could she kill two of your kind?"

"She kilt 'em, she did!" he shouted back. "I know it, cuz I found 'em dead and scalped, and I buried 'em at the camp! That's gospel, 'tis!"

Lieutenant Hockett held up his hands. "Be quiet, both of you, please. I want no shouting match here. It will avail us absolutely nothing." Turning to Benjamin One Feather, he said, "Please tell the woman to step forward. With your help, I want to question her. I may have to take her back to the fort for the investigation. Don't you understand? This man has made a grave accusation and it has to be addressed properly. Killing two white men . . ."

"Ikye!" Benjamin One Feather shouted. Suddenly, eight armed Absaroke braves, answering the alarm, materialized from the trees, rifles at the ready, covering the troopers on all sides.

"For God's sake, don't be foolish!" Hockett implored, his eyes bulging. "Call your men off. We're here only to investigate, not take up arms against you. I can't condone this kind of action on your part. It's foolhardy, and can only be held against you and your people. We don't want this, and the consequences ultimately will be to your disadvantage, I assure you. Now put the rifles down."

"Yes," replied Benjamin One Feather, "I certainly agree with you, but I see little advantage in taking this woman back to Fort Maginnis to be tried before a panel of white military officers who have nothing more than the word of this wolfer to rely upon. This doesn't sound like justice to me. You ask too much. This would anger my father, I also assure you, and the consequences you talk about might be to your disadvantage, too. Sometimes his ways can be very convincing."

"Are you making threats against the government?" Hockett asked. "Is this intimidation?"

"Not at all," Benjamin One Feather said calmly. "It's a promise. If you strike an unjust blow, we will retaliate. It's that simple."

"I see," Hockett said, stroking his moustache. "Then what do you suggest here and now to break this stalemate?"

"Simple again, Mr. Hockett. I suggest you ride to the place that this man Birdwell talks about and recover the bodies of his partners. He says he buried them. When you have the evidence of these killings, come to our village. The Nez Percé woman will be there. In fact, I'll oblige you and ride along to this campsite, wherever it is. Yes, I'll be your hostage until the matter is thoroughly investigated and concluded with proof that she actually killed someone. But for the present, you won't touch the woman." He smiled and looked at Hockett, then up at Sergeant Ketchum, whose face was flushed with anger. "I take it that this meets with the sergeant's approval?"

Ketchum glared threateningly at Benjamin One Feather. "You're a damned fool, pulling something like this, Injun boy. Putting your head into a noose, that's what, and I'll be there when they string you up." Reining to the side, he implored Hockett, "Don't listen to him, sir. We can't abide these conditions. We'll just be making a damned goose chase up in these hills. It's nonsense trusting these people. Call his bluff, sir."

"Jesus, what choice do we have, sergeant?" Hockett asked motioning toward the thickets where the Absaroke braves stood silently with their rifles raised. "His action is foolhardy, I agree, but not senseless. He has a point, and a good one. Only evidence will substantiate the charge . . . the bodies."

"No goose chase," Ulis Birdwell put in. "No, siree. I knows right where our camp is. You think I'd fergit that place? No, siree, not in a million years." He put his nose forward toward Benjamin One Feather. "I'm no liar, by gawd, and I kin prove it! What I says is gospel, 'tis."

Zachary Hockett sighed and turned back to his mount. Looking over at Benjamin One Feather, he said, "It is agreed, then. You'll ride with us to the site, and we may claim the woman at your village. Is this correct."

Benjamin nodded, and translated for his brothers and the women near the fire. Turning back to Hockett, he replied, "This is correct. You have my word."

With Ulis Birdwell leading the way, the group soon departed, Benjamin One Feather and Lieutenant Hockett abreast of each other directly behind the wolfer. Without conversation, they rode at a brisk trot along the main Bozeman trail until Birdwell finally paused at the foothills of Spirit Canyon. He pointed, telling Hockett that this was the trail to the campsite, about three miles up the small creek. Benjamin One Feather said nothing until the young officer finally commented on the beauty of the small valley. The air was chilly, the sun high, a small skiff of snow glistened in the mountain meadows. Aspen and juniper hugged the bottom, where grass was still green along the creekside.

"Do you know the land up here?" Hockett asked. "It seems almost pristine, primitive in nature."

"Ei, I know it," returned Benjamin. "No one comes this way, not unless he is carried. It's a sacred place to my people, once a ceremonial site, a burial ground for the ancient ones. Not used anymore. There are spirits up here."

"Ghosts?" Hockett said. "You seem to be a knowledgeable man, Mr. Benjamin. Tell me, do you believe this? Spirits, and such?"

Benjamin One Feather was silent for a moment, pondering such a foolish question, but obviously asked in innocence and sincerity. He finally said, "If I tried to explain the meaning of this place, I don't think you would understand. It's not that simple, unless you understand our many religions. Your religion is entirely too singular. You see, we believe in both nature spirits and human spirits, a spiritual universe for all beings and souls. I can only tell you this: My people take no more than they need from animal or plant, and we give back in thanks and respect. The spirits up here will do no harm as long as they are respected. Misfortune always follows transgression. This is a place of respect. If this fellow Birdwell came here to camp and poison wolves he was very foolish."

"But how would he know?" inquired Hockett. "How would I know such a thing if you had not told me?"

"Signs. The inner feeling" answered Benjamin One Feather. "Soon you will see what I mean, just above the small grove there, on the hillside, in the rocks." He pointed, and Hockett pulled to the side, directing his binoculars up the narrowing canyon. At first he saw nothing but the barren trees and outcrop of boulders. Several ravens came flying low, their harsh outcries echoing along the bottom. And then Hockett saw a few remnants of fluttering cloth, scaffolds among the sunlit rocks tracing multiple shadows across the inclines. In yet another place he saw a spire and great horns jutting out, guarding a mound of white boulders below. It was a burial ground, a majestic one, and as he slid his binoculars back into the case he experienced an unusual sensation coursing through his body, a tingling either of apprehension or anxiety, he couldn't comprehend which.

"Yes," he muttered, "I see what you mean . . . a burial ground, indeed."

"Tell your men to remain here," Benjamin One Feather ordered. "We will proceed by ourselves with Birdwell and Sergeant Ketchum. Yes, Ketchum, too. I don't want him to miss this."

The troopers dismounted and found places to rest in the sun by the small stream, where they lit up pipes and made conversation as their two leaders, Birdwell, and Benjamin One Feather rode on toward the aspen grove and meadow. When they drew near, Ulis Birdwell leaped eagerly from his saddle and ran toward the clearing. He was elated. After that afternoon of horror here, he had safely returned with the territorial law. His brother's death was to be avenged. But when he came into the small meadow his feet suddenly turned leaden, like heavy clods firmly rooted in the crusted snow. Transfixed by the unusually pleasant sight, he was unable to move. It was as though he had come to a virgin site, one untouched by any man or beast, as there was not a trace of the campsite, or the rock fire pit, or the tent poles so firmly lashed to the aspen.

Temporarily speechless, he gestured helplessly to the three men behind him. Finally in desperation he cried out, "This is it, I know it! It was right here. . . . " He ultimately bolted from his frozen tracks toward the rock-pile grave of his brother Amos and Sam Hanks. But here too there was only dried meadow grass, sprinkled with small skiffs of snow. Nothing. Not a trace of his great mound of rocks, the ones he had so laboriously carried up from the creek. He stood alone, stupefied at the serenity around him.

"Where are the bodies buried?" Hockett called to him.

"They were right here where I'm standing, goddammit!" Birdwell screamed. He stomped wildly about. "Right on this spot!" And he dashed madly back to the clearing, began to tear at the snow cover with his hands. "Fire was here . . . show you the ashes." He clawed futilely at the hard ground but turned up not one flake of wood ash. The earth was frozen, hard and unforgiving, and in desperation he stabbed at it with his knife. The other three men watched him as he fluttered about the scene.

Sergeant Bevis Ketchum began walking about, scuffing the hard ground with the toe of his great boot. He stared up at the scaffolds across the creek, the gaunt poles, feather, fur, and bone hanging to them, the weathered wood still miraculously intact in what seemed to be a sheer rock face. Shaking his head, he walked back and faced Hockett with a look of disgust. "This is no place to camp, sir. If they pitched here, they were crazy as loons. Reckon Birdwell is mistaken? Or he's fleeced the lot of us?"

Hockett turned about, carefully inspected the four directions. Ketchum was right. No one in his right mind would make camp here. He, too, shook his head, confused yet suspicious. "This place is as clean as the day God made it, Sergeant, almost too clean. If there was anything here, it has been dusted and picked apart, piece by piece, almost reverently, I'd say."

"Opinion or fact, sir?" asked Ketchum.

"Opinion only, and doubtful at that," was the reply. It was quiet, with only the barest rustle of twigs in the barren trees, the sound of the creek gurgling nearby, the flutter of several darting juncos. Even Ulis Birdwell, who had fallen to his knees, had spent himself. His emotions were strewn across the cold ground beneath him. Hockett looked across at the scaffolds, then surveyed the surroundings once more. He muttered, ". . . and we give back in respect and thanks."

"What's that, sir?"

Zachary Hockett shrugged. "Nothing, sergeant, only something our Indian friend over there said. Conversation along the trail, that's all."

Finally Benjamin One Feather called out, "Mr. Hockett, do you wish to look up ahead? Pursue this matter?"

The lieutenant waved him off. "No, sir, I think not. Obviously there is no evidence here, not even of a camp. I see no need to prolong this incident. As you said, it's a matter of proof, and you've played a winning hand this time."

Benjamin said, "Perhaps this wolfer had a bad dream."

"No, no," moaned Birdwell. "It was all here . . . real . . . they was scalped dead . . . blood, eyes gone. Jesus!" He turned on Benjamin One Feather and spoke with venom. "You knew it . . . knew it all the time! How could I dream such a thing? She did 'em in, she did! You covered her tracks. No other way, Injun, no other way." He mounted his horse, cursing, and leveled a finger at the young brave. "It's not over and done, hear? I'll be around these parts. Unceded land here, y'know. I have rights jest like you, boy. Yep, I'll be around sometime . . . pay that little bitch a visit, mark my words, Injun, mark 'em well."

Benjamin One Feather said nothing. True, the land was

adjacent to the ceded country of the Absaroke. It was free, belonged to those who chose it. He could not quarrel with that, but he entertained the thought that if Birdwell did have the courage to return, his stay would be short and very unpleasant. He watched Hockett and Ketchum remount. The officer turned to him. "Are you coming?"

"No," Benjamin replied. Pointing to the distant mountain to the east, he said, "No, I ride that way, that farthest ridge you see, another sacred place where the land and sky hold hands. Ei, that's my way, where I go to seek direction."

Hockett stared against the sun toward the ponderosa ridge, saw nothing more than a cold mountain, stark and silent. He turned back to Benjamin. "Sorry to have put you to the extra ride, Mr. Benjamin. Your point in coming up here was well justified, though, I must admit. But that little incident down on the trail, I'll have to report it, you understand."

"Understood," smiled Benjamin One Feather. "Next time keep your flanks covered."

"Rest assured, I will." On that parting note, he reined about and gave Benjamin One Feather a wave. Bevis Ketchum spat to the side and frowned. He was not a happy man.

Ulis Birdwell made one last outcry. "What about my hosses? The four hosses the woman stole?"

"Horses? What horses?" Hockett said over his shoulder. "Probably disappeared into thin air, just like your partners. Come on, man, come on, let's get out of this place. We've been whipped."

Benjamin One Feather came down into the village late that day from the upper valley. He was silhouetted against the lowering sun, but the women and young girls readily recognized him. They came running, with many tremolos.

In April, during the Moon of the Frogs, when the great renewal of Mother Earth commenced, scattered bands of Absaroke began to return to the main village. They had wintered in some of the adjacent valleys where game was more plentiful, and forage for the ponies abundant in the low meadows. There were many celebrations, both large and small, in the lodges. Clans were reunited, old friends came together to feast, dance, and enjoy the ceremony of the planting of tobacco, a traditional festival. As promised, the Goodharts came from their trading post on the Yellowstone to witness the marriage of young James and Little Blue Hoop, daughter of Man Called Tree, and there was great happiness and festivity among the people.

But far to the east in the Black Hills, the sacred Paha Sapa of the Sioux, conditions among these people were worsening. There was too little time for hunting and the celebration of Mother Earth, the essential elements in their nomadic way of life. The great Fort Laramie treaty of 1868 had been totally abrogated by the government, broken by the demands of miners and merchants who were running a hostile gauntlet into the traditional Indian lands searching for the rich rewards of gold. Sioux, once again joined by their brother Cheyenne, had begun to paint their faces and decorate battle ponies. Confrontations along the trails had become more frequent and travel was hazardous, even with military escorts.

All of this news was related to Benjamin One Feather by James Goodhart who, after a short stay of two nights in the village, returned with his new bride and parents to Manuel's fort. Barring the spread of hostilities, he allowed that the separation was only to be a short one, for already Big Cloud, the great Absaroke buffalo hunter and shaman, had placed his symbolic skull facing inward at the village perimeter. Meat was needed, and soon the spring hunt on the Bighorn for bull blackhorns was to take place. Big Cloud only awaited the proper signs to make his decision. As usual, the Crow hunters would stop for their customary reunion at the post, and James, at that juncture, had pledged to join his new in-laws in the hunt.

But before the buffalo, Man Called Tree had obligations to the west. After the marriage of James and Little Blue Hoop, a small group led by the Crow chief left for the Gallatin Valley, herding fifty head of green-broke ponies. Claybourn Moore was expecting the new stock to supplement horses that he and his two drovers were gentling down for the summer trade. Moore had been busy during the winter months, supervising construction of long cattle sheds in the Six Mile Creek bottom, most of which had been completed by calving time. A new line cabin also had been built up near the hot springs, where Ben Tree had acquired another large tract of land bordering the mountain wilderness. The six braves in the Crow party with him turned back toward home at the pass overlooking the valley, and Man Called Tree, his two sons, and White Crane and her new friend Two Shell Woman continued on with the ponies, skirting the frontier civilization of Bozeman City in the south.

They arrived at the ranch late in the afternoon. A light spring drizzle had set in, misty, low-hanging clouds skidding across the greening meadows, obscuring the great Rocky Mountains to the south. Clay Moore and one of the new hands, Robert Peete, came up from the main corrals to open a swinging pole gate and help move the ponies inside. From the main house Moore's wife, Ruth, beckoned the two women out of the rain, and they hurriedly dismounted. Pulling their ponchos tightly around their shoulders, grasping their bedrolls and bundles, they ran laughing into the warm kitchen. Once inside, Ruth grasped their hands and made them welcome, and then an awkward silence enveloped the room, broken only by small laughter and nodding heads, for White Crane and Two Shell Woman knew no English and Ruth, a Christian woman, had no knowledge of Indian tongues.

Later she was amazed to learn that even White Crane and Two Shell Woman could barely communicate between themselves, that each of them was from a different tribe. And she was astounded when she found out that Ben Tree and his sons spoke all three languages fluently. But eventually White Crane broke the language barrier, remembering the only word frequently used by Man Called Tree's family. "Hallo," she said, smiling. Ruth Moore was the first white woman she had ever met.

"Oh, yes," exclaimed Ruth, pressing her hands to her ruddy cheeks. "Hello, yes, hello!" She gestured to their wet ponchos and then to the table. While the two women removed their ponchos and took a seat at the table, Ruth hurried to the stove and poured coffee, brought them each a mug, steaming and fragrant. Two Shell Woman, remembering one of the few Absaroke words that she knew, muttered "*Aho*," much to the delight of White Crane.

But there was heartfelt communion among the women, even without conversation—the maternal bond most women covet, the advent of a newborn, for Ruth was heavy with child. She glowed, radiated, her fullness billowing the long gingham dress and apron. There were sighs, genuine happy smiles of admiration from White Crane and Two Shell Woman, and the bride of Benjamin One Feather cupped her hands in admiration, rocking them gently, and gestured with her eyes, "When?"

Understood, yes, but Ruth hesitantly pondered, finally held up two, three, four fingers, pointed skyward, and made a sweeping arc. In days, soon. The women knew. And when Ruth happily moved a finger slowly down the side of White Crane's cup and flung her arms outward, the women all exploded in laughter. At that point the door flew open and the men crowded in, eyes wide, astonished by the women's outcries, their peals of laughter.

"What is this?" asked Man Called Tree, first in English, then in rapid sign. "Do you all know each other so well as to make bad jokes already?"

White Crane answered, "We have spoken with our hearts," and she made sign, from the mouth, to each of the others, to the heart, clearly understood by Ruth and Two Shell Woman. They nodded eagerly.

Then, as Ruth stood smiling, Ben Tree, the great chief, introduced the women properly, who each one was, identifying Two Shell Woman as one who had been taken from her people by trappers, one day to be reunited with the Nez Percé. And then he too paused to admire Ruth's fullness and to congratulate Clay Moore. Indeed, a great cause for happiness.

White Crane spoke excitedly again. "*Iyke!* She says maybe two, three, or four days, very soon, maybe even before I finish my coffee!" She traced down the cup and opened the palm of her hand explosively.

Amid the laughter White Moon, with his customary drollness, said, "Then I shall leave now, find my place in the bunkhouse. I want no part of this." He paused at the door and glanced back at Ruth. "At least wait until after supper."

Ben Tree readily translated again, grinned, and looked over at Clay Moore. "I didn't allow for the communication problem, Clay. Might be a problem or two here before we clean country. As you can see, neither one of these women speaks English—one Crow, one Nez Percé—and most of the time I don't even know what language I'm talking. One of them makes a joke, and by the time I translate, or Benjamin there, time we get to the funny part, it's not all that funny anymore. Damned confusing, it is."

"Sign will make do, I reckon," drawled Moore. "Less racket that way."

Mimicking an old friend, Ben Tree said, "Ei, kee-reck!" He paused reflectively, took a cup of coffee from Ruth. "You said a line right out of the past, Clay. Gabe Bridger used those very words more than once. Ei, 'Sign will make do.' " Pausing again, he stared into his cup. "I can't believe it. . . . Almost twenty-five years ago we rode through here, down the middle fork of the big Mother River, right over the hill, through the Blackfeet, down the Musselshell, right into the Absaroke nation. Miraculous!'' He pulled a lock of his hair. ''See here, never lost a thread, either.''

Young Benjamin was rapidly translating both in sign and Absaroke. White Crane, who had never heard her father-in-law mention this story, asked in surprise, ''But why, father, did you do this crazy thing? Those Pekony tried to take me away. This journey, so dangerous!''

Man Called Tree laughed and replied, ''Yes, but it would be a damned sight more dangerous now. This was before the treaty-makers came. . . . No people fighting, only the Indians playing coup games among themselves. No, Gabe wanted to see this land one last time before the curtain fell. Fact is, he came back three more times. But as for myself, I just wanted to see it for the first time, the wilderness above the North Platte. At that time, I had no notion of staying or ever coming back.''

''But if you had not returned,'' White Crane said, ''just think . . . we would not be here this way.''

He sipped his coffee once and complimented Ruth on its taste. He went on, saying, ''Well, we stayed almost a month with Chief White Mouth's people on the Yellowstone. Did some hunting for the curly cows. Ei, went on up the Powder toward Fort Laramie. Even smoked a pipe or two with the Lakota. Didn't see a white man in four months, no roads, no forts, nothing but mountains and prairies. Ei, that was in fifty-two, first time I met Benjamin's blood father, three years before the boy was born down at Fort Hall.''

''You would not smoke with those Lakota now,'' said White Crane indignantly. ''*Eeyah,* they are the ones who chased my man one time.''

''Ei, and with good reason they chased him,'' Man Called Tree said with a smile. ''He and his young Fox brothers were caught stealing their ponies.''

''Only playing coup games, my father,'' rejoined an amused Benjamin One Feather. ''Your very own words.''

And then Two Shell Woman, her pretty dark eyes flashing, uttered her first words. ''I took four horses from the *cultis shoyapee* who beat me. The *piuapsiaunat* came and I saw plenty white men looking and pointing at me. I did not run, but they wanted to take me away. Benjamin One Feather said they wanted to hang me. These *piuapsiaunat* did not think taking those ponies was a coup game. Benjamin One Feather said *enimkinikai*! Go to hell, eh? He would not let them take me. I love him like a brother. I love White Crane like my sister. I love Man Called Tree like my father. He is the great Pootoosway to my people by the Tahmonmah, the great Medicine Tree. I tell you all, I am happy to be here, to know such white people who are not bad."

Benjamin One Feather glowed as he translated her statement, clapped his hands together, and everyone joined in the applause.

When Ruth went to the back of the kitchen to prepare supper, Two Shell Woman leaped up to help her. Too many hungry men for one woman to feed, she signed, too much work for a woman so fat in her belly. White Crane joined them and they heated up the bean pot; fried potatoes and fatback; baked hot biscuits. The kitchen was warm and beads of perspiration pebbled the young women's foreheads, but they spread the table with smiles and good food, and their men ate heartily.

Near the end of the meal, Ben Tree complimented Moore again on progress at the ranch. Sales of both cattle and riding stock were holding firm. In addition to supplying the nearby gold settlements, Moore had contracted beef to both Fort Ellis and Fort Maginnis, and he and a neighboring rancher, Adam Stuart, planned on moving over a thousand head of cows to the Salt Lake City stockyards in the fall. It was to be a drive of a month's duration, and because his two drovers were going, that would leave him shorthanded at the ranch. Benjamin immediately volunteered to help; he and White Crane would come for a fall visit and stay in the empty bunkhouse and share the chores. Agreed. This of course made Ruth happy—the prospect of having a woman's companionship. She would help White Crane with her English.

"We'd be obliged to have you," Clay Moore said to Benjamin. "Hay will be all cut and stacked, probably only some outriding to do, checking the stock. Give you a chance to try out the new place up at the hot springs. One good place to soak yourself. Reckon your woman would like it up there, too."

Benjamin nodded and translated to his wife, who eagerly nodded her head and flashed Moore a smile. Benjamin said, "There's your answer, Mr. Moore."

"Maybe when I get back we can even take a day off and do a little hunting," Moore added. "There's big bear up above, regular humpbacks, claws two inches long. Grizzlies. Boys got one last fall no more than two hundred yards from some of the critters. Good herd of elk, too. Some bulls, forked out big as pine boughs."

"A dangerous game with the grizzly," returned Benjamin, giving his father a sidelong glance. Certainly elk was not his game, not anymore. His stomach turned at the thought of killing such a magnificent creature. "Ei, I would like a bear-claw necklace such as the one my father owns, but I couldn't shoot an elk. That, Mr. Moore, would bring me dishonor, not to mention very bad luck. I'll have to pass that invitation. But a grizzly . . ."

"Bad luck?" He gave Benjamin a curious stare. He knew this young man was an expert with a rifle, an excellent hunter, almost as cunning in the mountains as his father. "What bad luck?" he finally asked.

Man Called Tree spoke up, explaining, "Elk is a taboo with Benjamin, Clay. His medicine comes from Shining Elk, a mystical source of power, the great Spirit Elk. He had a strong vision of this elk on a mountaintop early last winter. Ei, cached out one whole night by himself with a dead bull he and his brothers had killed. We don't quarrel with visions, only try to interpret them, seek out our purpose for being, what is meant for us. This is vision. It's the essence of the human spirit to seek a reason for being, ei?"

Clay Moore scratched his head thoughtfully. "I reckon I'm not much in step with the spiritual, Ben. Don't even know that much about the great book, but like you say, it's probably hard to quarrel with something like one of those visions if you have all of your faith wrapped up in it like a corn shuck. No, I wouldn't trifle with it. And I understand," he added, looking over at young Benjamin. He laughed lightly. "Hell, the only taboo *I* have is corn liquor. Tried it when I was a youngster. Gave me visions, all right, and made me damned sick in the stomach. That's when I figured somebody up there was trying to tell me something. Now, you never quarrel with your maker. That's about as close to a vision as I've ever had."

Sounding once again like his father, Benjamin One Feather commented dryly, "If someone spoke to you, it was good, ei? Among our people, whiskey has been as deadly as shot."

Then White Moon backed away from the table. Sighing, he gently patted his stomach. "You people make too much philosophy, too much heavy talk for such a good meal. No vision has come to me, but if I were among my brothers, I would make a great belch. Father says this isn't proper at the white man's table, so I will go outside and let the little night people know about this. If you hear a scratching on the door, you will know these spirits have heard my song of appreciation." He made a casual sign of peace to the three women and quickly gestured an explanation. White Crane and Two Shell Woman giggled. Everyone knew about White Moon's dry wit, his nonchalance, almost the antithesis of his serious brother. Holding his hand high, he disappeared into the night. Presently, one loud belch came from the darkness. Everyone laughed.

Shortly after midnight, Claybourn Moore was startled out of his sleep by a sharp outcry from Ruth. Bolting upright, he scratched at the night table, searching for the lantern, and as he hurriedly struck a match he whispered to her, "Is it time? What's happening?"

Ruth had her wrist resting on her forehead. At first she only shook her head, nausea sweeping over her. Then, finally: "I don't know. I'm wet . . . water." Moore jerked away the blankets and peered down through the dim yellow light. It was true. Ruth was wet, and so was the bedding. And then she whispered back, "Something's happening, a little twinge there. . . . Yes, oh yes, something is really happening!"

That was enough for Clay Moore. Pulling on his trousers, he bolted out of the bedroom into the small living room where Benjamin One Feather, White Crane, and Two Shell Woman were curled up in their bedrolls on the floor. The first one up was Two Shell Woman, and as Clay Moore struck up another lantern and pointed, she knew Ruth's time was near. Pulling at her long chemise, she ran barefoot into the bedroom, took one look at Ruth, then ran her hand over a damp, perspiring forehead. By then Moore was back, carrying several large towels. *"Tukug,"* Two Shell Woman said. You are right. And with that, she hurried back into the living room where she gave Benjamin a kick. "Get up, hurry, this man understands nothing I say, not even sign. His woman will have her baby this night. What I say, you tell him."

"Me?" said Benjamin despairingly. "No, wait, I'll get my father. He knows about these things."

"Nyah, Man Called Tree is sleeping. You will not disturb him! Come, now!"

Within a short time Ruth Moore was in labor, but Two Shell Woman had everything ready. There was little Clay Moore could do but sit in the kitchen over his coffee and wait. He thought about riding into town to fetch the doctor, but Two Shell Woman dissuaded him. Too little time for that. Besides, what any doctor could do, she could do just as well, at least when it came to childbirth. Twice before in her village she had assisted the old women, the midwives. This was an experience no one forgot.

So, as the moment drew closer, Two Shell Woman tried to make Ruth as comfortable as she could, bathing her forehead, positioning her hips and knees. White Crane brought water from the kettle and stood alongside. As Two Shell Woman gave orders, Benjamin translated to Ruth, and soon she was pursing her lips, taking deep breaths, slowly expelling. This went on for ten minutes, an agonizing eternity to a frazzled Benjamin One Feather, but then he suddenly heard Two Shell Woman whispering, "*tuz, taz.*" Easy, easy, and when he finally dared peer down he saw a reddish-pink protrusion of a tiny, fuzzy, damp head. Then shoulders and arms slipped out, and Two Shell Woman exclaimed, "*Kaizizyeuyeu*!" The slippery little body slid right out into her outstretched palms. "Greetings, little one," she said, amid several tiny bawls. "You are a fine little boy." Turning aside to Benjamin, who by now looked stunned, she said, "Tell her she has a baby boy . . . go fetch the father."

Benjamin One Feather gladly did so, and Ruth, her eyes wide, rose slowly to see her new son. By the time Benjamin had returned with Clay Moore, the baby's cord had been cut and tied and Ruth was pulling him up close to her breast. "He's a good one," Benjamin said, "and Ruth is fine. Congratulations to you both." Claybourn

Moore was speechless. He could do nothing but grin weakly.

White Crane leaned forward and kissed Ruth on her damp forehead. "What will you call this new man?" she asked. Ruth looked over at Benjamin One Feather. Benjamin said, "His name . . . What will it be?"

Ruth Moore closed her eyes and smiled. "Joshua . . . we will call him Joshua."

"Josh-u-ah," White Crane repeated slowly. "Josh-u-ah."

While the two young Indian women bathed Ruth and the child, Clay and Benjamin One Feather retired to the kitchen for more coffee. Once bedraggled and harried, they were now nervously laughing, expending the last of their anxieties. It was a full hour before the little house settled into quiet again. Fearful of disturbing his wife, Clay went to the bunkhouse and slept. But at dawn Two Shell Woman was up, rousting the others, making a fire in the stove, tending Ruth, bringing her the chamber pot, helping her from the bed. And while Ruth, both joyous and embarrassed, sat to the side, White Crane came and put a clean blanket on the bed. Soon all the men from the bunkhouse came to admire the new child, to take the breakfast of celebration that White Crane and Two Shell Woman had prepared.

Because of Joshua's birth, Ben Tree and the Crow elected to stay another day and night at the ranch. White Crane and Two Shell Woman were eager to assist Ruth. Man Called Tree, at the last moment, had decided to buy a wagon to take staples and gifts back to his people along the Yellowstone. And there was another matter, minor in nature, but Two Shell Woman thought it highly important. Even though Ruth Moore had prepared swaddling clothes and other necessities, neither she nor Clay had allowed for a cradle. The Nez Percé woman called this to Benjamin One Feather's attention, even suggested they could make one. Benjamin agreed that a cradle would make a nice present for the child, and since he and his father were going into Bozeman City this was a matter he would look into.

So that same afternoon, Ben Tree, Benjamin, and White Crane rode into town in the ranch buckboard. White Moon was helping Moore and his drovers break stock, and Two Shell Woman, who had passed through Bozeman City when she was with the wolfers, declined the invitation to return. She disliked that place; too many white people stared at her; she had to stay with the ponies while the men went into a big house; when they came out, the men smelled bad and acted crazy. No, she would not go back to this place called Bozeman City, so she stayed with Ruth and began to prepare a big stew for the evening meal.

In town the first stop was at the smithy's shed, where Ben and his son renewed an old friendship with Donald Blodgett, who still kept the ranch stock regularly shod. After a short talk they went on to the livery, where Ben Tree found several wagons for sale. He purchased a small one, and told the livery owner that he would be back the next day with a team. Leaving the buckboard at the stables they then separated, Man Called Tree heading for the bank to get an accounting while Benjamin and a wide-eyed White Crane went searching for the nearest mercantile. What her Nez Percé sister had said was true: A few white men were staring at her, making her feel uncomfortable. Benjamin One Feather said to pay no attention, that these people only envied her her pretty face and fine buckskin clothing. Of course, she knew this was not true. The white troopers, those buffalo soldiers, and the wolfers who had come to their land, they did not envy her people; they hated them.

But indeed, this place they called "town" was very unusual. These large houses had clear windows for the light, but many were obscured by writing, writing of all kinds, some large, some small. There were long places to walk here, made of wood, but to get upon them one had to walk through much water and mud, made only worse by the recent rains. She thought this was a bad place to have a village, because all of the ponies and wagons were in the middle of it, making a terrible smell. After leaping a few puddles and searching for high ground, they were on another wooden walk and approaching a great house with a long covered porch. This was one of the mercantiles, Benjamin One Feather told her.

Once inside the store, Benjamin inquired about a cradle. The clerk, aproned and bespectacled, was mildly surprised when he spoke English, very good English, and he could not refrain from inquiring. "Go to school somewhere?" he asked. "You speak better than most of the whites I get in here."

Benjamin, silently amused, translated to his wife and they both laughed. He then replied by asking, "Does our color make a difference?"

"Not to me, son," the clerk answered, "not as long as you have some money to spend. You just took me aback there for a moment. Sorry if I got a bit nosy. No, sir, money has no color." And he laughed heartily.

"Ei, that's what I thought," And Benjamin One Feather continued, saying, "No, I've never set foot in a school. My father is Ben Tree. He taught me, a taskmaster equal to any teacher."

"Oh ho!" the clerk said, his eyes suddenly alert. "Mr. *Tree*, well, well. Oh, I don't know him personally, saw him once, but his foreman comes in here, the missus, too." Suddenly, in recollection, he slapped his thigh. "Say, this cradle you want—is it for the Moore woman? She have her child? Is that it?"

"A boy, born last night," Benjamin answered.

"Well, that's a good piece of news, yes, sir, sure is." Turning, he motioned to Benjamin and White Crane. "Come on this way. Have two little rockers back here. You can take your pick—if I can find the darned things. Yes, and you give those people my regards, too." Finally, amidst the clutter of dry goods, tack, and assorted furniture, he pulled out the two cribs. White Crane immediately chose the largest. It would serve Ruth longer, until the boy's legs grew long, she explained.

Back at the counter, the clerk set the cradle aside while Benjamin began to show White Crane around the mercantile. She was fascinated. The Goodhart's small trading post on the Yellowstone was the only store she had ever been in, and while it had many fine tools, beads, trinkets, and staples, it was so small compared to this place. What use did the white man have for all of these things? How could he ever use so much in such a short lifetime? Benjamin One Feather took her from counter to counter, shelf to shelf, explaining, answering her questions as she excitedly pointed to many items she had never seen before.

Benjamin told her, "The white man's world is complex. Many things are needed to live in his society. The more things there are, the more he needs, and he often buys things he doesn't really need."

She shook her head, confused, bewildered by her husband's words. "But why would anyone buy something not needed? It is wasteful to take more than is needed."

"Vanity," he explained. "Usually because someone else has it, or a person thinks it's better than what he already has. If I own a fine pony, this is good, ei? I see another pony I think is better. Maybe I want that pony, too. I trade for it. I buy it."

"Foolish!" exclaimed White Crane. "You sound like a selfish man."

"If I see another woman I think is better . . ."

"You would not dare!" she said, cutting him off.

He laughed. "No, I would not, because there is no one better than you." He tapped her bottom lightly. "Ei, in all ways, you please me."

Embarrassed, White Crane quickly looked around. Only two men, both with beards, were in the store, and they were now busy talking to the man with the little round pieces of glass in front of his eyes. "You are too bold in this place, Benjamin One Feather," she whispered.

Shortly, Man Called Tree came in. Benjamin waved, and taking his wife by the arm, moved toward his father. At that moment one of the two men in front spoke aside to the clerk. "Better keep your eyes peeled, Lucas," he warned with a grin. "Those Injuns back there are apt to walk out of here with half the store under their leggings." The other man, thinking this a good joke, laughed loudly and clapped his friend on the back. Benjamin One Feather, too far away, did not hear the man's remark, but Ben Tree heard, and Lucas Hamm, the clerk, knew it. The storekeeper was furious. Before Ben Tree could even turn around, Lucas was in front of the two whiskered men, urging them to move toward the door. He had something to say and he whispered harshly, "Mind your tongue, man, don't you know who these people are? That fellow who just came in? Damnation, that's Ben Tree! That's his son back there, and they speak English!"

"Tree?" one of the men said. "You mean the man who—"

"Yes, Ben Tree," Lucas Hamm cut in. "He owns half of the valley out there, half of the bank, and the bank just happens to hold half of the mortgages in this town, mine included. Now go on, ease out of here before the damned roof caves in on us."

By then Ben Tree had turned to observe Lucas shoving at the men near the doorway. He called to him, "You having some trouble there, storekeep?"

Hamm shook his head, his muttonchops jumping on his florid face. "No sir, not a bit. Just showing these men the proper way out. Be right with you, only a minute."

Ben, however, already knew the problem, but he suppressed his anger, never so much as idled his right hand down to the side of the polished walnut handle of his revolver. At one time in his life he might have sought some form of retribution, taught the two men a lesson in propriety. Those were the old days. Now he had come to understand the nature of frontier men; some were simply ignorant, innocently blind to social injustice, and others were outright arrogant, social bigots. Ben Tree had mellowed, if the frontier had not, and in this instance he had a son and daughter-in-law to consider. This situation called for another tack, so he approached the startled men and held out his hand in friendship, the unexpected gesture dropping their whiskered jaws slack. Neither uttered a word, only shifted uneasily on the planking of the floor. "My name is Tree," he said calmly.

"Yes, we know that. Lucas here—" one began.

"Well, men, I'll allow you were only joking about my son and his wife back there," Ben went on. "Fact is, they're pretty good people, rather special to me. Oh, the young man might steal a pony or two out on the prairie to prove how clever he is. Our people have been playing games like that for years, long before the white man came along, ei. But stealing something in this store? Why should he? He has cash in his pocket. I suppose if he heard what you said, it might rile him a bit, too. Speaks good English, he does. So if you want to apologize to me, I won't even mention it to him. He's a bit hotheaded at times. Pretty damned good with that Colt on his hip, too."

"Glad to meet you," the largest man said, proferring his hand. "Well, you're right as rain, Mr. Tree. It was a joke . . . a mistake, for certain. We're not looking for trouble. Sorry if it upset you and Lucas here. Sorry, . . . not looking to upset anyone. We'll just move on out, if you don't mind."

"Oh, it didn't upset me," replied Ben Tree. "Nowadays, I'll allow any man a few foolish mistakes. It wasn't too long ago, though, a remark like that might have cost you your hair." He tipped a hand to his forehead. "Good day, gentlemen."

As they left, Hamm wheezed a sigh of relief. Hurrying behind Ben, he said, "My name is Lucas Hamm, Mr. Tree. Sorry about this. I just didn't want any trouble in the store. The boys don't see many Indians in here—your kind, that is. They just don't know beans."

"No different than most," Ben replied. "Cultures, like attitudes, never change over night, Mr. Hamm. Ei, sometimes never. Besides, you have to protect your business, not chase it away. No sense in scaring those old boys too much."

Benjamin One Feather, White Crane in tow, was approaching the counter. Inquisitive about the conversation with the two departed men, he asked, "What was that all about?"

Lucas Hamm said quickly, "Fellows wanted to meet your pa, that's all. You know how these people are . . . curious, all the stories they hear over the years. So, your pa here kindly obliged them . . . shook hands and all."

"No trouble?"

"No trouble," Ben Tree said, smiling, and he turned and spoke to White Crane in Absaroke. "Did you find what you were looking for? The cradle?" She proudly pointed to the side of the counter. "That's good," Man Called Tree said. "Ruth will like it, a great surprise." Bending down, he ran his callused palm over the tiny headboard, asked Lucas Hamm what the price was, and promptly paid him.

Benjamin One Feather then told his father in English, "You two go ahead. I have another chore . . . be along in a minute." He gave Ben a wink and nodded at White Crane.

"Good enough," was the reply, and shouldering the cradle, Ben Tree placed his other arm around White Crane and guided her toward the door. "Nice to have met you, Lucas," he called back. "Until next time." Lucas Hamm waved a hand in return. Then, staring over at Benjamin One Feather, the clerk said, "Aha, something for your wife, eh, on the sly?"

That evening after supper, Two Shell Woman and White Crane brought in the cradle from the buckboard. They tucked new bedding inside it, tied a snowberry branch on one of the spindles, and then carried it into the bedroom. The men were watching from the doorway as Ruth pulled herself up in the bed. Her eyes widened in surprise, and smiling, she clasped her hands to her breast, delighted at such a wonderful gift. Looking at Benjamin One Feather, she asked, "What is the word you use, that little simple one?" *"Aho,"* he said. "They all know it." Motioning to them all, Ruth cried out in happiness, "*Aho*!" Everyone applauded. Two Shell Woman, carefully taking the baby from the bed, placed it inside the cradle and gently rocked it. *"Sepekuse,"* she said softly. It is done. And the baby, Joshua, would be safe. The snowberry branch was there to keep ghosts away.

Later, when White Crane and Two Shell Woman were ready for bed, Benjamin appeared, holding his hands behind him. He had found gifts in Lucas Hamm's store. The two young women first exchanged curious glances, then smiles, and sat attentively before him on their bedrolls. First he brought out a small decorative tortoiseshell comb and presented it to Two Shell Woman. "This, my sister," he said, "is to make your hair even more beautiful than it already is, and I am happy to give it to you." Two Shell Woman held the comb close to the lantern, watched the sparkle in its amber-and-gold translucence. She sighed, got to her feet, and kissed Benjamin One Feather.

"I am honored and pleased at such a fine gift, Benjamin One Feather. You are my brother, now and always." And then with a giggle, she tried to peek around him to see White Crane's present. "Come, do not make us wait!" she pleaded.

Benjamin, with a flourish, swept his hand in front of his young wife's face, mirroring her image in the dim lantern light. She gasped, then cried out joyously, "A mirror!" She took it, reflected it against her face and laughed, then pulled Two Shell Woman to her cheek. They both stared at themselves and giggled like children. White Crane asked her husband, "Is this the vanity of which you speak?"

"No, this is necessity," he smiled, as she reached up and kissed him.

"Explain this to me as you always do, then," she said.

Benjamin One Feather replied, "Many moons ago, you told me these words: 'I am the woman within you . . . In every man there is the mirror of a woman.' Do you remember these words?"

"I have told you many things," she said with a smile.

"Well, look you there in this mirror and see the woman within me. Ei, and each time you take it up, you will be reminded of the one whose heart beats at your side."

EIGHT

Late in the Moon When the Ponies Shed, three scouts, Stone Calf, Old Dog Jumps, and Bear Gets Up, came back from a journey of six sleeps into the buffalo country. The report they brought back was mixed—good and bad. A few small blackhorn herds were moving down the Big Horn Valley, only about a day's ride from the Goodhart's trading post. This was good, for the meat-making would be within a reasonable distance of Man Called Tree's village. Much larger herds, with some huge bulls, had been sighted around the lower Rosebud Mountains, but great numbers of Cheyenne and Lakota also were arriving in that basin.

The appearance of the Cheyenne was no surprise to Big Cloud, the Crow buffalo seer. Rosebud country always had been a traditional hunting ground for the Cheyenne. Even after it was declared unceded land, the hunting rights for all the tribes had remained intact. But the Lakota! How could these people be so far north from their great reservation and hunting area of the Black Hills and the rolling plains down to the North Platte and Republican rivers? Were the Crow scouts mistaken?

Not at all, they said. They knew Lakota villages all too well, and in three separate encampments in the Greasy Grass there were already over three thousand people! More Indians were coming from the East, many more. Big Cloud was stunned. This was a contrary sign, one he could not fully comprehend. Neither he nor Man Called Tree knew that these Indians were restless hostiles who had moved west from their reservations, nor did they know that the government had dispatched three armies up the lower Yellowstone to engage them in battle and force them back to their reservations.

After a council, the Absaroke decided to conduct their hunt in the lower Big Horn Valley, a safe place far from the hostile villages reported to the south. True, there were fewer buffalo there, but the chance of confrontation with the enemy was slight, for the Crow were riding east to make meat, not war. And so it was that Man Called Tree's hunting party ultimately settled into a camp one day's ride southeast of Manuel's post. Farther to the east near the Yellowstone River, the Crow village of Plenty Coups also was hunting blackhorns, also many miles from the threat of Cheyenne or Sioux.

One afternoon five days into the hunt, Sitting Elk and Red Running Horse came into camp, reporting that they had spoken to their brother Absaroke from Plenty Coups' village. They were told that a large contingent of long-knives from Fort Ellis had been sighted coming down the Yellowstone Trail. No one knew where these pony soldiers were going, but word had come up the river trail of many men building a staging depot near the mouth of the Tongue River, a place where the steamboats often unloaded supplies for the freight merchants and packers. It was presumed that this was their destination.

This was curious to Benjamin One Feather, so after consulting with Man Called Tree, he decided to ride over to the big river and see these troopers who were crossing the Bird People's land. His Fox brothers, Old Dog Jumps and Red Running Horse, and James Goodhart elected to ride with him. Near sundown, they finally came upon the Fort Ellis troopers. They were busy finishing up a camp for the night at a wide bend on the river. One trooper and a man dressed in denims and a buckskin jacket met them near the edge of the field of tents. The civilian, a scout by the name of Henry Fuller, who spoke some Absaroke, knew Man Called Tree, and after discovering Benjamin One Feather's identity, he quickly motioned them forward into the camp, where they were greeted by a young officer and a sergeant.

After several inquiries by the officer the sergeant left, soon to return with a large pot of coffee and tin cups. Sitting on blankets, they all chatted until the commander arrived. He walked with a slight limp, was stocky, and sported a dark beard. Introduced as Col. John Gibbon, he was surprised that two of the hunters, Benjamin One Feather and his brother-in-law James Goodhart, spoke such good English. Fuller quickly explained. "This man," he said, pointing to Benjamin, "is the son of Ben Tree, the one who has that ranch in the Gallatin. This fellow here is young Goodhart, the trader's son, that place we passed early yesterday."

Colonel Gibbon leaned forward and shook hands. "And what are you doing way out here running with the Crows?" he asked, looking over at Old Dog Jumps and Red Running Horse. They were somber and silent, ever cautious about pony soldiers and their intentions, and now this man with whiskers and a large red nose.

"They are our people," Benjamin One Feather answered. "James is married to my sister, and I live in Man Called Tree's village. We came to hunt buffalo as we always do."

"Good hunting?"

"Not as good as it used to be," said Benjamin, "but we've taken almost what we need. Another day and we'll pack our ponies, head back up the river." He stopped to translate for Old Dog Jumps and Red Running Horse. Unsmiling, they said nothing.

James Goodhart spoke then, saying, "This is the largest bunch of soldiers I've ever seen. Where are you headed, all these men, the equipment?"

Directing his chin whiskers, Gibbon said, "Downriver a piece, a rendezvous, you might say." He seemed defensive, cautious, unaware that various scouts, the invisible ones, were likely to pick up his every movement all the way to his destination.

And that made Benjamin One Feather chuckle. "A rendezvous on the Tongue?"

Gibbon looked surprised. He said, "That could be, but it's not for discussion, I'm sorry."

Benjamin One Feather, moving his hand nonchalantly,

replied, "It's already known, Mr. Gibbon. It's no secret, all the unloading down there. The news has come up the river. Some of Plenty Coups' people told us today. We were only curious since all the activity seems to be along our hunting grounds. Ei, but we only hunt buffalo. What's the army hunting this season?"

"Well spoken," returned Gibbon with a slight flush. "The government intends to see that your land is used properly. Many of the Sioux at the agencies have left without permission. Many, in fact, didn't even bother to return for the winter. Our friends say they're spread out all over the prairie, and some have been waging war on the trails. Can't condone that anymore. Do you understand what I'm saying? We aim to thin them out, run the rest home. Understand?"

Benjamin One Feather nodded. "Ei, your intentions are obvious." He gestured around the camp. "I'll allow you are going to meet others of your kind, a campaign, but maybe these people you keep chasing have good reason to leave and move around. We keep hearing stories up here, some not so good. Broken words, meaningless treaties."

With a tight smile John Gibbon said, "You sound almost displeased, young man. These Indians are your enemies, the ones who raid your reservation land, your villages, kill your brothers. . . . "

"Not our village," interrupted Benjamin One Feather. "Not for many years. They hunt the plains up here, as all tribes have since the early days. No one tribe has ever claimed the buffalo grounds as territory, nor do we fight among ourselves over territory as the white people do. By treaty this land below us is unceded, free for anyone to use."

"Oh, no," Gibbon retorted sharply, "not anyone, young man! The commissioner has issued new orders. The Sioux and Cheyenne have been making too much trouble over in the Black Hills country. He's made the unceded land off-limits. They have no rights at all, not even for hunting, not anymore."

Somewhat surprised at this revelation, Benjamin One Feather spoke aside to Old Dog Jumps and Red Running Horse, who frowned and turned their palms downward.

Gibbon asked, "Does this trouble your friends?"

"No," Benjamin replied. "No, but we were wondering how this can be done without a great council of all the tribes. The treaty . . ."

"Treaty be damned!" said Gibbon, obviously annoyed. "These renegades are not on the agencies where they have agreed to live. They must go back, quit disrupting the country. Now, we intend to enlist the aid of the Crow. We'll meet Plenty Coups' people tomorrow, somewhere below here. We need good scouts. Stopped to see your father, in fact, but he's out there somewhere on a damned hunt. Wanted to give your people a chance to get in a few blows with us, take a lot of scalps, eh? You can go back and tell him this. Yes, of course, we'll be down on the Tongue a few days, so you'll know where to come. Tell your father that General Terry will be there, Colonel Custer, and myself. He can meet any of us. Be happy to see him, or any of your men."

Benjamin One Feather turned and spoke to his brothers again, and Old Dog Jumps smiled for the first time. Colonel Gibbon thought this was a better sign, smiled and nodded himself. A Crow brave delighted to go to battle against the Sioux. But Old Dog Jumps said to Benjamin One Feather, "I would rather kill something I can eat . . . buffalo, ei. I can piss on a Sioux anytime. This bluecoat eats fish!"

Gibbon asked them, "Have you seen any Sioux or Cheyenne over in the valley?"

Benjamin One Feather shook his head. "No, I've seen none. Our men say there are many far to the south in the upper Big Horns, but I warn you, Mr. Gibbon, their scouts are everywhere, and they miss very little. A movement this large . . . ?" Benjamin One Feather gave him a doubtful stare.

John Goodhart said, "There are Cheyenne already along Rosebud Creek, hunting, and more than a few; a village of a thousand or so, they say."

"Rosebud?" inquired Colonel Gibbon.

"That way, sir," Henry Fuller said, pointing south. "Good buffalo and antelope country. A two-day ride to the mountains, three or four days up the creek, maybe. With all the boys and gear, who knows?"

"Ei," Benjamin One Feather said, "when they find out Long Hair Custer is among you, they'll be happy."

Gibbon, momentarily perplexed, said, "I don't understand. . . . Happy?"

Standing, Benjamin casually drank the last of his coffee. "Washita, Colonel Gibbon, Washita. Custer massacred the Cheyenne. I don't think he'll ride into them at breakfast with his band playing. He'll have no Washita this time. There will be several thousand warriors facing him instead of sleeping women and children."

Gibbon simply shrugged, but his face turned red. "That was years ago, young man. What do you know about it? Dammit, tactics change. So do people. General Terry will be in command of this assignment, not Colonel Custer. You tell your father what I said. We'd welcome his participation." Curtly tipping his hat once, he limped away toward his quarters, displeased with the brief conversation.

Benjamin One Feather looked over at Fuller and grimly smiled. "But attitudes never change, do they? I know what my father will say."

"Have a notion I do, too," Henry Fuller answered. "Let them fight their own battles."

"Ei, something like that."

"More like go to hell," Goodhart opined, and they all laughed.

The day following this brief meeting on the river, the hunting Absaroke packed their ponies and travois and began moving west toward the Big Horn River. Although the hunting had been difficult because of the scattered herds, the small group had done well enough, making plenty of smoked meat from both buffalo and pronghorns. Big Cloud, however well satisfied, was still annoyed that the Sioux had blocked him from Absaroke land in the Greasy Grass country. His chief, Man Called Tree, dismissed this. Whether on the Greasy Grass of the Little Big Horn or the valley of the main river, Chief Tree's people never took more than they needed, anyhow. No more, no less, and in due time the Sioux and Cheyenne would move out; always did. For Man Called Tree, the safety of the Absaroke was paramount. As expected, Ben Tree had curtly brushed off Col. John Gibbon's proposal to join with the bluecoats as bad medicine.

To Benjamin One Feather it was also bad medicine. His last night at the buffalo camp had been a restless one, with such tossing and turning under his blanket as to even chase White Crane from his side. She complained that he had rolled like a village dog with fleas. On the trail this late May day he tried to explain, made an effort to connect his troubled thoughts. It was his vision. Was it coming to pass? Could this possibly be part of it, this gathering storm on the prairie? The signs pointed to it, the movement of troopers, the converging of Indians. This, he allowed, was an ominous prelude to terrible conflict, all to the east, a great fire. Shining Elk had taken him in that direction.

He asked White Crane if it was coincidence that this man, Red Nose Gibbon, whose life was dedicated to battle, walked with a limp. Or was this indeed a sign? The limping wolf in his dream had come from the fire. White Crane, too, rode uneasily, pondering Benjamin's words. She would have to watch him like a hawk, not let him fly away with Shining Elk on more dark missions.

Whatever troubled thoughts were hovering over these returning Crow, they swiftly took flight when they came to the long green meadow overlooking the Goodhart's trading post. Disaster had struck. Down below, the main building was little more than blackened timbers and ashes, a few whisps of smoke curling up from the charred ground. James, near the front file of Crow, cried out and kicked his horse ahead into a gallop, with Benjamin One Feather close behind. The first sight they came upon was that of the bodies of three troopers near the old stockade gate, their horses still fully saddled and calmly grazing nearby. By the time James rode into the small compound other riders were pounding down the hill, and soon everyone but those attending the pack ponies had gathered around the grim scene. The troopers were dead, and there was no sign of John and Molly Goodhart. Young James was soon joined by his wife, Little Blue Hoop, and White Crane, and they ran toward the second cabin, frantically calling out.

At the area near the gate, Sitting Elk bent over and examined the ground. After pointing around in all directions, he stood and told his brothers that Indians were responsible. Many of these tracks had been made by unshod stock. The braves then looked to Man Called Tree for direction, and with several of them following, their chief slowly walked the area, examining what was left and deciding what measures he must take.

Moments later, the old wooden door of the root cellar next to the barn rose and Molly Goodhart, her face distorted in anguish, appeared and cried for help. Climbing out, she threw aside the rifle she was carrying and motioned back into the darkness of the cellar. A startled Stone Calf was the first to see her. Shouting for James, he rushed to the cellar and took Molly by the arms as she wailed repeatedly, "John is dead! They killed him!"

By then, everyone had converged on the cellar. James, brushing back tears, finally led his mother to the second cabin, which he and Little Blue Hoop had only recently made their home. Benjamin One Feather and White Crane followed. Man Called Tree told some of the braves to mount up and follow the pony tracks for several miles to determine the direction of the hostiles and how much ground they were covering. From what he had determined, the incident had occurred much earlier in the day, the hostiles immediately making long tracks. They'd been gone many hours, and there was little hope of retaliation this day. When he turned back, he met Benjamin and Two Shell Woman walking back toward the root cellar.

Benjamin One Feather pointed and said, "She pulled John down there. Thought they'd come back and take his hair. She says there's another fellow there, too, shot in the leg, a trooper. Says he's barely alive. Lost a lot of blood."

Man Called Tree trotted along at his son's side. "Did she say what happened?"

"Not that much. She's all done in, but from what I could make of it John thought they were Cheyenne, maybe some Sioux, too. A big party, thirty or more, all painted. A platoon from Maginnis was here, taking rest, eating, and the Indians came in from two sides. Some of the soldiers struck a retreat right down the bottom, hightailed it. That's all she said. When the shooting started, John told her to run for the root cellar. Ei, she pulled both of those men down there."

"Damn!" cursed Man Called Tree. "If we'd left camp only a day earlier . . . They wouldn't dare come in here if we were around."

"They weren't after the Goodharts," Benjamin One Feather said.

"I know that," his father replied. "They weren't after hair, either, or stock. The troopers weren't scalped. Horses and mules are all corraled, some on the hill there. Hell, they didn't touch them. Only pony that is missing is John's riding mare, the big bay."

"Well, what *did* they want?" Benjamin stooped and peered into the cellar. "And why did they burn the house?"

"Rifles and ammunition," answered Man Called Tree. "Probably took what they could find in the store. Ei, and the rifles and cartridge belts of the three troopers, gone. Probably fired the building as an afterthought, getting even with the whites . . . and probably us for being here all the time."

Benjamin One Feather crawled into the cellar. John Goodhart's body was near the opening, blocking the passage to the back. The two men lifted the dead trader into the late-afternoon sunshine, setting off a wailing from the curious Crow women gathered near the opening. Two Shell Woman quickly covered the body with a blanket. Toward the back, Benjamin One Feather found the wounded trooper, curled on his side, a bloody bandage wrapped around his thigh. Molly had attempted to staunch the blood flow; torn linen littered the earthen floor. As Man Called Tree cautioned them to move the soldier gently, Benjamin and Two Shell Woman eased him up the stairway.

"Well, I'll be!" exclaimed Benjamin, staring up at Two Shell Woman in surprise. "It's our old friend, the lieutenant—that Hockett fellow!"

Man Called Tree asked, "You know this man?"

"Tukug," the Nez Percé woman said. "You are right, this is the one, the Hanging Soldier. He wanted to take me back to the fort, let his people hang me."

Bending over Zachary Hockett, the chief pressed a finger to the stricken man's throat. He felt a faint throb, very weak. "Well, he won't be taking anyone anywhere for a long time, not this soldier. He's alive, but barely." Glancing over at the young Indian woman, he added, "You want to take a look?"

"Why not? I know these things." She carefully began

to examine the leg, saw that Molly's last compress had held. "He has little more blood to lose. Look how white he is, like a ghost." Pointing to the shed, she said, "Take him over there in the hay. If he awakens, we'll try to feed him. This one has no strength left. He'll soon die without something in his belly. Have someone make hot broth, tea, anything. I will need water and more cloth, medicine from your bundle."

Benjamin One Feather turned and translated to Walking Woman, who nodded and immediately ran toward the second cabin.

By sundown, the Absaroke had secured the old post; the scouts had returned, reporting that the hostiles had fled up the Big Horn River trail and were at least four or five hours ahead of them; the three troopers, all young men, were buried together below the small compound; there was no ceremony, only Man Called Tree passing his hand over the mound of dirt once, asking that the One Above take their souls. John Goodhart's body, wrapped in blankets, was taken inside the shed. At sunrise he would go to his rest in the upper meadow where some of the Crow had already dug a grave, this by James's wish. Molly, her eyes red from tears, sat on the second cabin stoop, consoled by White Crane and Little Blue Hoop. Inside, Walking Woman and Red Bead were making soup, while on the perimeter of the post the rest of the Indians were building fires and erecting tipis.

Lt. Zachary Hockett awoke shortly after dark, was fed hot soup and strips of braised liver. After he had eaten, he slowly told his version of the attack, confirming Molly's story. Unable to grab his horse, much less ride it, he understood why his troops had panicked, but was surprised they had not returned, at least to reclaim their fallen comrades. Benjamin One Feather reasoned that the soldiers might have hidden on the river bottom. More likely, however, they probably crossed the river and headed back for Fort Maginnis for reinforcements.

Not much profit in that, lamented Hockett, not now. He told Benjamin that he and his men had been reassigned to Colonel Custer's Seventh Cavalry. They had intended to catch up with General Gibbon and ride with his troops to the Tongue River rendezvous. Hockett said he had not expected such poor luck on the Yellowstone, especially at John Goodhart's trading post.

Benjamin One Feather doubtfully shook his head. Almost prophetically he said, "Either way, your luck will be poor, Mr. Hockett. My medicine tells me your friends down below, and anyone else going that direction, are in for a bad time of it this summer. Better you die here in comfort than among the hot rocks of a prairie fire."

"Ah, then, you think I'll not make it?" asked Hockett. "It's that bad?"

Benjamin One Feather nodded toward Two Shell Woman. "This is the woman the trapper, Birdwell, accused of killing his brother and the other man. She is Nez Percé, the tribe of my mother. Her name is Two Shell Woman, and she calls you the Hanging Soldier. She says the lead is still in your leg, ei, up against the bone. It has to come out. If it doesn't, you damn well may die from infection. You already have lost enough blood to fill that water jug."

In pain and misery, Hockett closed his eyes and sighed. "Tell me honestly, Mr. Tree, did she kill those two men?"

"No."

"Never could piece that together," mumbled Hockett.

"My men and I killed them," Benjamin admitted. "They fired on us first."

"Had a hunch. . . . Not a shred of evidence," he said wearily. "So, what can she do to keep me alive?"

"She says she can get that ball out. She can remove it, but she doesn't know if you're strong enough to take it, being you have no Indian in you. Ei, and if you lose more blood, you won't make it. That's the size of it."

"Then I have no choice, do I?" he said, opening one eye and staring up at Benjamin One Feather.

"All we have is a little brandy."

"Tell her to do what she has to. . . . Give me something to hold on to. And yes, the brandy . . ."

And sometime later, with Hockett groggy and his hands wrapped around a shovel handle, Two Shell Woman did remove the lead shot, fishing it out with two pieces of wire she had sterilized in Man Called Tree's alcohol. After disinfecting the wound, she closed it with three stitches of sinew. She packed yarrow leaves and camphor balm under the compress, bound the thigh tightly, and stepped back. She told Benjamin One Feather that if the Hanging Soldier were able to stand in the morning and make urine, he would live. "If he makes urine in his pants, he will die." She then left.

Hockett, his eyes glazed, his mind numb, and his tongue thick, looked up at Benjamin and Man Called Tree. "She's gone . . . didn't even thank her. What does she say? Good or bad?"

Benjamin One Feather smiled and covered the young officer with a blanket. "She says you better get up and take a piss in the morning, ei, a good sign. If you piss in your pants, it's bad medicine. You're one of those goners. You die."

"Jesus!"

Near dawn, Lt. Zachary Hockett, U. S. Cavalry, stirred. Someone had kindly thrown another blanket over him. He smelled smoke, detected hushed voices, and in the distance heard women chanting, hauntingly beautiful. He brought a hand to his forehead, felt no heat, no fever, deduced he was better, certainly no worse. Tilting his head, he saw the source of the smoke, a small fire near the edge of the shed, a woman there too, huddled in a blanket and staring to the east. *The* woman? The Nez Percé woman? Good lord, he wondered, has she been here all night? He fell back, contemplating his next move, how he could adjust to the throb in his thigh, afraid to run his hand over the ache, fearful of discovering a sticky wetness there. But he could move his leg, slightly, ever so slightly, back and forth, once, twice. Stiff, yes, terribly stiff . . . He mumbled aloud, "Jesus, try, try just once."

Then the woman in the blanket hovered over him. *"Niez kunu?"* she whispered. Are you there?

Yes, she had spoken, and in the dimness he made out her fine features. She had the blanket curled around her shoulder. Her hair was long, pulled back tightly, and shell earrings dangled from her ears, ears only partially hidden by the slick sweep of her hair. This was the Nez Percé woman. This was a woman he did not understand in language or purpose. Why had she, of all these Indians, stayed at his side? My *miserable* side, he thought. Little wonder she called him "the Hanging Soldier." What could he say now, in the absence of duty? "Forgive me, young woman, and thank you"? He managed a smile, miserable there too, and did say, "Thank you . . . Understand? Thank you."

Two Shell Woman parted her blanket, reached down to him, and beckoned. Rise slowly, she was gesturing. Try, and I will help you. She moved to the side, picked up the shovel, and placed it at his side for support. Then, grasping her arm with one hand and pushing against the shovel with the other, he came up slowly, painfully. Two Shell Woman motioned to the darkness behind the horse shed. He knew what she meant. Using the shovel for a cane, Zachary Hockett, the Hanging Soldier, grunted. Was this not customary, a grunt of appreciation? Hobbling, he disappeared around the side of the barn, unbuttoned his pants, and urinated, the puddling embarrassingly as loud as a horse's. But, Jesus, he was saved!

When he peeked around the edge of the shed she was standing there, a small smile on her face. The sun was rising, burnishing her high cheekbones, sparking the faintest hint of white teeth behind a sly little smirk. She said simply, "*Sepekuse.*" So be it.

NINE

At Man Called Tree's village in the shadows of the Nah-pit-sei, the great bear's tooth, Lt. Zachary Hockett basked in the sun in front of the lodge of the old widow Looks Far Away, now a crowded refuge. After Little Blue Hoop's marriage to James Goodhart, Two Shell Woman and Looks Far Away had been the tipi's sole occupants. But now, following the disaster at Manuel's post, not only had Little Blue Hoop and James returned but also Molly Goodhart, as well as the recuperating young officer. The arrangement was only temporary, for James and his bride had decided, at Man Called Tree's suggestion, to go to the ranch in the Gallatin. Claybourn Moore needed another hand, and James Goodhart needed a job. Everyone agreed that the trading post, at least for the present, was a lost cause. Rebuilding would take time and money, and James allowed that it was no longer a safe place for his Absaroke wife and his mother. Molly had elected to stay on in the village with her old blood friends, who would help her heal from the loss of her husband, and the Absaroke were happy to have her.

Zachary Hockett, who had begun to stumble about on his lame leg, had no options. It had been four days since the attack at Goodhart's place, an eternity to the impatient young officer, and though he considered himself lucky to be alive he now found himself fretting about his immediate future. All he had was his horse, a horse he could not ride, the remnants of his pants, now patched and washed by Two Shell Woman, and the field jacket draped around his shoulders. Plain and simple he was a charity case, his welfare entirely dependent upon these strange but friendly Crow who had dragged him here on a travois and deposited him in a tent inhabited by a displaced Nez Percé woman, two widows, and a pair of newlyweds. Jesus, he thought, what's happening to me in this crazy, uncivilized world?

But at least he now could communicate verbally, if only in an awkward, roundabout way. Molly, God bless her, spoke English, and there were James and Little Blue Hoop, both of whom also afforded him translations. Often Benjamin One Feather came by to check on him, also the younger brother, White Moon, the crazy one who kept telling him that he was stuck here for life, that scheming village women with impotent husbands already had great plans for his services. Yes, and once accustomed to his new environment and the many rewards it offered, White Moon told him that he probably would not want to return to Fort Maginnis anyway. Besides, it was almost certain that the post commander had already given him honors for the dead, or dishonor for desertion. Jesus! But however amused by White Moon's visits and sage observations, Zachary Hockett nevertheless was always left with a feeling of complete helplessness, and how much longer this would continue he had no idea. He thought the Nez Percé woman might be a determining factor. That she was in sole charge, there was no doubt. She supervised his every activity, told him either by translation or by body language what he must do and not do. It was even she who, wrinkling her nose distastefully, had led him hobbling away to the creek on the second afternoon, helped him undress, and made him bathe. Refreshing, yes, but painfully embarrassing, the tinkle of laughter from others nearby who seemed amused and fascinated by his white skin. Of course Two Shell Woman admonished them. She looked to his needs, and she now understood the words "thank you." Jesus, she should! Hockett thought. I use it enough.

Early on the fourth morning she brought another woman

to examine his wound, a woman who wore similar shell earrings, one who also spoke the same unusual language. She was older, but graceful and dignified, slender and beautiful, and to his astonishment she also spoke a few words of English. Later White Moon told him that this was Rainbow, woman of Man Called Tree, and the mother of Benjamin One Feather, White Moon himself, and Little Blue Hoop. She was a Nez Percé woman, too, who long ago had left her people to live with the breed chief, Man Called Tree. Rainbow, pointing to Two Shell Woman, told Hockett that he was in good hands, not to worry, but he lamented that Two Shell Woman still called him "the Hanging Soldier." This was unfair, and it displeased him. Only a name, Rainbow replied kindly with a pretty smile. And she turned to her younger sister, saying slowly, "Hock-kett, Hock-kett." Two Shell Woman nodded, pointed at him, and repeated the name, precisely as Rainbow had said. With a twinkle in her dark eyes she added, "Thank you."

As he absorbed the morning sun, contemplating his predicament, returning smiles from passing women, teasing children who darted in to stare before fleeing, an old man, heavily wrinkled, came by and paused to scrutinize him. The ancient one mysteriously passed his hand through the air, said a few words, and pointed east. Benjamin One Feather and a fellow Fox warrior came along, listened, smiled, and made a sign of peace as the old man ambled away. Benjamin then greeted Hockett, asked how he was faring, if he had eaten breakfast. The trooper told him all was well. He felt much better, and yes, Molly Goodhart had prepared food and had eaten with him, flatcakes with dried berries, strips of freshly smoked meat, and coffee. Hockett nodded toward the old man, who was walking away. "Who was that fellow?" he asked. "What was he trying to tell me?"

"Ten Sleeps," answered Benjamin One Feather. "He makes medicine, tells the legends. I suppose your people would call him a teacher of sorts, philosophy, er, religion. He's somewhat of a prophet, too."

"Did you hear him?"

"Yes, I heard," Benjamin said. "He says you're lucky to be here instead of over the mountain. Same thing I told you, and I'm no prophet."

Hockett grinned self-consciously. "I don't know when I'm well off, is that it? Stove-up, out of commission, a bluebird without wings."

"Better stove-up than facedown," commented Benjamin One Feather. "You may have clipped wings, but at least you're alive."

"A prophet, is he? Now that's something."

"Hard to believe, you mean?"

Zachary Hockett shrugged. "Getting so I don't know what to believe, anymore. You people taking care of me, the Nez Percé girl, and that brother of yours, pulling my leg all the time."

"Not the bad one, I hope," Benjamin said, smiling. He turned and translated the conversation to Old Dog Jumps, who in turn managed a smile.

But then Old Dog Jumps' smile faded and he spoke seriously to Benjamin One Feather. Like many of his brothers, he was apprehensive about the intentions of all bluecoats, their arrogance, their ignorance of the land and its people, their poor manners, men he had met on the trail, men like the One Who Limps and the red-bearded one, Three Stripes, who said the Crow ate dogs and were dirty. He said, "Yes, this soldier is fortunate. If it had been one of us shot and found by his people would they have given us water? Would they have carried us away to their healing lodge? Ei, or would they have left us to die?"

Benjamin One Feather was silent for a moment, pondering his brother's question, wondering how Hockett would respond to such words. Finally he said to the trooper, "This is my friend Old Dog Jumps. He, too, was shot once, only by white men, the wolfers who attacked us. Your investigation, remember? Well, Two Shell Woman kept him from bleeding to death, so you understand why this woman is special to us. We would have never let you take her that day."

"That's a coincidence, isn't it?" Hockett said. "Jesus!"

"Ei, and Old Dog Jumps asks if he were found shot by your people, would they help him or leave him on the prairie to die?"

Hockett stared up at the two young men. He thoughtfully stroked his moustache. "How can I speak for others?" he finally asked. "I don't know. Myself? Why, I've never had such an experience, but I doubt if I could pass a friendly by, not without trying to help in some way. But I couldn't do what Two Shell Woman did for him or me, that's for certain." Then to Benjamin One Feather he said, "Jesus, tell him I'm grateful beyond words. If I can repay any of you, somehow I will."

Translating to Old Dog Jumps, Benjamin realized that his brother's question had achieved its purpose. When Zachary Hockett returned to civilization, he would do so with empathy, a better understanding of humanity and brotherhood, something not taught by his superiors. Old Dog Jumps nodded at Hockett. "Tell the soldier he better heed the omen of Ten Sleeps, too. If not, he will only have his maker to repay, not us." Benjamin smiled at this advice and repeated it, word for word.

"My God, what does your prophet know?" asked Hockett, almost in exasperation. "Maybe our scouts should talk to this old fellow. They sure could use some good information for a change. How does he come by these assumptions—omens, that is?"

Benjamin One Feather said, "Visions."

"You mean dreams?"

"More powerful than dreams."

"Well, these visions then," Hockett said. "Do they ever come to pass, actually happen?"

"Quite frequently."

"I'll be damned!"

"Is this so strange to you, a Christian? Aren't there many prophets in your book of religion, the book your blackrobes always quarrel about? Who was the greatest of your prophets?"

Scratching his head, Hockett said, "I don't rightly know. Well, there was Isaiah. Jeremiah, too, the one always predicting doom."

"What they foretold, then, did it come to pass?"

"Some of it, I suppose. That's what the book says, anyhow."

"Then why do you find it surprising our men are any different?" Benjamin One Feather asked. "They all answer to Bakukure, the One Above, the same God only by different name. Ei, he speaks to all of us, if not directly, through the spirits, through visions. Many of our people have visions, Mr. Hockett, even myself, but sometimes a vision isn't even necessary to foretell a happening or to guide your direction. What our own scouts saw over the mountains is enough to make a believer out of any man. Not all. Only men wishing to die will go there now, crazy dogs. Ei, crazy dogs, that's what our people call them, crazy dogs who throw their lives away. Stupidity."

"That sounds more like observation than vision." said Hockett skeptically. "Will your people go over the mountain and fight the ones who killed Goodhart? You have a reason, don't you?"

"My people aren't crazy dogs," answered Benjamin One Feather. "No, we'll not go over the mountain, not this time. The signs are bad. Everyone knows this, but I promise you, John Goodhart's death will be avenged. Ei, and many times over. Goodhart is not my *tribe's* business. He wasn't one of us by blood. It's *my* business, personal."

Benjamin One Feather owned a beautiful shield of polished willow frame and bleached buffalo hide. It was almost pure white, decorated with three eagle feathers and a dangle of ermine tails. Only recently, he had streaked a vermilion shaft of lightning across the face of it. More symbolic than practical, it was considered a source of power and it was deeply valued. White Crane handed it to him at the lodge entry, reached up on her toes and kissed him. "Come down soon," she said. "Don't keep me waiting, or I shall believe the great one with wings has spirited you away."

Securing the shield to a saddle strap, he shook his head, replying, "It's not good for someone so beautiful to worry. You'll get wrinkles long before your time. I'll be back, if not tonight, by the time Masaka warms the tipi."

White Crane sniffed at the morning air. "There is a mist, the sign of Rain Maker. It may be wet, the tipi cold."

"You make a fire if it rains," Benjamin told her. "I'll take shelter under the great tree. Where else?" He sheathed his rifle, and with a quick leap was in the saddle. Reining about, he slowly rode south through the camp, several curious children and their dogs trotting along by his side. Near the perimeter of the village his small admirers stopped and watched in awe as he disappeared into the brush. The children knew his mission must be a personal one, for seldom did a great brave like Benjamin One Feather venture away alone.

For a time Benjamin rode the trail up the broad canyon, his horse moving along in a steady walk. About five miles up he finally reined left, crossed the creek, and followed an old game trail leading toward the top of the ponderosa ridge. In isolated glades, small greening meadows where frightened cow elk and their calves loped away, he often paused to survey the side of the slope ahead of him. The great backbone of the ridge was hidden in the mist, and he allowed that White Crane might be right: Rain was near. Tugging protectively at his poncho he moved on, tracing one small trail after another until he finally came upon the well-worn game path on top. Here he stopped to let his pony rest, dismounted, and unexpectedly stood in sunshine.

Below him in all directions a great blanket of mist covered the land, broken only by small floating islands of pine and fir, green spires jutting up from the fluff. What a wondrous sight and feeling, to be a part of the heavens! He sat on a lichened old boulder while his pony munched on the tender new bunch grass growing among whiskers of maturing pasque flowers. Around him, bear grass was beginning to bloom. This was virgin high country seldom seen by man, the home of the eagle, the ram, the tiny pika, almost as near to Bakukure as one could get. Yes, this is where his old friend had come to die, to bare his soul under the canopy of the great ponderosa. The tree was up above somewhere, far up the ridge, standing like a sacred sentinel guarding the passage to Nah-pit-sei.

The great bull elk had led him here the first time, but on this return to make his giveaway, Benjamin One Feather needed no guide. He could have found his way on the blackest night. The mysterious magnetism of the ponderosa directed him. Although Spotted Hawk had endowed him with the keenest vision, Benjamin was unable to see the tree, yet he knew exactly where it was. After a drink from his small water bag he moved on expectantly, his heart now light and his mind free of troubled thoughts. This was the kingdom of the spirits, spirits with whom he would hold hands in friendship.

Within another hour, the tremendous ponderosa was in his sight. Magnificent! Once seen, who could ever mistake this lonely giant? Its ancient limbs fanned out like a great parasol, a mountain herald beckoning anyone who desired protection or comfort under its great shadow. Benjamin One Feather dismounted near the knoll and tied his pony to a smaller pine. Carrying his rifle and the shield, he walked under the huge canopy, and here on one of the bending boughs he fastened his giveaway, the beautiful white shield emblazoned with its bolt of red lightning. Then, spreading his arms outward to the bright sky, he slowly turned to the Four Great Ways, calling out, "Akbatatdia, Maker of Everything, you are first and always have been. This place belongs to you, and I only pass through with the spirit of Shining Elk. It is you who have created all things. In honor and respect I bring you this token. You are the one and one alone. Make your path come forth and show me the way."

With this prayer offered, Benjamin One Feather rested on the thick cushion of pine needles, sitting there for a long time, eyes closed, meditating. Time passed with the sounds of mountain creatures: a nutcracker harshly scolding him from a bent limb, chipping juncos, ravens calling in a canyon far below the cloud pillow, two pine squirrels battling each other in verbal duels, and a flicker punching holes. Leaning up against the big trunk, Benjamin finally dozed, hands across his breast, rifle in his lap.

Much later a sudden stiff breeze awakened him, and he saw a few heavy thunderheads moving rapidly toward him from the southwest. Soon the sun disappeared and the great gray mass enveloped him, bringing wind and heavy rain. The shield spun crazily, feathers and tails flapping against the white hide. Benjamin One Feather ran out and brought his pony to shelter, secured the halter rope to a waving limb. He then watched the massive clouds move swiftly to the east, obscuring the landscape of rolling hills and valleys far below. Suddenly, the sky was split with one tremendous streaking bolt of lightning that zigzagged across the eastern horizon for as far as the eye could see, illuminating the distant plains of the Greasy Grass.

After this, there was a hushed silence. The giveaway shield hung motionless. Below his token, for the first time, Benjamin noticed a small green plant growing from the mat of needles near the edge of the canopy. Strange, perhaps only coincidental, but it was close to the very spot where his brother elk had died. Why had he failed to notice this before now? Understandable, he thought. In the presence of spirits, the very spectacle of this high mountain kingdom, the appearance of one small plant would escape anyone. But he bent low to examine it, its leaves, its delicate white petals, a bush he did not know. It was beautiful, and Benjamin One Feather plucked one small, sweet-scented spray to take back to the village. He would present it to his pretty wife.

Soon afterward streaks of sunlight reappeared, slanted rays from a dying sun penetrating the shadows of the canopy. It was late in the day. Obligation fulfilled, offering made, his prayer given, there was little else he could accomplish, so he mounted up and began to walk his pony slowly back down the ridge. Though there had been no great revelation this time, Benjamin One Feather nevertheless was filled with contentment, his soul enriched, for high in the heavens he had felt the presence of Shining Elk, and this was good. Good enough for him.

As Benjamin One Feather had expected, White Crane had the front of the lodge open and was sitting there in the damp night air, her blanketed body silhouetted by the night fire behind her. In a small fret, she was waiting for him. She squealed once as he neared the tipi and she recognized him. He was carrying his saddle in one hand, his rifle in the other, and when he placed them by the entry, she leaped into his arms. The moon was high, the night half-gone, her vigil a long one. A dog barked, and an old woman in a lodge nearby complained about the noise. White Crane, giggling behind pressed fingers, led her husband inside and closed the tipi flap. First she kissed him, then whispered harshly, "You are too late, Benjamin One Feather. I expected you hours ago." He sat on a stool by the little fire and unconsciously extended his palm for warmth. He was not cold, only tired and hungry. Jerky and cold flatcakes had been his meager fare on this long day.

He spoke to her, saying, "You should have gone to your robes."

"Hah, you think I could sleep?" And then, as though reading his thoughts, she asked, "Are you hungry, my man?"

"What's in there?" he whispered, nosing at the iron kettle propped by the fire. She told him it was buffalo stew, filled with the white man's potatoes and carrots that Molly Goodhart had provided. Molly had brought many sacks and jars of food from the root cellar at the abandoned trading post, almost a wagonload. She was sharing this bounty with Man Called Tree's family and already preparing ground for a summer garden beyond the village. White Crane scooped out a large portion of the stew and handed Benjamin a wooden spoon. "For being so late," she said, "I should put you to bed with nothing in your belly." She felt his shoulders, his back, then started to ply him with questions. Why wasn't he wet? It had rained most of the day in the village. What had he seen on the sacred mountain? Had the ghosts come? And what about the Spirit Elk, the visionary who had given him his medicine? Smiling at her anxiety, Benjamin One Feather held up his spoon defensively. Enough, enough.

Hanging her head in mock shame, White Crane collapsed at his feet. She was sorry, but so happy to have him back. Patience, yes, but only for a short time. So, as Benjamin ate, he answered most of her questions by relating his experiences on the high mountain. When he had finally finished White Crane was silent, disappointed that Benjamin had not been given a sign. She finally lamented, "I thought you would see something, hear voices! You possess big medicine, the medicine of Shining Elk."

Benjamin One Feather smiled at her and set his bowl to one side. "I saw more than something," he said. "I saw the universe, felt its greatness from dawn until dusk. I touched the sky, and what I didn't see, I could feel. Don't you understand? The spirits didn't have to speak. They were there! I sensed their presence, something I cannot explain. And now my presence is there, too, hanging from the tree. I said to Shining Elk, "See this, and remember me." I vowed to return again, ei, and I will."

He went over to where his saddle lay and pulled out the small flower from the neck of his water bag, presented it to her by the fire. She smelled it, smiled curiously, and held it close to the light, fingering the many delicate flower heads. "I found it by the big tree," he explained. "I thought it was pretty, a flower I didn't know, but it reminded me of you—a beautiful flower on a slender stem."

"*Aho,*" said White Crane. "You have honey on your tongue, ei? I forgive you for being so late." Examining the flower, she said, "Benjamin One Feather, are you trying to play the part of Trickster, Esaccawata? I think you know the coyote too well. You pretend you don't know this flower, ei? Well, I do." With a devilish smile, she waved it in front of him. "This is sweet medicine. I know about it, have seen it many times in the valley. The old people tell many stories about sweet medicine."

Benjamin shrugged innocently. "But I didn't bring it for medicine. I thought it was pretty. It has a nice smell. . . . "

"*Eeyah,* you know nothing, my husband. This isn't for smelling. This plant is for making tea, a tea to help make a woman's breasts big, make plenty of milk, ei, to make her baby strong."

His eyes widened. "But you know I find nothing wrong with your breasts. How should I know these things?"

"Ask your father," she replied. "He knows all about flowers, plants, everything that grows in the mountains. Yes, I think you are a coyote." She picked up his empty bowl and started to turn away. Benjamin One Feather quickly reached out and pinched her rear end saying, "You're right. Don't smell the flowers, make some tea."

"*Eeyah!*"

The next day, when Benjamin related this incident, Man Called Tree chuckled along with his son. White Crane, sitting nearby, merely frowned and shook her head in exasperation. But then the chief fell serious, asking Benjamin One Feather more about his experience on the mountain, and after listening to the story he was silent for a time. He was trying to recall a legend told to him long ago by Buffalo Horn, the ancient one now buried above the medicine wheel. Remembering, he finally held up his hand. The real name of sweet medicine is baneberry, he told them. Jim Bridger had shown this flower to him many years ago. He in turn had identified it for a Jesuit priest, who had become interested in the medicinal values of prairie plants. But it was Buffalo Horn who related a legend about baneberry, the significance placed on it by the early ones.

It was told, Man Called Tree said, that an ancient Cheyenne medicine man transferred his sacred powers into the baneberry when he was dying. This old man's name was Sweet Medicine, and from that time on the Indians had used this name for the plant. The sacred bundle that he passed on to his people contained baneberry, the source of endurance, strength, and patience as decreed by the holy man. Man Called Tree said, "He had come down from the holy mountain with his bundle. Ei, after more than a hundred years, the old Cheyenne holy man knew the spirits were calling him. So he presented the bundle to the early ones gathered around him. He told his people, 'Do not forget me. This is my body that I give you. Always think of me.' With those last words, his spirit passed to the other world above the mountains. Ei, this is the legend as it was told to me by Buffalo Horn. Baneberry is sweet medicine, the one and the same, but to the early ones it's a remembrance of Sweet Medicine himself."

Man Called Tree looked over at his son and daughter-in-law, both transfixed by the story. "Interesting, isn't it?"

Benjamin One Feather sighed. "Interesting? I say *strange*. And what do *you* make of this?"

Man Called Tree nodded toward the mountains in back. "I don't really know. In this case maybe strength . . . the strength of your faith. Or as you say, maybe it was only coincidence, the flowers growing there."

"Sometimes the doubting white in me comes out," Benjamin said, deploringly. "It's a curse against my true culture."

"Ei, nothing unusual, son," Man Called Tree said. "I once had the same curse. It's a choice you make, either one way or the other. There's not much choice when you're in limbo, in the middle of the Great Hanging Road."

Benjamin One Feather mused aloud, "I wonder what Ten Sleeps would say? He has no in-between place."

White Crane gave him an anxious look, and with some apprehension said, "A sign. He would say this is a sign, the one you had to seek. Ei, you're a seeker now, remember? That one would surely make another mystery for you and give you a worse fire in the head. But a flower?" she asked skeptically. "A flower picked for me, one to make my breasts big?" She smiled and nudged him with an elbow.

"You know better," smiled Benjamin One Feather. "This wasn't my intention. I knew nothing about the flower or its meaning. I don't seek more beauty where none is needed." And Benjamin winked slyly at his father. "What do you think?"

Smiling back, Man Called Tree agreed. "You're right. I see no need for improvement, either. I think your wife enjoys a little joke. As for the sweet medicine . . . well, perhaps it has some significance in all of this. This may be part of your medicine, now. Take it for what it's worth. Put the flower in your bundle. It certainly won't do any harm."

White Crane, a twinkle in her eye, patted her man softly on the arm. "Your father's words are wise. If endurance is in the medicine of this flower, I say keep it. Ei, put it in the bundle. I shall search for more and make you some tea, too."

Later that day Benjamin, on his way to the creek, met Zachary Hockett. Hockett, supporting himself gingerly on a new cane, was accompanied by several small boys and their ubiquitous mongrels. The boys immediately began to swarm around Benjamin One Feather, several dashing in to snatch his blanket and touch his buckskin, then leaping away as if snake-bitten. This amused Lieutenant Hockett and finally, after the small fry had gone dashing away whooping at each other, Benjamin explained the commotion. These little ones believed that he possessed the greatness and cunning of Old Man Coyote, the legendary hero-rascal of the Absaroke, that the power of Esaccawata had been given to him by Man

Called Tree. Benjamin told Hockett that one of Man Called Tree's signs was the coyote. Of course they would never dare approach the great chief in this manner, but since Benjamin One Feather was a young brave, not an elder, he was fair game, and they were trying to steal some of his prowess for themselves. He had played the game himself when young.

After a short discourse on the tricks of Old Man Coyote at the trooper's request, the conversation turned to Hockett's tenure in the village. The lieutenant said he was grateful for the good treatment, particularly the daily attention from Two Shell Woman and Molly Goodhart. He also enjoyed White Moon's conversations, and he had absolutely no complaints. Why, even some of the men now greeted him. Yes, he sensed less hostility. Indeed, his life had been somewhat enriched by the Crow. (Benjamin One Feather smiled at this confession.) But now he was on the mend. What it came down to was, how much longer was this going to continue?

Benjamin contemplated for a moment. "Well, you can't sit a horse yet, not unless you want to reopen that hole," he finally replied. "Besides, how are you going to make it across the river, up the Musselshell, all the way to Maginnis by yourself? You were turned around coming down here in the first place, a full day's ride behind that idiot Gibbon. At least he knew where he was going, had old man Fuller showing him the way. Ever think about this? No, you're not paid to think, just to take orders."

Zachary Hockett sighed and said despairingly, "Maybe White Moon's right. Jesus, maybe I'll never get out of here. Damn that boy! Now every time I pull my blanket around me he calls me 'squaw man.' Says this is exactly the way your pa started out, shot in the hip and thrown in with a bunch of conniving women."

Benjamin One Feather laughed. "Oh, you'll get out. Quit worrying, and don't let White Moon get under your hide. His humor is about as sharp as a dull ax. No, Mr. Hockett, I think we're going to move you out within another week. My father mentioned it this morning."

Surprised, Zachary Hockett asked, "But what if I can't ride? Jesus, Two Shell Woman will have a fit. She told Molly I can't get near my horse until she says so."

"Ei, she's the boss," agreed Benjamin, grinning. "No, you won't be mounted. You'll be riding in a wagon, probably in back like cargo." Shedding his shirt, Benjamin One Feather started walking toward the creek.

The young officer anxiously limped behind, talking at Benjamin's back. "But I don't understand this. *Whose* wagon? And how in the hell can I get up to the fort from here in a damn wagon?"

"You can't," Benjamin said over his shoulder. Sitting on a boulder, he began undressing. "The wagon belongs to my father. My sister and James are going to the Gallatin to live." He tossed his moccasins aside, peeled off his pants, and grinned at Hockett. "They'll take you along, if Two Shell Woman agrees."

"Agrees?"

"Ei, I think that woman is beginning to like you, maybe has something on her mind you don't know about."

"Nonsense!" Hockett, his face reddening as he shook his cane at Benjamin. "You're as bad as that brother of yours. Jesus!"

Chuckling, a naked Benjamin One Feather leaped into the creek and disappeared into a deep pool. Directly, his head came up and he sputtered, spit water once. "Want to join me, Mr. Hockett?"

"Hell, no!" was the sharp retort. "Damned woman made me come down here already. Sun was barely up, and I almost froze my ass off." He sat glumly on the boulder vacated by Benjamin One Feather. "What about this wagon?" he finally asked.

"You go along, trail your horse with their stock. They drop you off in Bozeman City. You check in at Fort Ellis. When you're fit, they send you back to duty up at Maginnis. Simple, ei? How does this sound to you?"

A broad grin suddenly creased Zachary Hockett's tanned face. "I like the sound of it, damned if I don't!"

"Ei, I thought you would."

In afterthought, Hockett inquired, "What about Two Shell Woman? How do we handle her? Will she make the trip?"

Benjamin One Feather shrugged once, explained that the Nez Percé woman disliked Bozeman City, in fact had no regard for white people at all since her bad medicine days with the three wolfers. A bullet wound often healed quickly, a wound of the soul, sometimes never. That Hockett was alive and recovering in such good fashion seemed unbelievable to Benjamin One Feather. He told the trooper that, had the same circumstances befallen one of the wolfers, Two Shell Woman more likely would have removed his genitals than the bullet. Hockett shifted uneasily on the rock and winced at the young brave's assumption.

"But you won't be alone," Benjamin continued. "We always send along a party as far as the pass. At one time this was a necessity, the Pekony always coming down. More like tradition, now. A nice five- or six-day ride this time of the year, more like a campout." He jumped from the water and curled the blanket around his body. With a wink he said, "Oh, she might go along to the pass. That is, if she thought you still needed attention, or wanted it."

Kicking away one of Benjamin's moccasins, Hockett testily replied, "Look here, man, after all she's done for me, I have no intention of displeasing her. I am not an ungrateful clod, Benjamin, not in the least."

Zachary Hockett hobbled away, using his cane to whack a few bushes along the path. He found himself somewhat confused. These people, how incredible they were. Often free-spirited and light of heart, yet sometimes frightfully savage, they had actually captivated him. On one hand he was elated at the prospect of soon heading west with James and Little Blue Hoop, eventually finding his way back to Fort Maginnis. On the other hand he was dispirited, something he found it difficult to interpret. His gratitude was foolishly hypocritical and inadequate. Here he was, only a small part of a great scheme to subdue and contain the natives, inhibit their culture, and yet in their primitive way they had delivered him from death and sustained him.

Yet paradoxically, the thought of leaving was also disheartening. And this Nez Percé woman, what kind of an ingratiating spell had she cast upon him? Now he discovered that he was actually enjoying her nearness each morning when she inspected his wound and changed the dressing. He even enjoyed her proximity across the lodge in the darkness of the night, the security of her very presence. Was it her gentle efficiency, those proficient hands of healing she plyed against his leg? Jesus, I hope so! It was too incomprehensible that he, or for that matter she, he thought, could entertain any covetous intentions. Purely platonic, that was all, all within the parameters of medical attention, the healing process. Ah, but how rich in feeling he had become under this continuing care! Well, his imminent departure would cure this, but he admitted, grudgingly, that he would miss Two Shell Woman, miss her a great deal.

TEN

In the Moon of the Green Grass, two white men heading west appeared on the river trail, their four heavily packed mules trailing behind them. They had been sighted long before they reached the junction leading up to Man Called Tree's village, and when they did arrive at this point a party of six Absaroke was already there waiting for them. One of the men was a guide and scout, Jesse Bowden, the other a New York photographer by the name of Franklin Willard. Bowden, who made his living guiding both civilians and army personnel, was not surprised by the sudden appearance of the six Indians blocking the trail. In fact he had fully expected it, had already noticed that he and his friend were being closely observed as far back as four miles on the Yellowstone River Trail. He suspected these scouts were friendly Crow. His assumption was correct, but he was taken aback when one of the Indians, holding up a hand, asked in perfect English where he and Willard were headed, and how they had managed to come through the hostile country below unscathed.

To Benjamin One Feather, the condition of their stock, their full packs, and the weapons they carried gave a clear indication of unmolested travel. Bowden, allaying the alarm of Franklin Willard, quickly enlightened the

Crow, and Benjamin translated to his brothers. These two men had come all the way from a railroad stop on the Platte, had forded the Big Horn far south, skirted the lower Wind River Shoshoni, and had ridden cross-country to the Yellowstone. The photographer who sat nervously adjusting his spectacles was going into the Land of the Smoking Water to take pictures for the white man's government. Benjamin One Feather and his friends were impressed, for the route Bowden had chosen to arrive at the base of the Absaroke village was a hazardous passage between the Big Horn and Teton mountains. Bowden, however, explained that he had no alternative: The Bozeman Trail from the Tongue River country north to the Yellowstone was crawling with hostile Sioux, Cheyenne, and Arapaho. It was now a land also occupied by army troops, a circumstance making the Indians even more hostile.

After all of this information had been imparted, everyone dismounted and sat together in the late-morning sunshine. Tobacco was passed. Bowden proceeded to tell Benjamin One Feather that he had known he would ultimately come into the land of the Crow, that he had been this direction once before and knew of a good passage into the Smoking Water by simply following the Yellowstone River to its headwaters. His plan was to come in from the north and exit from the southwest, eventually returning to Ogden where Willard could make train connections for his trip home. All of this circuitous wandering for pictures amazed the listening Crow. No, Franklin Willard informed Benjamin, this was more than just a photographic journey. These photos were to be for an official record, used as a guide to chart the land's great attractions and its potential as a great park.

"No roads, no trails up there," Benjamin One Feather told him. "Who will go there to see these great things?"

Willard, a slight, agile man with a light beard, replied, "Not many for a long time, but it has been designated for future development. There are wonders up there never seen before, never recorded. This is my purpose, the assignment given to me."

"You're very fortunate, Mr. Willard, to have already come this far without getting yourself in hot water," said Benjamin One Feather. "God only knows how you'll fare up in that country, with steam and sulphur all around you." He looked at Bowden. "Did you see any of these troopers you mentioned, notice their movements?"

"See them?" laughed Bowden. "Hell, we *rode* with the bluebellies. Yep, all the way from Fort Fetterman to the upper creeks of the Tongue and Powder, and that's where we parted company, troopers going north smack-dab toward the Big Horn. Hell, I knows what they're up to. Hostile sign all over that consarned country. Reports coming down the trail almost every day from the Shoshoni."

Benjamin One Feather, somewhat confused by this news, asked, "Troops from Fetterman?" He had heard nothing of army movements from the south, only of General Terry's command that had been grouping on the Yellowstone far to the east.

Jesse Bowden nodded emphatically and blew out a stream of smoke. "That's where they mustered. Old George Crook, as tough as they come, has nigh on fifteen companies, mule train, and a passel of civilians tagging along like we was."

"Fifteen companies!" exclaimed Benjamin. "Why, that's . . . that's almost a thousand men!"

"A passel, for sure," Bowden said. "One of the general's boys tells me they're gonna run the hostiles outta that unceded country once and for all, get 'em back east of the Powder." He chuckled. "I remember the last time they was gonna do that, too. Didn't work out that way. Redskins whipped their asses and sent 'em back to Laramie."

"Interesting," mused Benjamin, and he then told Bowden and Willard about General Terry's Yellowstone expedition. It was now obvious that his columns were planning to converge on the Sioux and Cheyenne from the north. "Catch the enemy in the middle, corner him," he said. "An old ruse, but easier planned than carried out."

"Never snatch a badger when he's in his hole," was Jesse Bowden's dry comment. "Lose every finger on yer damned hand that way."

After another round of talk and translations, the two visitors stood, shook hands with Benjamin One Feather, and prepared to leave. Stone Calf spoke to Benjamin, and pointed toward the rim of mountains to the south. He made quick sign to Jesse Bowden, who then turned back to Benjamin One Feather. "Is this true, what he's telling me?" Bowden asked, nodding toward the distant ridges. "Shorter that way?"

"By at least three days," answered Benjamin. "Take a fork to the right, Rock Creek, around the lower side of the Beartooth. Ei, shorter, but steep, used only by the elk and sheep. My father has been that way many times; Bridger, Beckwourth, ei, and old man Colter, years ago."

"Colter's Hell," remarked Franklin Willard, his eyes lighting up. "It's here in my notes somewhere. That would be John Colter."

Benjamin One Feather nodded affirmatively. "One and the same. He came down that way. The early people were there long before him, though. Some believed the Smoking Water a sacred place. They went up there seeking visions."

"May we speak with your father?" Willard asked. "Would he tell us about this route, or would it be improper?"

Pointing up the nearby canyon, Benjamin One Feather said, "My father is Man Called Tree. You'll find him up there, the village two miles. Ask him yourself."

"Tree?" inquired Jesse Bowden, sucking in his breath. "By chance is that the white Injun, Ben Tree by name, that one?"

"The same."

"Shoot fire, I knowed him fifteen years back!" exclaimed Bowden. "He's a damned caution, he is. Why, I thought he was holed up down below here a piece. Why didn't you tell me he's yer pa?"

Benjamin One Feather smiled. "I usually don't volunteer such information, Mr. Bowden. If you know him, then you also know there are a few foolish men out here who still would enjoy the honor of killing him."

Later the small party came to the village, curious women and children standing to the side, silently observing the two strangers. A few dogs rushed in, snarling and snapping. No one seemed to pay any attention. Many of the women were still working on hides from the recent buffalo hunt, the great skins spread out in circles and pegged at the edges. No hint of friendliness here, thought

Franklin Willard, staring around uneasily, and he sensed that white men were not welcome in this village. Between two large lodges there was a wagon, several young men and women busy loading it with bundles of robes. The photographer adjusted his spectacles and took a closer look. He was not mistaken—there were several pieces of furniture, too, including a rocking chair. Was this booty from a homestead raid?

A tall, bronzed man near the back of the wagon was speaking in English to the others, who seemed to be enjoying the work. Franklin Willard eased up somewhat. He noticed that several of the men were smiling. This was a better sign, but they still were paying little attention to his approaching party. A shout from Benjamin One Feather finally brought them around, turning, but by then Jesse Bowden, grinning, cursing, was leaping from his horse and advancing on Man Called Tree with his hand extended. And it was true, Bowden did know the Absaroke chief, only it took a moment or two of recollection on the part of Man Called Tree. Then once again everyone sat down and talked, this time alongside the wagon. Ultimately the chief gave directions to the Smoking Water to Bowden and Willard, even to the point of sketching out a map in the hard ground.

Franklin Willard's curiosity about the furniture was finally satisfied when he learned of the trip to Bozeman City and the circumstances surrounding it. But hardly had that been dismissed when nearby he saw a white man sitting draped in a blanket, two women near him busily conversing with each other. The man made no attempt to get to his feet, only nodded and faintly smiled when Willard stared in his direction a second time. Once again the photographer's imagination skittered wildly away. Undoubtedly a captive, a white hostage of some sort, and yet another look confirmed it. Protruding from the bottom of the blanket were military boots. This young man was a captured soldier! Those women were watching over him, one even brandishing a stout cane.

Sitting next to Franklin Willard was another son of Man Called Tree. He had been introduced as White Moon, and his English, while not quite as good as his older brother's, was still quite proficient. And White Moon had noticed the apprehension in the photographer's face, his continuing looks at Zachary Hockett. There was very little that ever escaped the sharp scrutiny of White Moon. Willard, unable to contain himself any longer, finally whispered to White Moon, "Who is that fellow? What's he doing here?"

White Moon, feeling wily, casually peered around Willard. "Oh, that one? He's a bluecoat, you know, a soldier. He's been shot, ei, in the leg. We brought him in last week, big fight on the trail down below. Pow, pow, many shots, bodies all around. He hid in a cellar, tried to escape."

"Shot! My God, that's a pity," whispered Willard. "What's going to happen now?"

White Moon shrugged indifferently. "I don't know. Those women keep feeding him pretty good, but he's not getting very fat. Maybe they'll get tired of that and just settle for his liver. With that bad leg, he's not much use for work, ei?"

Franklin Willard's eyes whitened in alarm. "Good God, are you serious? What are you telling me?"

White Moon merely smiled, fox-like. He whispered back, "Are you a holy man? Why do you make a sign like this, a cross on your chest?"

Jesse Bowden and Franklin Willard spent the night in the Crow village, pitching their tent in back of Man Called Tree's lodge. Early the next morning Willard set up his tripod, adjusted his camera, and took photographs of Man Called Tree's family, White Moon in the back row grinning at him mischievously. Benjamin's wife White Crane thought the business of taking pictures great fun, but she was disappointed to learn that Willard would develop his plates later. However, somehow he would try to get a picture back to her. That was his parting promise.

At about the same time that he and Bowden were preparing to head toward the ridges of the Beartooth, James and Little Blue Hoop, with Zachary Hockett comfortably settled in the wagon box, were ready for the Bozeman Trail. White Moon, closely watching the photographer mount up, finally caught his eye. He grinned again and smacked his lips. In turn Franklin Willard, throwing his head back in a hearty laugh, shook a warning finger at the young brave. "You're a scallywag, Mr. White Moon!" he called over. "I'll not forget you!" The two parties, sharing laughter, moved away simultaneously in opposite directions.

Riding ahead of the small wagon, Benjamin One Feather gave a parting wave to his parents and White Moon. With Benjamin were Stone Calf, Sitting Elk, and Old Dog Jumps. White Crane and Two Shell Woman rode their ponies near the wagon's flank, and as they breasted the main path the Nez Percé woman called back to Man Called Tree and Rainbow, "*Taz algo, taz algo,*" good-bye, good-bye.

The small group then settled in and traveled a leisurely pace up the river trail, seeking out the best terrain with James Goodhart at the reins of the team pulling the small freighter. Although frequently jostled about, Zachary Hockett expressed no discomfort. The ride certainly would have been worse if he'd been mounted. He knew this. And among these people who were often so fierce and uncompromising, any outcry on his part would be taken as a sign of weakness. God bless his comforter, Two Shell Woman, for she had cushioned him with a huge hide and several blankets, all of which seemed to absorb most of the trail shock. No, he dared not embarrass her, or himself. But he thought perhaps that he might be just as well off if she paid a little less attention to him. Her smiling stare was almost continual. It made him feel warm under his blanket. But, Jesus, in four or five days he would be at Fort Ellis and in a clean uniform. He would endure, no matter what. Yes, by Jesus, he would.

Near the Stillwater River crossing, a light rain set in, so rather than continue in discomfort the group halted in a grove of giant cottonwoods and made camp, James quickly raising the canvas-wall tent owned by his late father, and calling the three women in out of the rain. The Crow men fashioned a wickiup, using saplings at hand and a few hides. After Sitting Elk and Benjamin One Feather had rigged a canvas fly over the cooking area, the women emerged with food they had packed and began to prepare the evening meal.

By dark, the rain had dissipated. Logs were heaped on the fire and, draped in their blankets, the small party spent half of the cool night in animated conversation. It was times like these, times of taking food freely offered, the campfire camraderie, sharing the warmth of a dancing fire, that made Zachary Hockett almost forget that these were not his people. But in truth their companionship, also freely given, was beginning to overwhelm him. Their warmth radiated like the flames of the fire, and for the first time in several weeks he no longer thought of himself as the infamous Hanging Soldier. To everyone he had finally become "Hock-kett." Staring vacantly into the flames, a sudden realization hit him: By Jesus, I'm not *enduring*, I'm *enjoying*!

Of course Zachary Hockett paid little attention to sleeping arrangements, not after his stay in the village. Everyone there had come and gone almost in complete abandon. He soon discovered that this new adventure on the trail entailed startling compromises in space allotment. The spaciousness of Looks Far Woman's big tipi now had been forsaken for a small corner niche in James Goodhart's tent. With Sitting Elk, Old Dog Jumps, and Stone Calf ensconced in the small wickiup, the young trooper found himself wedged in among two married couples and his ever-present attendant, Two Shell Woman. He had little choice in this maneuver. Two Shell Woman already had prepared his place in the corner, conveniently next to her own pallet. Among his Crow benefactors, to suggest some other arrangement would be out of the question, an impropriety to say the least, and it would have been embarrassing not only to himself but also to Two Shell Woman. Besides, this was a trifling matter at best, and he certainly had no taste for the alternative of sleeping outside under the wagon with an assortment of marauding insects. What difference did it make, anyhow? How many decisions had he actually made since the Nez Percé woman had assumed command of his crippled life? None. Jesus, not one! As White Moon had said to him in a moment of somber humor, "That woman not only carries the pipe, she smokes it." Well said, White Moon, thought Zachary Hockett.

And so, assuming a cheery air, he clambered into his robes next to Two Shell Woman, humming a soldier's tune: "tenting tonight, tenting tonight, tenting on the old campground." Though no one present knew this song, his small bit of whimsical bravado still provoked several chuckles. When he had settled in, he cautiously cornered an eye toward Two Shell Woman. She was uncomfortably close, but he could barely make out her features in the darkness. He took a closer look, discovered that her eyes were closed. Did he detect a tiny smile on her pretty face? Despite the coolness of the night air outside, it seemed so warm in the tent. When Zachary Hockett lay back and closed his own eyes, he heard a little giggle.

He had no idea how long he had dozed or what time of the night it was. For the most part, the keeping of time was an irrelevant matter among these people. What he did know was that muffled sounds had awakened him, sounds embarrassingly near, unmistakable sounds, the shuffling of robes, quickened breathing. Feeling somewhat breathless himself, even fearful of coughing, he managed a quick look across the shadowy tent and saw only one long protruding, outstretched leg. This was quite enough for Zachary Hockett and he sank guiltily back into his bedroll, pulling the blanket up over his ears. What free-spirited, uninhibited people! Obviously, someone besides himself had found sleep elusive, but had attacked the problem in an unconventional but natural way. Zachary Hockett ground his teeth, stifled another cough, shifted his body. His throat was as dry as a withered seed pod. Perspiration, however lined his forehead.

When the lieutenant finally stuck his head out to breathe, a new stillness greeted him. Outside, he heard crickets and the distant hoot of an owl. Inside all was quiet, not a rustle of robes nearby, not even a snore. He finally managed to clear his throat, then readjusted his blanket and sighed. Despite all, he would not let sleep evade him. He would prevail. His eyelids fluttered once and closed. But moments later, Hockett suddenly came alive again. He felt the slow glide of a hand across his cheek, tracing up to his damp forehead. Startled, he turned to discover Two Shell Woman hovering over him. She quickly pressed her fingers to his lips, shook her head, then to his astonishment, came down firmly pressing her mouth to his. Momentarily stunned, he gasped once, but suddenly found his hands fondling her long, tumbling tresses, returning her ardor in kind.

Two Shell Woman too had been a close witness to the

earlier scene in the tent, and this had aroused a longing want inside her. It had been too many moons since she had taken a lover on her own terms, one of her own choice. She was hungry to have this man that she now admired so much. Slowly drawing away, Two Shell Woman quietly threw back Hockett's robe and once again pressed her fingers to his lips. He understood: Be quiet, very quiet. Kissing him lightly, she motioned him up, at the same time sliding her lithe body from her own bedding. Then, with a blanket draped over her shoulder, she crept through the tent flap into the moonlight, leading Hockett by the hand.

Except for the cover across her shoulder the Nez Percé woman was totally naked, and to Zachary Hockett this was a shadowy sight to behold, her slim hips and firm buttocks swaying in front of him like a prancing filly. His spirits soared, his limp disappeared, and all of his previous apprehensions, his doubts, his fears of capitulation, went scattering crazily through the giant cottonwoods around him. Trembling as he trailed his own blanket, Hockett went willingly, joyfully, even suppressing a cry when he scraped his toe on a wayside rock. Soon, under the very wagon where he had earlier feared to sleep, he succumbed to his desires and those of an aroused Two Shell Woman.

When dawn broke over the Yellowstone, only a few of the Gallatin-bound party were up and about in the Stillwater camp. In the absence of the women, Sitting Elk had built up the fire and had a pot of water for coffee boiling. Stone Calf and Old Dog Jumps freed the horses from their hobbles and picket pins and led them downstream to water. Soon Benjamin One Feather and White Crane emerged from James's tent, spoke to Sitting Elk, then disappeared up the creek to bathe. By the time they returned, Two Shell Woman and Zachary Hockett had finally appeared. The Nez Percé woman smiled and immediately traded sign with White Crane who, at one point during the animated conversation, covered her face and snickered.

When Hockett saw this, it was obvious that the extended leg he had seen in the night had belonged to Benjamin's young wife. To avoid any embarrassment he quickly glanced away, avoiding any eye contact with her.

Taking up his cane, which he perhaps no longer really needed, he headed for the creek, soon to be followed by his shadow—now lover—Two Shell Woman. She stopped in the tent only long enough to pick up a large towel and a few strips of cloth. Following the limping soldier was nothing unusual, and no one paid any attention to her. After all, she had been attending the young officer every day since the hostiles' attack on Goodhart's trading post. As Zachary Hockett limped along upstream, he already labored with twisted thoughts, in addition to his gimpy leg, and vainly tried to unravel them.

Of course he knew what had precipitated such an amorous encounter under the wagon, but once done, was it likely to recur? Could such a moment of passion be relived? Moment! Jesus he thought, more like an hour! If only he could speak to this intriguing woman, sit side-by-side with her and just for once have a normal conversation! Her vocabulary was so damn limited—*Hallo, good, bad, shit no, shit yes*—the latter undoubtedly words taught her by the wolfers that Benjamin and his brothers had dispatched. At least Little Blue Hoop had politely informed her that the "shit no" and "shit yes" were taboo, used only by crude white men, and he hadn't heard those words for several days.

Testing the temperature of the stream, Zachary Hockett quickly decided it was much too cold for a full dip, at least for a white man, so he shucked his boots and socks, dropped his pants, and gingerly stepped in ankle-deep and began to cup water up against his stomach and crotch. This was no humane way to start the day, not in a frigid mountain valley creek. A barracks' tub filled with hot water had long been a distant longing of his. Preoccupied with discomfort, the chill at his loins, he was unaware that Two Shell Woman had come up behind him. "Hock-kett," she quietly called. When he quickly turned, she giggled and tossed him a bar of the white man's soap that Man Called Tree always brought back from Bozeman City. That he failed to catch it was no great surprise, for standing before him naked, her brown breasts stuck out like two molded biscuits, was his woman of the night, now resplendent in the bright sunshine of the day.

"*Kaiziyeuyeu,*" she said. Greetings, good morning.

That was one of the few Nez Percé words he understood. Without thinking, he protectively sat down in the cold water, felt the shock of it up to his eyebrows. Sucking for breath, he barely managed a weak "Hello."

"Hallo," she repeated, boldly wading in beside him. As though she were born to the water, she sat down directly in front of him, reached out and ran her hands up his thigh to his small bandage. Carefully peeling it away, she closely examined his wound under the clear water. Her pretty face lit up, and she nodded vigorously in approval. Unfurling the wrap of linen, she loosed it into the current and watched it swirl away in an eddy. *"Sepekuse!"* she exclaimed. It is done.

Curiously peering down, Zachary Hockett also smiled in quiet amazement. It was true: The angry red welt had glazed over into a new pinkish scar, now fully closed and free of drainage. He reached out to touch her, but laughing, she moved quickly away from him across the small stream, taking the bar of soap with her. As he watched wide-eyed and fascinated, Two Shell Woman, standing in water up to her thighs, slowly began to lather her body, presenting herself to him, unashamed, proud, and provocative. He was spellbound. Precious moments went by, moments that he knew could never be reclaimed. Suddenly she submerged, rolled over several times like a water nymph, then reappeared. Flipping him the soap, she grabbed her blanket and leaped away into the bushes, shrieking happily.

Moments later James Goodhart appeared on the bank, Little Blue Hoop directly behind him. James gave Hockett an amazed stare. "What happened? Did you fall? Do you need some help getting out of there?"

"No, not at all," Hockett replied, brushing suds from his chest.

"That water will freeze your balls off," James said. "Holy cow!"

"Not cold, not at all," stammered the trooper. "Just throw me that damned towel over there. I'll manage." And Zachary Hockett did manage. Wrapped in the towel, hugging his boots and pants, he went off into the bushes to dress. His body was as red as a lobster.

"Good-bye, red man!" Little Blue Hoop called merrily.

By the time Hockett had returned to camp, White Crane and Two Shell Woman were already busy over the fire preparing breakfast. They merely glanced at him and routinely carried on with their work. Not a word, not even a smile, as though nothing unusual had happened, as if this were just another new day along the Bozeman Trail. Shouldn't there be some self-satisfied smirks, a giggle or two? Astounding, Zachary Hockett mused, such casual indifference! But then again, what did he expect, the call of a bugle, reveille? How could he comprehend their quaint ways, their customs in three weeks? Or was it four? Jesus, he thought, I've even lost track of time! Well, regardless, there could be no dampening of his new found enthusiasm. Two Shell Woman had kindled his emotions, had filled him with anticipation and desire. Or was it lust?

Whatever, a twinge of remorse suddenly hit him when he was struck by the pitiful thought that perhaps her desire already had been fulfilled, that she now expected nothing more from him but kindly platitudes. He had to be realistic about this. Most certainly, there was no future for her with the Hanging Soldier, Hock-kett, who now was on his way home. If the beginning was to be the end, then that was that. He could do nothing more than accept it. Strange, though, the games Fate played. This woman who had every reason to hate white men, including himself, had now comforted and consorted with one. Why? You'd have to ask her. Impossible!

Benjamin One Feather came up and broke Zachary Hockett's confused musings, stepping close to hand him a cup of steaming coffee. Hockett thanked his Crow friend (he was always thanking someone in one way or another) and without thinking, he took a hasty sip from the hot cup and promptly burned his tongue. He cursed. Frozen butt, scorched mouth. Jesus, and the day had barely begun!

Benjamin was just finishing his own coffee when Stone Calf came trotting up, motioning toward the big river. Two riders coming in with three pack mules, he said, prompting Benjamin One Feather and Old Dog Jumps to reach for their rifles. They stood by the wagon and waited. And directly the men appeared, raised up a friendly shout, and each held a hand high. The Indians were surprised, for the man on the front horse was Henry Fuller, the same scout who had been leading Gibbon and his troops down the Yellowstone almost a month ago.

Fuller, slowly dismounting, grinned at them. "You fellers sure do spread your blankets around, don't you?"

"Ei," Benjamin replied. He moved forward and shook hands with the scout. "We manage to keep moving."

Fuller nodded toward his companion, a tall man dressed in denims. "This is Fred Gerard, one of my kind. Picked up your sign yesterday, figgered a party was up ahead." He raised his arm again and made sign to the rest of Benjamin's party. Turning back to Benjamin, he said, "Getting a late start, ain't you? Sun's up two hours ago. Skeeters already in the bottoms."

"We're in no hurry," Benjamin One Feather said. And he went on to explain the reason for the journey, finally pointing over to James and Little Blue Hoop. Fuller expressed his regrets. He and Gerard had passed the burned-out post five days ago and deduced what had happened. However the graves had puzzled them, and they were now both saddened to hear that John Goodhart lay buried in one of them.

Zachary Hockett, anxiously concerned, asked the men, "What's happening over that way, anyhow? Has there been any contact with the hostiles?"

White Crane had handed the two men cups of coffee. Henry Fuller, took one sip and set his on the edge of the wagon. With a surprised look he said, "You mean you haven't heard? The word's not up the trail?" Staring around curiously at the rest of the group, he received nothing but negative looks in return.

"We've heard nothing," Benjamin One Feather finally said. "Jesse Bowden and some photographer came by the other day, but they made a circuit around the buffalo grounds. They said Crook and some troops were coming up from Fetterman. That's the last we've heard."

"Well, there was contact, all right," said Fuller. "Contact, for sure, if that's what you're calling it. Not for myself, but old Fred here, he was in the thick of it up on the Greasy Grass. Almost got himself rubbed out. Allows he's lucky to be riding with me, now."

Grinning through his whiskers, Gerard said, "That's a fact, for sure."

Fuller continued, saying, "And we upped and figgered we'd had enough messing around with some of those fool soldier boys, so we headed out. Yes, sir, we're going south, plan to stay the winter, too." Looking over at Hockett, he added, "Meaning no disrespect for you, son, of course. Can't be that many fools wearing blue."

"No, of course not," Hockett said, shifting his eyes from Fuller back to Fred Gerard. "Then, there was battle of some sort, I assume," he said.

Gerard snorted sardonically, "Battle? Son, there was a regular bloodbath, that's what. Fact is, two of 'em." And then with occasional embellishments from Henry Fuller, Gerard, who had been scouting for the Seventh Cavalry, proceeded to relate the events of the past two weeks. Yes, it was true. General Crook had come north from Fetterman, and for a fact had engaged the Sioux and Cheyenne at a small canyon on the Rosebud. That was on June 17. No big victory there for Crook or the Indians, Gerard said, but Crook retreated unexpectedly back up to his main camp above Goose Creek in the Big Horns. A week later, Long Hair Custer came into the Greasy Grass with his troopers and was attacked by over two thousand Sioux and Cheyenne. His entire command had been wiped out. Gerard said that he had managed to escape the rout by riding over a ridge, where he took refuge with Major Marcus Reno's beleaguered troopers, who had dug in on a hillside. Half of his Seventh Cavalry troops perished, too, before the hostiles finally withdrew the next morning. He said there was very little left of the Seventh. In fact, every man on Custer's side of the hill had been killed.

Benjamin One Feather nodded toward Zachary Hockett, who was staring at the ground, dumbfounded by what he was hearing. "Mr. Hockett there, that's where he was riding, down to join the Seventh."

Fuller wagged his head, "Well, that's a how-de-doo, for you! Look here, boy, I suspect the good Lord was looking after you, he sure was. A ball in the leg is a heap better than an ax in the head. Yes, sir, and you couldn't have ended up in better hands, either."

"Yes, good hands," muttered Hockett without looking up.

Benjamin One Feather, also quietly shocked by the

news, yet not entirely surprised, asked Fuller, "Where were General Terry's men? And that idiot Gibbon you took through here?"

Fuller smiled. "Oh, you didn't forget the ol' Colonel Red Nose?"

"We remember him, we all do," Benjamin One Feather said, nodding toward Old Dog Jumps, and James. "Ei, the One Who Limps. His words were bad medicine, the words of a killer, not a peacemaker."

"Well, he was a day late and a dollar short," Fuller said. "Time we got to the Big Horn it was all over, hostiles scattering a dozen directions, war camp deserted, nothing left but bones and horseshit." He laughed once and clucked his tongue. "Whooee, ol' Red Nose was mad as hell he didn't get a chance to rub out a few redskins! Tell you the truth, after getting a look at that ridge above the creek, I was damned happy. Why, that jackass Custer went and split his troops, figgered he'd take that war camp from two sides. Young Reno didn't get the brunt of it at all, mostly women and youngsters at his end, but a few of those braves were mad as hornets. They came running and almost rubbed him out, too, leastways that's what we all allowed. Anyhow, when those bucks learned Yellow Hair was on the lower hill, there was no dilly-dallying. They went right up after him. Hell, it was all over in less than an hour, wasn't it, Fred?"

Nodding in agreement, Fred Gerard said disgustedly, "Assholes, the lot of 'em, paying no mind to the sign we done sorted out for 'em, and Armstrong the worst of all. Told the Colonel three times we had hostiles watching on both sides of us, and he kept pushing the boys, telling 'em they was gonna pull a big surprise on the Injuns. That man never paid a hill of beans to what *we* was telling him."

He looked over at Benjamin One Feather. "Back on the Yellowstone before he even gets down there, Gibbon tells him to wait 'til him and ol' man Terry comes along to join up. And by gawd, I tells him, too. Too many Injuns down there, I says. Hell, he thinks those bucks are gonna hightail outta that river bottom. Did jest the opposite." He gulped the last of his coffee and slammed the tin cup on the wagon gate. Glancing over at Benjamin, he added, "Few of your Crow brothers from downriver went up to the Big Sky along with ol' Yellow Hair. Lucky your pa didn't send some of your bucks down there with 'em."

"The signs were bad," Benjamin One Feather told him. "This was foretold. Anyone who ignores the signs is a fool."

Henry Fuller agreed. "Well, your pa is no fool, I'll allow that!"

James Goodhart, sitting to the side, had been translating the story and ensuing conversation, and Little Blue Hoop, with some knowledge of the Nez Percé tongue, had managed to tell most of it to Two Shell Woman. Few questions were asked, the group almost silent, neither happy nor sad but keenly aware that their great leader, Man Called Tree, had been wise enough to keep the sorrow of death away from the mountain Bird People. The women finally turned back to their task of packing, and Stone Calf and Old Dog Jumps began helping James with the wall tent. Benjamin One Feather harnessed up the wagon team and invited Fuller and Gerard to ride along the rest of the way to Bozeman City with his Crow party. Since they were in no hurry either, it was agreed. It was early summer—plenty of time left to reach the Oregon territory.

Later, when camp was broken and everyone was headed up the trail, White Crane, overwhelmed by curiosity, rode alongside Benjamin One Feather. For some time she had been thinking about the story told by the two scouts, how it coincided so strikingly with Benjamin's vision on the mountain, his mysterious encounter with Shining Elk. Finally she asked him, "Why didn't you tell them it was your vision that foresaw all of this?"

"It would have made no difference," he answered. "Ei, and I would have felt foolish pretending to be a prophet. No, among these whites some things are best left unsaid, woman. My vision is personal."

She said, "The One Who Limps escaped the fire, did he not? Wasn't it he who hid behind the rock?"

Benjamin One Feather smiled across at her. "*Ikye,* I see you've come to probe me again. Yes, this is what was foretold, but the fact is the man, Gibbon, didn't get there in time. Is this escape? I don't know. Perhaps the battle and fire are the same, ei, and this was in the east, too, on the prairie where the Lightning and Thunder Beings showed me their powerful medicine. This was the illumination of the Four Great Ways. This much, I see."

"The red fox? Where is his place in this?"

"Ah, now that one I don't know about," he said. "Ei, too many things I don't know about. Maybe they haven't come to pass yet. Too many beads are missing to complete the string. But I'll tell you this, I don't think we've seen the last of that man Gibbon. It's a feeling I have, one I can't explain, but it's here, right in my belly."

Her brow furrowed and she gave Benjamin One Feather a worried look. Yes, what he was saying was true, too many beads were missing. And from her standpoint, too many bad things were happening. Her man's vision was an ominous one, not pleasant, and this bothered her, caused her to fear for him. And she knew he would go over the mountain another time when a sign directed him. After the death of John Goodhart he had indicated as much, vowed to return to cleanse the anger that had crept into a corner of his heart. She said to him, "Shining Elk is your medicine, Benjamin One Feather. He has shown you illumination and the power of rebirth. You share a soul from that sacred place. I think you should look to him for guidance. That sweet medicine . . ."

Benjamin's head quickly turned. What had brought about this change of heart? Once she had gently chided him about the mysterious flowers, his very purpose in plucking a stem. "Sweet medicine? Then you believe it was a sign? You really believe this . . . not coincidence?"

White Crane shrugged. "How can I believe otherwise? As you, I've thought and thought about it. At the top of the sacred mountain you saw the clouds tremble and your heart trembled with it. You told me this. What you felt, I believe, and what you found, I also believe. There is no other explanation, my man. It must be. Shining Elk speaks on behalf of his dead brother. There is meaning here."

"Yes, the baneberry . . . sweet medicine," he said. "At the time I thought very little of it, those tiny white flowers." His voice trailed off, and staring ahead at the winding trail he mumbled to himself, "This is my body . . . do not forget . . . always think of me."

"What is this?" White Crane asked with a smile, staring over at him. "Are you talking to yourself?"

Smiling back, he waved her off. "No, just thinking aloud."

She tutted him, softly scolded, "Benjamin One Feather, it's not good to talk to yourself. Ei, your pony will go deaf and turn cross-eyed. Please, for his sake, don't do this anymore."

A day later, the party pitched camp up the Boulder River near a green meadow ringed by alder and willow, the grass thick and lush, ideally suited for the remuda. Once the chores had been completed, the three women, each confessing their immediate problems, wandered up the small river to bathe. For Little Blue Hoop, it was the worry of making another new home many sleeps from the Yellowstone, of how her man, James, would adjust to life on the big ranch, of how they would now become more white than Indian. Yet even with this anxiety, she knew that village life was not meant for James, and neither of them relished the prospect of returning to the trading post, not for the present anyhow.

However, Two Shell Woman saw only the bright side of this. Her new sister at least had a husband and a home. Her own home was far away over many rivers, and while the Absaroke had been kind to her, she longed to see her Nez Percé people. Worse yet, she finally admitted, she feared she was going to miss Hock-kett when he returned to Fort Ellis. Even though there was no future for her with a white man soldier, she had come to admire him, an affection that she realized never could be permanently resolved. And she confessed regretfully that this was all her own fault. She should have never allowed her emotions to become part of making him well.

White Crane, after listening to the translation by Little Blue Hoop, stood in front of her adopted Nez Percé sister and rapidly made sign. Saving another person's life, even a pony soldier, had brought Two Shell Woman great honor among the Bird People, and surely there was self-gratification in such a deed. She told her to take this as a measure of her goodness, feel joy in this reality, not sadness in unreality. White Crane herself had only one small lament, the fact that Benjamin One Feather had become so obsessed with his vision that she was afraid of where it was now leading him. Yes, and some of this was rubbing off on her. She had already lost her brother, Little Bull Runs, and now when her man was away, she had frightening thoughts and bad dreams.

The women chose a quiet pool flooded by the afternoon sunlight, its banks decorated with golden sand and tumbled boulders. The water here teemed with fish, darting streaks of silvery-gray, splotches of crimson and orange flashing between their bare legs. White Crane squealed and quickly found a place where the water was shallow and less threatening. But Two Shell Woman was delighted. These were trout that now flitted around her naked body, and they were delicious to eat.

Her sisters frowned. This was a good food source usually ignored by the Crow, and her sudden enthusiasm was not shared by either White Crane or Little Blue Hoop. Nevertheless the Nez Percé woman told them that she wanted to taste some of these trout, for in her life along the Snake and Salmon rivers she had eaten many trout and salmon. She was excited about this discovery. When they came from the water, she asked Little Blue Hoop to mention this to Benjamin One Feather when they returned to camp. He would know what to do.

But Benjamin, upon hearing her wish, was momentarily puzzled by such a strange request, the very oddity of the idea of catching fish. Why, he had never done such a thing in his life, even though his father had once told him how he and Gabe Bridger had killed them with a forked spear, had even cooked and eaten them. Fred Gerard, sitting nearby, told Benjamin that he and Fuller always enjoyed a batch of pan-fried trout, in fact considered it a delicacy. A further fact, he knew how to catch these fish, even had the tools to do it. All of this was duly translated to Two Shell Woman who, illuminated by joy, motioned to Gerard to come, she would show him this food treasure and they would all share in the feast. While she waited, Gerard went to his pack and, after a brief search, came up with twine and several small hooks. Slicing off a small chunk of fatback, he made sign to Two Shell Woman that he was ready. And off they went, Zachary Hockett and Benjamin One Feather curiously trailing behind the two.

The old scout's eyes bulged out like puff balls when he peered into the clear water of the pool. Trout were darting in all directions, now alarmed by this second intrusion of strange beings. Grinning, Fred Gerard smacked his lips, crumpled up a piece of the hogback, and tossed it into the eddy. The water suddenly boiled with hungry trout, lunging, rolling, tearing the meat to shreds. Gerard threw back his head and cackled. These were virgin trout, all right. While his companions watched, he proceeded to fasten line to a slender willow branch, bait up, and swing the hook out into the riffle.

His spectators laughed and clapped encouragingly when he began to catch fish after fish, and as swiftly as he beached them Two Shell Woman, her sharp knife flashing, slit them open and quickly ran her thumb down the cleft, spilling entrails into the damp sand. Even though Benjamin One Feather disdained fish, he nevertheless was highly impressed at the dexterity of Gerard, and he allowed this was one good reason such ingenious men never went hungry in the mountains.

That evening, while the Crow ate braised antelope strips, Two Shell Woman, Zachary Hockett, and the two grizzled scouts feasted on fried trout basted in cornmeal. And amid much derisive laughter, Benjamin One Feather ate several bites, placed in his mouth by the fingers of Two Shell Woman. He declined to admit this to his brothers, fearing more ridicule, but the fish tasted better than the antelope.

When darkness finally closed in, everyone found places around the night fire. There were smiles and a few chuckles as Sitting Elk related how that afternoon he had been nipped in the butt by one of the ponies while he was examining another one's rear hoof. Someone suggested that Two Shell Woman knew how to treat such bites, that he should look to her for sympathy and attention. This brought more laughter, then a few more humorous stories about contrary horses and mules. Fuller and Gerard being adept at sign, they soon were into the fun, taking turns telling stories not of battles, strife, and discord, but of the good times each had experienced in their many years on the frontier. These two men, much traveled and trail-wise, like their red brothers in the circle, had held hands with Mother Earth many times. Long ago they had learned that to do otherwise often only sowed the seeds of misfortune and brewed bad medicine. Their stories this night were humorous, frequently bawdy and self-revealing, and the men often stopped in the middle of a tale to laugh loudly at their own foolishness.

The three young women began to shriek when Henry Fuller stood up in front of the fire and related in great detail his experiences with rye whiskey and a Shoshoni woman with whom he had shared a cabin one winter down near Fort Bridger. Firewater had been a problem, he admitted, and his Shoshoni woman had finally tired of his drinking. After one bad night with red-eye, he awoke the next morning to discover that his beard had been cut off. Worse yet, he related with sweeping gestures and laughter, this woman had removed all of his pubic hair with her skinning knife. "This was too close," he sighed, grasping himself protectively, his face contorted in mock fright. "It gave me a terrible scare, and I drank no more whiskey the rest of that winter. I tell you, that made this woman mighty happy, too. She had a smile on her face every morning after that."

The women squealed and clapped. This prompted Fred Gerard to stand and begin gesturing. He also had a story of how he once had hidden a small bull snake in his woman's bundle of beadwork. "She made no complaint," he signed, "never mentioned the terrible fright of finding that darned snake. Oh, but I knows she found it, all right. A few days later, I gets this terrible itch in my bottom." Laughing, he paused to dramatize, scratching fiercely. "It was even worse than when Old Man Coyote ate too many uncooked rose hips and scratched his ass all night. That woman had done gone and put pine pitch in the crotch of my longjohns!" With that, he suddenly whipped out his harmonica, struck up a tune, and went jigging wildly around the fire. Fuller leaped up and performed a few intricate steps of his own.

The stories continued until the last scrap of wood had been thrown onto the fire. By then most of the men had taken a turn and Gerard and Fuller were finally exhausted from jigging and campfire oratory, the three women, though non-participants, happily weary from laughing. At least for now, all of their personal doubts and fears, and the woe of distant conflict, had been forgotten. Everyone began to prepare for bed. The two scouts had pitched their small tent next to the Crow wickiup, and after a few parting words with Benjamin One Feather, they retired to their bedrolls. Zachary Hockett tugged at his buffalo robe and blanket and then passed in front of Benjamin, explaining that since it was such a pleasant night he'd thought he might be more comfortable sleeping under the wagon. Sometime after midnight, when the camp was heavy with sleep and the moon at its highest, Two Shell Woman darted through the shadows and joined him.

ELEVEN

Farewells were exchanged at the narrow defile leading down to Bozeman City, at least one of them unexpected. Bidding the party good-bye were the three Crow braves, Sitting Elk, Old Dog Jumps, and Stone Calf, all of whom planned to hunt grizzly bear in the Rock Mountains for two sleeps before meeting up again with Benjamin One Feather and White Crane for the return trip to their village. These men knew they would soon see Little Blue Hoop and James Goodhart again, for they both had strong bonds of kinship in the Echeta Casha. But Two Shell Woman, their new friend, the woman who had saved Old Dog Jumps from death, was leaving, perhaps never to return again. This was a farewell none had expected. She had decided to join Henry Fuller and Fred Gerard and trail west to her tribe near Lapwai in the Idaho territory. The two veteran scouts, who had tasted her biscuits and pan-fried trout, were more than happy to have her company, and besides, she knew a shorter route to Oregon's Blue Mountains, a passageway through the Bitterroots that followed big streams down to the Land of the Winding Waters, the Snake River valley. To Benjamin One Feather, Two Shell Woman's decision was a great compromise, an expedient way to get her back with her people as he once had promised, and much sooner than expected. Now she would not have to wait for the Nez Percé arrival on the buffalo grounds. This sudden change in plans was understandably practical but distressingly sad. Everyone was going to miss this beautiful young woman who had helped heal them both bodily and spiritually, particularly Old Dog Jumps and the soldier, Zachary Hockett, who despite his remarkable recovery had begun to show some signs of despondency.

In the last two days, as the party had ridden closer to Fort Ellis, young Hockett's face had grown longer, Two Shell Woman's eyes more misty. This transition had not gone unnoticed. White Crane mentioned it to Benjamin One Feather, but only in reference to the lieutenant. Here was a man who had left their village with such great anticipation and was now becoming more morose and silent each passing day, with a look almost of despair upon his face. Had his bond with the Absaroke become so strong in such a short time? Or was it that he had become attached to Two Shell Woman in an impossible relationship? It certainly appeared more than casual. How could he possibly be any more sad than the rest of them? Of course, she already knew how the Nez Percé woman felt about the pony soldier. There had been a confession of sorts, that admission along the banks of the Boulder River about her emotions being askew, her desires impractical but so overwhelming. Now, her dark eyes were showing it.

Benjamin One Feather, as usual, listened patiently to the disguised logic in White Crane's questioning. He casually clucked his pony ahead. "I'm not old enough to be a wise man about such matters," he finally told her. "Nor is it any of my business, but what ails Mr. Hockett will probably go away once he gets back in uniform. Ei, she's healed one wound and opened another. The man is confused. She's been in the blanket with him and he probably feels that he owes her more than that. Right now it's more than he can handle, but he'll get over it. He'll get his pants back on."

"What are you saying, Benjamin One Feather?" she whispered harshly. "How do you know this? Did he tell you?"

Benjamin touched an eye with his forefinger. "When I'm on the trail, I sleep the one-eyed sleep."

"Eeyah!" she exclaimed. "How can you say this? Sometimes you snore."

"Ei, but always with one eye open," he grinned.

"You talk as if this were no more than an ache in his groin," she whispered across her pony. "What about *her*? What about *her* feelings in this matter? Have you thought about that, what this must be doing to her?"

"She paddles with the same oar," he replied. "She wants something she can never have. She must know this. Once over the mountains she will have to forget, maybe find herself a new husband. She is young, pretty, has much courage and intelligence." He sadly shook his head. "But no, I haven't spoken with the woman. How could I? I don't know how she feels, I only suspect. Did she say anything to you?"

"Only that she has come to admire him too much," White Crane answered. "Certainly nothing about tossing the blanket with him."

Sighing, Benjamin One Feather leaned over his saddle toward his wife. "It's none of our business, ei? These two have to find their own path, dismiss what cannot be, seek out the new. There's nothing we can do but wish them well when they go their separate ways."

"I shall do that, Benjamin One Feather," she replied somewhat crisply. "But I tell you this, you don't understand a woman. Dismiss it, hah! A woman can dismiss a man from the mind, but not always from the heart."

Early that afternoon they finally rode into the log and sod-chinked fort, with Fred Gerard, Henry Fuller, and Benjamin One Feather leading the way. Behind them came the wagon, James at the reins, Little Blue Hoop sitting beside him, and Zachary Hockett perched on a bundle of robes in the wagon box, straining his eyes in search of someone he might recognize. Trailing the small freighter were the women, pack ponies, and finally Hockett's big brown horse. The appearance of Indians caused no clamor at the fort, only a few troopers by the stables stopping to stare at the beautifully beaded neckpieces on the Crow ponies. Near company headquarters, one trooper did call out Henry Fuller's name, and there was a brief exchange concerning the recent fighting over in the plains. Obviously, the news about the Crook and Custer battles with the hostiles had come into Fort Ellis from the south on the telegraph, probably a week after the two disasters on the Rosebud and the Little Big Horn.

Since Fuller had been attached to the post, riding point for Colonel Gibbon, Benjamin One Feather decided to let the scout speak to the Officer of the Day to explain the circumstances surrounding Zachary Hockett's assignment out of Fort Maginnis and its subsequent failure. Hockett climbed out of the wagon but was intercepted near the steps by Two Shell Woman, who came trotting up leading his horse. In a disheartening moment, they briefly held hands and looked into each other's eyes. Haltingly and with deep affection she said, "Thank you, Hock-kett." And in Nez Percé he replied, "*Taz alago.*" Good-bye. After quickly kissing him on the cheek, Two Shell Woman ran back to her pony, tears tracing little paths all the way down to her outthrust chin. Then the rest of the party closed in, each member shaking Hockett's hand and wishing him well. He walked up the steps, sadly shaking his head.

After a short while Fuller came out of headquarters, followed by several officers and the lieutenant. One of these men, a major, expressed his gratitude for the care the Crow had given to Zachary Hockett. He said that they could stop by the quartermaster's office on their way out and pick up supplies of bacon, beans, flour, and coffee for their trip home, a gift from the army. After a final farewell, Hockett, crying out "God bless you all!" tossed his cane out to James, then limped away with the officers toward his new quarters. It was all over in less than ten minutes, but everyone knew it would take ten years to forget.

A mild depression then set in, and not much was said on the way into town, where a short stop at Lucas Hamm's mercantile had been planned. There was some shopping to do before the party rode on to the ranch for the night. The two scouts, anticipating their long journey ahead, needed to replenish ammunition and some clothing, and Benjamin One Feather, aware that Two Shell Woman carried only her bedroll and a few personal possessions, wanted to outfit her properly. This was the least he could do. Despite her gentle protests, Benjamin told her that he would not send her back to the Nez Percé destitute. After the unexpected windfall at the fort, only a few extra food items were necessary, and Benjamin was going to contribute a twenty-dollar gold piece toward these purchases.

Lucas Hamm immediately recognized Benjamin One Feather and White Crane. He quickly stepped from behind his counter and welcomed them, and in turn was introduced to Fred Gerard and Henry Fuller. When he learned that the two scouts were returning from the Little Big Horn, he quickly brought out some small black cigars and told them to take as many as they needed, allowing as, from what he had heard, they had earned them.

While they were striking up conversation, the three young women went down the long aisles ogling merchandise, giggling at so many strange things, this time James explaining and Little Blue Hoop translating into Nez Percé for the benefit of Two Shell Woman. She was astounded by all of the many objects, some on shelves, others hanging from long racks, and still more in great boxes and barrels. The smells were overwhelming—leather, linen, coffee, coal oil, and in one place even the delicate scent of spices. Benjamin One Feather, watching the women point, often touching their cheeks in surprise, told Lucas Hamm what he needed for Two Shell Woman: new blankets, a shawl and poncho, a riding skirt, denims, a pair of small leather boots, and anything else his wife White Crane might suggest of a more personal nature.

When all of this was done, Lucas fitted the clothes and boots and Two Shell Woman, flashing a broad smile, came close to Benjamin to show him what White Crane had chosen for her: a brush for her hair, two bars of the white man's soap, and some soft cloth for undergarments. Her once sad eyes had brightened, and, at least for the present, her farewell to Zachary Hockett had been forgotten.

When they finally came back out onto the boardwalk, a small knot of men had gathered near the rail where the wagon team and ponies were hitched. A few men were smiling, several others admiring the decorated bridles, saddles, and neckpieces on the Crow stock. One of the men, recognizing Henry Fuller, gave him a friendly shout, and Fuller, his arms loaded with supplies, nodded back, quickly deposited the goods in the back of the wagon, and went over and shook hands. All of this was friendly and without rancor until two other men, both wearing wide-brimmed hats, stopped near the group. One of them leaned over the walk and spat disgustedly near the hooves of the ponies. Fred Gerard was mounting his horse near the head of the wagon team when one of the two new arrivals called up, "Hey, partner, those squaws belong to you, or are you taking them back to the reservation?"

Gerard simply waved him off, saying, "Neither, friend, and why you asking?"

"I reckon you ain't been in town long, eh?" the man replied, taking a hitch at his suspenders. "Big ruckus with redskins east of here, massacred a lotta our boys over there. Got the people all riled up in these parts." Nodding at Benjamin One Feather and the women, he said, "If they ain't belonging to you, then you'd best be telling them not to hang around here too long. Y'see, Injuns have worn out their welcome here. Latch string is closed. They'd be asking for trouble."

Gerard threw back his head and laughed. "Massacre, is it? Is that what you're hearing?"

"That's the nut of it," the man said. "Ask any of these boys, they'll tell you."

A few grumbles came from the small gathering before Gerard, his smile now fading, glowered back at the man. "Listen, this man here is Henry Fuller. Some of you know him. Now me and Henry just came back from the little to-do you're gabbling about. Any of *you* there? Hell, no. And listen, wasn't no massacre at all. We got whipped, whipped damn good. That's the true nut of it." Staring at the stranger, he added, "And if you want to tell these friends of mine to keep moving, do it yourself. Tell it to that young feller over there, he speaks your lingo, and a damn sight better than you." Reining his horse, he motioned toward Benjamin One Feather, who had already handed the reins of his pony up to White Crane. Bristling inside, he quickly stepped up in front of the man talking with Fred Gerard.

"We came here to buy supplies," Benjamin told him. The drover's companion cautiously stepped to the back, out of the way. "Is there a law against this? We're not causing any trouble, mister. It's arrogant men like you with big mouths, ei, agitating others, who bring the trouble. Now we have what we need and we're leaving, but let me tell you, no one is making us leave. Is that clear?"

The man's face turned red and for a moment he was speechless, stunned by this curt reprimand, and from an Indian, no less. But certainly this young buck wasn't *all* Indian, not with such a quick tongue as that. A few of the people nearby laughed uneasily, one saying, "By God, that's telling him, son." But everyone was moving to the side, stepping into the dust of the street.

Urging his horse forward, Henry Fuller intervened, saying, "Come on, Benjamin, you had your say, now let's be moving out. I reckon this ol' boy understands right well, now. He's not looking for trouble, either."

Recovering, the man finally said, "I'm not ignorant, boy, and what I'm saying is the truth. I don't know where you come from, talking up big like this to whites, but you better do like the man says, get on your horse and move out. You're all the same, cut right outta the same cloth."

Benjamin One Feather, to everyone's surprise, suddenly laughed and shook his head disbelievingly. "Mister, I come from over the mountains there, but I own half of this boardwalk you're standing on. And you're telling me and my people to move out? What a joke!"

"Benjamin!" a voice suddenly called out. "Hey there, Mr. Benjamin, what's the trouble?" It was Lucas Hamm's voice. The storekeeper had suddenly appeared in the doorway, and he was holding a shotgun. Staring angrily at the group, he yelled, "What the hell are you gawking at, all standing around like a bunch of dumb chickens? All of you go on, get along and mind your business, before I dust some of your feathers. Don't be bothering these people. Go on, get! They're customers of mine, friends."

"Injuns?" exclaimed the lone man left on the walk. He suddenly had been isolated, his friend gone and the onlookers all now moving away. "These Injuns are your friends?"

Benjamin One Feather called over, "No trouble, Lucas." He leaped into his saddle and smiled at White Crane and Two Shell Woman, looking on in horror at the encounter. Neither woman had understood a word, but they knew anger when they saw it. And the shotgun that Lucas Hamm was brandishing! James Goodhart, elbows on his knees, his chin cupped in the hands that held the reins of the wagon, had a big grin on his face. To Little Blue Hoop, this was crazy. Her man seemed to be *enjoying* the boardwalk altercation.

Benjamin finally smiled down at the stranger below him. He said, "You have a pistol, I see. This is good, my friend, and I'll tell you why. If you ever again suggest that I or any of my friends get out of here, be prepared to use it. Ei, be prepared to use it for the last time." He turned away and moved alongside the wagon team.

Henry Fuller, to the other side, chuckled. He slipped his rifle back into its scabbard and gave Benjamin a wink. "You're a tad touchy, eh?"

"Ei," grinned Benjamin. "I allow if this were your Shoshoni woman, she would have trimmed his balls."

"Damn right!" exclaimed Fuller. "And maybe a little more to boot." He cackled shrilly, kicked his horse in the flanks, and with a tremendous war whoop went galloping off down the dusty street.

Back at the storefront, Lucas Hamm had set aside his shotgun. He was now throwing out his arms in frustration, berating the drover. "Why is it that almost every time one of Ben Tree's family of Indians comes to shop with good hard cash, some fool always has to open his big mouth?"

"Ben Tree? *The* Ben Tree, that one?"

"Yes, that one," huffed Hamm, turning back to the door. He cursed over his shoulder, "You're goddamned lucky you didn't get your crazy head blown off. That boy is his number one son."

When Claybourn Moore learned that James and Little Blue Hoop had come to stay permanently, both he and his wife Ruth were delighted. This solved some vexing problems for the ranch foreman, who, with more fencing, herd-counting, and irrigation work at hand, and first-cutting hay coming in, needed additional help. This also took care of another matter, for Moore no longer needed Benjamin to spell him for a month or so during the cattle drive down to the Ogden rail head in the fall. Perhaps more enthusiastic about the new arrivals than anyone was

Ruth, who now had the companionship of another woman, and one who spoke English. Even though Little Blue Hoop and James were planning to stay temporarily at the new line cabin by the hot springs, Ben Tree had sent orders to Clay Moore to hire some carpenters to build another house on the lower land next to Six Mile Creek. He wanted it finished by late summer, or at least by fall when the long months began. This would enable Ruth and Little Blue Hoop to be closer to one another.

A little disappointment finally crept into all of this excitement when Ruth was told that Two Shell Woman was going home, that she was making the trip west with the two old mountain men. Ruth Moore had both love and respect for the young Nez Percé who had so capably taken charge that night only a little less than three months past and had delivered her son, Joshua. Of course Two Shell Woman, upon arriving at the ranch, immediately went in to see the baby, and was pleased to find her small twig of snowberry still attached to the cradle. She spoke a few words to Little Blue Hoop, who translated for Ruth. Did the snowberry keep the ghosts away? Ruth, smiling at Two Shell Woman, nodded and motioned with her hands. Yes, far, far away.

Later that night, Claybourn Moore was not surprised when Benjamin related the story about the incident in front of Lucas Hamm's store. Understandable, he commented. The Custer affair had caused a lot of animosity around the valley, even down at Bannack and Virginia City where a group of volunteers had organized, even to the point of offering their services to Fort Ellis to fight Indians. By now any Indian in the area was suspect, because the people allowed that all of them were alike. No distinctions were being made. And Benjamin had to smile at that deduction. It had a familiar ring for Indians believed that whites were all one and the same. At least that was certainly the case in his own village, with only a few exceptions. He realized that there was no common ground in this inevitable clash of red and white cultures, no thought of trying to understand one another, no time for such nonsense. The white man's mind was committed to his livelihood, to survival, and there was precious little time over in his head for thoughts about the welfare of others.

They were sitting together at the big round table after supper, alone, the women in the kitchen, James, Fuller, and Gerard in the bunkhouse playing cards with the drovers, Robert Pette and Willie Left Hand, the Salish breed. Claybourn Moore, as if reading Benjamin's mind, finally said, "I know how you feel, Benjamin, it's a festering thing, just like a damned boil. But, as much as I hate to say it, the man was telling you the gospel. Until this Custer affair blows over, it's just not all that safe in this town. You have the women to think about, you know, although we both know you can handle yourself."

Benjamin gave Claybourn Moore a wan smile. Clay was no longer the lanky young man with the flapping duster, he was a foreman, and without a doubt one of the best, riding herd over thousands of acres. His words were good, too. Benjamin agreed with him, but only partially. He said, "It's not what he said but how he said it—trying to rile the others, find some stupid sheep to follow him. He's an Indian-hater. Sure, it's not safe out there with men like that running around. But is ignorance an excuse?"

"A lot of these folks have long memories," Moore said. "And there's two sides to this, as you well know. Not so much the Crow or Nez Percé, your people, but some of the others played billy-hell with wagons, homesteaders, and the like, and anything like this Custer thing always adds a little more fuel to the fire. Around town it gives them more to talk about, gets them stirred up. It's like poking a stick in an ant hole."

"Ei, but these folks always seem to forget who broke the treaties, even the bad treaties," Benjamin replied. And then he thoughtfully added, "But was there ever a good treaty?"

Moore laughed. "Was there ever a good Indian?"

Benjamin One Feather grinned back. "Only dead."

They were silent for a while, fingering their coffee cups, each man lost in his own thoughts, both present and past. Finally Claybourn Moore said, "Do you remember the first time we were here? Nothing but old man Coonrad's cabin and the horse shed, not a head of cattle on the place. I reckon you were about this high." He extended his hand out above the table.

"A bit taller, maybe. I think I was about thirteen or thereabouts. Never kept track too much in the village."

"Well," Moore went on, "you wore a hat, boots, pair of pants, and a buckskin jacket."

Nodding, Benjamin said, "Going on a big trip down to Virginia City, Fort Hall, all the big towns. Ei, civilization!"

"You sorta looked like a white boy with a good tan," Moore said. "Nice-looking chap. Quite a talker then, too."

"I remember those floppy pants," Benjamin recalled, smiling. "A good wind would have blown me away like a tumbleweed."

Pausing, Moore took a sip of his coffee. "Well, I was thinking. . . . When you go waltzing through town, why don't you get rid of that headband, those mocs, and dud out like you used to? That just might turn the trick and keep some of these rednecks off your ass. Hell, your pa dresses that way most of the time, and no one pays him any mind."

This morsel of friendly advice tickled Benjamin. Leaning back in his chair he chuckled, then swiftly drew up a finger and pointed it at Claybourn Moore. "Pow!" he went. "Now, *that's* the reason they pay my father no mind, Clay. Makes good sense doesn't it? My father can dress any way he damn well chooses. All he has to do is introduce himself. I've seen it more than once. He walks slowly up, big shoulders, barely smiles, looks right through you with those flinty eyes. 'My name is Ben Tree.' How-de-do and good-bye! That's it. Oh, he's taught White Moon and me a few things, like proper riding and shooting a sidearm, and he's given us advice on manners, even women. But I'm not my father, never will be the man he is, so I have to learn, do things my own way. Maybe I've inherited his philosophy, that's all."

"Just a suggestion," sighed Moore.

Benjamin grinned and pretended to holster his finger. "A good one, though, and I'll remember it. Ei, be a white man when necessary."

The next morning Benjamin One Feather was up early, cutting out a sturdy little mare and an extra pack pony for Two Shell Woman, further fulfilling his vow not to send her home destitute. Three of the four horses that she had taken from the wolfers were still back in the village, so he allowed that this gesture was only proper and fair. Within a short time all the ponies were saddled and packed, Fred Gerard and Henry Fuller chomping at their own bits to get under way. "Take care of the little woman," Benjamin admonished, and they both laughed. More likely it would be the other way around. She knew her direction. Another round of sad smiles and farewells took place, tears among the women, and with one last shout Henry Fuller, in the lead, turned west toward the Big Hole Valley. From there it was over the Bitterroots, through another pass, and on to the Salmon and Snake rivers.

Watching them leave, White Crane sadly rested her head against Benjamin's shoulder. Benjamin One Feather consoled his wife. The Tahmonmah was the land of his Nez Percé mother, Rainbow, and she still had relatives there. Perhaps one day he would go and seek out these people and take White Crane with him. Time and again trails cross, people are reunited. White Crane thought this was good, and she managed a smile when he predicted that they would see this woman again. So, with this last farewell out of the way, they turned away and began to pack their own ponies. They had decided to accompany James and Little Blue Hoop up to the line cabin and spend their final night there, then cut over the hills the next day to meet Sitting Elk, Old Dog Jumps, and Stone Calf on the pass.

With the loaded buckboard, the trip up to the hot springs took almost two hours, but once there it took only a few minutes to unpack and get James and Little Blue Hoop settled into their temporary quarters. The cabin, sturdy but small, had two bunks, an iron cooking stove, one cupboard, and a table and two chairs, sparse but adequate for the short time the two were going to use it. Surveying the scene outside from the plank doorway, Benjamin told James that his father had had several things in mind when he'd had the cabin built. It was a good location to supervise the upper range, was only a short ride to some of the long cattle sheds that he had set up in the nearby bottom, and in inclement weather it was a refuge, a dodge against sudden winter storms, the dreaded "whiteouts." In fair weather, it was an enjoyable place to bathe. The hot water steamed out from two giant crevices, bubbled into a deep, rock-lined pool, and finally cooled in a meandering brook below, where cattle and game came to drink.

Beyond the rocky outcropping of the springs, the land to the north swelled up into a series of broken meadows rimmed with pine and fir, behind which stood the high peaks guarding the upper Yellowstone and its headwaters. Benjamin One Feather pointed northeast toward the lower hills, which would be their direction in the morning. They would circle around into Bear Canyon, at the bottom of which he and White Crane would strike the trail leading to the pass and ultimately a rendezvous with their brothers. White Crane was happy to know this, that they were not going back through Bozeman City where the crazies made bad faces that caused her man to puff up like a prairie chicken.

By noon the following day, Benjamin and his wife had bottomed out in Bear Canyon and were preparing to follow the trail east up the distant pass. At this juncture he stopped and pointed to the damp ground near the creek bed, where only recently the grass had been trampled by hooves. Many animals had passed here. To the side was one set of wagon tracks, and he explained to White Crane that a large party with cattle and horses was somewhere up ahead; how far, he could only guess. Many hours at least. He thought it strange, but these tracks must have been made during the night. Rather than trail behind these unknown people they crossed the ruts, cutting up to the higher ground above the granite cliffs that overlooked the main trail. Up there the visibility was almost unlimited, the crude road far below only occasionally obstructed by towering pines or a winding bend around one of the steep hillsides. This was the high route, unsuitable for wagons but frequently used by Man Called Tree, who often reminded Benjamin that, when riding alone, it was much better to see the reality below than to chance the unknown above. But now, even from this high eagle's perch, Benjamin One Feather saw nothing of the wagon or cattle, and he had no way of determining who these people were or where they were headed.

White Crane, sensing his concern, asked, "Does this trouble you, my man?"

"No, only confuses me," he answered. "Where did this stock come from, and where is it headed?"

"Maybe to that fort where Hock-kett came from," she said, nodding to the north.

"Maginnis?" Benjamin One Feather shook his head doubtfully. "That's five, maybe six days from here. It's possible, but more likely they're going to one of those new spreads, ei, up in the valley of the Crazy Mountains. Wrong time of the year to be moving cattle for market. Back there, did you see? Some of those cows have calves with them, those smaller tracks all over the place." Perplexed, he shrugged, concluding, "Well, these people didn't buy them from us. Could have bought them at Stuart's place, or—"

"—stolen them," White Crane interjected, anticipating her man's next conjecture.

Benjamin shot her a quick look. With a wry smile he said, "Ei, you have a suspicious mind, woman, but that's something we may never know. I have the vision of Spotted Hawk, but even I can't see over that mountain. These men are too far ahead of us, maybe to the big river by now. We'll not see them this day."

This conclusion made White Crane happy. "This is good, Benjamin One Feather," she said, watching him from the side. "I had a fear of meeting them, more angry talk. Next time you should pretend you don't understand what they say, the way you do sometimes with those pony soldiers. Everytime you make the white man's talk, there is trouble. This is bad. Sometimes it's not a joke, eh?"

"These days they're angry with anyone, even themselves. When their army loses a battle everyone gets blamed, their leaders, our people. And their anger blinds them. Like a shedding snake, they strike out at anything."

"If you lost many of your people you would be plenty angry, too," she reminded him. "Ei, I know you, Benjamin One Feather. You would go to the Foxes, even the Muddy Hands or Lumpwoods, all of them, to make a big war party, that's what you would do."

"No," he said with a smile. "No, I would ask you first."

"*Eeyah,* what a liar!"

They rode on, up over the rolling hills to the right side of the trail, finally reaching the long saddle where the ruts in the distance slipped downward toward the far valley of the Yellowstone. They saw no sign of Sitting Elk, Old Dog Jumps, and Stone Calf. Moving slowly through a series of small draws, they finally approached a grove of pine and juniper, and here they came upon a profusion of tracks again. The cattle had come down through here. As Benjamin searched out the trail below he heard a shout, saw someone hailing him from the trees. It was Old Dog Jumps. Waving back, Benjamin One Feather clucked his pony ahead, White Crane and the pack horse trotting behind. When they reined up in front of Old Dog Jumps, he angrily gestured around. The small campsite was nothing but a shambles, the lodgepoles of their wickiup strewn about, hides scattered in disarray, and ashes everywhere. To the side, in the shade of a pine, stood Stone Calf, guarding over Sitting Elk who had been wounded. Benjamin One Feather saw that his brothers had no ponies or pack animals around.

White Crane leaped from her pony and rushed over to Sitting Elk. One eye was swollen shut from a blow to the side of his head. When she lifted the makeshift bandage she discovered that the deep gash across his cheekbone fortunately had already clotted under a thick matting of chipmunk tail, or what Man Called Tree always identified as "yarrow." With a wan smile, Sitting Elk told her that he was all right, only stunned when the white man rider had hit him with a rifle butt. This scar, he said, would now match the one on the other side left there by the Pekony that they had fought long ago in the river bottom.

It took some time to piece the story together, both Old Dog Jumps and Stone Calf talking, each relating his version or complementing the tale of the other. They had been in their camp eating, waiting for Benjamin and White Crane, shortly before Masaka was at his highest point. One white stranger came riding in and greeted them, making good sign and asking them if they wanted to take cows up to a place in the Crazy Mountains. He offered to pay one dollar each and give them food and plenty whiskey. Old Dog Jumps laughed at this. He told the man that one dollar was such a small amount for so much work. When Old Dog Jumps laughed a second time after an offer of two dollars, the white man became angry and rode away. But soon afterward he returned with another man, this time riding hard.

These men were yelling, swinging their rifles, and right behind them were many cows charging down the hill. At first the Crow believed the white men were making a joke, shouting and running the cows in such a crazy manner, but when part of the herd suddenly veered toward the camp, they realized that they were being overrun on purpose. By the time they had recovered, the drovers and their cattle were upon them and two more men were coming up from behind, one riding in a wagon, madly flailing his team of horses. There was much shooting, the Absaroke braves scrambling for cover, trying to avoid both bullets and flying hooves. Only Old Dog Jumps was able to retrieve his rifle, but his horse pounded away in the rush of cattle. He fired several shots at the wagon driver without success. Later, farther down the hill, he found a dead cow. "What made these crazies do such a thing?" he asked Benjamin One Feather. "They tried to kill us."

Benjamin's face was dark with anger. "Bigots, that's all, and they wanted you to do the rest of their dirty work. When someone below picks up those tracks, they'll come following, eh? Those cows were probably rustled, stolen. A good trick: They get you to take them the rest of the way, and if you get caught, you hang, not them. If you make it, all the better. They come later and get their share of the profit, and all you get is a lousy two dollars and bad whiskey." Benjamin spat on the ground in disgust.

Stone Calf spoke up. "Then we shall wait until these other men come, tell them what happened."

Benjamin One Feather waved a finger. "No, that could be another day, maybe even two or three days, who knows? We can't sit here that long, not now. We need your ponies, guns."

"Go back and tell some people in Bozeman City," suggested White Crane. "We can wait by that place called Bear Canyon."

"Go back to your friends?" smiled Benjamin One Feather sarcastically. He turned away and squatted in front of Sitting Elk, asked him if he could ride. His brother, laughing, jumped to his feet and clenched both fists. He was ready to go anytime. This was good. Benjamin One Feather then advised them that he would carry the pipe, that if they were willing to follow him and fight, they would get their horses and rifles back. Without discussion, they agreed. Then Benjamin One Feather carefully explained what they must do.

First they had to follow the drovers, this the easiest task. By nightfall these herders would stop somewhere to camp, he told them, a place near water, one where the cattle could feed and the men could hide and protect themselves. He believed that place probably would be where the Yellowstone came down from the south and the valley of the Crazy Mountains opened to the north. It was highly unlikely the cattle would be pushed another night. They were too tired and so were the men, and when men get tired, they often become careless.

"We have no weapons," said Stone Calf with a helpless shrug. "Only Old Dog Jumps has his rifle."

Benjamin One Feather pointed to his pony. "You'll have my rifle, brother, the one that shoots sixteen times, ei? In the pack is a shotgun. It shoots two times. That will be Sitting Elk's weapon." Patting his hip where his revolver was holstered, he said, "This will be all I need." He motioned around the broken camp. With only one pack pony, there was nothing here that could be taken, not even the great grizzly hide the three braves had brought down from the mountains. So they left, riding double, Sitting Elk in the rear by himself, astraddle White Crane's pack horse. There was no argument, only determined silence.

Out of necessity they rode slowly, but then they had no reason to hurry, for everyone knew that by the time Masaka had hidden his face they would catch up with the four men. And ultimately they did, almost precisely where their leader had said they might, two miles up the Crazy Mountains' valley, north of the Yellowstone crossing. A distant fire in the bottom glimmered, flicked on and off like a beacon, and the faint bawl of a calf was more than enough to convince the Crow that this was their target. Benjamin One Feather told White Crane that he was sending her back to the main river with the ponies, told her to hide in the cottonwoods and to come out only when called. She grasped his arm, held tightly, gave him one anxious look, and dutifully disappeared down the moonlit path.

It was almost five minutes before the young men finally managed to thread their way through the brush to a point where they could actually count heads. Flattened out, they bellied up close enough to hear voices around the campfire, discovered that only one of four herders was standing and he was in the darkness near a tree, a rifle resting in his folded arms.

Benjamin One Feather was astounded. In the face of imminent danger, these men were foolishly unprepared, almost oblivious to how vulnerable they were. Here they were, huddling around the fire like sitting ducks, drinking coffee from their big tin cups. Obviously they were not concerned about being followed this soon by the owners of the cattle, and Benjamin definitely had made up his mind that this was rustled stock. Benjamin's second surprise was his recognition of one of the men at the fireside. It was the ornery drover with whom he had quarreled in front of Lucas Hamm's mercantile.

After motioning his brothers back, Benjamin told them that it was unlikely the drovers would surrender to Indians, but he was going to make one honest attempt to call them out. He ordered each of his men to take a position on opposite sides of the camp, allowing them five minutes to get settled. As soon as he began to speak from his own hiding place, they were to fix their sights on the nearest target and be prepared to fire. Make your moccasins ready, he ordered with a grim smile, and they all nodded and crept stealthily away.

Time went by, always an eternity in crucial situations, each brave awaiting the sound of Benjamin One Feather's voice. It finally came. Without stirring from his place in the darkness, Benjamin spoke out loudly: "You there, you in the camp, we have you surrounded. Stand up by the fire clear of your rifles. You only have one—"

That was as far as he got with his warning. One of the men shouted, "Bullshit! Hit the dust!" Bodies flew in all directions, simultaneously with the barrage of erupting gunfire. Two of the drovers toppled, another went to his knees, turned, and shot back into the shadows, but a thunderous roar from Sitting Elk's shotgun blew out the back of his head. Rolling across the clearing, a fourth man scrambled into the shadows, making directly for the picketed horses, already rearing in panic at the deafening outburst. Benjamin, ducking around to the other side, leaped several logs and intercepted him just as he was grabbing a halter. One shot in the shoulder flattened the drover and his rifle flew through the air. He came down hard on his back, then rose up only to find himself staring into the face of Benjamin One Feather.

"It's you!" the man cried out, struggling to regain his feet. "I told 'em, Injun boy, I told 'em, you rascals is all the same."

Benjamin One Feather lashed out with his foot, pressing the drover back to the ground. "Ei, that you did, mister," he whispered. "That was your first mistake. Your second was on that hill back there, bringing dishonor to my brothers. You don't get a third." He pointed his revolver at the man's head and pulled the trigger.

Early the next morning, the Absaroke men and White Crane broke their impromptu camp by the river and went back to the drovers' camp to retrieve their ponies and weapons. They had little trouble finding the rifles and personal belongings that had disappeared when the hillside fracas took place. But catching up with the horses was a different matter, as some of them were almost two miles down the valley, feeding in the bottom with the spooked cattle. It was almost midday by the time the Crow had everything secured and packed, including all the confiscated supplies, and this time-consuming delay brought about another confrontation, this one entirely unexpected.

On the point, heading back, Old Dog Jumps suddenly whirled about and galloped back to the others, calling out that riders were coming, only a short distance from the river crossing. Since there was no time for consultation, Benjamin One Feather simply motioned everyone to take cover in the cottonwoods, but to ready their weapons. He unsheathed his own rifle, steadied his pony, and waited. A few minutes later the mounted men appeared, a group of seven. They almost rode over Benjamin before they noticed him. As they pulled up in a knot of heaving and snorting horses, one of the men was shouting,

"Whoa, goddammit, whoa!" Benjamin One Feather heard another exclaim, "Well, dammit all, Mr. Benjamin, what you doing down here? Where's your woman?"

When the horses had settled and Benjamin finally got a steady look, he immediately recognized Willie Left Hand, one of the Tree ranch drovers. The other two beside him he had never seen before, but one rather burly one with a drooping mustache was wearing a badge on his vest. "Hello, Willie," said Benjamin. "I suppose I could ask you the same, but I know you don't have a woman." Nodding to the other two men, he said, "I'm not alone." He raised his hand high, and White Crane and the three braves suddenly materialized from the trees.

Willie Left Hand quickly introduced the two men in front, the constable at Bozeman City, Bill Duggan, and Edwin Stuart, the son of Ben Tree's neighboring rancher, Adam Stuart. Constable Duggan told Benjamin that they were looking for stolen cattle, more particularly the rustlers who had taken them. Willie Left Hand then explained his own presence, to the astonishment of Benjamin: Some of the missing cattle belonged to Ben Tree. Somewhat sheepishly, Benjamin One Feather said no one had noticed any brands, but as far as the missing cows went, well, they were up the valley about two miles. Bill Duggan inquired about the men who had rustled them; how many there were, and if they were camped nearby.

"They're up there, four of them, all white men," Benjamin replied. "Horse thieves, too; stole my brothers' ponies yesterday morning." He gestured to the silent Absaroke to either side of the trail. "Ei, but we got them back last night. Heading home now, down the river."

"Trouble?" asked Duggan, sizing up Sitting Elk, who had been fitted out with a new bandage only that morning by White Crane. "Are those boys holed up down there, aiming to fight?"

"No trouble, now," answered Benjamin with a little grin. "They're all dead, Mr. Duggan. Saved you the trouble of hanging them."

All of the men shared incredulous stares, then looked at Benjamin One Feather. Duggan finally said, "Dead? All of them dead?"

"Ei, stone-dead," returned Benjamin. "We took their

horses and guns, figured it was a fair trade after what they did to us yesterday. Anyhow, they sure won't be needing them. Oh yes, they didn't want to talk with us last night. My brothers can tell you this. They tried to make a fight. Ei, it was a short one. That's it, go see for yourself."

Bill Duggan, exhausted, exasperated, heaved a great sigh, then shrugged. "What the hell, boys, let's go take a look and get your goddamned critters back."

"Anything more you want to know?"

Maneuvering his horse, Bill Duggan testily replied, "Hell, no, looks like you've gone and done it all. What more is there to know?"

Benjamin One Feather reined to the side, out of his way. "I'm sure glad you showed up. I hated the thought of riding back to explain all of this. The whites back there might not understand, especially about those cattle thieves being shot up. They just might have sided with them, for all I know. Lot of ill will in the country right now."

"Hogwash!" huffed Duggan. "Those boys done wrong, and you're Ben Tree's son, aren't you? His word is as good as gold in town. You know that."

Benjamin One Feather agreed, but with one reservation. "Ei, you may be right, Mr. Duggan, but if this had been one of my brothers over there trying to explain, his word wouldn't have been worth a shit to some of those troublemakers." With a sign of peace, he clucked his pony ahead. "Good hunting, men. Good-bye, Willie. You tell Mr. Clay to put James to work. Night-riding might be a good idea."

TWELVE

By the Moon of the Red Cherries, activity along the Yellowstone section of the Bozeman Trail was intensifying. Benjamin One Feather and his scouting companions sighted men and wagons, both civilian and military, almost on a weekly basis. Word also came regularly up the moccasin trail. The white man's army leaders, angered and humiliated by the Custer debacle, were sending in reinforcements and new commands, even building another fort on the lower Yellowstone at the Tongue River landing. But despite all of this activity, the far-ranging Crow scouts saw no more great concentrations of hostiles in the Big Horns. The Sioux and Cheyenne, after their victorious battles in the Greasy Grass, had wisely disbanded, scattering across the mountain and prairie land in smaller groups, some engaged in making meat, a few others skirmishing with the bluecoat patrols whenever they chanced to meet. The Indians were now playing a hit-and-run game, taking extreme delight in harassing these small, more vulnerable columns, decoying them into fruitless chases or sometimes boldly stealing their supplies and ponies.

These were among the stories from the moccasin trail. What Benjamin One Feather and his brothers were unable to see on their occasional scouting forays, they always heard from their neighboring Crow or passing friends, the Shoshoni. The whites were boiling up a retaliatory pot for the hostiles, even planning a winter campaign from the new fort, one they already had named Keogh in honor of a pony soldier killed in the Little Big Horn.

On one occasion, two officers had even come to Man Called Tree's village seeking additional scouting help for the renewed campaign, only to find out that the Absaroke breed chief was camping in the mountains below Nahpit-sei, enjoying the wilderness peace with several subchiefs of the tribe. One of these visitors, Lt. James Bradley, who had commanded Colonel Gibbon's Indian scouts, remembered Benjamin One Feather from a chance meeting on the Yellowstone in late spring. He knew that this was the same brave who had critically tested Gibbon's mettle with an exchange of rhetoric and knowledge. However, he asked Benjamin to speak and translate for him.

Of course Lieutenant Bradley's mention of Gibbon, the One Who Limps, immediately brought a few sour looks from the Crow circled around to listen to him. But the officer laughed loudly when several of the men held their noses after he had referred to Gibbon a second time as "Red Nose." Seeing him laugh this way at one of his own leaders eased some of the tension, and the Crow thought this bluecoat might not be such a bad sort after all. He reminded them somewhat of Hockett, their recently departed guest. And when he spoke unfavorably about Custer, a man hated by all Indians, everyone around the circle grimly nodded in accord.

Though Bradley showed little sympathy for the man everyone called General Yellow Hair (Custer actually was a colonel, only breveted to major general during the Civil War), he said that scouting information supplied by Benjamin's Crow brothers downriver had been invaluable, despite the Seventh Cavalry's annihilation. Quite simply, Custer had ignored most of the intelligence reports and was solely responsible for the demise of two hundred thirty-one of his troops and a few Crow warriors from Plenty Coups' camp. Of course this made little sense to Absaroke, risking life and limb to get such good intelligence on the hostiles, only to discard it like seeds in the prairie winds. The Greasy Grass battle, explained Bradley, had been a tactical blunder resulting in an ignominious defeat, one not likely to be repeated.

After hearing Benjamin One Feather's translation of this, Chief Shoots Far Arrow, Benjamin's father-in-law, told Bradley that in Crow society there was no room for defeat, that defeat was tantamount to disaster. All of this bad medicine across the mountains had been foreseen, and who but a fool would be a part of it? Man Called Tree's people were not *irise,* dumb. If the Lakota and Cheyenne had broken the treaty by making war, so had the great Indian Commissioner by disallowing use of the unceded lands across the great prairie. This was contrary to written law signed by all the tribes. This was even bad for the Crow, who often made their camps along the rivers and creeks in unceded territory. The Crow had used these great lands ever since Akbatatdia, the Maker of Everything, had created them. Why should Man Called Tree's men help this contrary commissioner who was making such bad medicine for everyone?

This brought a series of acknowledging grunts from those around the circle, and ultimately Bradley left, realizing that he had been wasting his words on friendly enemies. True, these people disliked the Sioux and Cheyenne, but while they held no personal grudge against him, they certainly mistrusted the words of his leaders, and understandably so.

And there were other incidents in the country of the Echeta Casha, some alarmingly close to the village, indicative of the changes that were now taking place. Several days after the departure of Lieutenant Bradley, Benjamin One Feather, White Moon, and Red Running Horse were riding above the hill overlooking the burned-out site of John Goodhart's trading post. Activity below them had caught their attention long before they emerged from the cover of the trees, so they dismounted well out of sight, crept close, and flattened themselves in the tall meadow grass. These were bluecoats below, at least twenty men, some standing guard near two wagons while a few others were waving back and forth from behind a tripod.

After Benjamin One Feather had watched for a while, he passed his binoculars to his brothers, who each took a turn. The soldiers were marking the land, that much was obvious, but for what reason, and why so far west from their new fort far down the river? After another few minutes the three Crow retrieved their ponies and rode over the crest of the hill, where they stopped several hundred yards above the surveying party. It took another few minutes before someone down below noticed the mounted Indians silently observing them. A shout immediately went up, and the startled troopers, grabbing their weapons, began to take up positions behind the wagons. Only then did Benjamin One Feather move forward.

With one arm to his side crooked upward, Benjamin gentled his pony slowly down the slope, with White Moon and Red Running Horse close behind. The heads of the troopers behind the wagon boxes began to pop up and down like wary turkeys, searching the perimeters for signs of more feathers. Finally one of the men came forward and returned Benjamin's greeting. He shouted a hello, then turned and called out, "Jenkins, get up here on the double! Find out who these fellows are, what they want."

An older trooper with long, graying sideburns and a full, speckled moustache, came ambling forward and stationed himself next to the officer. When the three Crow stopped a short distance away, he began to make sign, bringing a smile to Benjamin One Feather's face. This older man, his baggy trousers held up by stained suspenders, sweat hugging his soiled undershirt, had traveled many trails. He was very good with his hands, almost as adept as an Indian. "This man is my leader," Jenkins signed. "He wants to know what you're doing here. Who are you?"

Benjamin One Feather flashed back sign, finally glanced over to White Moon and Red Running Horse, and winked. Jenkins relayed this reply to the officer. "These men are Crow, sir, from up the river. They want to know the same—what are we doing here?"

"Curious, eh?" the trooper said.

"Most Injuns are, sir, and according to the map, we're sitting here right on the edge of their stomping grounds."

The officer scrutinized the three Absaroke for a moment: an impressive trio, formidable-looking in their leather headbands, buckskin vests, bare arms, and fringed leggings, and well-armed, all with repeating rifles; one man, the spokesman, even carried a pistol at his side. He finally said aside to Jenkins, "Two of them look like they have some white blood in them. You notice this?"

"Never pay much attention to it, sir, not anymore," Jenkins answered. "Trappers, drummers, whatnot, all been through here at one time or another. Who knows?"

"Well," the officer concluded, "tell them we're planning to run a better trail up here from Fort Keogh, make it easier for everyone to get back and forth with wagons, maybe put a telegraph station here by the river."

This was all fully taken in by Benjamin One Feather and White Moon, but Red Running Horse, who knew the game of pretense his two brothers often played, had to follow the sign of the trooper, Jenkins. And when the translation was completed, he was the only one who said, "Ahh."

Benjamin One Feather suddenly began to make sign again, stopping once to motion toward the small remaining cabin, the one James and Little Blue Hoop had shared for several months. Pointing to a large mound above the charred site of the main cabin, Benjamin made more sign.

Jenkins, nodding his head, finally emitted a low whistle. "This buck says we're on a homestead, a big one, more than five hundred acres. Man that owned it got killed by hostiles. So did some of our boys. They're buried over there in that hill. He wants to know why the people from the fort never came to claim their bodies."

"The hell you say!" the officer exclaimed. "My map shows no homestead, and where did the men come from? The ones he says are buried over there?" He stared curiously at the mound, now sprouting new grass all around the freshly turned earth.

Smiling, Benjamin One Feather finally spoke out in English. "They came from Fort Maginnis. Why don't you people reclaim your dead, bury them with honor?"

"Well, I declare," the trooper said, "you speak English! Why didn't you say so? Here we are, all carrying on, flipping fingers and hands, and you come out talking like you been at it all your life."

"We have," White Moon put in drolly. "We like to know who we're talking to, that's all. And what my brother says is true. This land you're on belongs to our brother-in-law, James Goodhart. Three homesteads were laid out here two years ago, papers filed in Virginia City."

"There's no indication—" began the officer.

But White Moon went right on, ignoring the trooper's attempt to explain. "My sister plans on coming back here one of these days," he said. "And she's a very mean woman sometimes. If she found a way station here, I think she would burn it down just like the hostiles burned the post. Ei, and there is her mother-in-law, too; Molly, they call her. She's as big as a mule and even meaner. She wants to put her garden back in, right over there. She's half-Absaroke and has a big shotgun. Boom, boom! Two shots, ei, makes plenty big holes. She says she wants those pony soldiers taken away from the ground by her garden. Bad medicine to have white ghosts around this place stealing her onions. She says they come out at night and make big moans, maybe hungry because they were buried without food, nothing to eat on their trip up the Great Hanging Road. You understand?"

Jenkins, who had stepped aside, had a wide grin on his grizzled face. The officer, overwhelmed by White Moon's rambling declaration, was momentarily speechless. It was Jenkins who recovered first. "Well, sir, seems like these boys know whose blanket was spread here first. I'll just mosey on back. Don't reckon you'll be needing any more sign today, leastways not from me."

"Soldiers killed . . . ghosts . . . mother-in-laws," muttered the puzzled trooper. "What's this all about?" He directly introduced himself. His name was Timothy Aubrey, a lieutenant; not a regular trooper, but an engineer and mapmaker. He was both apologetic and polite, offering coffee and biscuits to the three Crow, anything to get a straight, coherent explanation. They accepted, and Benjamin One Feather told him the history of Manuel's post, all about the recent raid by the Indians, the stories that he had heard from Man Called Tree, who previously had learned the legends from Jim Bridger. After an hour's visit, Benjamin, White Moon, and Red Running Horse mounted up, preparing to ride out to the east across the Big Horn River. Lieutenant Aubrey, thoroughly enlightened by the informative chat, told them that he would notify the proper authorities about the bodies of the three troopers, but allowed that Lt. Zachary Hockett probably already had done this upon his arrival at Fort Ellis. He also said that he would do his mapping on the other side of the Big Horn, well away from the homestead. He gave the three young men four prairie chickens that his men had shot earlier along the trail.

Departing, White Moon called back, "I forgot to tell you—watch your hair! Plenty of hostiles around."

"But we saw no sign of hostiles. . . ."

"They're like those ghosts!" White Moon shouted. "Mostly, they come around at night. Ahhhoooo!"

Chuckling, White Moon turned back to the others. His older brother was smiling, translating to Red Running Horse what White Moon had just told the army engineer. Red Running Horse simply nodded, finding no humor in this at all. He remembered that cold winter day when he and Hides Alone were with Benjamin One Feather at the Great Medicine Wheel, how he and Hides Alone had expressed some humorous skepticism about those mysterious rocks and the missing scalps of the two wolfers. That had been a grievous mistake, bad medicine. Later, a grinning coyote must have come in the night and pissed on his tipi, for soon afterward his favorite pony went lame; dogs chewed up his hide-skin mittens; a maiden he had been tootling for romance threw a piece of firewood at him, and he had to chew licorice root for a week because of a toothache. Unable to understand this terrible run of misfortune, he had gone for a visitation with the old wise one, Ten Sleeps, who after some meditation had told him that perhaps a ghost guiding the wheel thought ill of him and had invaded his body. Ghosts, Red Running Horse concluded, not varmints, had removed those scalps and taken them away to the Place of the Dead. He spent the better part of a day in the sweat lodge purifying himself. After that, it took him still another day to regain his strength. He knew now that he would not press his luck by laughing at White Moon's foolish remarks.

About an hour later, the three men were trailing along the rise of a long coulee where the sage grew as high as their ponies' bellies, searching for two things: a productive area suitable for their buffalo hunt in another month, and a secure place to camp for the night. Locating herds, predicting their movements across the grassland, had become more difficult because of increased hunting pressure exerted not only by all of the roaming tribes who used this land, but now by soldiers who were being fed buffalo meat. A few white hunters, scattered over the prairie but well within reach of the forts, were beginning to make their appearance. They came with Sharps rifles, powerful enough to slay the blackhorns from long distances. These white men salvaged the horns and hides for sale at the various trading points, and when possible sold the quarters to the army. When the distance to a fort was too great, they simply took the hides and left the carcasses to rot in the field, benefiting only the carrion-eaters.

Benjamin One Feather had heard of this wasteful practice down below the Platte, where the great southern herds roamed all the way into the Texas plains. However, only recently had the hide-hunters made an appearance in the north country. He knew that some of the Lakota tribes were complaining bitterly to the Indian agents about these men with their ponderous wagons and big guns. Man Called Tree told Benjamin that this kind of hunting had been inevitable ever since the railroad came across the North Platte country, and even the steamboats on the great Mother River were now taking back their share of the hides. His father said this was another way the ingenious white man had learned to profit from the land, a lucrative business pure and simple. But like the gold fields it could only endure so long, since Mother Earth's bounty was not boundless.

Benjamin One Feather reluctantly accepted these foreboding words, for Man Called Tree's prophecies were predicated not on high-mountain visions but on intellectual insight and experience accumulated during his many years on the wilderness and frontier trails. Despite this gloomy forecast, Benjamin vowed that if these wanton killers ever appeared in the land of the Absaroke, no *kahe* would be forthcoming from him. He had ideas of his own as to how to welcome them.

Late in the afternoon, under the threatening skies, the three Crow were crossing a small creek when White Moon suddenly pulled up and pointed to the side. There, in the damp grass, were fresh pony tracks, two sets, probably several hours old, coming from the northeast. This was puzzling sign, for one horse was shod, the other one not. The men could only believe that one of the ponies had been a military mount, stolen or taken after a battle.

Benjamin One Feather thought it too late in the day to backtrack far enough to determine where these riders had come from, but the men all agreed that the unknowns most likely were spying on the army surveyors, sizing up the strength of the column. From where they were now, it was only about five miles to the Yellowstone. The passing Indians could not possibly have missed seeing the troopers who were now settled in at the mouth of the Big Horn. Their tracks were now heading back south toward the distant Rosebud Mountains, at least a day's ride away, and Benjamin One Feather guessed that somewhere in that great tumble of creeks and coulees a small village was safely hidden, far from the eyes of the trooper's scouts. Red Running Horse, somewhat hesitantly, suggested that maybe these pony tracks had been made by two of their Crow brothers from Plenty Coups' village, out scouting for the new bluecoats down on the Tongue. This also seemed probable, but failed to answer the question of the shod horse.

White Moon, annoyed by all this speculation, said, "I don't care who these men are. A storm is coming, my butt is tired, and I say we find a camp along this water and spread our robes." Pointing up the creek he added, "They travel away from us, ei? This is good. They are gone. With some chicken in my belly, I can sleep in peace."

Red Running Horse agreed, and directed their attention to a large patch of willows. "We have to go no more than there," he said. "In the morning we can circle to the south and cross the Big Horn up above, come back down the other side of the river. The blackhorns follow the grass. Sometimes the grass over there is very good."

Once again there was consensus. Shortly, they had cleared out all the brush beneath the willows, fashioned a small wickiup in case of rain, and gathered up deadfall for a cooking fire. After picketing the ponies near the edge of the camp, Benjamin One Feather shouldered his rifle, telling the others that he was going to take a walk up the creek, follow the tracks a way. Maybe these men who had ridden through already had cleaned country and were far to the south. On the other hand, if someone had the same idea they had, of making camp for the night, he wanted to know who they were and how close. White Moon's joke about ghosts sneaking up in the night was not all that farfetched out here. White Moon cautioned him: If his older brother was not back by the time Masaka hid behind the dark clouds, his share of the chicken would be gone—and not eaten by ghosts, either. Consenting to make it a short hike, Benjamin One Feather padded away up the creek bottom.

For the better part of a mile he trotted, often leaping hummocks, sometimes a boulder, occasionally detouring around thickets of prickly rose and gooseberry bushes. Once he paused to search the land ahead, thought he detected a wisp of smoke. Uncertain, he slowed to a walk, finally came around a bend where the creek flattened and filtered through a marshy meadow. Beyond this, not more than fifty yards, he saw the source of the smoke: two Indians, one busy at a small fire, apparently cooking, the other resting his head up against a saddle, rifle in his lap.

Benjamin One Feather quickly hunkered, edged up to a clump of sage, and slowly caught his breath. There was little he could determine about the two men, not from his present position, nor could he see any way of skirting them without being seen, given the clearings below the coulees. His binoculars, unfortunately, were back at the makeshift camp, tucked away in his bundle. After several more long looks, he deduced that these men were not Crow. Shoshoni? Not likely, either. They never came this far east this time of year. That left him with Lakota, Cheyenne, or Arapaho, all hostile. From his vantage point two good shots could put them down, and while this thought did cross his mind, he also found himself wondering about the wisdom of it, the sanity of ambushing two human beings for no reason—enemies, true, but men he didn't even know. Perhaps their purpose in being here was no different than his own. And yet again, if the tables were turned, would they hesitate to pull the trigger on him?

Better to count coup by stealing their ponies and setting them afoot, to walk back to their people humiliated and dishonored. If they had been a part of the battles over in the Greasy Grass, they probably had plenty of ponies and new weapons in their village, anyhow. But the sun was sinking behind the dark clouds to his right, his time here almost spent. He smiled to himself at the sudden thought of his younger brother eating his share of the roasted prairie chicken, or pretending to. No, he saw little profit in an adventure here; best to return and tell White Moon and Red Running Horse about these two Indians, even if they posed no immediate threat. A distant rumble of thunder was more of a threat, and if he didn't move soon he knew he was going to get wet.

Just as he was preparing to slide back into the creek gully, he noticed a movement through the willows in back of the men. Their ponies were picketed in the thick cover, almost out of his sight. One of the horses, trailing rope, walked out into the open, leaned forward, and began to drink at the grassy shallow. Benjamin abruptly stopped, blinked several times, and took a steady second look. He noticed the white left foreleg, the deep brown body—a beautiful mare, yes indeed. Little doubt about it, this fine pony had once belonged to John Goodhart, had been his favorite mount.

Overwhelmed by sudden anger, Benjamin's mind swept him back in time to the trading post root cellar, recalling how he and his father had lifted Goodhart's body out of the darkness into the bright afternoon sunlight, the grief-stricken face of Molly, James standing nearby in stunned shock. That was a time of bad medicine, sadness, despair, and smouldering anger. Without a thought for the consequences, Benjamin One Feather went to one knee, shouldered his rifle, and took aim at the nearest man, the one by the fire. Little reason now to dwell on benevolence, sanity, or motive. He was outraged, and any rationale he might have entertained suddenly went thundering away with the roar of his rifle. The man in his sights flew backward and crumpled in a heap. But before Benjamin could get off a second shot the other brave was catapulting away, scrambling to the cover of the willows near the picketed ponies.

Unfortunately for Benjamin One Feather, Goodhart's

mare reared once, and with her hind legs kicking, swung right in front of the startled hostile, blocking any chance of a second shot. Later, when he cautiously peeked over the rim of the gully, all he saw was the mare and a pinto, their ears pricked, staring in his direction. At least his one shot had been true, for the body near the fire was unmoving. But now it was a matter of waiting out the man who had escaped into the brush, or help from White Moon and Red Running Horse, who must have heard the echo of the shot from down below.

There was no sign of activity in the willows, only the flapping of two magpies that came winging out, dipping up and down, soon to swing away over his head. Benjamin waited, breathed deeply, and waited some more. Time was on the side of the hostiles, as there was perhaps only an hour of daylight left, the heavens now heavy with thunderheads. But without his pony it was going to be a long hike back into the Rosebud Mountains, his likely direction if he decided to make a run for it. Benjamin One Feather, allowing that his own cover was now vulnerable, flattened and snaked his body forward under the slight overhang of the bank.

Once behind a clump of sage, he lifted his head for another peek. The ponies had calmed down and were now munching bunch grass at the edge of the clearing. He could even hear the grinding chomp of their jaws, that steady, rhythmic *crunch-crunch* sound indicative of contented stock. It was that quiet, almost deadly quiet; too quiet, Benjamin One Feather thought. Near the body of the slain Indian he could see the carcass of a rabbit still steaming at the edge of the little fire, and to the side of it, against a rock, the brave's rifle. His eyes then wandered over to the saddle where the other man had been resting, and there, too, to his great surprise, he saw another rifle, this one lying in the dust. And then it struck home: The second man must be unarmed, had been so thoroughly unnerved by Benjamin's blast from the brush that he had rolled away in sheer panic, seeking only to save himself from disaster.

But wait a moment, not *necessarily* unarmed, Benjamin thought in grim recollection. Had not Little Bull Runs died in his arms up in the Big Horns long ago? Ei, died at the hand of an "unarmed" warrior, a warrior who had in fact had a pistol, a pistol much like the one Benjamin himself always carried. The fatal wound of Little Bull Runs, his departed brother-in-law, was still embedded in his aching heart, and he suddenly hearkened to the recent words of Little Bull Runs' father, Shoots Far Arrow, who had told the bluecoat, Bradley, "In our culture, there is no room for defeat. . . . Defeat is disaster." Ei, the disaster of death.

Then Thunder Maker broke the silence. Benjamin One Feather stirred uncomfortably in his place of hiding, hardly daring to brush away the dust and pebbles filtering down from the disturbed overhang of his creek-side niche. His nostrils were filled with the pungency of the crushed sage he had wallowed through, intermingled now with the occasional odor of smoke and roasted rabbit. A few drops of rain began to dimple the slick of the creek, and as he lifted his brow to eye the lowering clouds, feeling the first gentle droplets against his forehead, a black form suddenly hurtled from the sky, momentarily plunging him into darkness. He rolled away, dirt spewing from his mouth, felt a terrible stinging pain in his left shoulder, tumbled clear of the weight on his back, and ended up on his knees in the middle of the creek. His enemy had successfully jumped him, snatched his rifle. Facing him now, only five yards away, was the other hostile, bloody knife in one hand and Benjamin's Henry rifle in the other.

What followed then was nothing more than a blur of action measured in seconds. The knife, the brave wiped across the side of his leggings, and with a defiant growl he sheathed it. The rifle that he had seized came up to his belly, but before he could touch off a round, the damp evening air was suddenly split apart by the roar of Benjamin One Feather's Colt pistol. Hit high in the middle, the impact of the heavy ball rocked the Indian backward into the bank. In reflex, he triggered off one shot from Benjamin's rifle, the bullet humming harmlessly away into the thunderheads.

Clasping at the pain near his back shoulder, Benjamin One Feather stood up in the water, and with his right hand took aim at the stricken man's head. The brave, eyes blinking, waited unafraid, but no shot was forthcoming, for Benjamin One Feather slowly lowered his revolver, then leaped forward and kicked the rifle away from an outstretched arm. After holstering his sidearm, Benjamin picked up the rifle, wiped it off, and stomped away. He crossed the small clearing and stood in the rain by the sputtering fire. He stared down at the first hostile he had shot, saw blood staining the front of the army shirt he was wearing, a shirt undoubtedly taken on the Greasy Grass from the body of one of Long Hair's troopers. Setting his rifle aside, Benjamin reached down and ripped away a sleeve, wadded it, pressed it up under his vest against his bleeding back.

The rabbit this man had been roasting lay to the side, a thick willow skewer still spiked into its body. Seizing the stick, Benjamin brought the meat to his mouth and tore off a large chunk. It was warm and juicy, but he barely tasted it. Ripping away more from the carcass, he chewed ravenously while his wild eyes frisked the small camp. He quickly examined the markings and beadwork on clothing, the exquisite decorations on the saddle lying by the fire. He now knew these men were Lakota, either Hunkpapa or Yanktonai, men who had been on the Little Big Horn as well as at Goodhart's trading post. He looked carefully at the rifles, both relatively new weapons, one a Winchester, the other a Spencer "needle gun" that smacked of familiarity. Upon close observation he saw a small heart-shaped imprint on the stock. Goodhart's brand, just like the bigger one on the rump of the brown mare.

Spitting out a shred of leg gristle, Benjamin One Feather turned his attention to the two ponies, now suddenly realizing that his brothers down below must have heard the shots and became concerned, were probably even on their way. The pain in his shoulder had become excruciating, and blood was trickling down his rib cage. But he was alive, if only by the narrowest of margins, the Sioux blade apparently having carved across his shoulder blade instead of plunging into his heart. A bolt of lightning ripped across the heavens, turning the landscape white, and the ensuing claps of thunder shook the ground. Benjamin One Feather lifted his face to the pelting rain, felt it coursing down through the grease and dirt, welcomed it. "*Aho,*" he said. "*Aho,* Great Lightning One, your spirit is in my body."

* * *

Far down the creek sometime later, amid slanting sheets of rain, Benjamin One Feather made out the shadowy forms of his brothers galloping along the muddy banks to meet him. White Moon, reining up first, immediately began to verbally flail him, cursing in English. "You damned fisheater, you scared the shit out of us! Plenty dumb-ass, you are, out in the rain like this! What happened up there?"

"Ei, I'm sorry, brother, trouble," Benjamin said wearily. He slapped his hand against the mare's wet neck. "Look what I found. Recognize this pony?"

Surprised, White Moon swore again, exclaiming, "Shit, yes! That's John's mare that—" He broke off, suddenly aware that his brother was holding his shoulder, noticing the widening splotch of blood now diffused by the rain. "You're shot! Here, let me see that." White Moon moved his pony closer, leaned over and pulled back Benjamin's buckskin vest and the wadding of cloth. "Dammit, you've been sliced. . . . A bad one, too, right down to the damned bone. Let's get out of here . . . patch this thing up. Shit, you got plenty blood all over your ribs and back!"

Before Benjamin One Feather could reply, Red Running Horse, also displeased by his companion's tardiness, admonished him. "You have trouble, you should have come back first, told us about these things, ei, that you found the ones who made the tracks." Then, for the first time, both he and White Moon noticed the mass of torn flesh and tattered buckskin tied to a rope behind the pinto. Red Running Horse was appalled at the sight, and at the ferocity of Benjamin One Feather. "Who is this man you drag like a piece of wood? *Eeyah,* he is nothing but red meat!"

"The Lakota who almost killed me," Benjamin said. "Ei, one of the men who killed the trader, Goodhart." He glanced back over his shoulder. "Cut him loose. His death was a brave one."

"*Eeyah,* dragging a dead man!" Red Running Horse slid off his pony and severed the rope near the brave's ankles.

"He was alive when I started."

Both White Moon and Red Running Horse exchanged

dark glances. More rain swept over the trio, and the Thunder Beings made deep, resonant rumbles. Red Running Horse cursed and pointed to the black clouds. "You see, they are angry up there!" Motioning ahead, he said, "Come, let us get away from this place; fix your wound, make a chant, and leave. Ei, ride in the rain over the mountain to the Place of the Big Trees. The spirit of this warrior will be plenty angry tonight; not a good way to die, not a good place to sleep."

White Moon grinned and looked over at Benjamin One Feather. "Ghosts? What happened to the other man?"

"Dead, too," was the reply. "Did you save me some chicken?"

"You may have my chicken," White Moon replied, staring back at the mutilated Lakota. "I'm not hungry."

"I'm not hungry either. I ate the rabbit they were cooking."

Red Running Horse, with another disapproving glare, asked, "You ate the dead men's food?"

"One rabbit."

Forcing a grim smile, Red Running Horse said, "You are a crazy dog, Benjamin One Feather. Ei, you have powerful medicine but a weak head. Before this night is over you will have two pains, one in your back and one in your belly. You should have left that rabbit for the spirits of the dead."

It was the following day, midmorning, and it was still raining lightly along the Yellowstone Valley. "You're a lucky man," Lt. Timothy Aubrey was saying, snipping the strand of gut. "If this had been an inch over, you probably would be back out there on the prairie somewhere under a mound, just like your friend Goodhart."

"That close, ei?" Benjamin said.

"That close."

White Moon, standing beside his prostrate brother, said, "He has good medicine. No Sioux will ever kill him."

"Is that so?" Aubrey, with a *humph,* went on dabbing a saturated cloth over the long gash, bringing out a small gasp through Benjamin One Feather's clenched teeth. "Well, he's not immune to this, is he? Stings a bit, eh, Benjamin?" Benjamin One Feather made no comment and the young engineer continued, now salving the wound, finally applying a gauze bandage. "And you probably were in luck that we were still around these parts. Time you got back to your village, this might have been infected. That would be a fine kettle of fish, wouldn't it?"

White Moon spoke up again. "We don't eat fish, so that wouldn't matter too much."

The lieutenant smiled slightly, looked at White Moon inquisitively. "If these hostiles were scouting *us*, why did they pick on *you*, carve up your brother this way?"

Shrugging, White Moon answered, "Ask him, he's the one who went looking for trouble, not me."

"A lot of trouble for a horse," commented Aubrey dryly. He patted Benjamin One Feather on the back. "You can get up now, but I wouldn't be using that arm for a while. You have a few muscles below the shoulder blade that are going to take some mending, a lot of healing to be done. And in about a week you can have someone snip those stitches. The meantime, I'm going to give you some bandage and disinfectant. Keep that cut clean, don't go out doing anything too hard, either, like breaking ponies, chopping wood—"

"We don't chop wood," White Moon put in.

"Oh yes, I forgot," said Aubrey with a grin. Then, somewhat sarcastically, "That's work for the women folk, isn't it?"

"No," answered White Moon, straight-faced, "we saw our wood with cross-cuts, just like you white folks do. We only let the women carry it. Ei, we let them build the fires, too."

Benjamin One Feather stood up and slipped into his vest, carefully tied the thong of leather at the top. His whole left arm ached, from the shoulder down to the wrist. He thanked Lieutenant Aubrey, the only man in the small troop who knew anything about stitching wounds. He would also thank Red Running Horse for riding out of his way on this gloomy, wet morning to locate the survey party. The soldiers had crossed the Big Horn and had pitched two large tents before the storm came in from the west, and with exception of a few men on guard duty, the whole troop was comfortably dry.

After some small conversation along with their coffee,

the three Absaroke finally prepared to leave. Red Running Horse left first, brought the ponies up to the big tent, stood outside, his poncho pulled up, and waited. Aubrey asked Benjamin One Feather what he intended to do with Goodhart's horse now that it had been recovered. But once again it was White Moon who came up with the ready answer, telling Aubrey that it was customary to shoot the horse by the grave of the owner so he could have spiritual transportation up the Great Hanging Road.

"You see, no one likes to walk up there," White Moon explained in all seriousness. "That's a long way up. The old wise men say it takes a year sometimes. That's for a healthy man like Benjamin here. Old people? Well, they maybe have to walk forever. That's why a good pony is needed. Saves a lot of time. You understand? No one likes to waste all that time, plenty walking. More to do if you get there in a hurry."

Watching Aubrey's face go slack in his attempt to follow his brother's logic, Benjamin chuckled. Aubrey cocked a skeptical eye at White Moon, then turned back to Benjamin. "No, he can't be serious, can he? Why would you ride all the way across the country to shoot a poor horse, for God's sake?"

Benjamin finally said, "No, we'll take it back to the village, give it to Goodhart's wife, Molly. That's only a small compensation, ei? But it will mean something. This fine pony has great sentimental value."

"Yes," nodded Aubrey, "I do understand," and he grimaced at White Moon.

White Moon said, "We'll give her the scalps, too, the hair from those hostiles."

"Scalps?" Aubrey said, his brows arching.

"Out there, hanging on the halter."

Lt. Timothy Aubrey cautiously peeked out the tent flap to where Red Running Horse was standing at the file of ponies. White Moon was not joshing this time, for there, suspended on each side of the mare's halter, were two dangling strands of hair, twisted and matted from the heavy rains. "My God, whatever will she do with them! That's no proper gift to present a widow woman." He shuddered slightly.

Offhandedly, White Moon replied, "Oh, she will probably spit on them plenty, curse those hostiles and throw their hair in the fire. That gives the spirits a plenty hot head, you know. Whoo-ee!"

Nonplussed at this casual savagery, yet with some understanding of tribal custom, Aubrey quickly averted his eyes from the grim mementoes. Following White Moon and Benjamin, he stepped out into the misty rain. Jenkins, the older trooper who had translated during the first encounter with the Indians two days before, had stopped in front of the brown mare and was fondling one of the damp strands of hair. Turning back to Lieutenant Aubrey with a grin, he said, "Hell, sir, these ain't scalps. This stuff is what we call Spanish moss. Hangs down from the limbs of those big pines back on the mountain there."

Benjamin One Feather smiled. "Ei, black tree lichen, that's what it is. That is White Moon's idea of a joke, just pulling your leg."

"But . . ." Aubrey began, searching for White Moon, who already had disappeared on the other side of the horses. "Your brother . . ."

"I know," Benjamin One Feather said, "he always does this. Ei, sometimes he even puts lichen on his face, makes a beard, and when the white men see this, they don't know what to think. *Eeyah,* an Injun with whiskers! White Moon is crazy like a coyote. I should have warned you. If you listen to him too much, you will lose both of your legs from pulling, ei?"

Giving Benjamin One Feather a boost up to his saddle, Aubrey managed a thin smile. "You have a very strange brother, Benjamin, very strange indeed."

Benjamin One Feather momentarily appraised the lieutenant, finally returned his smile. "Not so strange, my friend, not at all. No, White Moon is always here to remind us not to become too serious about ourselves. Take some enjoyment in life, otherwise too much of our time on Mother Earth will be wasted and to little avail." With a nod of his head, Benjamin reined away.

Red Running Horse came next, holding up his arm in friendship, and following him was White Moon the coyote. Grinning down at Lieutenant Aubrey, he reached above his headband and firmly grasped a lock of his black hair. "Watch out for those hostiles," he warned.

THIRTEEN

Benjamin One Feather's recuperation was slow and a bit frustrating. As Lt. Timothy Aubrey had predicted, the muscles in Benjamin's upper back were taking considerable time to knit. Because the young brave's usually active life had come to a standstill, nervous tension was gnawing at him, and at times he felt like he was standing on a hot rock. There was very little he could do about this without endangering himself. Handling the ponies, breaking the yearlings, making wood, all of these chores were out of the question. His brothers even balked at taking him along on the overnight scouting expeditions, and until the stabbing this had been his favorite pastime.

However, one ray of hope had popped out—White Crane. Even though she had chastised him for being away all the time, and for acting like a crazy dog over on the Big Horn, he soon convinced her that the incapacity of his left arm had not affected his ardor and passion. Pleasantly surprised, White Crane was equally receptive, joking that she was plenty thankful that his wound had not been elsewhere. She allowed that Shining Elk had something to do with this joyous renewal of love. That the spirit elk had intervened to save Benjamin's life she had not the slightest doubt, telling her man that this was his most powerful medicine, the great light that now guided and protected him. He had been spared, and his narrow escape from death, if nothing else, had brought renewed vigor to their marriage. They were both happy.

But neither Benjamin One Feather nor his pretty wife could find any signs relative to his vision in this latest experience on the eastern prairie. Where was the symbolism of the mysterious red fox, the fleeing animals that Benjamin One Feather had been bound to protect, and the leaping frog? Were these elements only incidental, or even meaningless to the great fire of battle and the dark shadows of death that had already passed over the prairie? In this instance, nothing seemed to correlate. Pondering this and seeking guidance, they left early one morning and rode up to the mountain where the great ponderosa stood, each believing that maybe another sign was forthcoming, something to indicate a new direction for Benjamin in one of the Four Great Ways.

The ride was relaxing, barely a strain on his sore shoulder, a pleasant outing on a warm sunny day, nothing more. One thing: The berries on the baneberry bush, the sweet medicine, had turned bloodred from snow-white, and though Benjamin One Feather was initially startled by this sight and sought some spiritual significance in it, White Crane told him that this was not too unusual. These berries often turned red in late summer.

And indeed this was deep summer, the Moon of the Black Berries, late July. While the troopers and a few freight wagons continued to move back and forth down the Yellowstone, the isolated villagers were now scattering across the hillsides and bottom, gathering the annual harvest of serviceberry, chokecherry, and plum, a time of picking, grinding, and drying. Children's faces were colored overnight, small thieves caught with stained evidence, purple rings around their happy mouths. Once the forthcoming buffalo hunt was over, this great wealth of berry mash, pulverized pits and all, would be caked into pemmican, the hardy winter staple of the Absaroke. Benjamin One Feather, for want of better things to do, often accompanied White Crane on these gathering forays, much to her amusement and delight. He, of course, was sharing her joy, whether in the berry fields of the day or their robes of the night, and he was beginning to realize, just being near her, how much he had really missed her.

It wasn't too long before he forgot about the excitement of scouting with his brothers, and when he wisely decided not to accompany his father on a business trip to the Gallatin Valley ranch, this quieted another small fret that his wife secretly harbored: the horrifying thought of returning to Bozeman City, where the crazies lived. She remembered the hazards of the last journey, the intimidating threats of angry white people, the frightful experience with the drovers and the resulting bloodshed. This was a place of bad medicine.

When she asked Benjamin why her father-in-law, Man Called Tree, never had such frightening experiences, he reminded her that this had not always been the case, that when his father was young and seeking his own true way, trouble had always followed his footsteps, often sought him out. He too had escaped death, several times, and only by inches, now carried the scars from a Pekony arrow in his side and a white man's bullet across his cheek and ear. But his medicine was strong, too, the sun, the coyote, and the tree. One by one his enemies were defeated, and soon his moccasin tracks were so big that no one dared follow him anymore. Benjamin One Feather said that the peace his father ultimately had found had been hard-earned.

They were sitting on a knoll overlooking the big river, some distance apart from the busy workers below who had discovered a large patch of buffalo berry. Contemplating her husband's words, White Crane said, "I think this is not a time of peace. I find it strange that peace only comes by fighting."

"Sometimes a man has to fight for what he believes is sacred and meaningful, not only to himself but to his people," replied Benjamin One Feather. "People who misunderstand each other will never find peace. Ei, and the greedy ones make it worse. What we have here in our valley is good, but you are right, woman, over the mountain there is little peace. This is because the people there judge a man by the color of his skin, ei, and as Mr. Clay says, by how he dresses." He stared across the valley and pointed a stem of wild timothy at the distant mountains. "Prejudice may never change, but we know the land is changing. This is why my father has made the big ranch. To him the ranch is a base of power for the family, security for all of us, a place where no white man can come in and tell us what we must do or not do."

Resting her head against his shoulder, she asked plaintively, "We will go there one day and live like James and your sister?"

"Only when the sanctity of the land is destroyed," he assured her. "Then, and not before." Gently, he caressed her long black hair. "Ah, but don't worry. This is too far away to think about. A woman like you wasn't meant to worry. Ei, never hide your smile from me."

She smiled up at him. "I can be happy with you wherever we go." But she secretly hoped that any move away from the village would be many moons away, and as her man said, "too far away to think about." But it was on her mind, difficult to conceal. She was afraid of the people over the mountains, their many strange customs. And some of these people were crude and ill-mannered, many somber and unsmiling, just like old women who had lost their teeth and slept alone. Two Shell Woman had told her about a few of these white people, and most of what she heard was bad medicine. And she could imagine, too, how silly she would look in the funny colored dresses and, worst of all, those ugly pointed shoes she had seen in Lucas Hamm's great store. Only one pleasant thought crossed her mind, and it was fleeting: to have such a grand house as Ruth did, with four rooms and a porch; yes, and big tub to bathe in; all of that might be nice.

Benjamin One Feather, now comfortably content beside his wife, leaned back in the mellowing grass and cupped his hands behind his head. He and his woman were silent for a while, lost in their thoughts, Benjamin chasing clouds in the summer sky, White Crane occasionally swishing away a horsefly with her dibble, watching over the man she loved so much. She had ridden out double with him this day just so she could wrap her arms around his middle, ignoring the titter of her friends, who chided her for this juvenile foolishness. Such riding was only meant for sweethearts, not man and wife. She had saucily tossed her head and laughed happily, knowing these women were just a little envious that she had such a handsome, attentive husband who still treated her like a sweetheart. This was good.

Some while later, a few shouts below aroused them

from their hillside reverie, and when Benjamin One Feather raised himself, he saw the women disappearing behind the bushes and trees. Except for Old Dog Jumps and Stone Calf, the bottom suddenly was deserted. He noticed that Stone Calf was motioning, pointing up the trail. When he and White Crane quickly directed their attention that way, they saw a few dark specks amongst a whirl of dust—pony soldiers far off, coming down the river trail. Waving back to the two braves below, Benjamin One Feather mounted his pony. White Crane took a hand and leaped aboard from the right side, her long bare legs moulding into the pony's flanks. Then Benjamin quietly walked the horse into the shadows of the high sage and juniper, where he stopped and waited.

The troopers finally came riding in at a brisk trot, slowed when they saw Stone Calf and Old Dog Jumps sitting their ponies alongside the cottonwoods. The Absaroke braves were both surprised and startled to see that the bluecoat in front was their friend Zachary Hockett, the young man they had trailed and camped with only two moons past, the Hanging Soldier that the Nez Percé woman had saved from death. Likewise, Hockett was surprised. Moving their horses close, the men exchanged greeting, shook hands.

The two Indians, pleased to see that Hockett was riding again, nodded and pointed to his leg, then to his horse. This is good, they gestured. Flat Nose, the Piegan breed interpreter, was there too, and after a few words with Zachary Hockett, he made sign with the Crow. In effect he said that the last time Hockett and his soldiers were in the Yellowstone bottom they weren't greeted with such friendship, being surrounded by angry braves who were protecting Two Shell Woman. Where were these braves today? How many were hiding in the trees? Stone Calf immediately answered, his hands moving swiftly.

Nodding, watching closely, Flat Nose finally grinned broadly, then turned and explained to the lieutenant. "They say, same as last time. You be seen plenty. Plenty squaw in trees, you no see. You look on hill, brave with plenty big gun see you. You no see him. He brother of Shining Elk. Plenty big medicine in sky."

Zachary Hockett, and several of his troopers who were within earshot, turned and looked upon the nearby knoll.

In the middle of a juniper patch was a lone black-and-white pinto pony with two red streaks of lightning painted on its forelegs. Around its throat, was a blazing red-and-white beaded necklace. Two Indians were mounted on the horse, the one in the front holding a rifle upright, its butt resting near the pommel of the saddle. In this instance what Hockett was seeing was not reality but more like a painting, silent, unmoving, but charged with rich color and emotion, a beautiful sight to be remembered. Pushing back the brim of his sweaty hat, he said to the others, "There's only one man in this country who can put on a show like that." Cupping his hand, he called out, "Benjamin! Hey, Benjamin, get your ass down here on the double!"

After a long *kahe* from the hill, women and a few children, their heads popping up like mushrooms, began to materialize from the trees. Flat Nose laughed and jerked a thumb at Hockett. "No bullshit, eh? Plenty Crow come, now see 'em, want candy, t'backy, what you got." Presently another call came from the hill, closer now, a woman's voice but lusty, mellow, and clear. "Hallo, Hock-kett, I see you." And it was Zachary Hockett's turn to laugh, and he did so, heartily. White Crane was learning English! Jesus, he was among true friends again!

After another round of greetings, Lieutenant Hockett, only recently reassigned to Fort Ellis, put his small troop at ease, the men retiring to the shade of the giant cottonwoods where they struck up their pipes. A few of the women went back to work in the bushes, but the small fry gathered around the soldiers and waited expectantly for anything that might come their way. They knew this man Hockett was their friend. Hockett did have some rock candy in the supply packs, and he was soon passing it out to their eager, outstretched hands. Meanwhile, he explained to the others why he was traveling east again, this time not to make war or investigate the death of trappers but to meet up with an army surveying party working somewhere down along the Yellowstone. The army had plans to connect the singing wires upriver from Fort Keogh to Fort Ellis.

Hockett was surprised to learn that Benjamin One Feather knew the surveyor, Lieutenant Aubrey, in fact had been with him only three weeks ago at Goodhart's place. When Benjamin pulled away his buckskin vest and related the story behind his fresh scar, Hockett was shocked, more so because he had met Benjamin's father and his Gallatin-bound party just a few days ago beyond the Boulder River. No mention had been made of any fight with the Sioux in the Big Horn country. However, there was some talk about the shooting affair with the cattle thieves in the Crazy Mountains. This story, after a great deal of circulation around Bozeman City, had become somewhat distorted, one of the latest versions being that young Benjamin Tree had stood up to four rustlers and gunned them down, a feat that had made him as famous as his father. The proof of this was that lawmen had found four bodies and recovered the stolen cattle, all because of young Tree.

Benjamin One Feather could hardly believe what he was hearing. His two Crow brothers, Stone Calf and Old Dog Jumps, who had participated in the shooting, laughed and slapped their thighs when they heard the translation. White Crane, on the other hand, was appalled. Now the white people, many of whom already disliked her man, were going to call him a crazy dog, seek him out as they had his father. Surely, he would never find any peace over the mountains. This was the worst of news. Zachary Hockett, discerning the fright written on her face, spoke to Benjamin, asked him to explain that these slain men were rustlers, criminals who probably would have been hanged anyway. In the white man's society stealing cows and ponies was very bad medicine, not a game of coup as played by the Indians. She listened but was not swayed. Killing white people, any kind, good or bad, was a grievous offense, not likely forgotten. Didn't these people have avengers? Was the white man any different in this respect than the red man? No, this wasn't something to be joked away as Old Dog Jumps and Stone Calf were now doing, so she scolded them.

Hockett's news about the far-ranging movements of the Sioux and Cheyenne was nothing more than Benjamin One Feather and his friends already knew. The fair-weather bluecoats were having a tough time of it, trying to catch up with the hostiles. But Hockett confirmed what the Crow had heard from people passing through Fort

Keogh, that indeed the army was planning a big winter campaign. This did not bode well for the hostiles, who disliked making war when Cold Maker came. For many it was a long period of hardship and difficult hunting, not a good time to be riding back and forth across the frozen prairie being chased by buffalo soldiers. Zachary Hockett, tracing a pattern in the dust with a twig, looked darkly at Benjamin One Feather. "It's all very simple: Now divided, they must fall. One by one, they'll go down. They'll be hounded from one end of the prairie to the other until they surrender or are killed off."

Benjamin One Feather was aware of this. He knew that it was impossible for the Sioux, Cheyenne, and their allies to sustain themselves in such a great concentration of power as they had done in the Greasy Grass, not in the middle of winter. Food supplies were too scarce to support such a gigantic war village, one of ten thousand people. In the winter the Indians had to disperse to survive, had to follow the wintering animals that ranged hundreds of miles searching for food themselves. He said reflectively, "The hostiles have already succeeded in what they set out to do. They destroyed Yellow Hair, the man who betrayed them in the Black Hills, the butcher of Washita. It won't matter much now to some of them, getting herded back to the reservations to get their chuckaway. Ei, we hear that many are already back, others have crossed north into the Queen Mother's Land where the army can't follow." He gave Hockett a wan smile. "I don't support them, but they have a just cause, that much of it can't be denied. My father told me long ago this was all a matter of organization, "logistics" as you people call it. Too many tribes fighting among themselves, unable to join forces against a common enemy, ancient rivalries never reconciled. Divided this way, they have no strength, no muscle to fight."

"Oh, that's an old story," Hockett said. "I remember we had a book at the army academy, historic battles, strategy and such. Striking similarity. The Greeks went down under the Persians and Romans the same way: city-states, never unified, picked apart one by one. The army's taking this one right out of the book. United we stand, divided we fall, that sort of thing."

"And the devil take the hindmost," added Benjamin One Feather.

"Well spoken, Benjamin. You're always surprising me."

Benjamin One Feather smiled. "My father brought many books into the lodge to help us read; ei, to teach us about people, the world. I was eager to learn, read them all, over and over, even the fairy tales, but through it all I've never been able to understand man himself, only that what may be good medicine for one is poison to another. The Great Medicine Wheel asks us to search for balance in our life, to seek out the wisdom of the Four Great Ways. The early ones listened. I'm afraid reality has blinded our eyes and deafened our ears. Ei, the Great Wheel is being torn apart, rock by rock. There is no balance."

Zachary Hockett listened with empathy to this young man of deep convictions, a man who already had lived a lifetime, who was wise beyond his years, a man who one day was destined to become a great chief among his people, as was his father. Hockett found himself seeking enlightening words of condolence, some middle ground of camaraderie. "Yes, your wheel," he finally said. "I remember that place, the little lecture you gave me about holy ground. Damn near froze my ass off riding all the way up there! Holy cold, it was. You made a fool out of me, Benjamin, spirits and all."

Benjamin grinned. "Human beings often work hand-in-hand with the spirits."

"And after all of that, you made me welcome in your village," added Hockett, somewhat sheepishly. "Jesus, I lived with your people, and under the circumstances never had a better time in my life. You already have this balance you're seeking, dammit. You're not involved in this mess over there. See here, Benjamin, you're damned lucky you aren't a part of all the confusion. Sometimes I wish to hell I wasn't either."

"*Aho,*" replied Benjamin One Feather. "You are learning, Mr. Hockett, but we're *all* a part of it now, whether we want to be or not. Remember this: Someday you will have to stand up and be counted. We all will."

Silence for a moment, Hockett still scratching the dirt with his twig. Finally: "Dammit all, I'll never forget that

Nez Percé woman. Strange, how it bothers me sometimes. Jesus, Benjamin, she's a special kind of . . . I don't know. . . . "

"Injun," interjected Benjamin, with amusement written in his dark eyes. "It's good to know you haven't forgotten. I thought maybe it was one of those nighttime adventures on the trail. Very common, you know, everyone being together that way. Things just happen, men and women. White Crane thinks it was something more than just fancy. Is this what you're trying to tell me, my friend?"

Hockett, with a helpless shrug and a small blush, said, "I don't know. Never experienced anything like that before, but it's damned frustrating. Something I'll never forget, not as long as I live."

"Ei, pleasant memories are the best," said Benjamin, "even if they sometimes cause a little pain in the heart. But everyone misses Two Shell Woman, don't you know this? She was good medicine for us all, a woman with many skills." Playfully tossing a pebble at the morose lieutenant, he added jokingly, "*Humph,* and you wanted to take her back to the fort to hang, ei?"

"Jesus!" The twig in Hockett's hand suddenly snapped. He looked curiously at the broken half, then tossed it over his shoulder. Abruptly standing, he dusted his trousers and methodically fitted on his dusty cavalry hat. Benjamin One Feather thought he detected a misty look in the lieutenant's eyes. But Zachary Hockett shouted with bravado, "All right, men, let's move out of here! Hit the leather!" He refused to lay his emotions on the ground in front of his red brother.

Benjamin One Feather missed Hockett's return trip to Fort Ellis two weeks later. He wanted to see his soldier friend again, but went with the buffalo hunting party down to the upper Greasy Grass near the mouth of the Little Big Horn River. This was one of Chief Big Cloud's favorite hunting areas—good grass, wallows, and frequently large herds of both blackhorns and antelope. The buffalo shaman needed good shooters, had asked Benjamin to go. Benjamin, preparing for this, had taken to exercising his shoulder each day, and while he occasionally felt a small twinge, he finally decided that his arm was sound enough for him to join the hunt. Some of his brothers had already ridden to the base of the nearby Rosebud Mountains, scouting for the hostile village from where the Lakota Benjamin One Feather killed may have been heading. They found only several abandoned camps. Pony and travois trails indicated that these people had moved south toward the upper Tongue and Powder river country.

The Crow scouts saw nothing of the bluecoats either, the men who were searching so futilely for the hostiles. However, on their circle back through the foothills near the Little Big Horn, they found the graves of many soldiers, some carefully disguised with sagebrush and rocks, and they knew this was where Long Hair Custer and his men had died. The bones and rotting hides of their horses and mules were scattered all over the hillsides. It was obvious that many wolves and coyotes had visited this place, some only recently, scavenging for the last decaying scraps. Padded footprints and spoor were everywhere in the sage-covered coulees.

At the hunting camp, Big Cloud went through his usual ceremonial rites, the smoking of sweet grass, the chants and offerings, his prayer for good hunting, calling out for the Great One to behold the buffalo that had been given to the Bird People. He chanted aloud, acknowledging "the chief of all the four-legged upon Mother Earth, for him the people live, and with him they walk the sacred path." But despite all these incantations, the first several days of the surrounds produced only meager kills, the blackhorns scattered and wary, not congregating in their usual great numbers. The hunters worked harder, ranging sometimes as far as five miles from the camp, and it was arduous work for everyone, men and women alike. But after the fourth day the drying and smoking racks were becoming heavy with curing meat, and there were plenty of hides, some pegged and fleshed, others bundled for later processing in the main village.

Near the end of this day Red Running Horse and one of the Lumpwoods, Bear Gets Up, came back to camp to report the sighting of four white men with wagons and mules about five miles to the northeast, near the Place of the Prairie Dogs. From what the scouts had observed, these men were making a camp near the Sandstone Buttes. This is what they told Shoots Far Arrow, their chief in the absence of Man Called Tree, who had not yet returned from the Gallatin Valley. Shoots Far Arrow, curious about this intrusion upon Absaroke land, immediately made plans to investigate, ordering Benjamin One Feather and Sitting Elk to accompany the other two to this place and make talk with the strangers.

What were these interlopers doing out here so far from the Yellowstone Trail? If they were up to mischief, Shoots Far Arrow wanted them off the land, back to where they had come from. Benjamin One Feather, however, already suspected their purpose, allowing that from what the two scouts had reported, these men were buffalo hunters who were coming to collect hides, and little else. When Shoots Far Arrow heard this his curiosity turned to livid anger, and he asked indignantly: ''Who has given these men the right to hunt on the land of the Absaroke? Certainly, the people at the Crow agency would not allow such a travesty.'' Incensed, his staff of authority cutting the air, Shoots Far Arrow said, ''Get rid of them!''

Chief Shoots Far Arrow did not elaborate, nor did any of the men press him for further instructions. ''Get rid of them'' could mean only one of two things: Order them off the hunting grounds, or kill them. Shoots Far Arrow, the great father of White Crane, didn't seem to care which course his men took, and with this in mind, they left in the darkness well before dawn for Sandstone Buttes. Since Benjamin One Feather knew the white man's tongue, his brothers elected him to carry the pipe, for they knew from experience that he would provide good leadership and great cunning. He had proved himself more than once. They were prepared to do his bidding whatever it was. Of course, White Crane was upset that her father had asked Benjamin One Feather to go on this mission, but she knew better than to question his authority, much less suggest that he appoint someone else. This was the business of men, not women, and well aware of her station, she wisely held her tongue. However she did get in a harsh word or two with her husband before he left, to little avail. She ended up caressing him, pleading with him to be careful, for she had not forgotten Benjamin's last misadventure in this country, or that a few years ago the life of her brother, Little Bull Runs, had been wasted up the river only a few day's ride.

Benjamin One Feather, usually imaginative, had no idea how he was going to bring about a confrontation with the white buffalo hunters, only knew that because they were usually well-armed, his plan had to be both cautious and cunning. All this was running through his mind when he and his men finally approached the buttes shortly before dawn. But after one look at the sleeping camp he knew exactly what his plan was going to be, and he quietly backed off, motioning to his three brothers to follow.

After securing their ponies they came back on foot, circled the camp, took up hiding places in the high sage, and waited. Almost an hour went by before a man finally appeared at the tent flap. He yawned once, stretched, and went over to the side and urinated. When he returned to the tent he said a few words, turned on his heel, and went to one of the wagons, where he pulled out a few chunks of scrap wood. Shortly he had a small blaze going inside a bank of rocks. A blackened coffee pot was perched to the side. Benjamin One Feather groaned inside as he watched the man stir the coffee several times with a long-bladed hunting knife. One thing that his father had taught him long ago, and he in turn had imparted to White Crane, is that there is nothing worse than stale coffee, no matter how hot. It's always as bitter as gall, even when diluted and laced with sugar, if one is lucky enough to have sugar.

Directly two more men emerged, pulling at their dirty trousers, scratching, and blinking at the rising sun. "Good day for buffalo gnats," he heard one lament. After the first man banged loudly on a frying pan, a fourth finally came out, exactly in the fashion of the others, scratching his backside and staring around as if he were lost. But this one Benjamin One Feather *knew*! No mistake about it, it was the wolfer they called "Birdwell," the same man who had accused Two Shell Woman of killing his brother and a fellow trapper up above the Great Medicine Wheel. This was unexpected good fortune for Benjamin, for he had looked forward to meeting this hated trapper again without bluecoats around. Since all four were now within his sight, he eased out from behind the sage and walked in, rifle cradled between his folded arms.

The man with the frying pan simply dropped it to his side and stared—an Indian, calmly walking right into the middle of their camp at daybreak! One of the others nearest a wagon reached for his rifle, leaning against the spokes of a wheel. But Ulis Birdwell was the first to find his voice. "What the hell you doing here, bucko? Long ways from yer diggin's, ain't ye?"

The man with the rifle looked over at Birdwell in surprise. "You know this Injun?"

"Hell, yes, I knows him," Birdwell exclaimed. He jerked nervously at his suspenders and his face twitched under his whiskers. "Jest keep him covered real easy-like. He's one of them Crows from upriver I was telling you about, took my brother's woman, he did. Knows every word yer sayin' too. Watch him, buster, watch him!"

Benjamin One Feather finally spoke, nodding toward the armed man near the wagon. "Put that thing away, it won't do you any good. If you shoulder it, you're a dead man. All of you stand where you are, very still, ei?" He called to the side, *"Ikye!"* Sitting Elk, Red Running Horse, and Bear Gets Up suddenly appeared from the sage like rising ghosts. They weren't more than twenty-five yards away, evenly positioned around three sides of the camp, and their rifles were pointed directly at the hunters.

"Oh, for crissakes, now what's this all about?" cried Birdwell. "Y'aint aimin' to roust us outta here, too, like we ain't got no rights? Is this what yer thinkin'?"

Pointing to one of the four wagons, this one already heavily loaded with hides, Benjamin One Feather said, "What did you do with the meat from those animals?"

"We et it," one of the men replied with a broad grin. "What'd you think we'd do with it? No business of yours, anyhow." He stared at the three Crow surrounding them. "Tell those bucks to put the guns down. We ain't looking to get shot."

"You won't," Benjamin One Feather said, "not unless you do something stupid. You realize you're on our land, killing our buffalo, wasting meat, leaving it to rot out there when many people on these plains go hungry?"

"Hah!" shouted one. "There's thousands of those critters out here and you know it; thick as fleas, they are.

And who says this is your land? This is ceded property, boy. Fact is, *you* ain't supposed to be here, not us."

Benjamin One Feather, nodding northeast, said, "Ceded land is forty miles north of here, mister, up near the big river. You've come too far this time, and it's going to cost you." He motioned his rifle barrel toward the first wagon. "All of you, get over there and take your boots off."

"Wait a minute, now!" the man holding the rifle interrupted hotly. "I ain't taking orders from no goddamned breed Injun! Shit, no, not on your life!"

Benjamin suddenly pulled the trigger of his Henry, sending a cloud of dust spewing near the protester's feet. Gawking in horror, the hide hunter threw his weapon aside and hastily started to remove his shoes. Huddled next to him, cursing lowly, the other three did likewise, then faced Benjamin with sullen glares. The smallest of the four, one who had not uttered a word, a young man no more than twenty years old, finally spoke up, asking, "Can't we talk this over, have some coffee, maybe settle up with you? We'd be obliged. . . ."

Benjamin One Feather turned to the side and fired a second round, right into the coffee pot, blowing it five feet from the fireside, a huge hole torn through its middle. "That stuff is not fit for any Indian to drink," said Benjamin. And then he pointed the barrel of the rifle to the northeast. "Well, what are you men waiting for?" he asked. "Go on, start marching, right back the way you came."

"For crissakes!" Ulis Birdwell protested. "No, man, you can't do this. Why, it's nigh on two hundred miles to Keogh! At least give us some grub and water, our boots back. Cricks all dried up out there, nothin' to eat but prickly pear."

"Go to the wallows where the buffalo go," Benjamin One Feather answered. "Go to the carcasses you left and get your meat. Go live like we do, off of the land. Ei, take what Mother Earth has to offer. You have no choice. Either die here, or take your chances out there."

Over his shoulder, and with venom in his cracking voice, Birdwell said, "Y'know goddamned well we can't make it, bucko. But I tell you this, if we do, we'll be back with the army to track you down. They'll get your hide yet, Injun. They'll peel you alive for this, let the wolves eat yer stinking red carcass."

"Yes," Benjamin One Feather said with a grim smile, "I know all about the wolves. They like white meat better, ei? We fed your brother and partner to them last winter."

By the time the four hide hunters were disappearing over a distant hill, their tent and three of their wagons were burning. The Crow had hitched a team of mules to the fourth wagon. It was loaded with good buffalo robes, Sharps rifles, and food supplies. Red Running Horse was sitting up high on the wagon porch holding the reins of the team, and he was smiling.

Benjamin One Feather looked up at him and said, "This is better than having the white men run cattle through your camp, brother."

"Yes, but we should have killed them like last time," Red Running Horse said. "They would have killed us if they'd had rifles in their hands. Ei, we should have killed them."

"We did," Benjamin One Feather said flatly. "Sometimes it just takes time to die."

FOURTEEN

In late September, the Moon of the Changing Seasons, many of the Crow began to move their lodges to lower country in preparation for Cold Maker. The cover near the bottom was better, forage for the pony herd more plentiful. There were too many ponies now, almost a thousand, the upper meadows grazed clean, and Benjamin One Feather, in response to Claybourn Moore's needs at the ranch, was busy cutting out a few to take to the Gallatin. Some of the village men, either through breeding or thieving, had accumulated more horses than they needed. They were eager to reap the rewards of the white man's increasing demand for good riding and pack stock. The animals would be sold to the ranch, broken and gentled, and ultimately resold at a profit.

After two days of thinning, Benjamin had a hundred head ready to move up the Bozeman Trail, including the eight mules taken in late summer from the hide hunters on the Greasy Grass. As usual, he had volunteers to make the journey west, a few with personal reasons, among them Red Running Horse and Stone Calf, who were determined to retrieve their grizzly hide from its hiding place near the Bozeman City pass. The claws were still intact, and these had great meaning and value to the men.

Three women were making the trip: White Crane,

Walking Woman (now the wife of Stone Calf), and Molly Goodhart, who had accepted her daughter-in-law's invitation to stay the winter in the new house on Six Mile Creek. James and Little Blue Hoop were expecting their first child sometime during the winter, an occasion Molly had no intention of missing. Walking Woman, one of Little Blue Hoop's closest friends, had heard about the fine new house of her sister, and she wanted to see this grand place with the great stone fireplaces and creek water that came into the kitchen from a long pipe.

White Crane also had her reason for joining the drive—the company of her husband. In the village she otherwise would have been alone, since her father and mother were joining Man Called Tree, Rainbow, White Moon, and Sitting Elk, among others, in a council at Plenty Coups' village. When she learned that Benjamin planned on driving the stock over the hills from Bear Canyon, bypassing Bozeman City, she was more than happy to go. This also pleased the men. Since the Custer defeat, the Crow were going out of their way to avoid any kind of a confrontation with the whites, most of whom never had been able to distinguish a friendly from a hostile.

Benjamin One Feather decided to take along the hide hunters' confiscated wagon. It would slow the pace, but because so many of the villagers selling their ponies had put in orders for staples, there was no way that Benjamin One Feather and the men could pack all the foodstuffs on horses for the return trip. Flour, cornmeal, and beans were heavy items; so were match blocks, ammunition, and flannel. Red Running Horse, happy about taking the big wagon, pitched in and helped Benjamin One Feather with the harnesses. And when the party finally headed up the trail, he was perched atop the freighter handling the reins, his pony trailing behind. Driving a team of mules was the only white man's custom that he really enjoyed. When Benjamin One Feather told him that Man Called Tree once had been a muleskinner, he beamed. To be compared, even so remotely, to a great chief such as Benjamin One Feather's father, was a great honor.

Even with the wagon trundling along they made good time, camping at their usual spots and sleeping in Goodhart's wall tent and one-hide wickiup. The days were warm for late fall but the nights cold, the grass and bushes girdled with hoar frost by daybreak. Molly had brought potatoes, carrots, and onions from her village garden, for the antelope and venison stews they all shared each evening. Ultimately, when they were approaching the pass, Stone Calf rode ahead and found the tree where the grizzly hide was hidden, only to discover that it was now worthless. Pine marten had thoroughly chewed out great sections of flesh and fur, and what they had missed the jays had finished off. However Stone Calf did salvage the huge claws, which the women could later fashion into fine necklaces or ornamental trim for jackets.

This was the sixth day on the road west. Near the peak of the hill overlooking the pass the Crow finally encountered the first travelers on the trail, a long double file of troopers winding up the grassy slope. Handing the reins of the mule team to Molly Goodhart, Red Running Horse leaped on his pony to help Stone Calf and his wife, Walking Woman, move the herd below the troopers, down toward the neck of the canyon. Benjamin One Feather and White Crane were waiting beside the wagon with Molly as the first soldiers approached. Benjamin, searching for the face of Zachary Hockett, saw nothing of his friend, and finally directed his eyes to the men at the head of the column. He immediately recognized two of them, neither of whom he trusted—Colonel Gibbon and two or three mounts back, another Indian hater, Sergeant Ketchum, the red-whiskered one. When they came abreast of the wagon, Gibbon raised his hand and the long column drew to a halt. As Benjamin One Feather stared down the line, he saw four canvas-covered wagons and several caissons bringing up the rear. Gibbon's troopers obviously were out for more than a trail ride, and Benjamin One Feather knew without asking that they were headed for the distant prairies, probably on another converging maneuver.

Colonel Gibbon, recognizing Benjamin, greeted him like a long-lost friend, momentarily setting the young brave back in his saddle. Since their last meeting hadn't been all that pleasant, Benjamin One Feather allowed that only a man seeking a favor would be riding in with folded gloves and a smile on his face. After introducing the officer at his side, one Major Marvis Canty, Gibbon casually inquired about the trail—whether there was any activity along the way, where the Crow were taking the horses—all of this nothing but small talk. Finally, he got around to asking about the land beyond the Big Horn. Had any of the Crow traveled along the Rosebud Mountains lately? Benjamin told him that many of his people had been that way, some only recently, both scouting and hunting. Much of this was their land, and they used it regularly.

"Any sign of the Sioux or Cheyenne?" Gibbon inquired.

"Plenty of sign," Benjamin One Feather replied. But he thought to himself that if Gibbon wants to know how fresh it was, he's going to have to find out for himself.

"Villages? Any villages?"

"Far to the south, Colonel, far from our land now," answered Benjamin One Feather. "I'm afraid you and your men are in for a long ride; maybe, like the last time, for nothing. There are no hostiles anywhere in the Greasy Grass. We hunted there in peace late in the summer. Our scouts have been over since then, down the Yellowstone too. All we see or hear about is the surveyors for the telegraph. No, I'm afraid there are no Indians for you to kill." He peered down the line again. "I don't see any good scouts with you . . . Gerard or Henry Fuller. They told me no one listened to them last spring. Gerard almost got himself killed. Maybe that's why they're not along, ei?" Benjamin knew that by now the two old scouts were in the Oregon territory, probably toasting each other with rye whiskey.

Gibbon stiffened, and his big nose turned rosier. Here he was, confronted again with this impudent, English-speaking Indian, and yet again he resented the snobbish attitude and impertinent questions of this arrogant Crow brave. "The only one who didn't listen, young man, was George Custer," he retorted. "And I wouldn't give too much credence to the words of either Fuller or Gerard. They left us in the field, deserted their duty to carry on. Quitters, the both of them. Good riddance."

Benjamin One Feather grinned. "I don't blame them, Mr. Gibbon. What good is intelligence when it's ignored? By jingo, if I had three thousand armed hostiles looking down my throat, I'd slap leather too, and plenty fast. I wouldn't go charging in with two or three hundred men."

Then Major Canty, sensing the building hostility between Gibbon and Benjamin One Feather, finally spoke up. "Tell me, sir, what have you heard about Dull Knife, the Cheyenne?"

"Ah!" Benjamin softly exclaimed, his eyes lighting up. "So you're not interested in the Sioux? This was the goose chase I thought you were going on, Sitting Bull and his people. . . ."

"What about Sitting Bull?" Gibbon asked curtly.

"He's gone," Benjamin said, whisking his hand through the air. "*Poof,* just like that. You're too late again, Mr. Gibbon. Your General Miles, I hear, chased him for two or three weeks. Many of his people are back home already, ei, but not the great chief. No, not old Sitting Bull. He's up in the Queen Mother's Land, drinking good whiskey." Benjamin One Feather glanced back and forth, first to Gibbon, then back to Major Canty. They had sour looks on their faces. Neither man seemed to appreciate what he was telling them. Allowing that this news about Sitting Bull had never come out of the field yet, Benjamin continued, saying, "You need to get these singing wires connected. All these surveyors seem to be doing is riding up and down the river pounding sticks in the ground and enjoying the scenery. The moccasin trail is much faster these days. We seem to know more than you do."

This was enough for the One Who Limps. He had taken all the abuse that he was going to from this brave. "And one of these days, Mr. Tree," he gruffly put in, "you're going to have to quit riding the goddamned fence, make up your mind whose side you're on in this campaign, quit your talking and start fighting." He nodded curtly and motioned his men forward.

Glancing over at Molly and White Crane, Benjamin One Feather shrugged. "Not even an *aho*."

Canty, reining to the side, asked again, "Dull Knife? What have you heard?" He leaned close to Benjamin One Feather and nodded toward the departing Gibbon. "Look here now, it's obvious you don't like old Red Nose, and damned few of us do, but it's our skins on these saddles, too. Now, what about Dull Knife?"

Benjamin One Feather grinned. "He's up in the Big Horns, a big village, somewhere around the upper Tongue, but I wouldn't count too much on catching up with him, not with that fool leading you. He's apt to get you all rubbed out, just like Yellow Hair."

Canty politely tipped his hat and rode on. But this wasn't the end of the conversation. Bevis Ketchum, who had an ear cocked to part of it, stopped briefly to add a few words of his own. With his horse nervously prancing back and forth, Sergeant Ketchum nodded at the mule train. "Hey, fancy talker, thought you people didn't deal in mules. Where'd you get these beauties, anyhow?"

Benjamin One Feather, his suspicion immediately aroused, replied casually, "On the prairie . . . A gift, you might say."

Ketchum smirked back through his red beard. "Is that so? Now, if that don't beat all! A gift, you say? Well, some of the boys from Keogh found a boy on the trail about a month ago, almost all done in he was, half-starved and bug-bitten. Said some fancy-talking Injun chased him and his buddies off the buffalo grounds. Yep, made 'em walk out. The boy's name was Harley. . . . Harley Frame, as I recall. His partners didn't make it, I reckon. Leastways, no one found 'em. Now that's some story, ain't it?"

Benjamin One Feather shrugged casually. "That's a pity. I thought with all of those buffalo they've killed on our land, they'd have plenty to eat along the way. Ei, this is hard to believe, Sergeant. We even showed them the way out. I'm sorry to hear this."

"Yep, I sure bet you are," Ketchum said stonily. "Well, boy, you better watch out, watch your step. No one gives a shit what your name is. One of these days the law ain't gonna be on your side. No profit in killing white folks. Get yourself hanged doing it."

"And I suppose you want to be on the other end of the rope?" said Benjamin One Feather. Venting his anger, Bevis Ketchum suddenly made a cutting pass with his quirt at Benjamin's face, but just as swiftly the young brave jerked his head back and grasped the sergeant's wrist in midair. He held it firmly for a moment, then shoved it away. "If you ever try that again," Benjamin One Feather said lowly, "I'll kill you, uniform or not."

Then, lashing out with his foot, he caught Ketchum's horse on the forearm. It bolted backward and the sergeant, fighting briefly for control, finally reined the big black in and trotted away. "You ornery sonofabitch!" he cursed. "I'll see you in Hell!"

Molly Goodhart, her dark eyes sparking outrage, watched Ketchum ride toward the head of the column. Shaking her fist, she exclaimed, "You vile man!" Turning back to Benjamin One Feather, she said, "He needs a good thrashing, carrying on that way! Who does he think he is? My gracious!"

"Three Stripes," said Benjamin. "That's what we call him, Three Stripes. Red Whiskers." He moved closer to the wagon as the caissons trundled by. Several troopers raised their hands in friendly salutes, for they had seen this Crow brave before, and a few of them knew he was a friend of Lieutenant Hockett. Benjamin One Feather attempting to smooth Molly's ruffled feathers, told her that this wasn't the first time he had exchanged words with Three Stripes. It had become a habit to duel with the man.

White Crane had a startled expression on her face. She pulled her pony close to her husband. "Three Stripes. Do you see this? Three times you have crossed this man's path, Benjamin One Feather. Ei, three times!" Her wide eyes then followed the departing soldiers, penetrated the back of Ketchum. "This is not coincidence, my man," she said. "As surely as the brown hawk crosses the sky, that man is the fox!"

"The fox?" Molly said, still agitated. She stared curiously over at White Crane, who was sitting quietly with a frightened look on her face. "Why, he looks more like an ugly ruffian to me. Acts like one, too. Fox, indeed!" Gathering up the reins, she gave them a quick snap and the mules moved ahead.

Near the mouth of Bear Canyon, Benjamin One Feather unexpectedly took over the reins of the mule team, advising his friends that pulling the wagon up the canyon was unsafe—too much of the hillside was rocky; in many places it was covered with downfall. Instead he had decided to drive the team on into Bozeman City, telling his companions to ride over the hill to the line cabin and that he would meet them later in the day at the ranch. He was aware that no one particularly cared about riding through a hostile town, and thought this a practical solution. White Crane, of course, expressed some concern about the change in plans, but Benjamin assured her that there was no need to worry. He wasn't begging for trouble, only intended to stop by Lucas Hamm's store to arrange for the supplies the Crow had ordered. He planned on leaving the wagon and mules at the livery where they could be picked up the following morning. This much decided, and with White Crane wagging a finger of warning, Benjamin One Feather proceeded on by himself and did exactly as he had said. By late afternoon he was riding through the gate of the ranch on his pinto, just about the time the pony herd and droving party came trotting into the main corral.

There was a lot of celebrating that night, as everyone gathered in James and Little Blue Hoop's new house. The women had prepared a feast of ribs, corn fritters, biscuits, and wild honey. The Crow marveled at the sight of water coming through a spigot into a basin, and a handle that could stop the flow by a mere twist of the hand. When Little Blue Hoop, her belly already fat as a melon, showed Walking Woman the new feather bed, she squealed delightedly, and then almost disappeared from sight when she was asked to try it out.

Later Benjamin One Feather and Claybourn Moore, with tiny Joshua riding his shoulders, went back to the foreman's house to look over a few memoes of transactions Moore had been preparing for Ben Tree. There was one interesting note: The recently completed cattle drive had netted over forty thousand dollars profit for the ranch, this recently deposited in the Bozeman City bank. Lately James, Robert Peete, and Willie Left Hand had been busy completing the last of the long wintering sheds in the Six Mile Creek bottom. Even though Claybourn Moore thought this was a rather extravagant venture just for field critters, he never questioned Ben Tree's prophecy that sometime down the line these shelters would pay off overnight. In Ben Tree's opinion cows were stupid, defenseless animals with absolutely no sense of direction. The blessing of protection given to the buffalo by the

Great Maker of Everything never had been afforded the cow.

While Ruth Moore was putting Joshua to bed, James came in and joined Benjamin and Claybourn at the table. They sipped fresh coffee while Benjamin tried to answer his brother-in-law's questions about the fighting in the Big Horns. Whatever he knew Benjamin told, often venturing an opinion on what was likely to happen next—futile chases, small skirmishes until winter set in, then the inevitable. The hostiles, for the most part, would be herded back to their reservations. The bluecoats now had them surrounded on four sides, with forts in every direction. Subjugation was imminent.

James expressed his thanks again for getting back the brown mare, Nell, that his father had favored so much. Lately he had taken to riding her on trips to the upper ranges near the line cabin. James said that it was not only good for the horse but for himself as well, spiritually. But when he asked more about the Sioux, details about Benjamin's fight, he was appalled, distressed that Benjamin had taken such a chance, especially when he saw the ugly scar for the first time. Smiling, Benjamin adjusted his buckskin shirt, telling James and Claybourn that it could have been much worse, that only his spiritual guide had saved him. It was obvious to his listeners to whom he was referring, the great Shining Elk. They had heard the story of this mysterious creature of the skies from both Man Called Tree and Little Blue Hoop. This brought a faint smile to Claybourn Moore's tanned face, the recollection of Benjamin's polite refusal to hunt bull elk above the ranch and the mystical reasoning behind it. But no matter, Moore had come to understand the Indian mind in his long association with the Tree family. Animals bring visions, and the spirits of these animals distribute powerful medicine to only a chosen few. Shining Elk had become Benjamin's protector and guardian in this spiritual transfer of power. This was Benjamin's belief and Claybourn Moore would not belittle it, but he did give him a friendly repartee.

"Benjamin, if I had a guide like that," he said with a smile, "I wouldn't eat elk meat either. I can see why those legs of your pony are all painted up. Now, *that's* something new. Streaks of lightning."

Benjamin laughed. "That's White Crane's doing, not mine. I don't quarrel with her ideas. Sometimes she sees things in my medicine that I miss, and most of the time she's more right than wrong. Lightning is the medicine of the Spirit Elk. She figures when I'm sitting that pony, he's a part of me and he shares in my medicine. Ei, that's what she thinks. Fact is, he eats and craps just like the rest of them." He looked up over the rim of his cup at the two men and grinned. "One of these days, though, I expect him to take off flying. . . . Hope I can hang on, because it would be one helluva buckoff from way up there."

Ruth Moore came back in the front room and refilled the cups, and it was only a few minutes afterward when the men heard riders coming up outside. Claybourn Moore went to the door and peered out, wondering who would be calling so late. Shortly, Donald Blodgett appeared in the light of the doorway, followed by his son Henry. When the smithy entered the room, he immediately pointed at Benjamin. "Ah-hah," he said, grinning, "*there's* the rascal I'm looking for!" Everyone shook hands and Ruth brought two more cups. Meanwhile, Blodgett began to explain. Earlier that evening his son Henry had stopped by the Antler saloon, where he'd overheard several men talking about young Benjamin Tree being back in town, one of them a brother to Jim Clancy.

Benjamin gave Blodgett a blank look. "Who's Jim Clancy?"

"One of the rustlers you and your boys shot up over in the Crazies," Donald Blodgett replied.

His son interrupted then, saying, "His brother's name is Dupee. Leastways, that's what I heard. Only been around a few days. Dupee Clancy. Dupee . . . Damned funny name, if you ask me. Anyhow, he's all riled and drunked-up, and I hear him saying someone oughtta take care of you, and maybe he just might consider doing it himself. He's jawing away about a fair shake, Injuns taking the law in their hands, and all that crap." Henry looked over at his father. "Well, pa says we oughtta come out and warn you."

Claybourn Moore spoke up. "The constable, old man Duggan, is the one you should be telling this. He'd run that drunk over to the jail to cool off."

"Tried that," Henry replied. "He wasn't in, only a keeper in his place, that's all. Said he didn't know where old Bill was, so I let it go, told pa. That's the size of it."

Pouring coffee, Ruth Moore said, "Go tar and feather that scamp!"

Donald Blodgett took a sip of his coffee, looked across the table at Benjamin. "You could probably blow this Dupee fellow over with a broom straw. He's a drifter, roustabout, just like Jim was, always looking for something easy. Now that's what got me addled. It's fellows like this you just can't trust. Regular folks don't hold with this line of thinking about those cattle thieves. Hell, no, they'd pin a medal on you, but this jasper, why he's apt to sneak around some barn and—"

"A bushwhacker," Benjamin interjected.

"Right," said Blodgett. "You hit the nail right on the head. Or like his brother, he could go getting a few others of his like all riled." Blodgett grunted with disgust. "Anyhow, I knew you were coming back in tomorrow to get that wagon, so thought maybe it best to warn you. I know damned well that jackass won't come looking for trouble out here. He'd get his feathers dusted."

Benjamin unconsciously tugged on an earlobe for a moment. He thanked the two Blodgetts for riding out with the news, decided the best way to avoid trouble was not to seek it. If White Crane and the others had no wish to go through Bozeman City in the morning, neither did he. The least thing in the world he wanted to do right now was shoot down some drifter in a town already filled with Indian hatred. But then again, the thought of conceding to the crazy whims of some drunk by the name of Dupee in a town half-owned by the Tree family curdled his blood. Before he could make a decision, Claybourn Moore made it for him.

"Old man Hamm got your order, right?" Moore asked. Benjamin agreed that yes, everything was already arranged. "Well," concluded Moore, "I'll pick up that load as soon as the store opens, pay Lucas off, head out, meet you over at the canyon where you came out last time." He shot Benjamin a questioning look. "How's it sound?"

"Under the circumstances," Benjamin said, "it solves a small problem. Don't mention it to the others. No use in them worrying about some damned drunk. Ei, Stone Calf just might want to sneak into town tonight and make the man's body disappear."

James asked, "But how you going to explain riding over the hill with them, the wagon being in town and all? Holy cow, maybe they'll think you've lost some of your medicine, that kind of stuff."

Benjamin tapped the side of his head. "James, most of my medicine is right in here, ei? Always has been. Besides, I like riding in the hills with my people. Let Mr. Clay here handle those mules. I sure can abide that." He grinned. "Red Running Horse is the only one in our crowd who likes to play muleskinner, but it would take a powerful lot of persuasion to get him snaking that whip through town."

This matter settled, the conversation turned briefly to business, matters of the ranch, and rumors of new gold strikes two days west of Bozeman City. Donald Blodgett allowed that with all of his work ahead for Ben Tree, he was going to set up a forge for his son Henry in one of the ranch sheds. Clay Moore figured there were at least sixty horses on hand that had to be shod. A shop on the ranch would save a lot of riding back and forth. After another round of coffee, the smithy and his son left. It was almost nine o'clock.

The next morning the Crow party got away early, pausing long enough at the line cabin to take a plunge in the hot springs. White Crane, although she held her tongue, was suspicious of her husband's most recent change in plans—riding with her instead of handling the wagon—but she was too happy about having his company to even question the decision. She thought Clay Moore's explanation was rather lame—he was driving the mules so Benjamin could visit the hot springs again. It wasn't until later, when they all came down to the mouth of the canyon, that her suspicions were confirmed. Something was amiss. White Crane not only saw Moore waiting by the wagon, but with him Robert Peete and Willie Left Hand, two of the ranch hands. And when Moore waved a goodbye and rode away on his horse, both Peete and Willie Left Hand stayed behind, began to move their ponies ahead of the wagon and on up toward the pass.

Easing up to her husband, White Crane finally asked,

"What has happened, my man, that these two ride with us? They must have work at the ranch more important than this?"

"It's nothing to worry about," Benjamin One Feather assured her. "They only go as far as the pass."

But her perception was too keen for him. "Bad white men always worry me, Benjamin One Feather. I see these things better than you think. Are the people still angry with us because of Yellow Hair? Or have the friends of the cow thieves come to haunt us like ghosts?"

Benjamin gently tutted her. "Mr. Clay thought we should have some company, and I didn't want to argue the point. Next to my father, he has the final word. He says there are road agents about, men who steal on the trail. With all of these supplies, a few gold coins for our people, it would be bad medicine to return with empty hands."

White Crane thought this answer somewhat evasive but she silently accepted it, realizing that she was unlikely to get anything more definitive from her man this day. Since he had become a pipe-carrier, it was contrary to his medicine to let others worry. Their trust was explicitly in him, their welfare in capable hands wielding great power. But White Crane thought perhaps her husband had forgotten or did not realize that his followers were also deeply concerned about his well-being. She foresaw many dark clouds on the distant horizon, prophecies unresolved. Her man was going to need his greatest medicine, and much help from these people, to find his way through this threatening maze.

But five sleeps later, and without incident, Benjamin One Feather and his followers arrived in their village. It was a clear morning, Masaka's face unhidden, the brisk autumn wind giving the falling leaves a rollicking good ride across the browning landscape. The supplies were unloaded, gifts distributed, and the people were happy. Homecoming was a time of joy. All of this was plenty good.

FIFTEEN

May, 1877

It was the Moon When the Ponies Shed before Benjamin One Feather and his brothers once again began to notice an increase in travel along the Yellowstone River trail. This was in part because war between the bluecoats and their enemies, the Sioux and Cheyenne, had almost ended. Winter had been a bad time for the Indians. Sitting Bull and some of his Hunkpapa fled to the Queen Mother's land during the cold months; Dull Knife's village of Cheyenne surrendered after a battle with Col. Raynald Mackenzie's Fourth Cavalry; Crazy Horse and some of his Sioux finally gave up to Gen. Nelson Bearcoat Miles, after a bitter campaign in below-zero weather on the Tongue River. But as Benjamin One Feather had predicted, Colonel Red Nose Gibbon's trek to the prairie once again proved fruitless, the One Who Limps and his bluecoats having been two days late to participate in the battle with Dull Knife.

Now the Crow scouts were regularly sighting patrols from Fort Keogh and occasionally a platoon from Fort Ellis, all of these generally riding the Yellowstone River trail. Lt. Zachary Hockett, reassigned to the cavalry at Keogh, showed up one spring day to report that in March he had visited James and Little Blue Hoop at the ranch and met their new daughter, Melody. Two new ranch hands had been hired, a drover and Molly Goodhart, who now worked as the bunkhouse cook.

This conversation took place on the Yellowstone. Seldom did Benjamin's Crow meet anyone on the cutoff leading south to Fort Fetterman and the main Oregon trail. Even though the Lakota no longer contested the Bozeman Trail through the Big Horns, its traffic had diminished dramatically. Most immigrants heading west were now riding the iron road, the Union Pacific's route, some stopping at the Utah stations where they outfitted and traveled on north into the Idaho and Montana territories. So it was a surprise this day when Benjamin One Feather and his brothers sighted a train of wagons winding down the lower Tongue River bottom. The Crow were hidden from view on a distant sagebrush knoll, where Benjamin was carefully glassing the oncoming party.

He saw fourteen wagons, most them ribbed with canvas, a few men riding ponies alongside the grinding wheels. At the rear several others were herding a conglomeration of horses, mules, and cattle. After taking turns watching, Benjamin One Feather and Sitting Elk agreed that these were immigrants, probably farmers, destination unknown. Sitting Elk, after a careful second look, handed the binoculars back to Benjamin. One of the men riding near the front of the file looked familiar, like the scout who told funny stories, the man who had once led Red Nose Gibbon's troops into the Greasy Grass. Benjamin One Feather said that this had to be Henry Fuller, who, with Fred Gerard, had ridden toward the Oregon territory the past year with Two Shell Woman. He thought it strange that Fuller was already back in plains country, but then allowed that the lack of hostiles probably had something to do with it. The trail was safe again. White Moon dryly commented that it was more likely a lack of money, for only someone who was broke and badly in need of a grubstake would be guiding such a sorry assortment of pilgrims. His assumption proved to be the right one.

Circling back, the Crow came down in front of the wagon train about a mile downriver. There were a few moments of panic among the movers when four buckskinned Indians armed with rifles suddenly appeared, blocking their way. This sent the outriders into a hasty retreat behind the wagons, where they began to scan the line of cottonwoods for signs of ambush. When they saw Henry Fuller riding boldly into them and then shaking hands, they began to cautiously edge out, everyone down the line with their necks craned, wondering who these Indians were, the first they had encountered on the long trail up from the North Platte.

After Fuller had introduced the man in charge, Sam Meeker, a carpenter by trade, they retired to the shade of the trees, spread blankets, and began to talk. As White Moon had presumed, Fuller, without money, had come back across the southern route until he struck up with the guiding job offered by Meeker. He was leading these people up to Fort Keogh, where white men were already congregating, erecting a few buildings and makeshift cabins of log and sod near the fort, and calling this new settlement Milestown.

Milestown! This always bitterly amused Benjamin One Feather, how the white people always seemed to name their villages and forts after dead pony soldiers or men who had marked the land. Keogh, Fetterman, Kearny, Smith, Bozeman, Stevens, and now Bearcoat Miles, a general who wasn't even dead yet. To Benjamin this was ironically arrogant. Many of these places were ancient Indian landmarks, now bearing the names of white men who, in many instances, had been vain, foolhardy, and ill-prepared for the frontier endeavors that had led to their deaths.

After some discussion about hostiles, or the lack of them, Benjamin One Feather inquired about Fuller's trip across the Bitterroots into the land of his mother's people, and the disposition of Two Shell Woman. Fuller told the Crow that all had gone well, the journey pleasant and without incident. He joked that they had caught good-eating trout in every stream all the way to the Salmon, beautiful, clear waters in pristine canyons, some filled with fish as long as his arm, that Two Shell Woman had taught him and Gerard how to prepare a mouth-watering chowder using bacon, fish, flour, camas, and wild onions. As expected, the Crow turned up their noses to this.

Two Shell Woman was now with her relatives in the

Wallowa, Fuller told them. In early spring Fred Gerard had headed up toward the Hellgate country in Montana territory while he packed east, finally ending up along the North Platte. However, when Fuller came back through the Salmon and Snake River valleys he discovered that Nez Percé were becoming alarmed at new encroachments on their reservation, this time not by miners but by ranchers who were ranging their cattle on tribal land in the rich coulees of the Wallowa.

"Seems like the Wallowa is being reopened to settlement, leastways that's what they're claiming," Fuller told his listeners. "That parcel of land was sealed off for the Injuns in seventy-three. Course I reckon that don't mean much anymore, government and all siding in with these farmers. I hear some chief name of Joseph is trying to get it settled, but it ain't looking too good. Some of those bucks of his are hopping mad, and that's a new twist. They been so damned peaceful long as I can recollect. Go out of their way to make a man comfortable. Hell, old Fred and me stayed on for three days and didn't turn a lick. Sang and danced a bit, though."

Benjamin One Feather, reflecting momentarily on what his father had told him about the Nez Percé from the days when he had lived with them, finally said, "That's been their problem, Mr. Fuller. They try to please too much, and then the sodbusters walk all over them. They have no treaty, never have, only imitations of treaties. Years ago when my father first married my mother, he was already a famous man, a spokesman for many tribes. He told the people across the mountains the first treaty was a bad one, the second one even worse. They didn't listen. The government and cross-bearers misled them and stole them blind. There are no treaties left anymore, only pieces of paper that are meaningless." His dark eyes flashed with anger and he crossed his throat with the edge of his hand. "I tell you, the Nez Percé should have fought long ago, chased all the *shoyapee* from their land, killed a few. Ei, to give up everything without a fight is a dishonorable and slow way to die."

Sam Meeker, the wagonmaster sitting next to Henry Fuller, listened in alarmed silence to this harsh indictment from a young Indian who spoke better English than most of the whites in the wagons behind them. Had his bitter words been uttered in more civilized surroundings, they certainly would have brought most men to their feet, angrily shaking their fists. But not here, not in this wild, sage-covered country of the red man. After hearing several more references to the brave's father, Sam Meeker finally asked, "Who *is* your father? Is he still in these parts?"

Benjamin One Feather answered, "Man Called Tree, chief of Absaroke. He is a friend of Mr. Fuller here. Yes, he's here. Long ago he was everywhere across this land. He was called by many names—White Ghost, Crow Man, Medicine Tree, ei, the White Wolf. That's when he was a white man."

Sam Meeker studied Benjamin One Feather curiously. "You mean your father is white, like us here? I don't understand."

"Ei, white, but not like you or anyone here," Benjamin One Feather replied. "He gave up his white blood many years ago."

Henry Fuller spoke up. "Benjamin here is named after his father, Ben Tree. Ben Tree was long-running these trails even before I came this way, and hell, I'm ten years older than him."

Sam Meeker was silent for a moment, lost in distant recollection. Finally: "Read accounts about a man called Tree some years ago, but this fellow lived in the mountains. More legend than man, I reckon. No one ever saw him, and I thought that all of this reading was more tall tales than gospel."

Fuller chuckled, saying, "Reckon that's why some of the boys called him the White Ghost. In those days it made a lot of people real uneasy just hearing he was around, red and white alike. First time I met these boys' pa, he was riding a Cheyenne stud, four scalps hanging from his hackamore. Ben had a couple of big eagle feathers dangling from his own hair, a scar from his cheek plumb to his ear. Damndest sight I ever saw. Why, it was said he could steal your horse right out from under you, too, leave you sitting there reaching for air."

"Is that a fact?" Meeker said, his eyes widening.

White Moon, who had been silent as he listened to more legends being born, said, "This is the reason we're out here, looking for some ponies to steal, maybe a scalp or two. We were up there a plenty long time looking over this stock, seeing how many women you have." He stared indifferently down the line of wagons, "Not much good here. Ponies look skinny just like the women. Maybe we have to ride over to the main trail, see what we can find there. Man Called Tree gets plenty mad when we don't bring home something good. He hates skinny women. Too hard to sell." Looking Meeker in the eye, he asked, "You have a young woman hiding in the wagons you want to trade? One my age? I have a plenty good rifle, two gold pieces."

Sam Meeker, startled by such an outrageous proposition, stonily contemplated White Moon, then glanced at the two braves closest him, Sitting Elk and Red Running Horse, both somber of course, the English conversation beyond their comprehension. Nearby Fuller was merely shrugging, and Benjamin One Feather had only the smallest trace of a smile on his face, nothing forthcoming from any of them. Meeker's mouth puckered and he gave White Moon a sour look. "I'm afraid we don't trade our women, not our custom, understand? Besides, we only have four here and they have menfolks; you know, wedded women, and all of them have younguns."

White Moon's face went blank. "Younguns? What is younguns?" He leaned across and spoke seriously to Henry Fuller. "Is this bad medicine, like bugs? I think if these women have younguns, I don't want them. I had a woman who had lice. That was plenty bad. Had to put all my blankets and clothes on the ant hills. Ei, the ants ate all of those little bastards. I scratched like a crazy coyote for three nights just thinking about those lice."

Benjamin One Feather finally translated all of this for Sitting Elk and Red Running Horse, who both began laughing and scratching their sides for mock lice. Sam Meeker, still perplexed, forced a smile and shrugged helplessly at Henry Fuller. "These fellows don't seem to understand my lingo, Henry."

"Oh, they understand," Fuller assured him with a broad grin. "Some of these bucks will put a cockle burr in your pants every chance they get. They done heard plenty of this 'dumb Injun' shit. Dumb, hell! Why, they'll go back and cackle like geese about this, how they went and bamboozled some greenhorn white man. Dammit, this is their way of having fun once in a while, eh, boys?''

Benjamin One Feather told Meeker, ''If you listen to my brother too much you'll go blind and deaf, the worst thing possible if you enjoy playing with rattlesnakes. Ei, this day you have been bitten.''

''Oh, bushwah!'' the wagoner exclaimed with a hearty laugh, pointing an accusing finger at the Indians.

White Moon, unsmiling, said, ''I will trade you two rifles for one fat woman without younguns. This is my last offer.''

Despite this brief levity at departure, Benjamin One Feather came away despondent, the bad news from the land of the Nez Percé nagging him. He knew that his father and Nez Percé mother, Rainbow, would be upset to hear what Henry Fuller had just related. The distressing part was that there was nothing to be done about it. It was a hopeless situation, a giant boulder on a hill, slowly starting its roll toward the precipice, gradually picking up speed, then thundering along and crushing everything on its fateful path to oblivion. Ei, too many boulders, no one to stop them.

White Moon, sensing his brother's worry, and at the same time sharing it, tried to rationalize. Perhaps by now the treaty problem had been resolved. If there were any conflict, news of it it would have come down the moccasin trail by now. After all, Fuller had left the Salmon almost two months ago. This was true, Benjamin One Feather admitted, but the shadow inside him, his *iraxxaxe,* was restless, his vision beginning to crystallize in the spiritual mists. He was an uneasy man.

On their homeward journey, the four Absaroke scouts forded the Big Horn River and made their way through the high mountains to the west, where they killed two fine sheep, both with great curls of gnarled horn rimming their heads. They feasted, packed on quarters of the rams, and two days later came into the valley of the Clarks Fork and then to rest in their village.

Benjamin One Feather first told Big Cloud that the buffalo country was free of hostiles, that he and his brothers had found no sign of hide hunters, either. He traced a map in the dust outside the chief's lodge, pointing out several areas where they had sighted isolated herds of blackhorn. This was good. The buffalo chief was awaiting only a few more favorable signs before he placed the symbolic skull at the village perimeter, and he promised he would soon announce the time of the early hunt. Later, White Crane and her husband went to the big tipi of Man Called Tree, where they all ate and talked.

As expected, Benjamin's father was unhappy to hear the news from Henry Fuller about the most recent trouble of the Nez Percé; unhappy, but not surprised. He explained that their lands, spacious and wide, had long been envied by white settlers who were forever clamoring for more ground to plow, more range for their ponies and cows, more gullies to wash away in the search of gold, all of this in the name of progress and civilization. The chief said that powerful men in government, including some who had fought Indians, were unlikely to impede these territorial advances by upholding the rightful claims of the Nez Percé. In the white man's new society there was no room for compromise or benevolence, especially if it interfered with economic progress. For the Nez Percé it was too late to fight—too many forts, too many trodden trails, too many squatters, too few warriors to protect the diminishing land. He knew some of the men Henry Fuller had mentioned: Young Joseph, White Bird, Looking Glass, and Ollokot. And there was Gray Hawk, the brother of Rainbow, the uncle of Man Called Tree's children. All of these men had been peacemakers. It was his belief and hope that these leaders would find some solution to the Wallowa dispute, even if it meant ceding another portion of the land, since battle was alien to them and would only lead to humiliating defeat.

Benjamin One Feather, aware of his father's wisdom, listened to these discouraging words, some familiar from Man Called Tree's prophecies. Even though Benjamin's entire life had been spent with the Absaroke, he often read a message of sorrowful lament in his Nez Percé mother's eyes when the oppression of her people had been discussed. Benjamin's blood was Nez Percé, too. He vowed secretly that if his blood brothers were ever forced to fight to protect their ancient heritage, he somehow would assist them, however insignificant that help might be. He realized now that, in some inexplicable way, this was part of his vision, the conflict of people, the signs of the evil coming from the shadows of the West, his call to the Great Bear of the West to help the fleeing, all of these images unresolved.

And there was his great guide, Shining Elk from the North, who had endowed him with special power. *Spread your wings and use it.* How was all of this to be resolved? And when? He contemplated the rugged features of his father for a moment, this great man who had been around the mountain so many times, a man of wisdom and courage. Benjamin One Feather said, "In all my years I've never disagreed with your words, your counsel, your advice, but I tell you now, our people in the Tahmonmah are going to fight. There is no other solution. My medicine tells me this and I can't believe otherwise. *Sepekuse.*"

"You may be right, son," Man Called Tree agreed. "Ei, you're man enough now to voice your opinion. You have proved yourself many times, but there's little we can do about it here but pray these people come to an agreement of some kind." He contemplated his son, gave him a fatherly smile. "If a man burdens himself too much with the misfortunes of others, he often loses sight of his own worth and responsibilities. No one in this lodge, ei, your pretty wife, wants this to happen to you, *barakbatse,* my son. One day you'll become a chief of the Absaroke, take your place in the council as a leader. Always keep this in mind, ei?"

But White Crane, sitting by Benjamin's side, her dark eyes downcast, knew her man's mind, his heart as well, for in loving him she had become a part of him. His heart was heavy with what he foresaw, and time and events were casting him adrift on troubled waters. For the present, she knew there would be no homecoming in the Land of the Winding Waters where her husband had once promised to take her, no reunion with their friend Two Shell Woman. Her only consolation was that all of this bad medicine was far over the mountains, many sleeps away from the peaceful Absaroke. For this, she was thankful.

Spring mellowed into summer and activity on the trail burgeoned, wagons creaking back and forth, the continuing hustle of the pony soldiers, the telegraph crews stringing the singing wires. After the buffalo hunt, many of the villagers took their tipis into the cool, pine woods below Nah-pit-sei, ranging their ponies in the high mountain meadows far away from the wary eyes of the white men. But news still filtered in, mostly from what the scouts picked up along the moccasin trail.

Benjamin One Feather wasn't alarmed to hear stories of war between the troopers and the Nez Percé, this only confirming how powerful his vision on the sacred mountain had been. He heard how General One Arm Howard had rousted Young Joseph and his tribe from the Wallowa, how white men had raided the Nez Percé pony herd while crossing the Snake River, shooting and killing a young Indian boy. Angry Nez Percé returned that same night to recapture their ponies, and they killed eight of the thieves as well. This precipitated all-out war, and One Arm Howard immediately attacked the Indians in White Bird Canyon, only to be dealt a crushing defeat by Joseph's men, who outmaneuvered and outfought him in this first brief battle. There was word of a later fight on the Clearwater River, this one inconclusive, but the Nez Percé once again had escaped Howard, humiliating the trained militia now out to destroy them.

Even though Benjamin One Feather had fully anticipated the war, he was surprised that his Nez Percé brothers, so unaccustomed, so inadequately prepared for battle, were actually defending themselves with a zeal, strategy, and skill that far outmatched the West Point officers now harassing them. When he and White Moon, along with White Crane, arrived at the ranch during the Moon of Red Cherries to help with branding and culling the herd, Claybourn Moore told them that the settlers were getting angry with One Arm Howard's repeated failures in the field. More, they were fearful that the Nez Percé were now likely to raid the Idaho settlements in revenge for the injustices heaped upon them at the Lapwai reservation. Moore said reports in the Virginia City newspaper about the Indians' whereabouts were so confusing that no one knew what to believe.

Some of these conflicting stories were laid to rest two days later when Fred Gerard unexpectedly showed up at the ranch. On his way east from the Bitterroot country, where he had recently guided a party of sodbusters, he had firsthand news both startling and ominous. Only several days past, over three hundred Nez Percé, led by Joseph and White Bird, had appeared in the Bitterroot Valley. Gerard in fact had long discussions with some of the people that he and Henry Fuller had stayed with the year previous. Most astonishing to Benjamin and his friends was that Gerard also had met Two Shell Woman, her brother and sister-in-law, who were among Joseph's party. Two Shell Woman was packing a baby on her back, a boy more white than Indian, nine months old. Benjamin One Feather and Clay Moore exchanged surprised glances. White Moon, thoroughly pleased, grinned and translated to White Crane, whose hands suddenly exploded against her cheeks. "Hock-kett!" she gasped.

Fred Gerard nodded affirmatively. "Reckon so. Sure wasn't me. She's calling that boy by a Christian name, too. Killed two birds with one stone—Little Joseph. Reckon the chief won't mind if the little bastard's named after him."

"But how did these people end up in the Bitterroot?" Benjamin One Feather asked, startled at this bizarre turn of events. "What are they doing *there*, of all places?"

Gerard sat on the porch stoop and fetched out his pipe. "Seems like they been chased there," he said. He struck a match on the railing and puffed several times. Then, blowing out a stream of blue smoke, he went on. "Ol' Big Whiskers Howard and his army's behind them, somewhere over in the mountain country. He ain't no big problem, dragging cannon and a mule train over the hills, mebbe two or three days back. He's still licking his wounds." He stopped and grinned broadly, as if he were going to leap up any minute and start to play his harmonica. "Lemme tell you something crazy, here. Some of those greenhorns from Fort Missoula, bluebellies without their feathers yet, tried to stop the Percies in Lolo Canyon, built a big log barricade, got themselves all set up behind it. Ol' Joseph, he comes down and parleys a bit, gets himself a good look. By gawd, the next morning he sneaks over the ridge, comes down several miles below them." The scout chuckled and puffed on his pipe again. "If that don't beat all! Slipped around 'em slick as a whistle, he did. Be calling that place Fort Fizzle, now. Some of those sodbusters playing soldier jest shouldered up their rifles and went home, plumb gave up. Seems as though they didn't hanker to fight either."

Benjamin One Feather asked, "Where are the Nez Percé camped?"

Gerard shook his head. "No place permanent like, jest a night here, a night there." Pointing the stem of his pipe northward, he said, "There's the problem, the other direction. Your ol' friend Red Nose is coming down from Fort Shaw. Leastways, that's what the Hellgate people say. Supposed to link up with Howard, catch the Percies up the valley somewheres. Oh, I wouldn't bet on it, though. Time Red Nose gets in the valley, those boys of Joseph's are likely to be clean out of the country, mebbe all the way to the buffalo grounds."

"The buffalo grounds!" White Moon exclaimed. "Why, that's a two-week trip across the mountains! You think they're going hunting with all those pony soldiers behind them?"

"Headed east they are, for a fact," answered Gerard, with an emphatic wave of the pipe. "Talked to White Bird himself. He says they're gonna kill a few curly cows, then mebbe head on north and link up with ol' Sitting Bull across the border, get away from all these ornery white folks. Ain't exactly how he signed it, though. I think mebbe it was more like ornery assholes." He cackled again and looked at Benjamin. "Yep, appears to me they're heading right for Crow country, eh?"

Benjamin One Feather, his mind swirling, suddenly conjuring up mountaintop visions, hunkered down in front of Gerard, smoothed out a small patch of dust with the heel of his hand. He began to trace a map with Gerard's discarded match stick. "Ei, I understand what you're saying, Mr. Gerard, but which way will they go? The Bitterroot is south, not east, and Gibbon is coming from the north, Howard from the west. They'll try to catch Joseph up here." He marked an X in the dust. "Unless he goes over the pass and moves south into the upper Salmon."

"Gimme that," Gerard said, plucking the stick from Benjamin's fingers. "Lookee here, now. He could take 'em up the Salmon, sure, but that would leave him in a pickle in the Lemhi. He ain't gonna let those soldiers from Fort Boise get a shot at him, too. No, he's gonna cut east right here, same ways ol' Henry and me and little woman came through when we left here last year. He's gonna take his people into the Big Hole, probably cross the Grasshopper into the Big Mountains of the Smoking Water." Scratching a sharp line in the dust, he said, "That would take him right through here, no more'n a two-day ride from where we're sitting." Gerard spat to the side, saying, "Show me a place I ain't been, eh? Only one hitch here," he continued. "If they tarry along the way, they ain't gonna make it this far. They'll get shot down and scattered around like melon seed."

White Crane, listening to White Moon's translation, looked anxiously at Benjamin One Feather. "I would like to get Two Shell Woman and her baby away from this bad medicine. Sometimes those soldiers kill the women and children—ei, even the old ones who bend when they walk."

Gerard listened, then glanced across at Benjamin. "What's she saying?" After another short translation, Gerard gave White Crane an understanding smile and made quick sign. "I asked Two Shell Woman if she wanted to trail this way. She said no, she's staying with her brother's family, her people." Gerard hesitated, then turned back to Benjamin. "Reckon that's best, the baby and all. Not much that soldier boy can do for her now, not in this place."

White Moon, with a dour expression on his bronzed face, commented, "Ei, *that* soldier has already scattered his melon seed, but in a better place."

SIXTEEN

Benjamin One Feather and White Moon, presently discouraged but determined to seek out their Nez Percé uncle, Gray Hawk, stopped to rest on the third day of their wide circuit to the south. So far their journey had proved fruitless, no sign of Indians anywhere in the country. They had hoped to cut the tracks of the Nez Percé, or at least intercept Joseph's wandering band of fugitives within a three-day ride of the ranch. When they finally came down to the upper Big Hole by way of Bannack, they met one rider loping off in the distance, hailed him, and discovered that he was headed for Virginia City with an urgent dispatch. When they asked him about signs of the Nez Percé, he hastily pointed to the northwest, and without pausing further, shouted, "They're coming over the river there, the whole shebang of 'em!" He took off again at a gallop.

The two Crow headed out, following the pony tracks of the dispatch rider, but ultimately lost them when they came down to the Big Hole River. Fording the stream, they kept bearing to the northwest, searching for signs of mounted riders, believing that at any moment they were likely to encounter a few scouts in advance of the tribe.

The first signs of their brothers came about midmorning—not scouts riding point, but a few women and children who immediately began to scramble for cover at their approach. Benjamin One Feather shouted to White Moon, "It's these damned hats we're wearing! They think we're whites!" And with that he shoved his drover's hat down under his bedroll at the back of the saddle. White Moon followed suit, and with their long hair flying, they made a turn around several of the women, calling out in Nez Percé, *"Taz, taz,"* take it easy. *"Kaiziyeuyeu!"* yelled White Moon. At this greeting, one of the women rushed up and pointed frantically toward the distant hills. "The *piuapsiaunat* are over there killing my people!" she cried. "It is time to find places to hide, to save the children, and wait until our men come for us." This much said, she rushed away to join the others.

"The damned army caught up with them before we did," Benjamin cursed, jerking off his denim jacket. This, too, was tucked away behind him. From a trouser pocket he pulled out his beaded headband, adjusted it, and swept his hair back. Moments later, he and his brother were galloping toward the hills. There was no mistaking the proper direction, for another band of women and children, some leading ponies draped with wounded men, was moving along their path. A short time later they could hear the sporadic sharp cracks of rifle fire. Up ahead, nestled in among willows and aspen, they finally saw the cones of the lodges, a layer of smoke drifting away in the morning air. Beyond the village, on the slopes of sage and lodgepole pine, an occasional puff of smoke spit from the shrub; these, Benjamin One Feather reckoned, came from the present position of the soldiers.

Dismounting far out of range, he and White Moon tethered their ponies near a creek, one of the many tributaries of the Big Hole, then followed its protective line of willow to edge up toward the camp. A few women were still huddled together in small groups under the bank-side cover, their faces filled with fear and anguish. Numerous bodies, both of soldiers and Nez Percé, were lying about the left perimeter of the shattered village. In some of the nearby gullies flanking the camp, warriors had taken up defensive positions and were now peppering the adjacent hillside with their rifle fire. Obviously, the village itself had been the site of an earlier battle, the witness to this being the dead of both sides strewn about at the far end of the village nearest the timbered slopes above.

Benjamin One Feather was horrified to see the body of a young woman and her child, flies already swarming about the crushed head of the baby. His first thought was of Two Shell Woman, but this woman was younger, no more than seventeen or eighteen years old. A young Indian, crouching low, came up and grasped Benjamin by the arm. "Who are you?" he asked hurriedly, in sign. "Where did you come from?" Benjamin One Feather spoke back in Nez Percé. "We are Crow from Man Called Tree's village far across the mountains. We are also Nez Percé. Our uncle is Gray Hawk." He nodded toward the carnage. "This is bad medicine."

"Yes," the brave answered, "but we are now winning. Our leaders have rallied. We fought the *piuapsiaunat* here hand-to-hand, beat them back to the hill." The brave identified himself as Wallitze. He pointed to the other side of the village. Over there somewhere was Gray Hawk. His woman, Rabbit Runs, was tending some of the wounded far down the creek. He quickly related that the camp had been attacked by the soldiers at dawn while many of the people were still in their tipis. Many women and children were shot trying to reach the safety of the creek bottom. The soldiers came in long lines accompanied by *cultis shoyapee,* bad whites. Now the troopers were digging holes and hiding behind the trees and rocks. "Come," he said, "I will show you the way to Gray Hawk. I must get back to my place in the line. No time to waste. We are going up those gullies to get them."

A short while later Benjamin One Feather and White Moon scrambled up a small ravine under a sage and juniper knoll, where a knot of men were huddled listening to the talk of a bare-chested brave attired in nothing more than his decorated apron and elkskin moccasins. Noticing the newcomers, he stopped briefly to ask what they wanted. Benjamin One Feather answered, "We are looking for our uncle. He is called Gray Hawk."

"That man is Gray Hawk," the leader said, pointing to one of the group, and he immediately went back to his conversation with the others. Gray Hawk, his eyes widening in surprise, slid down next to Benjamin and White Moon. Grasping them affectionately by the shoulders, his voice choking with emotion, he said, "What is this? I haven't seen you since you were little boys. *Eeyah*, you are men! Ah, but you have come to visit at a bad time. You shouldn't have come to this place. Bad medicine, a time of great danger for us all." Tears suddenly welled in his eyes.

White Moon replied, "No, uncle, this is a good time. We didn't expect a fight like this. Ei, but we are here, and we have our weapons."

"Your father?" Gray Hawk asked. "Is he with you?"

"No," Benjamin One Feather replied. "He's at the village. We came up from the Gallatin, where he has his cows. The man, Gerard, told us you were coming this way. We saw him four days ago."

Gray Hawk shook his head sadly. "We didn't expect this either. Not so soon, ei. We have lost many people, little ones, only a few of our men. Some of these shoy-apee were drunk. They were like crazy men, striking out at everyone, setting some of our lodges on fire." He motioned to the man talking. "This one is Penpenhihi, the white men call him White Bird. We make plans to keep the soldiers surrounded, ei. They have lost more men than we have. We have some good news with the bad." He patted each of them on the shoulders again. "Can you shoot as well as Pootoosway, your great father?"

White Moon managed a thin smile. No one shot better or faster than Man Called Tree, Pootoosway to the Nez Percé. But he boldly answered, "Just as good. He's getting old like you. We aim well, hold steady."

"Ei, he has taught you well then," Gray Hawk said. "Come listen to Penpenhihi. I will tell him who you are. He's a friend of your father. Hinmut-tooyah-latkeht, the one called Joseph, and Looking Glass are up in the middle. Yellow Bull and Ollokot are on the other side. We listen to all of them, ei? They chased the bluecoats back this morning. Now, we see what happens."

A few minutes later several of the braves crept off in different directions, and White Bird turned to Gray Hawk, listened intently as he explained the presence of Benjamin One Feather and White Moon. When he heard that they both spoke English like their father, he nodded, smiled, the corners of his eyes wrinkling into tiny crevices. This was good. He said that before the battle was over they might put their English to good use, if the soldiers decided they wanted to talk about surrendering. He was going to tell Chief Joseph of their arrival.

Benjamin One Feather, surprised at the confidence White Bird exuded, told him that he and his brother were prepared to do more than talk. They were ready to fight. Penpenhihi smiled at this, told them they could join Gray Hawk and several others who were preparing to strengthen the right flank of the Nez Percé line. His men were getting ready now to push the soldiers back up the hill and surround them on three sides. Penpenhihi was voicing enthusiasm; the situation, dire at first, was much better now, and he said that many of the settlers who had joined the soldiers were dead, many others had fled back to the pass after his warriors had stopped the initial onslaught in the village. Benjamin's eyes smouldered when he learned that the soldiers were being led by Colonel Gibbon rather than One Arm Howard. At last, the One Who Limps had managed to get his troops into battle, and ironically, like Yellow Hair, he was about to be rubbed out.

Along with Gray Hawk, Little Bear, and Rabbit Leggings, Benjamin and White Moon made a wide circle to the right of the village, and by early afternoon they were coming down a small draw that overlooked the flank of the entrenched bluecoats. But they were out of shooting range, and without adequate cover to creep in any closer. Glassing the area, Benjamin One Feather saw movement through the pines above the soldiers, soon could make out a few men hauling a howitzer and a caisson toward the middle of the hill. Meanwhile the Nez Percé marksmen were putting up a steady barrage of rifle fire, directed at Gibbon's men dug in on the brushy hillside.

Handing his glasses to Gray Hawk, Benjamin One Feather said, "If they get that cannon in place, they can bring their shot across your middle. Ei, and we're too far away to get off a few rounds at those men dragging that big gun."

After several moments of indecision, Gray Hawk said, "We can go back to the trees over there, climb up and cut across, get above them."

"In back of their lines?" White Moon questioned in a whisper. "That's a bad risk. They'll have shooters on the rim of their circle."

"Ei," Benjamin One Feather smiled grimly. "A risk, true, but if we opened up a barrage on them from above, surprised them, they might bolt out of there like scared chickens. Give those men below better targets, and maybe a chance to claim that higher ground."

Little Bear, listening to these strange Crow who spoke Nez Percé, said, "Penpenhihi would say this is a good way to shoot their assholes. I can climb like a ram, go up this hill pretty fast. Those *piuapsiaunat* killed my sister and her boy this morning when I was in my robes. I have no robe now, but I have this good rifle taken this morning from a dead *shoyapee*. I say we go and chase them off that hill."

Benjamin One Feather, inspecting the rifle, saw that it was a new Winchester, and Little Bear had been smart enough to retrieve the cartridge belt as well. The young brave's words were enough. Without further discussion, and with Little Bear leading the way, the five of them climbed the incline, using the brushy north slope as cover. When they were above the tree line, Benjamin One Feather ventured out to take a look, saw no one above them. Motioning to the others, he crept down into the trees until he finally spotted the howitzer crew, laboring far below and to his right. Beneath these men, another hundred yards away, he picked out at least a dozen soldiers tucked in the rocks and behind small mounds of dirt that they had excavated with their bayonets.

In deference to his uncle, Benjamin turned for his decision. Gray Hawk, making sign, was predictable—hit the howitzer first, rake the area below with rifle fire, then retreat to their present position in case reinforcements came from inside the flank.

Moving stealthily across a series of small depressions, and using the scrub pine for cover, they got within thirty yards of the approaching men with the small cannon before they were spotted. But by the time the alarm had been sounded, Benjamin and Gray Hawk, nearest the six soldiers, opened fire, knocking two of the howitzer crew down. Little Bear, ducking through the trees, felled another soldier, but the remaining three made it to the lodgepole forest and kept right on running. At the same time White Moon and Rabbit Leggings began to pick out targets in the brush below, and true to Benjamin's words, the soldiers were soon leaping out of their cover, making a mad dash toward the middle of the hill. From far below, the Nez Percé stationed on the flank opened up, dropping at least three more soldiers before the rest ducked away into the main encampment.

Gray Hawk and Benjamin, with a few shots whistling over their heads, managed to send the howitzer trundling down the slope. It crashed into a boulder, made one flip, and landed upside down in the sage brush. The caisson met a similar fate. This diversion, as expected, brought a few troopers out from the trees opposite Gray Hawk and Benjamin One Feather. But no sooner had they appeared than they were chased back by a round of fire touched off by Little Bear, White Moon, and Rabbit Leggings. All five of the party held fast until the Nez Percé below began advancing to find new positions on the hill.

By late that afternoon the left side also had been secured, and Colonel Gibbon found himself effectively stymied on three sides, unable to attack without coming under a withering fusillade from the warriors. When darkness set in, the Indians on the flat retrieved their dead, buried many of them, and set up chants that lasted most of the night. It was an eerie, frightening sound, one that Benjamin One Feather knew the white man dreaded to hear.

Benjamin and White Moon became part of this lament, too. They located Two Shell Woman shortly after nightfall in a partially destroyed tipi far back of the village. Crestfallen, almost in a state of shock, she nevertheless greeted them like long-lost brothers. Her brother, Red Owl, had been killed; his wife, White Wing, shot in the back, had just died in her arms. Grateful that they had come, she already knew that Benjamin and White Moon were in the village, had heard word of two Crow, the sons of Pootoosway, who had arrived to fight with the Nez Percé. To make sure, she had gone down to see their ponies picketed in the bottom and immediately recognized the trappings.

Now, as they quietly talked, the *tewat* came to the tipi

for the *pasapukitse,* the blowing of the ghosts away. While he chanted and blew smoke in the four directions, Two Shell Woman, rocking her baby back and forth under her blanket, lamented and moaned a song of death. And the medicine man left to make more incantations, for as Gray Hawk had reported sixty-nine women and children had been slain by the enemy, plus nineteen men—a costly victory for Chief Joseph and the other chiefs. Benjamin One Feather was heavy at heart when he heard this appalling news.

It wasn't until the following day, after a council, that Benjamin One Feather discovered the terrible toll the Nez Percé had inflicted upon Red Nose Gibbon's contingent. Hinmut-tooyah-latkeht and his men had decided upon a strategy to deceive the One Who Limps, and it was Benjamin One Feather, because of his knowledge of the white man's tongue, who was asked to carry out the first part of the ruse.

Shortly after noon he left the broken village on his pony, dressed in his drover's clothing of brimmed hat, denim jacket, and chaps. He made a mile-wide circuit around the beleaguered area and came into the enemy camp from the back, talking briefly with several sentries until an officer arrived. The officer was none other than Major Canty, the same man that Benjamin had met once on the Bozeman Trail with Gibbon's mounted infantry. This amused Benjamin, that the very first officer to greet him was one who probably disliked Red Nose as much as he did. After Benjamin had explained how he and White Moon had appeared on the scene for the purpose of visiting relatives, Canty, beset by disillusionment and humiliation, accompanied him to see Colonel Gibbon. But he warned the young Crow scout that the colonel was distressed, angered because the honor he so keenly desired, that of defeating and capturing Chief Joseph, had been denied him. His stature as a military leader, one seeking recognition and promotion, was being eaten away by a band of underrated pack rats who were stealing his greatest chance for victory.

Soon Benjamin One Feather learned that Gibbon was not only distraught and sick at his stomach with colic, he also had been wounded, shot in the leg. Benjamin had to chuckle at this revelation, and when he suggested to

Major Canty that Gibbon now might inherit another name, the One Who Limps Twice, Canty actually smiled for the first time in two days. For Gibbon's men, there had been very little to laugh about. Major Canty, to Benjamin's astonishment, said that twenty-nine soldiers and officers were dead, over forty wounded, and a half-dozen civilians either killed or missing. One third of Gibbon's command had been put out of commission. The situation, Canty said, was deplorable.

"Why didn't he wait for General Howard?" Benjamin One Feather asked. "Isn't this what he told Colonel Custer last year, to wait?"

Canty replied, "When he sneaked over the hill the first night and saw all of those lodges being pitched, he thought he had the cat in the bag. All in one cluster right below him. Simple strategy. Move in at dawn unexpectedly and destroy them." Canty heaved a sigh of despair. "Our capability is gone now. He's a vain man."

Benjamin One Feather grunted disdainfully and eyed Canty from the side. "A *sick* man, much like Long Hair Custer. Do you realize there are almost seventy women and children dead down there? Ei, children with their heads crushed in like broken gourds. I should have brought one of those babies up here and laid it at his feet, ei, so he could step on it one last time."

"Some of the civilians' fault, there," Major Canty said. "They were liquored up a bit, drinking all night. The old man's orders were to take no prisoners, but I don't think he meant the outright murder of women and children. They could have wandered. . . ."

"The hell he didn't!" angrily replied Benjamin. "That's how your officers win their promotions, by killing Indians. Baker did it to the Blackfeet, Custer on the Washita, Chivington to Black Kettle, all the same damned way. Kill anything that moves, even the poor dogs!" But Benjamin One Feather could vent no more of his pent-up rage, for they were approaching the makeshift quarters of Gibbon, a thatch of boughs and canvas up against a big white boulder. A surge of lightning suddenly coursed through Benjamin One Feather's body, sending a tingling sensation from the base of his spine all the way up to his skull. Here in front of him was the limping wolf, taking refuge behind the white rock! The distant image on the Sacred Mountain was so strikingly similar that he almost swooned. But reality came just as swiftly when he heard Gibbon bark, "What the hell are *you* doing up here? Things are bad enough. How did you get here?"

It took a moment for Benjamin One Feather to recover. Small visionary sparks were still blistering his brain, and now the harsh, shattering outcry of the damned. "I rode here," he finally said. "Ei, right back there, up the hill just like you. The Nez Percé are my people. They asked me to come and talk with you."

"Your people?" Gibbon snorted. "You're down there with them? Why, you don't know who your people are, never did! You're a Crow, and that's where you ought to be, back home with your people, not these hostiles."

"My mother is Nez Percé," Benjamin One Feather said calmly.

Colonel Gibbon, sweeping away a horsefly, shot Benjamin a look of indifference. "What does it matter, and what do you want of me? This talk business. . . . Why are they sending an upstart like you up here? Where's Chief Joseph, Ollokot, White Bird? They're the ones who should be answering to me. Shot some of my best officers. They're the ones who brought all of this on. Why didn't they stay back at Lapwai like the rest of the tribe, respect the law and order of the whole?" This brief outburst left Gibbon's face florid, and he puffed and groaned once, then patted the bandage on his wounded leg. "A scratch, just a scratch. Some fool down there leveled in on me. Damned poor shot."

"Ei, you were more fortunate than some of the others," Benjamin One Feather said. "They died here. And you? Well, you'll probably die in bed someday, but not too peaceful. Too many bad things out there to haunt you, children dead, others without mothers. . . ."

Colonel Gibbon curtly waved Benjamin One Feather off with a huge hand. "Enough, Mr. Tree, enough, don't labor me with sorrowful tales. For God's sake we're at war here, and I'm not a sentimental man. I'm a soldier. I do my duty. Now, get on with this. What do these people want of me? What kind of favor this time?" He groaned again, belched once, and wiped a small trace of drool from the corners of his mouth.

Benjamin One Feather blinked several times and stared incredulously at Gibbon. Certainly his eyes were playing tricks on him, an illusion, a fantasy, Old Man Coyote at work again. Could anyone else have seen such a thing? A little black toad? He glanced curiously at Major Canty, then at the two other officers nearby. All were expressionless. He heard Gibbon rasp again, "Well, come on, Mr. Tree, what is it?"

Benjamin laughed uneasily. "That toad in your throat, I thought I saw it leap out."

"Good Lord, Mr. Tree, I have a touch of colic. Now let's get on with it."

Benjamin One Feather, still mystified by what he had seen, or imagined, gathered himself and began by explaining, as he had to Canty, how he and White Moon had merely chanced upon the battle. After this brief opening, he went on with his subterfuge, Colonel Gibbon's face ranging from red to purple. "The council says if you and your men retire from the field, they will do the same, go on to the buffalo grounds and hunt in peace. They don't want more war. Some of them want to go to the Queen Mother's Land, where there are no quarrels about the land. When the hunt is over, the others will return to the reservation at Lapwai. They say if you don't withdraw they plan on attacking, and from what I've seen, you'll all go down."

Gibbon, outraged, pounded his fist down on his good leg and his eyes rolled wildly. "That's it?" he fumed. "They sent you here to tell me this? What kind of a fool do they think I am? I'm not able to withdraw from the field, not under any such threat! We are well fortified here, have the hostiles under scrutiny at all times. Why, we're under *no* pressure!"

"They have you boxed in on three sides," Benjamin One Feather said. "You're under siege now. You can't mount an offensive without getting cut to pieces. There's only one way out, the way you came. Not my observation, but one made by their scouts. They only lost nineteen men. You've lost one-third of your strength already, and by tomorrow—"

"How do you know how many casualties I have?" Gibbon interrupted testily. He shot an angry look of accusal around the circle of men. "This is none of your damned business."

Shrugging, Benjamin One Feather said, "No, that's true, but it's obvious from one look around here. And on the lines, you're spread about as thin as bacon grease." He nodded in back of him. "Allow you're short on rations, too, else these boys wouldn't be carving up that dead horse. Your supply train is still in the Bitterroot, trying to get through the rocks and trees."

Gibbon assumed the posture of a bloated toad. Obviously he was a tired man, ill in the stomach and now sorely tested by the impertinence of a young man twenty years his junior, without military rank, without status even among his own people, and ill-mannered to boot. Worse yet, the intelligence on his command was embarrassingly true! "Get out, Mr. Tree, before I have you arrested for interfering in military matters . . . treason, if you will. Go back and tell those men the only way they can get out of this is to lay down their arms and come back with me to Lapwai. Their leaders will be tried by a court of law, punishment meted out accordingly. You tell them exactly what I said. There is nothing more to discuss here. Now, good day to you." Gibbon held up his hand. "Wait a moment. One thing more: You'd better clear their camp, or you'll be charged along with them. Complicity, they call it."

Benjamin One Feather tipped his hat. Gibbon's message was plain enough, even for an Indian to understand. And satisfied that he had accomplished what the council had intended, a diversionary bluff, he adjusted his white man's hat, turned on his heel, and walked away from the One Who Limps Twice. Benjamin thought to himself that it was true, that this man *had* lost his soul, and by the Great Spirit, Gibbon was destined to die in his sleep searching to reclaim it. To Benjamin, this was much worse than dying on the field of battle, perhaps attaining undeserved honor.

Major Canty stepped up alongside Benjamin One Feather and together they began to walk toward the back of the encampment, threading through the wounded stretched out under the trees, a miserable lot—soaked bandages, refuse scattered about them, a scant supply of water on a hot afternoon, the air filled with horseflies.

Major Canty, staring straight ahead, told Benjamin One Feather, "I warned you about old Red Nose; no man to trifle with, that one. He's worried as hell about this, the repercussions, but he's all soldier. As bad as this is, he's a soldier, I'll grant the bastard that much."

"Soldier from the neck down," Benjamin replied sarcastically.

"We can hold out. Another day or two, at least until General Howard arrives. Regroup, that's on the colonel's mind. He hates to lose."

"Ei, I know all about Old One Arm. So do the Nez Percé, but at least Red nose won't fight again. He's been whipped, disgraced. If Joseph had fifty more men, none of you would get out of here alive. It would be Custer all over again." Benjamin eyed Canty carefully before planting one last seed of doubt. "Ei, and when the council hears Gibbon's words, they may even decide to come in tonight, overrun your positions."

They paused at the perimeter where Benjamin One Feather had tied his pony and shook hands. Major Canty, with a nod toward the dense woods, warned, "Don't turn your back going through there. Understand? You know more about what's going on up here than most. That could be a bit dangerous, especially for one with your reputation."

Pulling his rifle from the scabbard, Benjamin said, "I understand, but Penpenhihi has a white man tied up down below, a fellow with a broken arm. If I don't get back, he'll have two broken arms, maybe worse." Doffing his hat, he moved off slowly through the trees.

A short time later, Benjamin realized that Canty's warning had not been without reason or purpose. He kept edging his pony to the side, first to the right, then left, his eyes scanning the timber behind him. It was that keen inner sense, the instinct that one always seems to muster up when being watched. First it was a scurrying pine squirrel darting along the downfall, then the flicker of jays coming to scavenge on horseflesh, and ultimately it was what he had suspected, a patch of dark blue suddenly glaring in a shaft of sunlight. No doubt about it, Benjamin knew that he was being followed.

Shying away from the open, grassy clearings, he turned toward a small ravine and rode halfway through it before slipping from his saddle. He gave the pony a pat on the rump and watched it trot on through, finally disappearing in the thick lodgepole on the opposite side. Benjamin One Feather checked his rifle and, crouching low, sneaked around the neck of the ravine, where he flattened himself behind the buckbrush to wait. He had barely positioned himself when he saw a soldier softly treading directly toward him, his body in a running slouch, rifle lowered but fully ready for an easy swing to the shoulder. Near the middle of the gully the man abruptly stopped, leaned forward, and began to search the terrain ahead, his head finally turning to the side, trying to catch the direction of the moving horse.

Slowly coming to his knees, Benjamin One Feather brought his Henry to his shoulder. "Up here," he called softly. The soldier below swung quickly around, bringing his own rifle to play, but before he could target in on his quarry, one shot cracked out like a bolt of lightning, splitting the stillness of the forest, and a big blue shadow flew backward into the ravine. Leaping from his cover, Benjamin half slid down the incline and quickly came up over the dead soldier. He was sprawled on his stomach, both arms flung out as though he were reaching for some last thread of salvation. Heaving him over, Benjamin looked down into his face. Benjamin One Feather flinched once and slowly backed away, disbelieving what he saw. It was the sergeant, Three Stripes, Bevis Ketchum, his eyes still open, lids unmoving, one final, tobacco-stained grin etched in his red beard.

That same afternoon, White Moon moved Two Shell Woman and her child two miles below the stricken village, secluding them under a shelter of a robe stretched out over the creek-side willows. From his pack he prepared a hot meal of bacon and bannack, but with death all around them they took little joy in the feast. She had no family left among the Nez Percé, although Gray Hawk and Rabbit Runs had offered to take her with them to the buffalo grounds. White Moon solved this, deciding to take her and Little Joseph back to the Gallatin, where she could find refuge with Little Blue Hoop and James. She would be among friends, and happily welcomed. With this decision made, White Moon left to find his brother; by dawn, they would be on their way back to the ranch.

Meanwhile, now that Benjamin One Feather had returned from the meeting with General Gibbon, the Nez Percé were prepared to carry out the last part of their diversionary plan. They were well aware that General One Arm Howard was coming up to reinforce Red Nose, probably within another day or two. Hinmut-tooyahlatkeht and White Bird allowed that there wasn't any profit in prolonging the standoff with Gibbon and possibly subjecting their people to another disaster when Howard made his appearance. And Gibbon, now convinced by young Benjamin Tree that the Nez Percé were going to maintain their siege, if not counterattack that very night, was keeping his fatigued men on the lines busy around the clock. He was badly off-balance, unprepared for what was to follow.

Toward midnight, the Nez Percé, as planned, quietly began to withdraw from their positions, a few at a time. By dawn the war camp was entirely deserted, the Indians far up the valley taking a circuitous, confusing route that would eventually lead them into the Land of the Smoking Water. They had left Colonel Gibbon behind, stranded on the sandy hill like a beached crawfish, incapacitated, his troops shot up, disorganized, and too weary to mount any kind of an effective chase. Departing for the ranch with White Moon and Two Shell Woman, Benjamin One Feather made one last *taz alago*. He promised Gray Hawk and Rabbit Leggings that he would see them again soon on the other side of the great Beartooth in the land of the Absaroke. This was to the East, one of the Four Great Ways, a part of his vision, and he was destined to seek them out.

By the end of the second day Benjamin One Feather, White Moon, and Two Shell Woman had come down into the Beaverhead, where they pitched camp for the night in a patch of creek-side alders. They were only a half-mile from the trail used most frequently by traders riding between Bannack and Virginia City. The water here was crystal-clear, and the grass plentiful for the three ponies and two packers they were trailing from the Big Hole.

By now Two Shell Woman had begun to recover

slightly from the devastating experience of these three harrowing and sorrowful nights along the banks of the battlefield creek. At least she had begun to talk again. Once there had been no hope, but now she was looking forward to a homecoming of sorts with White Crane and Little Blue Hoop. She was excited about seeing Little Blue Hoop's daughter, and while she didn't confess this to either Benjamin One Feather or White Moon, she was anxious to present her own new child, Joseph, to her adopted family. She had no shame that she was without a husband. She was happy to have her son, fortunate that both she and the baby had escaped the fate of many others, those who had been needlessly murdered by the men of the One Who Limps. What was ahead of her now was as much better than what had been left behind as survival is better than death.

Fate had played a part in her plight. She had been swept away by the events in the valley of the Winding Waters, had joined with her brother and sister-in-law in the exodus only because of them, not because she herself had wanted to leave Lapwai. The people of her first man were still there and, though not blood relatives, she told Benjamin and White Moon she had a distant hope that she might return to her land again. She knew some of the men and women who had stayed behind on the reservation. This was too far in the future to worry about, Benjamin One Feather told her. For now, at least, she had security and a home for herself and the child. Everyone agreed that this was good.

On the third morning Benjamin, White Moon, and Two Shell Woman met their first travelers, a group of about twenty men riding west along the trail that they had covered the previous day. They were white men, and two of them broke off from the file when they saw the three coming out from their camp in the alders. Two Shell Woman, frightened at the sight of more *shoyapee*, wanted to go back and hide in the trees, but Benjamin quickly allayed her fears by touching the brim of his white man's hat and imparting a wink and a sly smile. The riders, as both he and White Moon had suspected, were a group of volunteers, these from Virginia City, out seeking hostiles reported to be passing through from the Big Hole Valley. The spokesman, large, with a drooping moustache, and wearing a sheepskin jacket, identified himself as Emmett Hodge, a deputy from the marshal's office. He wore two revolvers on his hips, a habit which, whenever Benjamin previously had noticed it among white men, always amused him. Why anyone needed two hand weapons was beyond his imagination. There were few men who could handle one pistol expertly, much less two of them. Hodge, whatever his appearance and his armament absurdity, was cordial and well-spoken, and his greeting was hearty. After the brief introductions and explanations of purpose, he asked Benjamin and White Moon if they had crossed the trail of Indians.

White Moon was the first to speak up about this, saying, "We didn't cross their tracks, but back over the pass we saw a couple of men booting it up toward Bannack. Didn't even take much time to talk with us, they were in such a hurry. They did mention something about seeing some Indians."

"Hostiles?" inquired Hodge.

White Moon shrugged innocently. "Didn't say. Just Indians." He gave the officer a questioning look. "Who are these hostiles, anyhow?"

"Chief Joseph, the Nez Percé," Hodge said, almost haltingly. Then, curiously searching their faces, he asked, "Just how long you people been on the trail? Why, the news is all over, hostiles headed this way, shooting and looting along the way. Big trouble, boys, big trouble Damned lucky you didn't run into them; you'd be afoot or dead, for sure."

"Well, that's sure something, ei?" White Moon said, looking over at Benjamin. "Looks like we really did have luck, cutting across that valley."

The deputy asked, "Just where you coming from, anyhow?"

"Fort Hall," White Moon lied. "Took my little wife here down to see her folks. Kind of a 'potlatch,' they call it, eating, dancing, all that sort of thing. Damned good fun, when you get the hang of it."

"Damn, that's a far piece of riding," Hodge said. Then, impatiently, he went on. "But what did those men say about the Indians, the ones they told you they saw?"

White Moon, posing thoughtfully, scratched behind his ear for a moment. "Let's see now. Seems to me I remember them saying these particular Indians were moving right down the river. That's about it."

"A big party, or just a few? Did they say how many they saw?"

Looking at Benjamin, White Moon shrugged again. Benjamin One Feather said, "A whole village, was the way I got it."

"By God!" Hodge exclaimed. "That's for certain the Nez Percé, then." He gave his partner an excited glance. "A day ahead of us, Jake. What do you think? Some of the soldiers are down that way, too. It's possible. . . ."

White Moon cut in again, saying, "We just got the idea they must be moving to the buffalo country; never heard anything about hostiles. I suppose if you wanted to catch up you could ride on down the valley here to the lower river, and cross over. Seems most likely that's where they'd be coming out. If they're hostiles, they'll probably stay clear of the settlements."

"Didn't realize it was all that serious," Benjamin One Feather said, and whistled low.

"Serious!" exclaimed Hodge. "Boys, there's a war going on, a regular war, so keep on your toes, hear?"

The man called Jake reined away. "Come on, Emmett, let's ride, catch up. Those army boys can't be too far behind, either." They wheeled away, collected the rest of the men, and rode by in a cloud of dust toward the north, waving and shouting at Benjamin and White Moon.

"Good luck!" called White Moon, waving back.

When Two Shell Woman heard this story in Nez Percé, she smiled for the first time in many days. It was good to be back with such good friends, but she couldn't believe that White Moon had told such a big lie to the *shoyapee*. Then she fell serious again. What if they came back along the trail somewhere to take revenge for such a bad story? This was no problem, Benjamin One Feather said, pointing across the hills. "By the time the *shoyapee* return to their homes, we'll be two days ahead of them and almost home ourselves."

"Ei," agreed White Moon, his face somber. "All they want to do is kill some crazy Indians." Aiming a finger at his brother, he cried, "Boom!", then said, "Good Injun, dead Injun."

They rode on, following the road to Alder Gulch and Virginia City, and finally arrived at the big gold camp near dusk. Because of Two Shell Woman they shared some apprehension about riding through the town, but were surprised to see very few people on the long, winding main street. This was not the place Benjamin One Feather remembered from almost ten years ago, when he and his father had come to do business with Arthur Clawson, the lawyer. At that time men crazy with gold fever were crawling like ants over the hillside gullies; the street was filled with wagons, mules, and milling people. Had Mother Earth given up so much so soon? Had all of the hair been pulled from her head? They stopped at a mercantile, where Benjamin went in and bought fresh food for their nighttime meal, and within ten minutes they were gone, riding over the twisting road down toward the middle fork of the Mother River.

Late the next afternoon they pulled up their ponies at the line cabin in the Gallatin Valley, where they found Willie Left Hand by himself, preparing supper. After some conversation and a bath in the hot springs, they rode on down to the main ranch, arriving in the darkness and immediately arousing the dogs. This brought Claybourn Moore scurrying from the foreman's house carrying a lantern, and within minutes everyone was quickly gathered around at the corral, exchanging handshakes and back slaps, and sharing a few hugs and kisses from the women.

White Crane, after a brief moment with Benjamin One Feather, took the baby from Two Shell Woman and rushed away to the big house of James and Little Blue Hoop, where she could see the child in light. All of the women huddled around to admire the new Hock-kett, and not long afterward everyone was in the big log home, listening to the unbelievable tale of the battle of the Big Hole. It wasn't a pleasant story. Benjamin and White Moon related it with bitterness and sorrow, paradoxically intermingled with some elation. But the fact was that the Nez Percé had fought the army to a standstill and then had escaped capture. This confirmed the brief reports that had come in this very day to Bozeman City. White Crane was appalled when she learned that Benjamin and White Moon had actually fought the bluecoats, for two days helping Chief Joseph's men kill soldiers. This was frightening, contrary to what her man had told her of his plan to visit his uncle, to try to encourage Two Shell Woman to return with her child. Her anger, however, was slightly tempered by thanksgiving that he and his brother had returned safely. And she had to smile at White Moon's attempt to pacify her.

"We were there," White Moon said by way of explanation. "What else could we do? Not even long enough to eat, and they had us out shooting at those soldiers. Ei, I was plenty damned happy when our people decided to sneak away from that place. Bad medicine now, all those ghosts around, all mad as hell at the One Who Limps. Ei, and he is mad as hell too, shot in the leg. My brother here talked to the Red Nose and gave him another new name—the One Who Limps Twice." White Moon merely nodded in somber approval as some of the others laughed. Looking over at Molly and James Goodhart, he said, "You remember that Three Stripes bluecoat we used to meet on the trail sometimes, the one who was with Hockett when Benjamin had to ride all the way up to that wolfers' camp?"

Molly immediately snorted indignantly, recalling another incident on the Bozeman Trail when Three Stripes had swung his crop at Benjamin One Feather. "That man with distemper? Hah!" she huffed. "No, I don't forget one like him, not at all."

"Well," concluded White Moon, "he's dead."

James, mildly surprised, said, "Now, that's some twist, ain't it? Of all the people who hated that scamp, some Nez Percé who didn't even know him got in the last lick. That's damned peculiar, all right."

"Not just *some* Nez Percé," White Moon replied. "*That* Nez Percé." And he nodded at Benjamin One Feather.

Everyone stared at Benjamin, who at that moment wasn't particularly interested in discussing the incident. White Moon was the only one he had told about it, and even then he hadn't imparted the significance of the killing, how it so strangely related to his vision. Nor did he want to belabor the story now. But he sensed that White Crane already had understood a small part of what had just been revealed by his well-intentioned brother, because she was talking to one side with Molly in Absaroke. Finally, without elaboration, he said simply, "We ran into each other on the hillside. I just happened to get a round off quicker than he did. He was going to kill me."

White Crane, her pretty face troubled, had already moved away. She found a seat by the big rock fireplace, where she sat down to stare vacantly at the great bearskin rug, a present to James and Little Blue Hoop from the ranch hands. Molly Goodhart finally turned to Benjamin One Feather. "She says this was the fox, same as she told me on the trail that time. I still say he was more jackass than fox." Patting Benjamin on the arm, she added, "You did the right thing. He didn't like our kind at all."

But Claybourn Moore, on the other side of Benjamin One Feather, seemed to understand this moment of quiet discomfort and his young friend's detachment. He said quietly, almost in a whisper, "Your old guide with the horns was with you?"

Benjamin One Feather nodded. "Someone was."

One sunny fall afternoon during the Moon of the Drying Grass, Sitting Elk, Hides Alone, and Red Running Horse came down the backtrail from a scouting trip to report what everyone had been expecting: The Nez Percé were now on their way out of the Land of the Smoking Water. In one of the high canyons, only a two-day ride, the scouts had watched some of One Arm Howard's troopers chase Nez Percé braves into a rocky defile, only to be trapped themselves. The Indians, like billy goats, had slipped over the ridge and disappeared while their brother snipers, hidden in the high rocks, had wreaked havoc among the soldiers below them. After observing this successful ruse, the three Crow, attempting to cross the rocks and make contact with the Nez Percé on the other side, were fired upon by Indian scouts working for the army, scouts that Sitting Elk angrily declared were Crow from one of the downriver tribes. Before they were chased from the mountains, they determined that the troopers had retreated back toward the Smoking Water country, the Nez Percé having eluded them by sending the decoys up one of the box canyons and then escaping out another.

All of this was told to Chief Man Called Tree and several other tribal leaders who, after a short council, decided to try to intercept the Nez Percé and make talk when they made their appearance on the buffalo grounds. By Man Called Tree's way of reckoning, there was little doubt now where his brother Nez Percé would enter the Yellowstone valley: due south of his village. Coincidence, or not? Benjamin One Feather confirmed his father's suspicions when he admitted that while he was in the Big Hole Valley he had scratched a crude map on one of Chief White Bird's robes, indicating the two best ways of exiting the Smoking Water from the northeast. Benjamin explained that to help these people flee evil was part of his vision, that he was only carrying out his part of the Sacred Mountain pact he had made with Shining Elk.

His father had no argument with this. His only concern now was the movement of the troopers, the possibility of extending the running battle into the land of the Absaroke. He didn't want this. And he was incensed at the report that some neighboring river Crow were riding as scouts with General Howard's troops. He would never allow his own tribe to assist in the harassment of people who had been driven from their rightful land, nor did he want his mountain Crow to be drawn into a conflict with such an inevitable conclusion. As much as he detested the tactics of the bluecoats, he wanted no mourning among his men and women because of them. By wise leadership, strong words, and careful alliances, he had spared his own people this kind of misery. Now fearful of making some blunder that would lead him into this war, he sent scouts out in all four directions to ascertain the movements of army troops, allowing that if Chief Joseph and his band came through the upper Yellowstone, he would at least know the best way to help them avoid confrontations.

Two days later Man Called Tree, Shoots Far Arrow, and Four Bears rode out with a small party of braves toward the upper Clarks Fork. Early in the afternoon they met the scouts of the Nez Percé, told them to go back and report to their leaders that they were waiting to have council with them. The Crow chiefs, dressed in all of their ceremonial finery, spread their blankets and waited, with Man Called Tree sitting in the middle of the half-circle. It was at times like these that Benjamin One Feather always admired the magnificence of his father, the colorful attire that he had come by over the years: the shiny bone breastplate trimmed with fur; spangles of silver; the full eagle bonnet, sweeping down almost to his hips; the beautiful bear-claw necklace; and the decorated crooked staff, the symbol of supreme authority.

Shortly the Nez Percé came, led by Hinmut-tooyahlatkeht himself, Thunder Rolling in the Mountain, the great chief called Young Joseph. Beside him were White Bird and Looking Glass, and behind them Ollokot, Gray Hawk, and Yellow Bull. Despite the ordeals of their recent battles along Canyon Creek and Camas Meadows, and the rugged, tortuous terrain they had covered, they appeared hardy and cheerful, and upon dismounting walked proudly forward to accept greetings from the Crow. The leaders all finally sat in the circle, and the usual ceremonial pipe was passed. To Benjamin One Feather, this was an occasion of great significance, one he would never forget. He had received friendly smiles and raised palms of recognition from both Joseph and White Bird, and he felt so proud to be a part of this that tears welled in his eyes. His medicine was indeed powerful, and this was good.

The council lasted almost an hour. It was made clear by Chief Joseph that he and his people only wanted to move on to the buffalo grounds, but that One Arm Howard, always behind them, was determined to destroy his tribe. They now had no time to hunt the blackhorns, even though they had successfully eluded the troopers for the fourth time. All he wanted was safe passage across the Yellowstone. Eventually, he would lead his followers to the Queen Mother's Land. Man Called Tree, speaking fluently in Nez Percé but making sign for the benefit of his Crow chiefs, told Joseph that as long as he and his people were on the territory of the mountain Crow, they would be protected. He said that his scouts had returned, reporting no bluecoats within three sleeps, the only exception being One Arm's men, who were still floundering in the high mountains in an unfamiliar land. It was agreed that Man Called Tree's braves would escort the Nez Percé across the Yellowstone country and show them the way north to the Musselshell. But once across the Echeta Casha, their destiny would be their own.

White Bird was the last chief to speak. After thanking

the Crow, he looked directly into the eyes of Man Called Tree and said, "We were young men together once on the Tahmonmah. We hunted the big sheep together. We shared meat around the fire. You have the blood of our people in your family, your woman one of us. My brother, I ask you one last favor."

"We are friends," Man Called Tree said. "Say what you wish."

"I want that man to show us the way." He turned and pointed to Benjamin One Feather.

After a moment's pause, Man Called Tree replied proudly, "He is a great man. *Sepekuse.* So be it."

After the council had ended, the Nez Percé made camp for the night near the creek. Despite the fact that there were no soldiers in the area, lookouts were posted on all sides of the village. Man Called Tree then named a party of five, including his son White Moon, to contact the Crow tribe that had given assistance to the bluecoats. Chief Joseph had told him that these scouts not only had shot at them but also had raided their pony herd, stealing fifty head. This news infuriated Man Called Tree. He told the departing braves to advise his neighbors to the east that if the ponies were not returned, he would personally make a visit within three sleeps and bring one hundred armed warriors with him. Taking White Moon aside, he said, "You deliver these words, son. Tell them that these poor people are fighting for something the Crow already have, freedom to live on their own land. Tell them I'm damned unhappy about such treatment to friendlies who have never done any harm to us."

"I think they'll get the message," White Moon said. "Maybe scare the shit out of them."

Man Called Tree smiled. "That's a bit blunt, son, but you have the right idea."

Although White Crane was proud that the Nez Percé chief, White Bird, held her husband in such high esteem, she thought his participation in their exodus was too dangerous. Yet she could see that the great power of Shining Elk was guiding him around the Great Circle. His direction now was to the Great Way of the North, where wisdom reigned under the sign of the Great Buffalo. Shining Elk had received his greatest power from the North. Even so, there were dangers omitted in the vision on the Sacred Mountain, and these were more real than spiritual. Yet she foresaw no threat to her man's life. By his vision he had already come through the worst of times, but if he chanced to be caught aiding the hostiles, as he had dared to do in the Big Hole, she was well aware of the possible consequences: death, or imprisonment in some faraway place.

White Crane shared these thoughts with her mother-in-law, Rainbow, in the big lodge as the night fire was getting low. Rainbow knew all about these frets, for she had seen her own great man depart on many perilous treks across the wilderness frontier, fortunately always to return.

"I always look across the river," Rainbow said. "The day comes when I see him riding in proud on his great pony, and my heart sings with joy, even to this day. It is bad medicine if your man deserts you for another woman, not so bad if he leaves for a just cause. When the cause has been won, he will always return. Ei, but with another woman, who knows?" She laughed, her face still radiating beauty, even after forty-three winters. She said, "You please Benjamin One Feather in all ways. Trust him, for he possesses the spirit of his blood father, Henri Bilodeau, who always traveled a safe trail, and he has learned from Man Called Tree. These things make legends of our men, and legends always survive, ei? This is my belief. It sustains me in times such as these. Worry only makes wrinkles—not so good, for one so young as you."

When she returned to her robes that night, White Crane knew that her worries were not shared by Benjamin One Feather. Oblivious to her arrival, he was sound asleep, making tiny whistles through his parted lips. In the morning she presented him with a fine new buckskin shirt, beautifully beaded, its sleeves fringed, the shoulders decorated with ermine tails. It was bleached pure white, the color of the Great Way of the North. She said to him, "This will let those Nez Percé women know you have a good wife, one who dresses her man plenty good."

Admiring its beauty and fine details, he quickly slipped it on. It felt good against his body, as though it had been melted onto his skin. "But this is too fine to wear on the trail," he protested gently.

"It is not for beauty alone," she answered, almost mystically. "This is a shirt of lights, the color white."

"Ei, this is plain to see, but . . . ?"

"But my man, you don't see, ei?" she said with a smile. "It doesn't matter. Wear it, and think of me."

Mystified, he smoothed down the shirt, and White Crane tousled his hair playfully and kissed him. She had all of his trail necessities prepared, including several bundles of food for his parfleche. She was happy for him, not herself, but the reassuring words of Rainbow bolstered her spirit, kept her from crying. Yes, this man she loved so much would return, and he would carry much honor. He would appear across the river like his father, riding proudly on his great pony with the legs of lightning.

She rode along with Benjamin and a group of twenty braves and other friends and relatives down to the trail. These braves, all heavily armed, were to ride escort for a distance, then return to the village. In the meadow the Nez Percé were waiting, several hundred men, women, and children, some of them whooping wildly and racing their horses down through the drying grass. This was prompted by the appearance of a large band of ponies trotting toward them, neighing loudly and picking up familiar scents as they approached. White Moon and the other Crow braves were returning with the stolen Nez Percé ponies.

After a small impromptu celebration and a few more farewells, the tribe headed up the river to a crossing that Benjamin One Feather had selected. And by late afternoon that same day they were skirting the Bull Mountains, making directly for the Musselshell River. By the time they had reached the timbered bottoms, only two Crow scouts were still among the Nez Percé, Benjamin One Feather and his Fox brother, Sitting Elk. Man Called Tree had kept his promise, to guide the Nez Percé across the Echeta Casha in safety. To further assist in this pledge, he had sent a few men down the trail to cut the new singing wires, disrupting communications between Fort Ellis and Fort Keogh.

Once across the Musselshell, Benjamin One Feather and Sitting Elk scouted far ahead for several days, sometimes accompanied by one or two Nez Percé braves, always searching out the safest trails. The two young Crow led Joseph's band west of the Big Snowy Mountains, up to the Judith Basin, following this valley for one day before cutting right and heading for the Mother River, the River That Scorns All Others. This was the fourth night of a journey without incident, but not without apprehension. Somewhere far to their rear, they knew General One Arm Howard had picked up the wide trail they were leaving behind across the sage and bunch grass plains. Howard was as relentless as they were cunning, but now it was a ride of only a few days to the white rocks separating the Queen Mother's Land from the Montana territory.

On the sixth day they approached the freight depot on the Cow Island landing, a place where the Missouri river steamers often unloaded supplies during the low-water season. Benjamin and Sitting Elk came back and reported that only a dozen troopers and a few civilians occupied the landing, and these men were totally unaware of the tribe's presence. Allowing that their people needed to replenish supplies, Joseph and White Bird elected to scare off the soldiers by a show of force, capture the landing, and make the Missouri crossing from Cow Island. Despite Chief Joseph's wish to avoid an outright fight, the small entrenched garrison behind the depot opened fire when the Nez Percé were discovered advancing from across the river.

The resulting skirmish lasted most of the day, the troopers refusing to budge from their outpost, the Nez Percé unwilling to sustain casualties by overrunning the soldiers. However, during the night, the Indians claimed the fifty tons of supplies on the landing, took what they needed, and bypassing the beleaguered soldiers, headed due north, Benjamin One Feather leading the way. His direction was toward the Bearpaw Mountains, as from there it was only a one-day ride to the border.

When the Nez Percé finally came down to Snake Creek at the foot of the Bearpaws, Chief Joseph, out of dire necessity, decided to make camp. This was at the beginning of the Moon of the Changing Seasons, and his women and children were now weary, the ponies tired, many sore of foot. There was good bunch grass here, the water clear, and the weather had been kind to the tribe—sunny days and cool nights. A few of the leaders protested any further delay, pointing out that in just one more day they would find sanctuary across the boundary, the reality of peace and security they had sought for so long. But they were overruled, and Benjamin One Feather, Sitting Elk, and several Nez Percé fanned out, scouting as far as five miles in each direction. They saw no sign of bluecoats.

It seemed as though the little valley below the Bearpaw Mountains was indeed isolated, at least safe enough for a one-day respite. So lodges were erected and a few protective trenches dug along the coulees and perimeters of the camp, for this had become routine practice since the fight in the Big Hole. Everyone then took a well-earned rest for the remainder of the day. The following morning, Joseph planned to strike the lodges and head for the Queen Mother's Land.

Early the next day, one of the young boys cutting out ponies from the big remuda saw unidentified mounted men riding away across one of the ridges to the east. In short order an alert was sounded, and several scouts were dispatched by White Bird to follow the strangers. It wasn't long before these men returned with the alarming news of an approaching column of troopers coming in from the southeast. But by this time one-third of the village already had been prepared to move, and several hundred ponies were milling about the village perimeter. These Nez Percé were just under way, moving to the north, when the first long line of bluecoats appeared on the crest of the small hills. Benjamin One Feather and Sitting Elk were on their ponies, urging those who had already packed and mounted to begin moving down the creek. There were over a hundred men, women, and children in this first party.

Not long afterward, the soldiers came charging toward the scattering villagers. White Bird, having placed his warriors in strategic positions all along the mounds and coulees, met the advance with a devastating barrage of accurate rifle fire, dropping almost half of the soldiers from their mounts. This unexpected and fierce resistance brought the riders abruptly up in their saddles, and within minutes they were retreating, leaving their dead and wounded in the field.

Meanwhile, another troop charged off after the party

of escaping Nez Percé being led by Benjamin One Feather and Sitting Elk, only to have forty warriors suddenly swing back and attack them in the creek bottom. These soldiers also were overwhelmed, some shot off their horses, the remainder retreating back toward the village and hotly pursued by a few screaming Nez Percé braves. After Benjamin One Feather and Sitting Elk had successfully led this first big escaping group across the distant Milk River, they returned to the battle ground, arriving shortly before noon.

The soldiers, their first two charges having been beaten back, were now trying to dig in on three sides of what was left of the wrecked village. Sporadic rifle fire split the air. Benjamin One Feather saw bodies scattered about, most of them bluecoats who had penetrated the south edge of the grounds during a second charge, only to be killed in close-quarter fighting. There were two Indian scouts among the dead, and from what Benjamin could make of it, they were Cheyenne. A wounded soldier had crawled into a gully, only to be dragged out and brought back to the rear by two angry Nez Percé braves. White Bird, later that evening, took Benjamin One Feather to see this man, a young sergeant who had been shot in the shoulder. His wound had stopped bleeding, the bullet having passed completely through to exit just beside the shoulder blade. Someone, during all the turmoil had been kind enough to bandage him.

Benjamin, staring down at the wounded man, finally leaned over and said, ''If you don't get infection in that hole, you may live.'' Surprised that someone spoke English, the sergeant gaped but could barely speak. Benjamin called for water, this being immediately attended to by one of the women, who appeared in short time with a hide bag. Then, after a moment, the soldier said hoarsely, ''Thanks.'' He winced once at the pain in his shoulder and looked up hopelessly at Benjamin One Feather. ''What's gonna happen to me? I don't want to die here.''

''Nothing will happen,'' Benjamin said. ''You have to rest. I'll see what I can do for you, ei?'' Nodding toward the distant ridge, he asked, ''Who are we fighting over there? Who's in command?''

''General Miles, Fort Keogh,'' was the raspy answer.

"Three battalions. I'm with the Seventh. Haines, William Haines."

"The Seventh cavalry? Custer's old outfit?"

"All new, sir," Haines said. "Back in the field again."

"For the present, at least," Benjamin One Feather said with a smile. Then after a moment he asked, "Do you know an officer by the name of Hockett? He was at Keogh."

Haines perked up a bit at this. "Lieutenant Hockett? I sure do know him. He was with us this morning. Is he here too, shot up like me?"

"Not at all," Benjamin replied. "I know him from another time; once a friend, perhaps now an enemy."

"He's a good one, sir," Haines said. "Hope his luck's better'n mine."

Benjamin One Feather turned away and related to White Bird what had just transpired. These soldiers were from the fort down on the Yellowstone, and they were being led by Bearcoat Miles, a general who had fought the Lakota and Cheyenne. This explained the presence of the two dead turncoat Cheyenne scouts, but White Bird was perplexed why Indians who had fought the pony soldiers so fiercely all these years would now turn around and help them. Benjamin One Feather wasn't able to answer this, was angered himself that the Cheyenne had led the soldiers to Joseph's village and were here to count coup themselves. White Bird wanted to know the whereabouts of One Arm Howard, but the young sergeant had told Benjamin that no one knew where Howard was, only that he had troops in the field somewhere south toward the Yellowstone. Benjamin then suggested to the chief that it might be possible to learn more about how serious a situation the Nez Percé were in if he returned the wounded soldier the next day to the bluecoats. If Zachary Hockett hadn't been shot down, there was a good possibility that such a benevolent ruse might be profitable. It would at least give Benjamin a chance to look around, maybe get a few enlightening words from his friend.

After a few moments of consideration, White Bird agreed. He believed the worst of the battle had already been fought, and much the same as at the Big Hole, the soldiers had been taught a severe lesson already and were not strong enough to storm the Nez Percé lines. However, if General One Arm arrived on the scene, the balance would change dramatically. Now it was a matter of precious time—how to escape this Bearcoat Miles before One Arm came with reinforcements. "I will die fighting these *piuapsiaunat.*" White Bird said, "I will never surrender." And he said this bitterly, because among the eighteen dead this first day were Looking Glass, Ollokot, Pile of Clouds, and the medicine man, Tuhulhutsut. White Bird was to learn the next day that the soldier's losses were double those of his brothers, and it would be Benjamin One Feather who delivered this news.

Cold Maker came unexpectedly later that night, bringing flying wet snow that hung like glue to the hide shelters scattered along the coulees. This was a miserable night for both sides, what with burying the dead, trying to keep warm, fearing to build fires because of the snipers. Wrapped in their blankets and big robes, the Nez Percé warriors huddled in trenches out of the wind while many of the women and children placed makeshift lodges in coulees to the rear. By dawn, little had changed but the weather. It was brisk and cold, the sun poking a bleary eye through the hazy, drifting clouds that were now moving swiftly to the east. Benjamin One Feather left Sitting Elk near the left side of the gullies by the creek and went to the rear to get his pony. He munched on cold bannock from his pack, and without hot coffee, swigged at his white man's canteen, chasing down the heavy dough with cold water. He was wearing a Hudson Bay robe over his jacket, and because of the great chill he had resorted to wearing his drover's hat, now more impressive since his thoughtful wife had attached three beautiful eagle feathers to the leather band. This is the way he appeared when he rode around the soldier's flank carrying a white piece of cloth on his rifle barrel and with the sergeant, William Haines, mounted double and slumped against his back. There had been only a few shots fired during the early hours, mostly as a reminder that the lines were still being manned. As Benjamin moved along, everything suddenly became quiet.

When Benjamin One Feather came in behind the lines, he drew a few curious stares, continued on until finally two soldiers came running from a tent far back to pluck Haines off the pony. They took him away to the field hospital, and that was the last Benjamin ever saw of the man. Another soldier nearby stepped up and motioned to Benjamin One Feather to follow, making gestures and pointing below to where several field tents were pitched, this area undoubtedly housing the leaders of the campaign. Benjamin's keen eyes swept the perimeters on both sides. He saw men tucked in behind shelters, several Cheyenne scouts, guarding in small knots at the various points, and in the distance some of the Nez Percé ponies the soldiers had captured the first morning. There were two long coulees leading into this area, and beyond the coulees nothing but free space, no soldiers anywhere in sight. All this he firmly implanted in his mind.

Directly, he came to the first of the two big tents and met two troopers standing guard. The officer escorting him once again made a series of gestures, opened the flap of the tent and beckoned Benjamin One Feather to enter. Dismounting, Benjamin shouldered his rifle and flag and finally spoke, saying crisply, "Thank you," to the astonished soldier. Once inside, the officer found his tongue, quickly began to explain that Benjamin had just brought in a wounded cavalryman. This brought an exchange of amazed looks between the officers who were all gathered around a small wooden table. Papers were cluttered over the top of the table, one a small map with scrawls of black ink, dots and crosses, probably detailing the nomenclature of the strange land they were now visiting for the first time. Benjamin One Feather smiled inwardly at this. He had been here only two days and not only that: he had been ten miles north to the Milk River but knew at least three ways in and out. *His* map was in his head.

The first words he heard were, "Get one of the interpreters in here, on the double." This came from a bearded officer seated on a stool near the middle of the table, and Benjamin One Feather allowed that this must be Bearcoat Miles. He was wearing an army field coat with trappings on the shoulders and a very big, furry hat. He looked much like a bear, even though his coat was only of heavy wool.

"I don't need an interpreter," Benjamin One Feather said, "unless you want to talk in Cheyenne. I don't know much about their tongue, but I've shot a few in my time."

This remark, obvious in its reference to the Cheyenne

scouts outside, brought several smiles from the officers attending General Miles, but not the general himself. He merely acknowledged Benjamin's presence with a toss of his hand, then said, "I appreciate your gesture, bringing back one of our men. What's your name, and why have you done this? Is there some message you bring from the other side?"

"No message," Benjamin One Feather said. "The other side, as you call the Nez Percé, fares well, considering the weather. A fire or two would be welcome, but your men seem to be shooting at anything that moves out there. No one wants to go out searching for wood." This brought more grins. "My name is Benjamin One Feather. I come from the land of the Absaroke. My father traveled this country many times before the forts were built to protect it, ei, and destroy it. I thought it best to return your sergeant because the Nez Percé have no place to treat him, no great tents like this to hide in. He has a neat hole through his shoulder, not bleeding now, but it could get bad if infection comes. We believe a man's life has some value."

General Miles remained unperturbed. "This is your only reason for being here, then, not a word from Chief Joseph? I would expect him to realize he's been caught this time. He should understand this, be willing now to lay down his arms and return home. When you go back, tell him this is what General Miles has suggested, not to prolong this war any longer. It's useless. This is the end of the war for him."

"They're going to the Queen Mother's Land," Benjamin One Feather said. "Many are already there, the ones who got away yesterday. There will be more."

General Miles shook his head. "No, you're mistaken, young man. We have men coming up the river. Escape is out of the question now. You tell Chief Joseph we have him surrounded, there is no way out. Tell him I want to talk with him, make terms. This is for the good of his people."

With a grim smile, Benjamin replied, "He would ask you, why you didn't want to talk yesterday morning instead of sending in your men to kill his people. Ei, that's a good question, General."

This immediately brought Miles to his feet, but the

question went unanswered. He promptly dismissed Benjamin One Feather. "Now, if there is nothing more, I'll bid you good morning. Thank you again for bringing our sergeant back."

But Benjamin abruptly raised his hand. "One more thing. I have an old friend here. His name is Zachary Hockett. I would like to see him before I go, wish him well."

Miles looked questioningly at the other officers. "Hockett?" he asked. "Is there a Hockett among us?"

A major standing nearby said, "Yes, sir, Lieutenant Hockett. He's with the Seventh, a transfer down from Fort Ellis last summer. I know the officer."

"Well, get someone to call him out," Miles said, "so this man can be on his way, for God's sake."

There was a line of squad tents back near the brow of the hill, and a few minutes later from one of these Zachary Hockett came on the dead run, meeting the departing Benjamin One Feather, who was shouldering his white pennant with one hand and leading his pony with the other. "Jesus!" he cried out, "I knew it was you! They said some smooth-talking Indian was asking about me, and I knew it just had to be you." He extended his hand for a hearty shake, then stood back and admired his friend. "What the hell are you doing in this place? How did you get involved in this damned mess?"

Benjamin One Feather quietly explained his presence as they walked toward the back of the war camp, finally voicing his opinion that conditions now appeared grim for the Nez Percé, that he saw little hope of anything but surrender for Chief Joseph, this a tragedy since they were so near their destination. There was some sympathetic response from Zachary Hockett, and at the same time he expressed bitterness that the fight had been allowed to begin without an attempt on the part of General Miles to talk with the Nez Percé beforehand. "We just had orders to form our lines and attack the village!" Hockett said dispairingly. "That was it, and they slaughtered us. Damned poor execution. General Miles cost us one-third of the command. Jesus!"

"Bad medicine," Benjamin said. "He doesn't have enough men left to mount another attack, ei?"

"Hell, no," Hockett answered. He nodded toward

some tents to the side. "More than fifty men in there shot up. At least thirty missing or dead. And the only reason I'm here is because one of your friends shot my damned horse instead of me." He stared at Benjamin One Feather incredulously. "Jesus, Benjamin, you're crazy coming all the way up here! They're calling out every trooper in the country to get their asses up here and corral these people. Why don't you and Sitting Elk sneak out, go on back home? You've done what they asked. What more can you do?"

With a wan smile, Benjamin One Feather replied, "Do what I can to help, that's all; maybe stay around until I can kill some of those Cheyenne over there watching me. I think they know damned well who I am. They've disgraced their own people." And then as Benjamin One Feather had expected, the big question finally came.

Hockett, with a worried look, said, "Have you seen her? She isn't over there is she? Her people?"

Benjamin leaped on his pony, saying, "No, my friend, Two Shell Woman isn't here."

"Thank God for that," Hockett wheezed.

Benjamin reined around and hoisted his small flag. Looking down at Zachary Hockett, he smiled. "Fred Gerard stopped by about two months ago. Made a special effort to see us, said he saw Two Shell Woman in the spring. She has a white child, Little Joseph, named after the great chief your people are trying to kill. You're a father, Mr. Hockett, and I offer you my congratulations." He nudged his pony ahead, threading his way through the tents and gawking soldiers to finally disappear into the brush.

Zachary Hockett's soaring elation over the news that Two Shell Woman wasn't in the Nez Percé camp suddenly collapsed and fell to the cold ground beside his boots. With a despairing moan he stared through tearful eyes at the desolation, the ugliness of the camp. Good grief, what a wretched place! What a cruel world! He had a son! The woman he loved had born him a son! But reality as cold as the ground smashed him in the head. Jesus, his beloved Two Shell Woman and a little child he would never see! Zachary Hockett was sick at heart, terribly sick.

* * *

The stalemale in the Bearpaws continued, and while it did plans were carefully made by a few of the Nez Percé for eventualities. Time was now running on a short wick for them. Chief Joseph, unable to move his people safely without further losses, finally went over to a council with General Miles. He was accompanied by Yellow Bull and Benjamin One Feather. White Bird had adamantly refused to meet with Bearcoat Miles, claiming that the general was no better than One Arm Howard or Red Nose Gibbon, neither of whom he had ever trusted, and with good reason. After an unsuccessful attempt to get favorable surrender terms, Miles finally called off the proceedings, but for some inexplicable reason he detained Chief Joseph in the bluecoat camp. This breach of conduct angered not only the Nez Percé but some of Miles's officers as well, including Lieutenant Hockett, who since Benjamin One Feather's disclosure about Two Shell Woman was beginning to take the war a bit more personally.

After several heated exchanges by both sides, Chief Joseph was returned on the fourth day, but his detainment by Miles had served its purpose. The great chief Thunder Rolling in the Mountains had been convinced there was no alternative but surrender. A runner had arrived from the Missouri River station at Cow Island—One Arm Howard was on his way, expected within twelve hours. General Miles had led Joseph to believe that he and his people would be returned to Lapwai. This was good. Joseph wanted no negotiations with One Arm that might interfere with this promise, so he pledged to Bearcoat Miles that he would lay down his arms the next morning before Howard made his appearance. His word was his honor.

Chief White Bird, thoroughly disillusioned, had been expecting this decision. But he had also vowed never to surrender. He told Joseph that he couldn't remember one instance when the white man had kept a promise, and furthermore, he had no honor to uphold. Accordingly, he went directly to the man who had led the Nez Percé to the Bearpaws—Benjamin One Feather. White Bird, Gray Hawk, and several others from the Clearwater band huddled together in a coulee and listened intently to a plan Benjamin already had advanced to the chief the previous day.

Meantime, news of the imminent surrender spread quickly through both camps, and by nightfall, warming fires were popping up on both sides of Snake Creek. For the first time in four nights, soldiers and Nez Percé warriors had a chance to relax and not worry about getting shot. All of this was working to Benjamin One Feather's advantage, but he waited patiently until the fires were at their lowest ebb and many of the soldiers had bedded down. Then, in selected groups, White Bird's men and women, carrying saddles, tack, and all of their belongings, began quietly to disappear, moving along the creek bottom to a distant coulee almost a half-mile northwest of the makeshift village. Beyond this was the open space Benjamin One Feather had carefully observed when he'd first visited the soldier's war camp. Where once four sentries had been posted below in an adjacent draw, now there were only two, and the land in back of them was free of guards.

The two soldiers were at the edge of the meadow where many of the Nez Percé ponies had been herded. And to Benjamin's surprise, these men also had a small fire burning, were sitting next to it on two empty ammunition boxes, quietly talking, their rifles resting to the side. This was becoming easier than he had anticipated. Using the sage cover, Benjamin One Feather, Sitting Elk, and two of the Nez Percé quietly crept to within twenty yards of the soldiers. Benjamin finally spoke out in a low voice, "Do not move, do not shout, or you are dead men." At this, one of the bluecoats turned slightly, but by then felt a rifle barrel resting against the side of his head. Before Benjamin could intervene, the two Nez Percé angrily clubbed both soldiers with their rifle butts. "Put out the fire and leave them," Benjamin whispered, and the two braves quickly threw dirt and rocks over the small blaze. Meanwhile Sitting Elk, in a low crouch, was running for the pony herd, and the two Nez Percé soon followed. Within five minutes they were quietly walking more than fifty head up the coulee toward the far ridge.

Benjamin One Feather ran back through the lower draw, up over the hill and down to the next bottom, where White Bird and many of his men, women, and children were waiting. Only one group had failed to arrive, but within minutes Benjamin made out their shadowy forms near the bottom of the draw. Without waiting any longer everyone set out, making directly for the top of the long ridge where the ponies were being driven by Sitting Elk's men.

The long procession, with Benjamin One Feather and Sitting Elk at the front, filed slowly through the dips and over the sage-covered knolls for almost nine miles before they came in sight of the Milk River. Over this distance no one had spoken a word, but when Benjamin suddenly raised his arm and swept it grandly toward the valley ahead, those nearest him began to whisper to each other, and the excitement rippled down the long file like a small tidal wave. There were sudden cries of joy, and the women and children broke ranks and began to race ahead toward the stream.

"From here, straight ahead, the direction North of the Four Great Ways," Benjamin One Feather told his uncle Gray Hawk. "Following the first creek. It will lead you to a new place. By first light, you'll be there. Ei, if you don't like it, come back someday to my father's village. Your sister will welcome you."

Gray Hawk saluted his nephew. "I will go with my people, make a new home. You have a powerful guide, my nephew. Your Shining Elk is good medicine."

"Go in peace," Benjamin One Feather said.

"*Taz alago.*"

"*Taz alago,* brothers!" Benjamin One Feather called aloud. And many happy calls echoed back to him in the cold night air: *Taz alago, taz alago.* He reined away slowly, feeling great happiness in his soul, and in the moonlight ahead he imagined that he saw two familiar little men approaching from the Way of the South, his direction now. The little tree people! They were dressed in white buckskin shirts much like his own, his shirt of light, and once again they were carrying a long pipe, calling out to him, "This is Mother Earth, take and become part of her." Tears in his eyes, Benjamin One Feather opened his arms to the silent heavens. To the East he had gone; to the West he had gone; to the North, and now to the Way of the South. He had traveled the Great Circle.

EIGHTEEN

Late one cold afternoon in November, the Moon of the Geese Going, a solitary rider came up the river trail a few miles from the Crow village of Man Called Tree. Dressed in a buffalo coat, and with a wool shawl pulled up over his ears under his brimmed hat, he occasionally stopped and searched the slopes and canyons to the south. Hides Alone and Stone Calf, in the nearby bottom hunting for stray ponies, watched this man for a short while before they rode out and hailed him. Obviously he was looking for sign of some kind, probably smoke; at the time they didn't know it was their own village that he was seeking. They met along the frosty trail, and because of the stranger's heavy winter garb and the great scarf that half hid his face, neither of the two Absaroke braves recognized him. It was only after he had made several stumbling attempts at uttering a few Crow words that Stone Calf suddenly raised up his hand in greeting and said, "*Kahe,* Hock-kett, *kahe*!" Then both of the Indians opened up with broad grins, pointing at Zachary Hockett's absurd white-man's winter dress.

Gesturing, making simple sign, Stone Calf asked what had happened to his soldier clothes, why was he wearing the white man's hat and the white woman's shawl? Hockett, smiling sheepishly back at them, quickly understood the meaning of their sign, allowed that his winter attire, however humorous to them, had served its purpose; he had made it across the prairie and back to his friends without freezing to death. Motioning back down the river toward Fort Keogh, he then thrust out his hands flatly and passed them back and forth across each other several times. Finally, he clenched his fist and made the gesture of throwing to the ground. Both of the Crow nodded, Stone Calf sighing a long, "Ah."

Their friend Hockett had left the big soldier house down the river; he was finished, had cast away the bluecoats. And when Zachary Hockett finally positioned his forefingers and thumbs together, making the sign of the lodge, and placed one finger to the back of his hat, they knew he was looking for the tipi of Benjamin One Feather. They both grinned again, and with a beckoning wave kicked their ponies away into a trot. Zachary Hockett, looking like a great bear with a toothache, sighed a steamy breath and trundled his horse along behind them.

He received a warm welcome in the village. Stone Calf shouted out his arrival, and a few women and children, bundled up in blankets and woolens, ran beside his horse, calling out his name, Hock-kett, Hock-kett. They hadn't forgotten him, but he felt bad that he had no rock candy to toss out to his admirers. Waving with one huge mitten, he rode along, following Stone Calf and Hides Alone directly to the lodge of White Crane and Benjamin One Feather, where another group of curious women and children began to gather.

There was no doubt about this being Benjamin's tipi. Two great crimson streaks of lightning stretched up its sides toward the apex, both bolts bordering a pure white figure of a bull elk with black antlers and silver tines. Directly the tipi entry parted, and White Crane's face appeared in the chilly November air. For Zachary Hockett, this was a wonderful sight to behold, for her beautiful mouth parted into a flashing smile, and her black eyes widened into two huge ebony gumdrops. "Hockkett!" she cried out happily in English. "I see you! Come my house. You welcome. *Aho*, I thank you."

Then Benjamin One Feather appeared. Parting the flap, he stood there with hands on hips, a small smile playing across his brown face. "This is not the best time of the year to be making a visit, my friend, but we're happy to see you.''

Zachary Hockett, without even thinking, impetuously gave White Crane a hug and a kiss, and all of the children around squealed and leaped up and down. One shouted gleefully, ''Hock-kett has come to steal Benjamin One Feather's woman!'' And this brought another round of shrieks, but these quickly subsided to happy sighs when Benjamin and Hockett embraced, slapping each other affectionately on the back.

Inside, sitting by the radiating warmth of the fire, Zachary Hockett explained his presence. Holding a mug of coffee between his cold hands, he said that his commission had expired two weeks ago, that he'd declined to sign the papers for another hitch. All of the persecution and killing had soured him and drained his soul. The experience in the Bearpaw Mountains had devastated him—not only the poor military judgment of General Miles, and the needless deaths of his comrades, but the poor treatment of the Nez Percé that followed. Contrary to the promises of both Miles and One Arm Howard, the band of Chief Joseph had been taken down the Mother River by steamer and barges. They were being moved to the Indian Territory in Kansas instead of to their reservation in Lapwai. More good words, more broken promises, lamented Hockett. He said that almost everyone at Fort Keogh was upset at the discouraging turn of events, the betrayal of Chief Joseph, particularly those who had become acquainted with him during the long trek back to the fort.

''He's a gentle man,'' Hockett said forlornly. ''Dignified, sincere, only concerned about his people. The army command is making a big mistake by moving him to Kansas, one they'll come to regret. They're making a big man out of him, oddly enough, by trying to disgrace him. Hell, most of the people think he's a hero already. I don't think this was the army's intention. It backfired.''

Benjamin One Feather, sorrowed by this distressing news, stared at the dancing flames for a moment. He was reflecting on White Bird's words in one of their last conversations: ''I can't remember one time when a white man has kept his word.'' Or what his father had once told him: ''Stay away from bluecoats and treaty-makers, for they are harbingers of the plague." Then, as though he were addressing the mysteries of the nearby flames, he said, "There are small men who become big men by way of legends, sometimes misdeeds, ei. And we know who these men are. But I tell you, it takes more than legends to become a *great* man."

They were silent for a while, absorbed in their own thoughts and recollections of distressing events, both past and present, simply watching the fire, a small reunion in difficult times. Finally Zachary Hockett said, "You know, they were mad as hell when they found out all of White Bird's people were gone. Old One Arm blew up and jumped all over General Miles. Sent me and a whole troop north looking for them. Long gone." He grinned knowingly at Benjamin One Feather. "I sort of figured you and Sitting Elk had a hand in that, but I got a bit worried when I didn't see you around. Thought maybe something had happened, or maybe you'd gone on across the border with the others."

"*Someone* knew we were around," answered Benjamin with a slight scowl. "First day coming back, there were three Cheyenne on our tails. Sitting Elk got two of them, one got away, but that's not much compensation for the damage they did." Crouching near the fire pit, he moved a piece of wood into the hot embers, then nestled back close to his wife. "So, what are your plans? Why have you come this way, instead of heading down the river to civilization?"

Zachary Hockett stared into his cup. He knew that Benjamin's perception was too keen for such an empty question. "Don't know for sure, but you know damned well I can't go back without seeing her. My son." He gave Benjamin a forlorn look. "Jesus, does this sound crazy? Is it hopeless? What the hell should I do? I can't go back with this hanging over my head, and I'm damned near broke as well."

"Wrong time to be heading for the Mullan Road to the Palouse country," Benjamin One Feather opined. "Not much traffic this time of year through the valleys. Snow. Cold."

White Crane, listening, trying to understand some of what was being said, finally interrupted to ask her man to translate. And after he had, she said with exasperation, "Well, tell him to go to the ranch and fetch his woman and child, go away somewhere, or take her back to Lapwai where she belongs." Then, looking squarely at Zachary Hockett, she went on brokenly. "Get woman, good. No get, bad. You good, no get hurt in heart," and clasping her breast, she winced in pain as though she ached.

Smiling, Benjamin One Feather said, "She's getting better by the day, ei?"

"She's damned good," Zachary Hockett answered. He reached across Benjamin's lap, seized White Crane's hand, and kissed it. He said, "*Aho,* you are a good woman. Say it for me—I . . . am . . . a . . . good . . . woman."

White Crane blushed and tossed back her head and laughed. Then, peeking around her husband, she repeated slowly, "I . . . am . . . a . . . good . . . woman."

"Yes, indeed, you are," Hockett said, and laughed.

Benjamin One Feather put his arm over Hockett's shoulders. "I have an idea, Mr. Hockett, one that might solve a part of this problem. Why don't you ride on to the ranch, see Mr. Clay, and tell him you need a job for the winter? Now, since he'll allow that my father sent you, he'll find some work for you, ei, earn your keep over the winter. You know horses and such, so it won't be like you're a greenhorn. Come spring, you can make up a pack and head out for Lapwai. Now, that is about the best I can come up with." He grinned and added, "Molly's over there now, cooking. She'll keep your belly happy, anyhow."

While Hockett sat and wondered at his sudden salvation, Benjamin One Feather translated for his wife, who promptly stared upward into the tipi vent and emitted a great sigh of futility. She huffed at him, "You did not tell this man his woman is there!"

"He doesn't deserve to be told everything," Benjamin One Feather said. "Let him find it out himself."

That night Zachary Hockett, light of heart, his welfare kindly accommodated by a thoughtful and understanding Benjamin One Feather, went to the tipi of the old widow woman, Looks Far Away, where he piled his bedroll next to that of White Moon. He was welcome in this lodge, for Looks Far Away had been one of those, along with his beloved Two Shell Woman, who had cared for him when he was wounded. And the company of White Moon was certainly appreciated. Hockett had come into the village cold, disheartened, and belabored by doubt. These people, indeed, were great healers, not only of the body but also of the soul. Their medicine was good, and this particular night hilarity was the medicine of White Moon.

It was a long time until the laughter from the big lodge finally subsided, and before it was over White Moon had arranged for a small party to accompany Zachary Hockett to the Gallatin. Despite the advent of Cold Maker, they thought a camping and hunting trip to the west was a good idea, an excellent way to relieve the boredom of early winter. With luck they could bring back plenty of meat on their packs from the elk, deer, and antelope and for the people of the village. This was always good.

Benjamin One Feather was content to stay at home with his wife, mainly because she would be discontented to see him leave again so soon. He had no desire to read sad disappointment and anxiety in her dark eyes once again. They shared the belief that the many mysteries of his vision had been solved, his mission fulfilled. Shining Elk had led him in all directions of the Four Great Ways. The land he had seen was in a great circle, the circle a mirror of understanding, and the reflection that he had discovered within it was that of a total man.

But a melancholy settled over him, and he realized with sadness that the spokes of the Great Medicine Wheel were now being broken, their shattered shafts scattered across the plains like his Indian brothers. The center of the Great Hoop was being torn apart, the center of balance lost forever. "Ei," he whispered to himself, "only the spirits endure, those left behind to guard over the Wheel." Sprawled in front of the little fire, he saw visions dancing in the embers. White Crane was close by his side, watching too. She said, "What do you see, my man?"

"Ghosts."

"Ghosts? What kind of ghosts, good or bad?"

"All kinds, but they are animals, the spiritual ghosts

of our people, many weeping, some frightened, searching. . . ."

"Searching for what?"

The flames flickered, and a small log burst into flames. Benjamin One Feather said, "They are searching for the gift of life. Rebirth. Ei, they are running across the land seeking purpose, direction, and humanity, a happy place of their own, free of oppression, where they can all die in peace."

Looking forward . . .
In January 1994, Signet presents volume three in the Ben Tree Saga. The following is an excerpt from *White Moon Tree* by Paul A. Hawkins.

July 1881

Most people called him Moon, the second son of the breed Ben Tree, who owned one of the largest ranches in the Montana territory. His close-knit family, however, still referred to him as White Moon, his given name among the Absaroke or Crow Indians with whom he had lived most of his life. After White Moon and his older brother, Benjamin One Feather, had arrived to share in the family ownership of the giant spread in the beautiful Gallatin Valley, their given Crow names had proved to be a bit incongruous in the white man's society. So, they resorted and made do with what many people around Bozeman City usually called these two well-versed young men—Moon and Young Benjamin. They had been at the ranch over a year now.

After the beginning of the demise of the buffalo herds on White Moon and Benjamin's native land in the Yellowstone, the tribe of Man Called Tree had slowly disintegrated. Many of the villagers forced to new homes on the great reservation were living the usual life of reservation lassitude in meager comfort, accepting the food supplements supplied by a benevolent government, the same government that for years had attempted to tear apart their culture. Ben Tree, or Chief Man Called Tree as he was known by the various tribes, long ago had foreseen this slow, insidious destruction, the inevitable consequence of civilization's encroachment upon the Indians' West.

Through homesteading, politics, and a great sum of money that he had both earned and inherited from a prosperous freighting business during the great migration years, he established the Tree Ranch in 1868, hired capable men to manage it, all in preparation for his family's future in the white world. The future of the West as he envisioned it, was beef and horses. And this had come to pass. The Tree Ranch holdings now encompassed twelve thousand deeded acres of choice range land and watershed. With the great unceded portions of the distant Yellowstone rapidly diminishing to the realm of range cattle and the plow, White Moon and Benjamin One Feather, their freedom harnessed and tribal friends disappearing, had finally moved to the Gallatin to take up their inherited duties.

For White Moon, the duty on this particular day was working on the upper range above the hot springs' line cabin with Zachary Hockett and Willie Left Hand. Willie, a breed of Salish origin and a bachelor, had been working for the ranch six years, while Hockett, an ex-army lieutenant, had arrived four years past. Hockett, married to a young Nez Percé by the name of Two Shell Woman, lived with her and their four-year-old son, Joseph, in the line cabin, once a one-room bunk house now converted into a three-room home. The three men were riding near the north end of the property bordering open range this afternoon in July when, in the distance, White Moon saw for the first time in his life a band of sheep grazing up near the edge of the timber. And this was the day that he was to meet Divinity Jones, another first in his young life.

After exchanging surprised glances, the drovers reined over and headed up toward the sheep to investigate, searching ahead for signs of a herder. White Moon, who spoke English, thanks to the literacy and tutelage of his great father, finally said to the others, ''Now, what do you suppose this fellow is doing bringing those woolies up this way? Old man Stuart's going to have a conniption when he hears about it. By jingo, he hates those fuzzy critters.'' Moon's reference was to Adam Stuart, a neighboring rancher who shared part of the big open range with the Tree Ranch.

''He'll be sore, that's what,'' Zachary Hockett said. ''But there's no markers on this land, so whoever's up here has his rights, too, just as on this side, it's our problem, not Stuart's. We'll just tell this herder to move on up the canyon.''

With some annoyance Willie Left Hand spoke up. "I told Mister Clay one of these days we was gonna have to put wire and a gate up here. Ain't no way a man can know where the hell he is. Wire'd keep Stuart's stock where they belong, too. If old man Stuart wants the free grass, he can herd his cows over from the other side of the ridge, stedda letting them mix in with our critters all the time. Just makes work double later on, sorting 'em out this way all the time."

"I see somebody," White Moon said, pointing.

"A wagon?" Hockett asked, obviously puzzled. "A covered wagon?"

Willie Left Hand laughed derisively. "That's a sheep-herder's outfit, you damned fool. Hell, I see those things down south of here a couple of times on the drives to Utah. Even got a cooking stove inside. See there, that little old stack sticking up? Bunk in that contraption, too, regular moving cook house, it is."

Frowning, elevating his nose, White Moon said, "I smell those sheep all the way over here, I can smell them."

"Yep," Willie Left Hand chuckled, suddenly becoming the authority on sheep. "Right peculiar smell they has, and they crap just like a big old jack rabbit, eat the grass, weeds and all, just like a jack, too, right down to the nubbin. Oh, I sees these critters before, but not up in this country. Lots of them coming in other side of the big mountains. Come winter, they's all gone, far south. Trims them up, they do. Come spring and the grass is up, they moves them back to the high country again."

As they approached the wagon, a lone figure attired in baggy pants and a large denim jacket stepped out from behind it. None of the three men could make out a face because of a huge, weather-beaten hat hiding it, but they clearly saw the double-barreled shotgun protruding from the great gathering of sleeve. This made Willie Left Hand grin. He said aside, "Looks like one of them damned scarecrows the sodbusters use to keep the blackies outta the grain. Now, look at that, would you!"

A former cavalryman, Zachary Hockett's reaction was a little less lackadaisical. He knew all about weapons, and a shotgun at close range was nothing to trifle with, not in his manual of arms. "Jesus, it's a kid aiming that sucker at us!" He abruptly reined up and held out a protesting hand. "Hey," he shouted, "put that thing down. We're coming in to talk and mean you no harm. Go on, boy, ease off, you hear?"

A small voice came back. "State your business and don't you come any closer, either."

"Aw, now," Willie Left Hand said, slowly dismounting, "if you touch that buster off, it mos' likely'll knock you on your ass, kid. Just put it aside. Hell, we're just looking for a few strays, that's all, cows from down below, always sneaking off on us in the timber up here to get away from the skeeters."

"Ain't no strays here."

White Moon, frisking the campsite with his quick, dark eyes, saw two mules grazing nearby, one pony, and, hanging on a rear wheel of the wagon, a man's coat. His first thought was that perhaps another weapon was close by, probably aimed right at their heads. It was almost a certainty that there was someone else with this outfit. He said easily, "Where's your folks?" Then edging in toward the wagon, he added, "You're not alone up here, are you?"

"My paw's up there with the dogs," the youth nodded. "We got strays, too."

"Well, how about your mother?" Moon asked. "She hiding in there?"

"Ain't got no maw. She's been dead four years now" was the reply. "And don't you come up here. That's far enough, mister."

"Well, you shouldn't go letting your stock go wandering back there," White Moon said, nodding toward the adjacent woods. He stopped to stretch out his nearly six-foot frame, casually removed his hat, and swept away the perspiration from his forehead. Except for his black hair and dark eyes, he had the features of his famous father, angular face, straight nose, the identical chin with a small cleft in the middle. And there wasn't the trace of a hair on his smooth, olive-skinned face. "There's all kind of critters in the timber there," he went on. "Killed a grizzly right about this spot last week. Ate up one of our cows plenty good. Six feet high, at the least. Claws on him three inches long. Bad medicine, I'll tell you that. Why, one of those woolies wouldn't amount to no more than a hotcake for that critter.'' Moon's jaw suddenly dropped and his eyeballs went white. *''Ikye!''* he shouted out in Absaroke. ''Look there, boys, there's one of them now!''

Even Zachary Hockett and Willie Left Hand, both of whom had been duped by White Moon too many times, took a quick look. So did the youth with the shotgun. But before anyone saw the great phantom bear, Moon Tree had leaped headlong five feet and wrested away the gun. Flattened out by the wagon was the young boy, scratching at the grass, cursing, and trying to retrieve his great hat. Only it wasn't a boy. It was a young woman, her blondish hair tumbling crazily in all directions, and her steel blue eyes spitting sparks. She came up flailing her arms like a molting goose, spewing a string of curses that would have put a muleskinner to shame.

''Jesus!'' exclaimed Zachary Hockett, ''she's a woman!''

''More wildcat,'' opined Willie Left Hand, hopping quickly to the side.

''Well, what the hell did you think I was!'' she screamed, wiping at a grass smear on her chin. ''You think I'm some kind of a monkey in the medicine show? You dumb bastards!'' With her fingers crooked like claws, she shouted, ''Get back or I'll scratch your goddamned eyes out!''

White Moon, with a wry smile, flipped out the shells from the shotgun and tossed it back to her, and she snatched the weapon in midair. He said, ''How were we to know what you were, that garb you're all decked out in?'' He stared down at her feet and grinned. ''Those clod-hoppers you got on, those trousers, big enough to—''

She made one angry swipe at his legs with the barrel of the shotgun, but Moon Tree deftly leaped away, laughing. Thrusting her chin out, she cried, ''What the hell you expecting I'd be wearing out here in this shitty place, a getting-married dress? You assholes are all alike, drinking, chewing, never paying no mind to nothing.'' Suddenly she sat on the grass, wildly beat her hands up and down and started bawling, great tears dribbling down her cheeks, leaving shiny little trails across her dirty face.

For a moment the startled men just stood there quite helpless, and stared disbelievingly at this bizarre sight.

"Oh, Jesus!" Zachary Hockett finally mumbled. He kicked his boot out at White Moon. "Look at what you've gone and done. Dammit, maybe she just doesn't have anything better than what's she's wearing. You've offended her, got her all riled up."

"Well, I'm sorry, miss," Moon Tree offered lamely, trying to suppress a smile. Never in his life, even among angry squaws, had he witnessed such a crazy performance, from venomous bravado to a frazzled fit of weeping, almost within the flick of an eyelash. It was beyond him, all women were beyond him, always trying to get under a man's skin or give him an itch.

Hockett shot him another dirty look. "Oh, shut up! Get her on her feet, dammit. Help her up, and let's get out of here. Jesus!" When White Moon, fearful of putting his hand into a nettle patch, hesitated and shrugged, Zachary Hockett cursed again. "Oh, hell, get out of the way." Bending over, he put his hands under the young woman's armpits and heaved her to her feet. He pulled off his bandana and gave it to her. "Here, wipe off those tears," he commanded. Snatching away the red scarf, she promptly blew her nose, a very loud honk, bringing another smile to White Moon's usually solemn face. "What's your name?" Zachary Hockett asked.

"Divinity," she said with a final sob. "Divinity Jones."

And in the next few minutes Divinity Jones wove an amazing yarn for the men, laced with colorful invectives, how she and her father, Burleigh, had run their two hundred sheep all the way from the Idaho Territory up into the Madison Valley and had crossed over to the Gallatin. They were making a circuit for the Coombes Livestock Company, now planning to head west and graze the band back through the Beaverhead and then go home. Two dollars a day and grub, boasted Divinity, handsome wages. A rancher down near the Targhee country had already rousted them once, had even threatened to kill their two sheep dogs. Coyotes had stolen at least a half dozen of the lambs, and at one time it rained for three straight days, miring their wagon in the mud. Their extra mule was stolen, probably by wandering Bannock Indians. The mosquitoes had been ferocious, and now the deer flies were beginning to hatch. She allowed that it hadn't been a pleasant trip. Besides all of this, Divinity said her pa was a drunk. There wasn't much Zachary Hockett, White Moon, or Willie Left Hand could do about her plight except stare at her sympathetically. This young woman was no more than eighteen years old.

Presently, Burleigh Jones made his appearance, riding in, followed by six sheep and the two dogs. The dogs chased the sheep back toward the main band, and Burleigh, a ring of froth around his whiskered mouth, went straight for the water bucket. He took one dipper full, drank only a teaspoon or two, gargled once, and spat disgustedly to the side. "Bad stuff," he said. "Bad stuff." Eyeballing the three visitors, he settled in on the closest, who happened to be Moon Tree. "Don't tell me," he asked forlornly, "we's on your land, ain't we?"

"No, sir," White Moon replied. "No, this is open range. 'Course, with those woolies, you aren't too welcome with all of the cattle in the neighborhood, and our neighbor over the ridge ten miles or so, he'd take exception to this, I'm certain. Fact is, you sort of surprised us. First time we've seen sheep this far north. Private land is half mile below here, markers out."

Burleigh, the exact counterpart of his daughter in dress, pointed to the west. "Heading that way tomorrow, anyhows. Yep, back around the horn." He sized up the drovers again, one by one, this time chose Zachary Hockett, who appeared to be a tad more white than White Moon or Willie Left Hand. "Reckon you're the ramrod, eh? Wouldn't happen to have a touch of whiskey, would you?"

"Nary a drop," Hockett replied. "Sorry."

"Sorry, shit," groaned Burleigh Jones. "I'm the one who's sorry. Little green feller with a big red nose lives in my belly. Thirsty little bastard, he is. Been naggin' the hell out of me for at least a couple days now. Reckon he's about done in 'til I swings by the diggin's."

Divinity, slumped disconsolately against a wagon wheel, glanced away, a forlorn look on her tear-stained face. Zachary Hockett gave her a friendly tap on her droopy hat and tried to put some cheer in her. "You take care, hear?" he almost whispered. "Things will get better."

And Moon Tree, mounting up, said woefully, "Sorry

about jumping you that way. Those shotguns aren't much for welcoming, you know."

Divinity Jones simply waved him off. Good-bye, asshole.

The three drovers turned and slowly rode away without so much as a backward glance. But they all were sharing thoughts about the Jones family encounter. White Moon spoke up first. "I've never seen my brothers look as poorly as those two. The Great Maker of Everything, Akbatatdia, must have been looking the other way when they passed through the gate, ei?"

And Zachary Hockett agreed. But he had made an observation, one that went deeper than dress and grime. "That young woman would be downright pretty if she could afford to take care of herself, get some of that money her old man wastes on whiskey. She has a lot of grit in her, too."

"Ei," smiled White Moon. "Most of it on her face and tongue. Who-eee, Divinity Jones."

The housewarming at the new home of Young Benjamin and White Crane was underway this same July evening, a few friends from Bozeman City and Adam Stuart's spread in attendance. The big log and frame structure had been built several hundred yards above Benjamin's brother-in-law's place, adjacent to Six Mile Creek. It had one long porch across the front, a large parlor with a rock fireplace, a spacious kitchen, and three bedrooms. Unlike James Goodhart's home, where water came into the kitchen by a gravity-flow pipe from the creek, Young Benjamin had built his kitchen over a hand-dug well, and a cistern with a shiny red handle pumped water into a huge basin. White Crane, the slender, pretty wife of Benjamin, was several months pregnant with her second child.

Most of the conversation at the housewarming concerned the news of the Northern Pacific Railroad's extension of track westward up the Yellowstone River. This, of course, was beneficial to the ranchers now multiplying in the great basin country, who were to have better access to the lucrative cattle markets of the Midwest. And it was Ben Tree's idea to capture more of this market by establishing a central shipping point somewhere along the Yellowstone, thus eliminating the arduous month-long drives to the rail heads in Idaho and Utah. The cattlemen far to the east were already moving stock south by rail from the Dakotas, some of it even dressed and packaged. It was time to firm up the Montana Territory's market with an operational base within a reasonable moving distance, and Ben Tree had suggested investing in a stockyard and perhaps a packing plant on the Northern Pacific line. Claybourn Moore, his longtime ranch foreman, had already approached several ranchers about the venture, including Adam Stuart. Most of the men were enthusiastic but without adequate funds to become partners. Presently only Stuart was still talking business, and his voice wasn't too loud. Ben Tree, however, promised Claybourn Moore that one way or another, he was going to conclude his enterprise before one of the British cattle companies expanded in this direction. Several of the English lords now appropriating much of the unceded range were building up herds by the thousands in the Judith basin country, all the way east to Milestown.

While some of the evening's guests continued talking about cattle and the brisk business in horse sales, the women were busy bringing out huge portions of food to the makeshift plank tables spread out under the long porch. Finally, Benjamin One Feather, holding his son Thad, made a short speech, then invited his friends to take up their plates and begin helping themselves. A smattering of applause here, and his invitation was quickly accepted, and before long, everyone had found seats either in the shade of the porch or beneath the huge cottonwoods fronting the new house. White Moon, the Hocketts and their son, Joseph, sat on blankets under one of the trees, soon were joined by Melody, the five-year-old daughter of James Goodhart and Little Blue Hoop. Melody doted on her Uncle Moon, followed him like a camp puppy, rode in the saddle with him when he was around the corrals, and sometimes called him in for a good night kiss if he wasn't in the bunk house playing poker. Moon had another admirer present, too, Jessie Stuart, the daughter of rancher Adam Stuart. But Jessie was no little girl. She was eighteen, had the same large dark eyes of her mother, Ellie Stuart, was slim, slightly buxom, and displayed two dimples when she smiled. And this was quite often, particularly when she was around Moon Tree. She found him a handsome young man of dry wit and humor who always made a lot of people laugh and smile. In bygone days in the Crow village of Man Called Tree, Moon's brothers had come to identify him closely with the Trickster, Esaccwata, the legendary Old Man Coyote, the perpetrator of humorous tricks. Mrs. Stuart, along with her daughter, thought Moon Tree a suitable catch, despite his half Nez Percé blood, but her husband, Adam, was apprehensive about this possible union. Moon didn't have the serious mettle or business acumen of his brother, Young Benjamin, and his addiction to gambling was somewhat disturbing, too.

Young Jessie Stuart wasn't dissuaded in the least by this dim paternal appraisal. After all, in the spacious Gallatin Valley, there weren't all that many eligible bachelors around, and those few who were usually owned nothing more than their horse and saddle, not exactly a prosperous outlook. Jessie was on the wide porch steps, seated with Young Benjamin, Lucas Hamm, owner of the largest mercantile in town, and James Goodhart. Her eyes were constantly drifting over to the cottonwood grove where Moon Tree, Melody in his lap, continued to eat and talk with Zachary Hockett and Two Shell Woman. Jessie was hesitant to join them because of a slight language barrier. Moon and Two Shell Woman together held some of their conversation in Nez Percé. Both of these women were embarrassed by their English deficiency. When the conversation became one with a series of accompanying gestures, Jessie Stuart had difficulty following. She thought it amazing that Moon Tree spoke Crow, Nez Percé, and English equally well. It would have been more convenient for her purposes if he only used the latter.

Zachary Hockett, who like Benjamin One Feather possessed the eyes of an owl, was silently amused, observing this small flirtation, and not for the first time. Jessie Stuart had been out on the range more than once with Stuart's drovers, including her brother, Ed, often sidled up near White Moon to pass a few words. On several occasions when Moon hadn't been among the outriders, she made her usual inquiry of his whereabouts. This always prompted some hearty teasing back in the bunk house where White Moon lived with the other drovers, Willie Left Hand, Robert Peete, and Peter Marshall, the "Quiet One." Nodding toward the porch, Zachary Hockett said to Moon, "Why don't you do something about that girl, dammit? You two have been playing cat and mouse for six months now. I should think in this amount of time you could come to some kind of mutual agreement, some romance even."

White Moon, gnawing on the last of a chicken leg, flipped the bone at one of the ranch dogs. "Bad medicine," he replied casually. "You want me in your boots? I have plenty trouble around here with critters, more than enough than to be getting myself tied down with a filly like her. No, I do all right by myself, no woman to tell me what to do."

"But she's a good-looking woman," Hockett replied.

"Ei," agreed White Moon. "Plenty of spirit under those petticoats, too, but if I claimed every good-looking pony I ever saw, I would have a hundred."

Two Shell Woman, listening intently, picked up part of this short dialogue, and she frowned at her husband. She finally said, "You want him toss blanket, no good. Maybe he no have heart song for woman. Bad, bring plenty pain in heart for woman. You hear me, I know woman inside me." And she reached over and pinched Zachary Hockett on the thigh. This short declaration had meaning, and both her husband and White Moon knew the subtle inference. Long ago during the Indian wars, she had saved Hockett's life, nurtured him to health from a bullet wound, only to fall hopelessly in love with him. Separated by the events of those tragic days, she thought she was never to see him again, bore his child, ultimately took haven at the ranch during the Nez Percé war. That he had returned a year later searching for her was the miracle in her life, her gift from the Great Spirit. But her heart had ached for many moons before this came to pass. She knew about pain.

Zachary Hockett tried to explain. "I didn't say anything about him tossing the blanket with her, dammit. I was just saying he ought to get together with her a little more. She's taken a shine to him, understand. Makes big eyes."

"No business, you, my man," Two Shell Woman said,

wagging a finger of warning. Then in Nez Percé she told White Moon, "You listen to his words, and you'll find big trouble. If you make a child and don't love her, this is bad with these white people. You must get married or run away and hide somewhere. Maybe our people don't care, but her father would be plenty angry with you, my brother, maybe shoot you between your legs where this trouble all began. *Sepekuse,* so be it. I have spoken enough about this."

Zachary Hockett looked curiously at Moon. "What's she saying now?"

White Moon said solemnly, "Says that old man Stuart's liable to shoot my balls off one of these days if I'm not careful."

"Oh, Jesus!" moaned Hockett in frustration. "How'd we get into fornication! I never even suggested this 'tossing the blanket' crap. She's putting words into my mouth again."

With an indifferent shrug Moon said, "Human nature, I suppose, one thing leading to another." He gave Hockett an impish grin. "She's just not forgetting what you put into her on that pack trip back to the fort that time. Boom, boom." And when White Moon translated this fully, Two Shell Woman giggled. "Plenty good," she replied with a small blush.

"Uh-oh," Zachary Hockett suddenly mumbled, and the others looked up in unison to discover the exuberant and pretty Jessie Stuart approaching, holding her arms open to Melody Goodhart. As she embraced the child, she said, "May I join you? The men are over there talking business again, saddles this time. I figured you people were talking about something more interesting than tack, at least."

"Welcome, Miss Jessie," Zachary Hockett answered, getting to his feet.

"Oh, do sit down," she protested. Holding Melody, she gracefully tucked in her dress and sat beside them, smiling at Two Shell Woman. "How are you, Shell?" she said. "You look so nice, your dress, and your pretty hair all swept back. Ah, but you always look this way. Someday I'm going to steal those pretty earrings."

Two Shell Woman returned her smile and politely responded, "Hallo, thank you. Happy I see you." She turned to White Moon, as usual, and said a few words in Nez Percé, and he, as usual, uttered a quick translation. "She says when you get some holes in your ears, she'll give you some earrings, be happy to. Makes them out of quills, shells, and beads."

"Holes like me," Melody Goodhart said, tilting her head, presenting an ear resplendent with a tiny gold ring.

"Will it hurt?" Jessie asked Melody.

Melody answered, "I don't know. Uncle Moon says I came this way. A fairy spirit gave me these. I kept them."

Jessie Stuart, giving Melody a hug, looked over at Moon Tree. "I never knew you told fairy tales, only tales. And where have you been this past week? Working or playing cards?"

"Riding up the far end with Mister Hockett," Moon said. "That's his country up there, and I just follow orders."

"Evenings, too?" she asked slyly. "Night riding?"

"Some of the boys been trying to get even," he admitted. "I have to give them their chance. Hard to walk away a winner in the bunk house, not like in town. Ei, big difference when you play with fellows you work with. That's fun. In town, it is business."

The talk then wandered, and near dusk Lucas Hamm and Willie Left Hand struck up their fiddles in the big parlor of the new home. Young Benjamin and White Crane had only sparingly furnished the house, so there was very little furniture to move. One carpet and two huge buffalo robes were pulled away, and soon most everyone was taking a turn at the circle two-step, French jig, and a schottische or two. Both White Crane and Two Shell Woman finally threw off their white woman's footwear and danced shoeless. While this was amusing and rather fascinating to several of the guests, it didn't faze Jessie Stuart. She dared to join them, and amid a few surprised stares, she went waltzing away across the shiny new floor with Zachary Hockett. As they swept around the room, she finally asked, "What am I going to do about that man? He sees more in a deck of cards than he does a woman. I am a woman, don't you think? Too brazen for him?"

"Oh, he sees you," assured Hockett. "He's just a different cut, that one. He watched both his sister and sister-in-law fetch men, knows how you women operate. Refers to Benjamin and James as goners now.'' Zachary Hockett chuckled. ''He puts me in the same category, too. He doesn't want to get trapped that way. I'd say give him some time. Let the cream settle and one of these days, he'll come around to lick the topping. I think you're too much of a woman to be denied. I reckon you overwhelm him a bit. But you're sure right about the cards. He has an affair going there, calls her 'Lady Luck,' and she takes up a lot of his spare time.''

Her eyes gleamed and she said boldly, ''If ever I get hold of him, I'll make him forget Lady Luck in a hurry.''

And Zachary Hockett smiled inwardly. This, undoubtedly, was what young Moon Tree was worried about, a woman of desire and ambition who would put a snug halter around his handsome face and inhibit his newly found avocation. And as Hockett made a graceful sweep, turning Jessie Stuart on her pretty toes, there in the open doorway suddenly appeared the bedraggled Divinity Jones, mouth agape, her floppy hat down around her ears staring directly at him. ''Jesus!'' exclaimed Zachary Hockett. He abruptly dropped his arm from Jessie's slim waist. ''It's Divinity Jones!''

''You know that person . . . ?'' Jessie's words dribbled off at the unexpected spectacle. She had never seen such an unkempt woman.

''Sheepherder's daughter,'' said Hockett. ''Met her and her old man today on the high line.'' Suddenly the fiddles screeched away on discordant notes, and Willie Left Hand let out a long moan. ''What the hell . . . ?''

Then from the silence, the hushed whispers, Divinity Jones announced, ''My paw's dead. Kilt. Drovers, five of them, they kilt him. No place else to go but here. . . .''

Claybourn Moore moved up quickly beside her, followed by White Moon. Moon said to the foreman, ''This is the one I was telling you about, sheep, up above the line cabin. Her name is Divinity.''

''What drovers?'' Claybourn Moore asked her. ''What the hell happened?''

Shoulders sagging helplessly, Divinity Jones replied, ''Drovers pushing horses. They comes right through our sheep, yelling like crazy men, chasing their shitty horses. I was at the creek fetching water, and I hears the shots.

I comes up and the bastards are riding hell-bent over the hill. My paw is dead by the wagon, dogs just sitting there by him, moaning like."

Jessie Stuart slid a chair under a wavering Divinity Jones. Clay Moore asked her the location of the wagon, and she said just over the ridge from where she had seen the three drovers earlier in the day, near a creek and some rock spires. Her father, Burleigh, had thought it best to move on after the first encounter with the Tree Ranch cowboys.

Young Ed Stuart spoke up, "That's Finger Butte where she means. Hell, that's over on our side, twenty miles from here. Damnation!" He stared across the room at his father. "Hey, Pa, ain't we got horses up that way?"

"Forty or so head," Adam Stuart acknowledged. "Mostly mares and colts. Do you reckon . . . ?"

Clay Moore said, "You bet I reckon, Adam. Horse thieves, and I'd say that was some of your stock. Those fellows ran into the old man probably by accident. He got a look at them and paid the price, didn't know what the hell was going on."

At that moment Divinity Jones fell from the chair and collapsed in a heap at the foot of Zachary Hockett. "Oh, Jesus, she's fainted away," he yelled. "Get some water." Young Benjamin, pushing several people aside, lifted the young woman into his arms and, followed by White Crane, carried her away to one of the back bedrooms.

By then Clay Moore was in action, ordering Moon, Willie Left Hand, and Robert Peete to start riding for Finger Butte, allowing that the rustlers were leaving a well-trodden trail and one that he knew White Moon was capable of following in the darkest of night. Adam Stuart, who had arrived at the party in a buggy, told young Ed to latch up and ride with the Tree Ranch drovers. In the meantime he and his wife and daughter would stop in town and advise Bill Duggan to get some deputies out by first light. This amused Moon Tree, and pausing at the porch steps, he winked at Jessie Stuart. Then, over his shoulder, he said "By dawn we'll probably be to hell and gone, Mister Stuart, somewhere over in the Madison country. If Duggan's boys come, tell them to bring some grub, ei?"

At the corral, Clay Moore had a few last words for White Moon. "Zachary and Pete Marshall will be up there in the morning to look after those damned sheep. Wrap the old man in some blankets and we'll bring his body down here, do him up proper like. From there, God only knows." He grasped White Moon's arm. "And for crissakes, be careful, son."

Back at the house, the guests were beginning to leave, everyone discussing the strange turn of events, such a bizarre conclusion to a housewarming. Molly Goodhart, now supervising the care of Divinity Jones, fed her some of the food from the evening's feast. In between a few grateful sobs, the frazzled young woman devoured it all. And staring wide-eyed from one passing benefactor to another, she was unable to comprehend any of it. These were grand surroundings, but strangely most of these people looked like Indians, some lighter than the others. A few even talked in a language that she had never heard before. And the women were wearing such beautiful clothes, the kind that she had only seen in the fancy stores once long ago in Ogden. How could this be? How could they be so rich when she, a white, was so poor? The Shoshoni and Bannock she often saw in the Idaho Territory lived in teepees and sod shacks. They were just as poor as she was, certainly dressed no better.

"Are you ready for a good hot bath?" she heard the kind, older woman asking. "Make you feel better before you go to bed."

Divinity Jones' eyes widened in further amazement. "Who are you? You some breed Injun, too, like the rest?"

Molly Goodhart laughed heartily. "Molly's my name. Yes, I'm part Absaroke. Oh, gracious, we have all kinds here at the ranch, some Absaroke, a few Nez Percé, and Willie, he's part Salish."

"You mean to let me stay here tonight . . . in this place?" she asked, bewildered by all the attention. "What about my pa up there, all dead and cold?"

"The men folks are looking out for all of that," Molly soothed. "Ei, you stay here for tonight. Tomorrow, they'll decide what to do about all of this. No worry, now. Take bath, go to bed. Get you some clean clothes, too. Store man is going to send out some things for you first thing in the morning."

Divinity Jones' pale blue eyes clouded with tears. "I'm pretty shitty, ain't I?" She stared down at her tattered trousers, her oversized boots. She shrugged forlornly. "Feller laughed at me today, you know. Said he was sorry, but I reckon he had reason to laugh." And as Molly led her away to the great tin tub in the kitchen, huge tears rolled down Divinity Jones' cheeks and melted away in the dust of her faded jacket. In her bitterly jaded world someone had given her a spoonful of kindness.